THE GIRL
ON THE
PLATFORM

BOOKS BY ELLIE MIDWOOD

The Violinist of Auschwitz
The Girl Who Escaped from Auschwitz
The Girl in the Striped Dress
The Girl Who Survived

ELLIE MIDWOOD

THE GIRL
ON THE
PLATFORM

Bookouture

Published by Bookouture in 2021

An imprint of Storyfire Ltd.
Carmelite House
50 Victoria Embankment
London EC4Y 0DZ

www.bookouture.com

ISBN: 978-1-80019-869-2
eBook ISBN: 978-1-80019-868-5

To Vlada and Ana. We weren't born to the same mother, but you shall forever be my sisters. Thank you for being so fiercely, unapologetically you. Love you.

Chapter 1

Berlin. Spring 1933

"Your new desk." With a somewhat theatrical sweep of his hand, Erich Tischendorf, the head of Metro-Goldwyn-Mayer Studios' publicity department, indicated Libertas' new workplace.

With mounting horror, Libertas observed stacks of papers towering over the typewriter and not one, but two black telephones buried among magazines and binders.

"Forgive the mess." Herr Tischendorf—*"call me Erich, please"*—inclined his meticulously coiffured head to one side. "We have just finished cleaning up the house and certain positions haven't been attended to in a few days and sometimes even weeks." He accompanied those last words with a dramatic gaze to the ornate ceiling.

It occurred to Libertas that he belonged on the silver screen rather than a managerial post of the publicity department of the American MGM's Berlin branch. Everything about him appeared thoroughly rehearsed and even more thoroughly performed. A Clark Gable type—though, sans mustache—he was a polished, refined version of a person, but somehow utterly devoid of personality.

"You ought to dismiss the people in charge of cleaning." In an effort to lighten the mood, Libertas permitted herself a tentative smile as she motioned her blond head toward the cluttered desk. "If that's what my desk looks like after their best efforts."

There was a pause, during which Erich's expression shifted a few times. He blinked like a confused owl, scowled, blinked again, and at last brightened and burst into relieved laughter. "*Ach*, you're such a delight! At long last, a media relations person with a healthy sense of humor. That is precisely what this studio needs. Fresh, sparkling blood to revive this swamp. Marvelous!"

And with that, he grasped Libertas' palm, gave it a warm parting pressure, and was gone, still chuckling mutely to himself.

It was Libertas' turn to gaze after him uncomprehendingly.

The true meaning of his words—*we have just finished cleaning up the house*—dawned on her much later that week; her very first day was spent in a sort of dreamlike state, wandering the studio's long corridors smelling of floor wax and expensive perfume and admiring the photos of the MGM's most celebrated actors, directors, and producers: Greta Garbo, John Barrymore, Jean Harlow, Clark Gable, Edmund Goulding who'd shot the Oscar-winning hit *Grand Hotel*, and Irving Thalberg, under whose guidance all of these stars had been born.

In her initial investigation, Libertas noticed that a few of the portraits were missing, only golden nameplates were left, indicating those whose likeness graced the wall not that long ago. A worm of a suspicion stirred somewhere in the back of her mind, but she dismissed the thought with her usual idealistic, youthful nonchalance.

Must be replacing them with newer ones, she decided and felt her breath catch in her throat when her gaze fell on another nameplate under the empty spot: Erich Pommer, producer.

Erich Pommer! Unable to contain her excitement, Libertas traced her fingers across the engraved letters of his name in awe. *The legendary trailblazer, the founder of the very first German production studio Decla Film, the face of the Weimar film production as the leading producer of the UFA studios, the man who discovered Fritz Lang himself!*

However, Libertas' exhilaration was abruptly interrupted by a workman's indifferent, "Beg pardon, Fräulein."

Moving her out of his way, he set his toolbox on the carpeted floor, produced a screwdriver and began to whistle a nationalistic tune to himself as he worked on the screws.

"What are you doing?" Libertas demanded as soon as she had recovered herself.

The worker regarded her as though she had just asked him something impossibly idiotic. "Removing this nameplate?" He arched a thick, unruly brow.

"I can see that." Her cheeks reddening—more from annoyance rather than embarrassment—Libertas crossed her arms over her chest, challenge audible in her voice. "What I want to know is why you're removing it? Do you even know who Erich Pommer is? He's one of the founders of the entire German cinematic—"

"That may very well be so, Fräulein," the worker interrupted her, "but his name is on the list and so the nameplate must be removed."

"What list?" Libertas pressed, growing more and more irate at the man's indifference.

"This list." Just as unperturbed, he extracted a folded, oil-smudged piece of paper out of the pocket of his overalls and handed it to her.

Snatching it out of the man's hands, Libertas swiftly scanned the wrinkled document bearing the stamp of the Ministry of Propaganda. It didn't explain much, simply enumerated names in alphabetic order—actors, actresses, directors, screenwriters, producers—not a single profession was spared a seemingly random purge that still made not the faintest sense to her. Annoyed, she gave it back and made a mental note to take up the matter with her immediate boss, Tischendorf.

But then sorting out the binders on the desk occupied the next few days, and by Thursday, new portraits filled the empty spots in the gallery, and on Friday, Libertas was to meet her uncle Wend and the issue had slipped from her mind entirely.

The Anhalter Bahnhof, the city's main railway artery, pumping blood in hundreds of different directions from the country's heart—Berlin—was unusually silent that evening.

"One sort of an SA parade or another is taking place near the Linden," the bored-looking ticket seller explained. "Torches, banners, all business as it should be. They say the Führer might make an appearance."

"Oh, well," Libertas said, nodding knowingly, "that explains the empty stations and dead streets."

"People love him," the ticket seller uttered in a toneless voice and something told Libertas that the ticket seller himself didn't. Noticing a Party pin on her coat's lapel, he regarded her over the rim of his glasses as though in silent demand, *And why aren't you there, Fräulein?*

"I'm meeting my uncle," Libertas explained, gesturing toward the platform, embarrassed, for no apparent reason, at being taken for a zealous Nazi proudly displaying her pin to everyone who cared to look.

The truth was much more prosaic: Libertas had only joined the Party because the same uncle Wend—now, he was a zealous Nazi indeed—had insisted that it would be much easier for a Party member to secure herself a job in Berlin, and that was the extent of Libertas' NSDAP affiliations. An artistic soul at the tender age of nineteen, she wasn't interested in politics and cared about the current state of German affairs even less. The leading Party in power had never affected her life at any rate—a long, aristocratic Prussian lineage combined with a few recent successful investments of her family had long seen to the fact that Libertas could enjoy a lavish lifestyle without working a day in her entire life. But she soon grew bored of the remote familial mansion, horse rides, and writing half-decent poems, deciding that bohemian Berlin suited her much more. She dreamt of the motion pictures but scoffed at the idea of considering acting herself and set her views on something much more meaningful, something that would immortalize her name for years to come, something that—

"Arriving now at platform two—" The voice of an announcer sliced into the glorious pictures her vivid imagination was painting.

Torn away from her rosy dreams, Libertas checked the ornate clock hanging on the opposite platform. The typical Prussian militaristic love of order drilled into her by the serving members of the family, Libertas arrived at the station much too early. Growing bored, she strolled into a first-class women's restroom, powdered her pale skin, pining for the gorgeous tan she'd sport at this time of the year at her former boarding school in Switzerland, drew a dark-cherry lipstick across her lips and fixed her already immaculate platinum curls. Her most recent admirer had claimed she looked like Greta Garbo. The one before him had compared her to Marlene Dietrich. Libertas had only laughed at them both and declared that she wished to be the novelist Erich Remarque, but from the early twenties, when he was still a journalist, and she laughed even harder at their astounded expressions.

Her aspirations were a man's aspirations. They only saw a doll-like face and a body to die for in her and that was the reason she left them both and hadn't looked back since.

The restroom attendant pushed the door open for Libertas and thanked *gnädige Frau* profusely for a generous tip. Outside, the platform was once again empty, the great swarm of arriving passengers already disappearing through the doors where taxicabs were awaiting them, into the underground tunnel leading to the Hotel Excelsior, and into countless high-end shops selling the latest Parisian fashion for exuberant prices. On one of the polished benches, a commuting businessman was studying the economics section of the newspaper with a look of utter concentration about him.

"*Scheiße!*"

Startled by the crude curse, Libertas looked up at the man hidden almost entirely by the shadow of a tall limestone column. Dressed with great taste but obviously in some sort of distress, he was struggling with a box of matches, which, judging by their abundance at his feet, must have been wet; cursing at the blasted rain the day before, at the man-servant who had misplaced his favorite lighter, at the entire damned world that could very well go the devil as far as he was concerned—

"Here." Flicking her silver lighter with the familial crest on it, Libertas brought the flame to the man's cigarette.

His face obscured by the rim of his elegant felt hat, he took a deep pull and released a sigh full of such inner torment, Libertas thought someone close to him must have died... or that he had just lost a few millions to a bad deal.

"Rotten day?" she probed gently.

"Rotten life." He finally removed his hat, raked his hand through his dark hair, and gave Libertas a grin she was familiar with from countless magazines and newspapers.

Fritz Lang. *The* German director; the genius behind the marvel of the cinematography *Metropolis*; the mad genius behind the serial killer thriller *M* that shook the entire world; the dreamer who had sent a film rocket to the moon; the Berlin star always surrounded by cheering crowds of awestruck fans... standing alone in the shadows with a single suitcase at his feet.

Something about the picture should have stirred Libertas' suspicion, but she was much too excited to process it all. A gasp was already threatening to break off her lips, to turn into a full-blown squeal of pure adolescent delight—

"No, please, don't!" There was such terror in Lang's voice, such urgency at the manner in which he grasped at her forearm to pull her further into the shadows, Libertas grew all at once silent and concerned. "I have upset you," the great German director softened his voice at once, his expression growing wistful. Only now did it occur to Libertas that the signature monocle Fritz Lang always wore in his left eye was missing. His face was still too recognizable without it. That must have been why he replaced the felt hat back on his head, pulling its rim low as it had been before. "Forgive me, please, for ruining your first impression of me in such an inconsiderate manner. I assure you, it was never my intention. I'm only..." He searched for the right words. "I'm only trying to make this particular train ride incognito, if the higher powers allow it to be so."

"I promise not to make a ruckus and won't tell your wife that you were traveling to see your lady friend if you sign an autograph for me." Libertas offered only half in jest, in an attempt to lighten his mood. Some very dark shadows lay around him; she glimpsed their reflection in his hazel eyes, tired and lost, with deep half-moons under them as though he hadn't slept a night, or even longer.

Lang released a desolate, ghostlike chuckle and shook his head, grateful for the distraction. "I wish my tangled marital affairs were the biggest of my troubles, my darling, but I'm afraid that's no longer the case. My wife and I have just signed our divorce papers and my lady friend... It's anyone's guess if I'll ever see her again. But enough of my problems. Now, what's your name, sweetheart?"

"Libertas," she offered breathlessly, handing him her small leather notebook and a fountain pen.

"Libertas!" Lang exclaimed, regarding her with a renewed interest. "That's some name. A freedom fighter's name."

"My grandfather, Fürst Philipp of Eulenburg, was a composer."

"Was he now?"

"In his *Fairytale of Freedom* one of the characters is named Libertas. I'm named after her."

"And what do you do, with such an artistic genetic pool?" Lang asked teasingly, writing something in her notebook.

"I work for the MGM Studios here, in Berlin," Libertas announced with pride, itching to see the message Lang was presently inscribing.

"You don't say?" Lang stopped writing for a moment and looked up at Libertas, this time with a professional interest. "How splendid! You're not an actress, are you?"

"No. Media Relations department. I haven't the faintest idea why they hired me in the first place!" Feeling more and more at ease with Lang—he truly did have such a charming personality,

Libertas couldn't help but notice—she began to chatter. "I'm fresh out of boarding school; no work experience; no clue how to do this job whatsoever and they take me on the spot."

A playful smile slipped off Lang's face as though someone had just cut the strings from his mask.

Libertas bit her tongue, sensing that she had just said something very wrong at a very wrong time and to a very wrong person, but no matter how much she searched her mind, she failed to come up with a reason.

"They hired you because someone *has* to do this job." Even Lang's tone was tinged with ice now. "So many empty positions. Someone has to fill them."

"What do you mean?" Libertas searched his face, genuinely at a loss.

He narrowed his eyes at her Nazi Party pin, just now noticing it, then shifted his gaze back to her face. "How old are you, Libertas?"

"Nineteen," she replied, feeling guilty for no apparent reason.

After that admission, the director's expression relaxed, the corners of his stern mouth softening, pulled to a rueful smile. "That explains it. Still so young... Do you like this Party business then?" He gestured toward her badge with the pen, as though the very thought of touching it disgusted him.

"This? No!" Libertas tossed her head, covering her pin with a silver fox collar. Persuading him was suddenly a matter of paramount importance. "This was only to obtain a job. My uncle told me that the vetting process... something to do with the Party members... must be of the reliable political status, or some such rot," she kept grasping at the words in desperation.

When Lang chuckled softly at the final word so unbefitting the well-bred young aristocrat in front of him, Libertas breathed a sigh of relief.

"I assume you know nothing of the recently passed Law for the Restoration of the Professional Civil Service? No, I thought not."

Lang closed the notebook and pressed it gently into Libertas' hands. For a few moments, his palms were encasing hers while he peered intently into her eyes. "They dismissed all Jews from your studio. From all studios. From all spheres of civil service. Theater, movies, law offices, banks, administrative positions, hospitals. Beautiful, purebred Aryans like yourself must take up their places. This is how you got your job, my darling."

The whistle of the arriving train pierced Libertas' chest. Or was it his words that did it? Swaddled in a column of steam, she couldn't quite tell.

"This is me." Lang finally released her hands and picked up his suitcase. "Paris, one end, no return ticket… if they don't arrest me on the border. Never know these days, eh?" He laughed carelessly, but Libertas suddenly felt tears stinging her mascaraed eyes. Lang's image was swimming in her vision, already dissolving into nothing, just like Erich Pommer's name, just like so many celebrated names, pried off the walls, deleted from the lists, doomed to oblivion.

"I'm sorry," she whispered, unsure if he heard her behind all the mechanical noise, all the cries of the porters and conductors, all the cacophony of the Bahnhof. "Please, forgive me… I'm so sorry."

"Don't be. Just be braver than me. Don't run. Fight."

With her eyes tightly shut, tears rolling from her dark lashes, Libertas felt his lips gently touching the skin on her burning cheek.

"Little freedom fighter."

Lang's train was long gone when Libertas finally found the strength to open the notebook—and cried anew at the message he wrote for her:

Live up to your name, little Freedom Fighter. Perhaps one day I shall make a film about your bravery.

Good luck!
Fritz Lang.

*

"It was an idiotic thing he did." Fürst Friedrich-Wend zu Eulenburg und Hertefeld—Uncle Wend only to Libertas—proclaimed at the family dinner that Sunday. The titled head of the familial estate Schloss Liebenberg, dressed in his Sunday finest, raised a crystal goblet to his lips and sipped his wine, before adding in a tone of chill distaste, "Snubbing Minister Goebbels' generous offer in such a manner. Minister Goebbels offers that half-breed a position of the head of a new agency that would supervise motion picture production in the entire Reich and even proposes to make Lang an honorary Aryan. And what does Lang go and do? Leaves for Paris the same night." Wend shook his regal head in disapproval. "A typical Jew. First swears that he loves Germany more than life, but at the sign of the smallest challenge runs away with his tail between his legs."

This entire time Libertas had sat in silence, pushing a piece of duck from one side of the monogrammed plate to the other, but at those words something flared up in her; some spark of resentment she couldn't even explain to herself. "Now, I don't think that's fair, *Onkel*," she protested, dropping the silver fork onto her plate louder than she had intended. "That anti-Jewish law they have just passed cannot, in all good conscience, be called 'the smallest challenge.' And neither can Herr Lang be called a coward. He fought for his native Austria in the Great War and was decorated for bravery several times."

"Lang fought in the war?" Her uncle arched his brow in mild surprise. "Hm… I wasn't aware of that. Oh!" His expression suddenly brightened as he turned to his fellow officer, changing the subject. "You will not believe whom Minister Goebbels has just appointed to the position of…"

Wasn't aware or simply didn't care one way or the other, Libertas mused grimly to herself, losing all interest in the political gossip and resuming pushing her food around the plate. She loved her

Onkel Wend, but this was always the case with him—rejecting or dismissing anything that didn't fit his narrative.

"Perhaps, you'll get a chance to see your favorite director's newest motion picture Minister Goebbels has banned," Wend called out to her teasingly over the gilded candelabra. "He plans to have a private screening for his guests after his birthday dinner. You're invited as my date. Delighted?"

"On account of Herr Lang's film, yes," Libertas grumbled under her breath.

At once, Wend broke into laughter. "A feisty little thing, my Libs, isn't she?" he demanded from his uniformed audience just to be met with a grumble of approval and subservient chortles from both the army officers and industrialists.

Wend was one of the biggest donors of the Nazi Party. It was one of the NSDAP's obligations to laugh at his jests. Even his niece's defiance was regarded with a sense of amused adoration instead of condemnation. They all looked at her as though they found her positively delightful just then, a young girl too pretty to understand what she was saying.

"Libs, be a darling, play accordion for us," Wend asked and pressed his hand to his decorated chest as he turned to his guests. "You ought to hear her play. She is a wonder with an accordion."

Suppressing a sigh of resignation, Libertas rose from her chair and went to retrieve her accordion, wondering how it was possible to be so disillusioned in Berlin in a span of a few short days. She had come here hoping to make a difference and a name for herself; now, she saw precisely what she was for the men of the new Reich—a beautiful ornament for a dinner party whose words didn't matter and whose voice was only valuable when it sang patriotic songs for them.

Freedom Fighter, her foot. A usurper who had unwittingly stolen a position from an unfortunate Jew, who was certainly much more qualified for it than her. That's all she was.

Chapter 2

Berlin. May 10, 1933

The commotion outside her office window was certainly unusual that morning, but Libertas was too preoccupied with her duties to pay any heed to the shouts of SA commanders and grumbling of truck engines that appeared to be in constant motion since dawn.

"May I speak with Herr Best, please? Libertas Haas-Heye, MGM publicity department… Certainly, I can hold for a couple of minutes."

With a black phone squeezed between her ear and shoulder, Libertas was writing a memo from her last conversation: Die Dame *magazine agreed to review* Dancing Lady *as well; requested an interview with Joan Crawford—see if it's possible to organize; Frankfurter Zeitung wants new photos of Gable and Astaire from the shoot itself—call Hollywood pub. dep. and request to send some for their June issue. Organize a reception for Hardy—*

A familiar voice on the phone interrupted her train of thought. At once, Libertas' face blossomed into a well-rehearsed smile. "Herr Best!" Glimpsing the time on her golden wristwatch, Libertas noted with a sense of surprise that scarcely a minute had passed. All of the celebrated editors of the glossiest periodicals, who used to make her wait on the phone for twenty minutes and force her to call back multiple times a day pretending to be thoroughly busy and utterly unavailable, now snatched up the phone from their assistants within moments of her name being announced. "How *are* you today? It is *such* a *pleasure* to be talking to you again. Oh, the flowers?"

The editor was gushing about the bouquet Libertas had sent to the editor for the glowing review his team had written for MGM's latest sensation, *Dancing Lady*. A small personal touch that caused discontent and grumbling among the publicity department's accountant, but which Libertas' immediate superior Erich Tischendorf found perfectly ingenious.

"That was the least we could do to express our utmost gratitude, Herr Best." She lowered her voice confidentially. "Promise not to tell anyone, but—and I'm saying it on the most reliable authority—*Film Kurier* is MGM's favorite magazine. You have my word! Ha-ha, Herr Best, you are *such* a *darling…*"

If only Herr Best knew that Libertas repeated the exact same words and heaped the exact same praises on every editor she dealt with, no matter how big or small, he would most certainly lose the smug expression Libertas strongly suspected he was wearing. But it was precisely such flattery and well-rehearsed intimacy she had cultivated with the press in the course of one short month that had shot Libertas' star straight into the Berlin MGM's stratosphere. Erich Tischendorf wouldn't stop singing her praises to everyone who agreed to listen and ran to Libertas for "expert advice" whenever an issue with one periodical or another arose or a stubborn star refused to be bothered with another interview.

The studio's head himself, Frits Strengholt, was known to pop into Libertas' office for a cup of coffee—an unimaginable occurrence for a man who usually ignored the greetings of his employees as though they were invisible and unworthy of his attention.

"Naturally, Herr Best. I'm quite certain an exclusive can be arranged with the director."

Libertas cringed at the particularly loud series of shouts filling her office through an opened window and silently cursed an SA blockhead issuing them. Pulling the cord after herself, she took the phone to the window and, after placing it on the sill, pulled the window closed. Behind the glass, ant-like men in SA uniforms were running to and fro, building a pyre of sorts as their commanders looked on. In the distance, a great number of trucks covered by tarpaulin were lined up.

"Oh no, he'll agree to it all right. Don't fret, I know how to talk to him." Almost genuinely, she laughed at the editor's, *I have no doubts in your abilities, Fräulein Haas-Heye*. "I know, I know; he imagines himself God's gift to mankind, but what can you do? You know those directors, and particularly gifted ones. They're all a bit full of themselves. He won't say no to me though, I can personally guarantee you that... Oh, Herr Best, you're such a flatterer! It's all settled then. All right. I know how busy you are and won't take up any more of your precious time. I'll contact you as soon as I set up the meeting with him... Of course! You too... Always my pleasure. Good day."

Libertas had just returned the phone back in its place when one of the studio's photographers, Inge Bissen, burst into the office, camera at the ready.

"Libs, I need a photo for tomorrow's special issue of the *Beobachter*. Sit at your desk, give me your widest smile, and make it snappy! They never bother to warn us, which means I'll be developing these all night again. There go my date-night plans..."

At those words, Libertas' smile emerged genuine and bright, reaching the corners of her pale blue eyes. Fixing the white lace collar of her otherwise professional black woolen dress, she sat in her chair and folded her hands over the countless memos and glossy magazines.

"What is it for?" Libertas inquired after Inge finished snapping a few shots.

The photographer widened her eyes at her MGM colleague. "I told you, for the special issue, dedicated to tonight's burning of the books."

"Burning of the...?" Libertas blinked a few times, drawing a complete blank.

"Oh, that's right, you were away on assignment and missed the meeting." Inge waved her hand dismissively. "Nothing major, we'll just all head outside after the workday is over and help the SA fellows organize everything. Then Minister Goebbels will make a speech, Reichsmarschall Göring too should be in attendance, if I'm not mistaken, and then we'll all take a nice handful of the recently banned literature and hurl it into the flames. The photos ought to come out great. Night shots with the fire and all that business. I can hardly wait!"

Inge's dark eyes shone in eager anticipation, but inside Libertas, a dark mixture of suspicion and disgust stirred. With great reluctance, she feigned a smile in response to Inge's parting wave.

The night descended upon the capital, shrouding the Opera House Plaza in black. At its center, a large pyre towered ominously, smelling faintly of gasoline and something inexplicably menacing. Her hands thrust in the pockets of her trench coat, Libertas felt herself shivering against the chilly May wind. All around her, the crowd shifted and waited, hungry eyes trained on the pyre, licking their lips in anticipation. There was something primeval, savage, about the entire affair, it suddenly occurred to her. They must have burned witches in the same manner, in this very spot, not that long ago.

Across the pyre, the podium was erected for the Reich's main inquisitor—Minister Goebbels. From the backs of the trucks, the Brownshirts were hauling stacks and stacks of books tied with twine. Their black-clad colleagues from the SS were gallantly bringing them forward, cutting the twine and handing the books out to the "guests" occupying the front rows, accompanying their "gifts" with smiles and a polite, "*Bitte.*"

After a young SS man enclosed a few editions in her gloved hands, Libertas slowly turned them this way and that and felt a scowl growing deeper and deeper on her face. *They're burning*

Mann? Brecht, her favorite songwriter? Freud? Remarque? Certainly,
not Remarque…

Her throat suddenly constricted as though in the grip of barbed
wire, and Libertas tried to swallow, but the lump inside was too
thick.

In the distance, Minister Goebbels' cultivated voice, with a
faint trace of the Swabian accent he so desperately tried to shed,
carried long and far about the purity of blood, race, and thought.
The Minister of Propaganda may have lacked in stature and Aryan
looks, but he certainly made up for it with the nationalistic fervor
shining out of his black eyes and the poison dripping from his
diabolic, eloquent tongue.

Torches were flung into the pyre and Libertas couldn't tell any
longer whether her eyes stung from the smoke or her tears. Helpful
SS hands in white gloves were already nudging her toward the fire,
the sparks of which landed dangerously close to her feet, danced
around her hair, singed her skin at a particularly harsh gust of wind.
But she was grateful for the pain just then. It distracted from the
thoughts that were much more painful than any fire and darker
than the night itself.

That night, she helped burn independent thought, the works of
the freethinkers and, all at once, her own name—the embodiment
of personal freedom itself—seemed to be a mockery.

Next to her, Inge was staring, as though hypnotized, into the
raging flames that turned freedom to ash. "I shall never forget this
day," she uttered with almost religious reverence.

"Neither shall I," concurred Libertas, but meant something
entirely different.

Chapter 3

Berlin. August 1933

"What is this?" Mystified, Libertas studied what appeared to be a train ticket slipped inside a binder that Erich Tischendorf had just deposited on her desk.

"Oh! Completely escaped my mind." With his typical theatrical manner, the head of the publicity department rolled his eyes supposedly at his own incompetency. "You're going to the Nuremberg rally. The Party people are making a documentary about it and, from what we've heard, it's not contracted. Meaning, the UFA with that *Arschloch* Klitzsch in charge haven't gotten their greedy hands on it yet. I want you to go there, befriend the person who's making it, and try to get him on our side. MGM has been making remarkable profits with the German market and Herr Mayer thinks the studio will benefit even more if we prove to the Ministry of Propaganda that we can produce German documentaries as well."

Libertas leaned back in her chair, hands crossed over her chest, a look of skepticism on her face. "Isn't Herr Mayer Jewish? Whatever does he want with the Party documentaries?"

Tischendorf's answer came in the form of an evasive hand gesture. "Businessman first, Jewish second. I gather it matters not to him where the money comes from as long as it keeps coming. Besides, he lives in Hollywood. He doesn't care what happens here in Germany as long as his profits keep growing. He even consented to Dr. Goebbels' censor, Consul Gyssling, editing their American films so that they could be tailored to our German audience. *The Mad Dog of Europe* got canceled after Gyssling got himself in an uproar over it. Rightfully, it should be noted," he added hastily. "It was pure enemy propaganda aimed at alienating the rest of the world from Germany over our purported persecution of the Jews."

Purported? Libertas felt a surge of something dark and poisonous inside and hid her gaze from her superior so that he wouldn't notice the pure resentment in her pale-blue eyes. It was convenient for him to forget about his former Jewish colleagues. For Libertas, the wound was still too fresh, smarting each time she passed through the hallway, where, in place of Erich Pommer's photograph, some smiling blond starlet's portrait now hung; each time she opened her notebook and saw Fritz Lang's inscription inside. Local movie circles' rumor had it that both the director and his loyal producer were presently filming something in France—out of sheer desperation, having left Germany with nothing but the clothes on their backs and whatever meager cash they had in their wallets.

"At any rate," Tischendorf's upbeat tone sliced into Libertas' dark musings, "you're our best asset when it comes to publicity. If you can't befriend that documentary director, no one can." He placed a hand on her shoulder, his expression so grave that one would think he were a general sending his second-in-command to battle. It took Libertas great effort not to snort with laughter.

"Can I at least have the name of this mysterious director?" she asked with a sigh of resignation.

Tischendorf's scrunched-up face was eloquent enough. "Afraid not. Even Herr Strengholt himself hasn't the faintest idea who the fortunate fellow entrusted with such a monumental task is, and Herr Strengholt has a direct line to Minister Goebbels himself."

"Splendid," Libertas muttered under her breath and that very evening began to pack a small suitcase.

*

Nuremberg. September 2, 1933

Nuremberg was crumbling under the waves of rally-goers, most of them dressed in colorful dirndls and lederhosen, pouring down the city's streets like an army of invaders. From their height, somber granite statues looked on at the children armed with small bright-red *Hakenkreuz* flags who wormed their way to the front lines. There, the legs of SS and SA soldiers served as live cordon, their hands clasping each other's leather belts, two soldiers facing out, one soldier facing the crowd. Young blond girls, with their hair braided, had already occupied the coveted strategic position on the cobbled ground, firmly holding onto the SS men's tall jackboots and refusing to yield even a few centimeters of space facing the road leading to the rally. They had the Führer and their favorite Party dignitaries to throw flowers at; their little counterparts, who hadn't been savvy enough to arrive at dawn, should stay at the back. Not enough nationalistic spirit and devotion as far as the girls were concerned.

By midday, the air was soaked with the heavy smell of sweaty woolen uniforms, warm leather, wurst, beer, and, unavoidably, urine. Exhausted, Libertas dropped to the freshly cut lawn, kicked off her shoes and, paying no heed to the spectators around her, pulled up her skirt and began to unfasten her stockings. The sun hadn't yet set, but she'd already had enough of the day, of the blasted rally, waves and waves of black and brown whirling and shifting around her, glassy-eyed, fanatical, one big funeral adorned with wreaths and bloody banners.

Good luck finding a film crew in that mass madness, she thought to herself, rolling down her ruined stockings and massaging her swollen ankles. For the first few hours, Libertas had tried to reason, beg, and even flirt with the uniformed cordon, but all of her efforts were met with smirks and condescending explanations that the inside of the rally was *men only*. Women—a thumb pointing over the shoulder—ought to watch from the back and cheer their brave leaders.

"But I have a work assignment!" As a last resort, Libertas had shoved her credentials into their faces—a line-up of mass-manufactured Teutonic Knights. "I work for MGM!"

Her claim had produced no effect whatsoever.

"Good for you, sweetheart; now, get in the back."

Frustrated, her sensitive skin burned by the sun, Libertas was muttering curses under her breath when a young woman, dressed in slacks and a short-sleeved shirt, dropped to the grass beside her.

"You too then?" the brunette asked by means of introduction.

"Me too what?" Libertas grumbled, not too disposed for a friendly chat.

"Can't access inside due to the absence of male genitals?"

The coarse reply of a typical Berliner made Libertas snort in spite of herself. Still laughing, she turned to the woman and felt her eyes snapping wide in astonishment. It was impossible not to recognize the striking face that had graced every wall of Berlin just months ago; that smiled mysteriously out of the cover of every other glossy film magazine.

"Fräulein Riefenstahl?" Libertas asked in disbelief.

"The very same." Grinning, the actress and aspiring director offered Libertas her hand. "Drop the formalities, though. I can't bear them for the life of me. Leni."

"Libertas." Still unable to believe her good fortune, Libertas grasped Leni's hand and gave it a thorough shake. "Oughtn't you to be inside, with all the celebrities?"

At first, the actress made no reply, searching her pockets for cigarettes instead. If she hadn't been sitting so close, Libertas would never have recognized her in her simple attire. Her hair, naturally wavy, was undone and constantly got in her face. No makeup, not even a trace of lipstick on her; just intense dark-brown eyes staring with defiance at the uniformed masses.

"I would have been, if I'd been more agreeable," Leni ventured at last, cupping her hands around the match and turning away from the wind. Under an SA man's disapproving look, the actress threw the match down onto the ground and blew him a mocking air kiss. "If I just opened my legs when Herr Minister of Propaganda Goebbels asked me to, I would have been filming this entire affair with no trouble whatsoever, instead of being cursed at and told to get lost at every turn."

"I'm so sorry," Libertas murmured, genuinely meaning it.

"Mm." Leni gave an indifferent one-shoulder shrug. "When you're an actress, you get used to dealing with that sort of thing. He's not the first, he won't be the last." Blowing out a cloud of smoke, Leni narrowed her gaze at the podium from which Göring was presently speaking—something profoundly cringeworthy about blood, race, and Germany's rightful place in the world order, his voice amplified by hundreds of loudspeakers. "I only wish he didn't make my already difficult job even more difficult."

Libertas was about to inquire further when a young man with a camera in his hand squeezed his way from inside the crowd toward them and, handing Leni the camera, sprawled on the grass as though he'd been shot. With his arms wide open, Libertas saw that his underarms were entirely wet, turning the color of his light-blue shirt to indigo.

"Please tell me you at least shot some footage." Leni regarded him pleadingly.

"I at least shot some footage," he repeated in a voice that was entirely exhausted. His eyes were still closed, dark lashes throwing shadows over his cheekbones.

"You're just pacifying me, aren't you?" she pressed.

"What do you think?" the fellow asked with great sarcasm, opening his eyes to give Leni a dirty sideways glance. "Your good friend Dr. Goebbels kept turning his head away each time I aimed the camera at him."

Leni moaned, wiped her face with her hands, and suddenly broke into mirthless laughter. On her lap, the camera lay forgotten. "The Führer will get me shot."

"No, he won't," the man retorted, brushing off Leni's claim with wonderful nonchalance. "Not your fault."

"Do you think he shall express any desire to get to the bottom of whose fault this is?" Annoyed by such a dismissive attitude, Leni swiftly descended upon her unsuspecting colleague in an explosion of ire. "He ordered me—*me*—" she jabbed a finger at her chest, "to make this documentary. Not Goebbels, not Goebbels' Party people, but me. *Ordered*, despite my initial refusal. Everyone knows the Führer's orders *must* be obeyed, no excuses. And I can't even get inside of this blasted rally!"

Her mind dulled by the scorching sun and the abundance of people, scents, shouts, and emotions, Libertas watched them bickering for some time until her brain slowly began to put together the puzzle of the hand camera, Leni's words, and the very reason she, Libertas, had been sent here.

"Wait a moment." Libertas stared at the two, incredulous. *Didn't Tischendorf say the documentary director was male? Could it be that he simply made a mistake by assuming it?* "Is it you who's directing the rally documentary?" Libertas probed, almost holding her breath as she shifted her gaze from Leni to Leni's camera and back, too afraid to jinx her good fortune.

"*Liebchen,* look at me. Do I look like I'm directing anything?" Leni tilted her head to one side and arched an expressive brow. "I took this job because I was ordered to. I had to borrow the money for the expenses from my father because my former partner in film production, Herr Sokal, disappeared to greener pastures aboard with all of the money he owed me. I have only these two miserable boys working for me as my film crew," she gestured vaguely toward the crowd where a second cameraman must have been working, "and the chances are, I shall be editing the entire affair in my kitchen with scissors against the window. Directing, my foot." She shook her head in great disdain.

But Libertas, undeterred, was already fishing in her pocketbook for her business card. "Fräulein Riefenstahl—" she began, forgetting herself.

"Leni."

"Leni. I work for MGM's publicity department. Would it be at all possible to organize a meeting with you after you're finished here? We should so love to sponsor your editing and we will be more than happy to reimburse all of the expenses you've already gone through. Please consider this and give me a call when you're back in Berlin."

Much to Libertas' relief, Leni took her card, studied it with apparent interest and placed it in her breast pocket. "I will, Libertas."

"Libs. Friends call me Libs."

"Libs." Leni gave her a reciprocal warm smile. "We girls ought to stick together, no?"

"Absolutely."

"All right." Suddenly bolt upright, Leni slapped her palm on her hip, clutching the camera in the other hand. "We can sit here on our behinds all day and mope or we can go and shoot some half-decent footage, which I shall later cut into something watchable just to spite that sod and his Party people from the *Promi*." Rising the camera like a weapon after cursing out Goebbels and the Propaganda Ministry—*Promi*—he was in charge of, Leni turned to Libertas for a final goodbye, before motioning the cameraman to follow her. "Keep your chin up, doll-face. We'll show them yet."

"Yes, we will," Libertas whispered to their retreating backs, admiration shining in her eyes.

*

Berlin, December 1933

Libertas had no doubt in her heart that Fräulein Riefenstahl would indeed make "something watchable" out of her rally footage, even if driven solely by her desire to spite Goebbels. But when the documentary premiered at the UFA Palace on the first of December, it turned out that Libertas, dressed in her finest, as the rest of the invitation-only crowd around her, still hadn't been prepared for the newest German star's genius.

As though under a spell, Libertas watched the footage, wondering if it was the same rally she had attended just a few months ago. Instead of the stench of thousands of human bodies and the smirks of SA men, she looked at the faces of noble heroes and saw immaculate formations of present-day knights. In spite of herself, she felt a rush of excitement whenever the crowds burst into ecstatic cheers, driven to near madness by the inspiring words of their beloved, godlike leaders, observing their overjoyed, devoted subjects from the height of their podium adorned with wreaths and flags. How Leni had managed to transform their shared miserable experience into a cinematographic miracle was beyond Libertas' comprehension. The desire to spite the Minister of Propaganda must have been great indeed.

Libertas grinned to herself as she applauded the woman on the stage, who was bowing gratefully to her euphoric audience, her hand, weighed down by rings and bracelets, pressed against her heart.

From his seat, Joseph Goebbels looked on with a sour face. For some reason, it made Libertas feel vindicated, even though she had no part in the complicated affair whatsoever. Perhaps it was the woman in her, rejoicing at another woman's success and a powerful man being put in his place, and rightfully so. Just for that she raised her hands over her head and applauded Leni even harder.

Later that evening, when she approached Leni to personally congratulate her, Libertas didn't expect Fräulein Riefenstahl to remember her. However, it appeared that Leni not only remembered her, but took her away from the clamoring crowd and began to apologize profusely instead.

"I hope you will find it in yourself to forgive me," she said, her hand still on top of Libertas' elbow. "When I submitted the footage to the *Promi* people, I requested specifically for MGM to be put in charge of the production and attached your name and phone number to the paper. But as soon as that odious serpent heard about it—" Leni meant Goebbels, to be sure, and it took Libertas all of her powers not to burst out laughing at such a telling characteristic, "he purposely ordered that UFA should be the studio producing it. I should never have said anything."

"Please, Leni, it's not your fault," Libertas rushed to assure her. "I understand entirely! He *is* an odious serpent indeed," she added, lowering her voice conspiratorially.

At once, Leni's black eyes ignited naughtily. "Did you see his face tonight?"

"I sure did." Libertas readily broke into hushed, vindictive giggles along with the actress. "He looked like he swallowed something rotten!"

"He did. His pride." Leni's gaze turned steely and triumphant. "And serves him right. I know he'll make it a point of honor to turn my life into hell from this night on, but I'll be damned it was worth it."

As Libertas was watching the brightly lit streets of Berlin glide behind the window of the taxicab carrying her home, she wondered if she could make them come alive the same way Leni did on film. After all, Leni only had a few years on her; it wasn't impossible to learn a director's trade from someone capable. And then, it would be her standing on stage—a woman who had achieved something, a woman who had created, a talent of its own, not attached to some man, but her own person, with her own successful career…

Dreaming of endless possibilities, she had fallen asleep with her temple against the cold glass and only woke up when the driver knocked politely on the window, waiting to open the door for her. As she took his hand to step outside, Libertas imagined the UFA Palace entrance before her and cameras commemorating her every move.

Chapter 4

Frits Strengholt, the head of the Berlin MGM studio, was going over a Christmas publicity schedule for Libertas as she took notes. She owed "the honor" of such a personal reception to Martin Tressler's efforts. One of the freelance journalists employed by the prestigious *Film Kurier* magazine, Martin wrote such an outstanding article for MGM's latest release, *Sons of the Desert*, that the German market had exploded in profits. It was just as well, since Libertas had long tiptoed around the studio head with a personal request she'd been too anxious to voice before the notoriously stern man.

"And don't be upset about the rally documentary contract," Strengholt concluded before dismissing her. He was in wonderful spirits indeed. "You did everything that was in your power. Unfortunately, Fräulein Riefenstahl doesn't decide which studio shall be awarded with a contract, the Propaganda Ministry does. And the *Promi* decided that the German UFA was a much more obvious choice than the American MGM." Signing a piece of paper, Strengholt handed it to Libertas. "A reviewed and approved list of magazines featuring our newest release. This shall be the last for today."

He was already busying himself with paperwork, but Libertas still stood next to her chair, refusing to be dismissed.

"Anything else?" Strengholt asked without looking up.

"Yes, *Herr Direktor.*" Libertas shifted from one foot to the other and wetted her lips. "Are there any assistant director positions currently open?"

This time, Strengholt not only deigned to look at her, but removed his glasses altogether, studying her with interest. "Why?

Has someone promising expressed his interest? Have you his résumé?"

Her cheeks assuming a faint blush, Libertas shook her head. "It's not a *he*, *Herr Direktor*. I was asking for myself."

At that, Strengholt burst into boisterous laughter and receded only after Libertas hadn't joined him.

"Oh, you were speaking seriously then. Hm." He cleared his throat, still chuckling, much to Libertas' annoyance. "Surely you understand why no one in their right mind shall hire you, a *female* assistant director?" He looked at her as though he was finding her positively ridiculous. "What next? A woman in the Reichstag? A woman leading the country, perhaps?" He snorted with great disdain.

"Surely," Libertas mocked him, feeling the heat rising in her neck, "one doesn't have to be a man to make great films. As you, yourself, saw, Fräulein Riefenstahl is an incredibly talented director who is admired by the Führer himself. If she could learn how to make films, so can I."

"She learned how to make films because her then-director Fanck was besotted with her. Only for that reason did he permit her to film sequences for his mountain films. And she had an opportunity to do so because she had that Jewish banker, Sokal or whatever his name was, to support her directorial efforts." Strengholt inclined his head, regarding Libertas a trifle mockingly. "Do you have a director who's besotted with you and a Jewish benefactor ready to sponsor your efforts?"

Libertas considered arguing the point, explaining that there were no such benefactors and Leni had to borrow her father's money for an initial investment, but realized that no arguments would suffice against the rumors the studio higher-ups delighted in. And so, she replied with a simple "No," and set for the door.

"You're a great asset to the publicity department, Libertas," Strengholt's voice called after her. "You have all of those critics, editors, and journalists in your pockets just because you're a wonderful flirt and they love you. No man could do your job so efficiently. Consider it an advantage, eh?"

"Why do you sound so mournful?" Martin demanded on the other side of the phone line, still chewing.

Libertas had considered submitting her resignation and never coming back to the office, let alone making use of her "advantage," as Strengholt had called it.

Chauvinistic pig.

But then she had thought of Leni and her words—*chin up, doll-face; we'll show them yet*—and, grinding her teeth, had picked up the phone. The *Film Kurier's* editor wasn't in; Martin Tressler, his newest find, answered the phone, his mouth still full of lunch he had to eat at his desk, unlike the big boss, who always had a table reserved for him at the Josty.

"No reason. Could you just tell him that I called?" Libertas replied.

"Of course." Martin must have washed his sandwich down with coffee, for now he sounded much clearer. "How's work been?"

"Don't ask." Libertas rubbed her forehead tiredly. They had only made their virtual acquaintance over the phone a few weeks ago, but for some reason, Libertas felt a certain kinship with Martin that she hadn't felt even with her immediate MGM colleagues. His sense of humor and just the sound of his voice on the other end of the line never failed to raise her spirits and just for that, she was eternally grateful to the journalist.

"You sound like you could use a drink."

"I could."

"It's Friday. Why don't you come out with us to the Adlon after work?"

"What's the Adlon?"

"I keep forgetting you're not a native Berliner." Martin chuckled good-naturedly. "The Adlon, Libby, is the biggest journalist haunt in the city. You truly ought to come! You'd be right at home."

"But I won't know anyone there."

She didn't know anyone in Berlin, with whom she could go out for drinks, if Libertas was entirely honest. So far, her life in the metropolis had consisted of work, more work, and an odd dinner with Wend when he had time to meet up with his niece. Otherwise, it was just her and her lonely, rented apartment; not even a cat to keep her company at night. With Libertas' work schedule, the poor thing would have starved to death.

"On the contrary, these are the very people you deal with on the phone every day. Only, tonight you'll meet them all in person. It won't be such bad fun, I promise. We aren't a boring bunch."

Before too long, a grin was back on Libertas' face. "Well, all right then. What time?"

"Say, six?"

"Six it is."

At six o'clock precisely, Libertas exited her taxicab in front of the Hotel Adlon. A liveried doorman opened the door for her, instantly transporting Libertas from the snowed-in street into a gilded warmth of Berlin's most famous hotel. She found her party without any trouble after crossing a lobby with its leather armchairs in which foreign dignitaries smoked their cigars, faces half-concealed behind newspapers.

At the bar—all polished wood, marble countertops, crystal ashtrays with the hotel's logo in gold, and liquor that most Berliners could afford only by the glass and never by the bottle—Libertas was instantly swept into a bear hug she hadn't expected.

Martin, his jacket draped over the back of the barstool, had to shout in her ear over the upbeat music and boisterous laughter of his colleagues. "I'm so glad you could make it! What are you drinking?"

Libertas considered asking for a glass of champagne but instead tossed her head at the drink Martin held in his hand. "What's that?"

"Gin and club soda."

Under his surprised gaze, she took it from his hand and took a healthy sip; pondered something for a few instants and, much to Martin's colleagues' delight, signed to the bartender to make her one.

"After the day that I had…" She didn't have to finish her thought. Everyone present had already broken into cheers and sympathetic chuckles.

"I can only imagine," Martin replied. "You're not the only person driven to alcoholism by that *Arschloch* Strengholt, if you pardon my French."

"He is though," a wiry man with a receding hairline, but the liveliest face Libertas had ever seen, inserted. "One has to be a veritable *Arschloch* to divorce his wife just because she was Jewish as soon as Hitler came to power. Before that, her heritage didn't matter all that much as long as her daddy, the banker, paid Strengholt's bills and promoted his career. Willy Brandt…" He thrust out a hand to Libertas. "I work at *Film Kurier* with Martin. We spoke on the phone before, but it's such a pleasure to finally meet you in person."

Libertas' face instantly brightened in recognition. "Of course! How are you, Herr Brandt?"

"Please, it's just Willy. Herr Brandt is my father," Willy said with an expressive roll of his eyes. "An old conservative who disowned me years ago for pursuing a career in journalism and writing all that liberal *Scheiße*, as he calls it, instead of following his steps and joining the Army."

Libertas discovered that she was laughing, genuinely and without restraint, for the first time in weeks. "You have my sympathies. My uncle is the same exact sort."

"Has he disowned you too?"

"Not yet, but I'm actively working on it."

After a few minutes, a circle formed around Libertas and she discovered that Martin hadn't lied when he insisted that she would know all of these people. While the editors dined at the restaurant across the hall, the journalists Libertas had befriended over the phone in the course of the past few months chose to undo their ties, roll up their sleeves, and go over every dirty-laundry detail of those very editors, as they shared a drink and a laugh at their arrogant bosses' expense.

"They're not the old kind, who actually knew and loved our trade," Martin explained with a somewhat wistful look about him. "You would have loved our old editor."

"He was a gentleman," Willy agreed, raising his glass in a toast.

"Dismissed last March." Martin gulped down his gin and signaled the bartender for a new one.

"Jewish?" Libertas asked sympathetically.

"Worse. An active member of the KPD." Willy shook his head, playing with his glass on the marble countertop. "He never let it interfere with his work. We're the entertainment section of a newspaper, you understand? So, he ensured that all we reported was entertainment. His political views were his private business, he explained to me back in 1932, just before the elections. But the Party people who had dismissed him still painted him a Bolshevist of the brightest crimson and claimed that he used his position for spreading communist propaganda."

"MGM dismissed all of its Jewish workers as well," Libertas said, nodding her thanks to Martin, who helped light her cigarette. "They even removed all of their portraits from the prominent figures' gallery. Such a shame," she added in an undertone.

"It is a damned shame," Martin conceded, giving her an amicable, light clap on her shoulder. There was something inexplicably pleasant about the gesture; it was one of inclusion, of acceptance, of camaraderie and shared sentiments in a circle of friends who made her feel welcome and at home for the first time in this big, alien city. "Blast it all, how I miss Weimar!"

"Don't rub the salt into my unhealed wounds!" Willy protested with a groan full of pain. "That was a golden decade indeed. Bars, cabarets on every corner—"

"Opium sold in the pharmacies!" one of the journalists joined in at once, reveling in the communal memories as Libertas watched on, her eyes growing wider and wider in wonder.

"Legalized prostitution."

"I'll drink to that!"

Another explosion of laughter.

"Oh, freedom of speech, how I long for you!" Martin drew his gaze upward, his hand pressed against his chest. "How much I miss writing actual film reviews, critiquing cinematography and actors, instead of writing columns and columns of nationalistic propaganda for each new release."

"I miss Max Reinhardt. The theater shall never be the same."

"We lost our best talents!"

"Do you remember the revolving stage Reinhardt invented?"

"Do you remember Grosz in his cowboy outfit, strutting into the Romanisches as though there was nothing to it?"

Wistful murmurs; mist in everyone's eyes.

"The entire Dada movement was insane!"

"I drank with him at that Count's estate. What a wild weekend that was! I woke up in a bathtub, still wearing my tailcoats and someone's pince-nez."

Her head swimming slightly with gin, Libertas listened to their excited chatter and found herself transported into a world she'd never known and regretted it something fierce. They spoke of a Berlin she didn't recognize; a veritable Babylon where artists created everything out of nothing; where the old was demolished, paving paths to something new and utterly exciting; where women were free to love whoever they wanted, and men kissed men in the open—one never-ending celebration of life she had missed. She felt the absence of these experiences as a sharp pain under her ribcage, where a feral heart was beating that didn't belong in this new somber, SS-infested city.

It was nearing twelve when the men began to bow out, staggering with bohemian elegance in the direction of the exit, where the doorman was already signaling taxicabs for them.

Libertas and Martin were the last ones at the bar—two single, lost souls who didn't rush to get back to their cold, unlighted apartments.

"Thank you for inviting me out tonight," Libertas said, poking at the unfinished crème brûlée with a small silver spoon. They had eaten their dinner in the same casual manner, right at the bar and in between lively conversations. "Made me feel alive. As though I were…"

"One of the guys?" Martin supplied with a grin.

"Yes." Libertas nodded a few times, a warm feeling spreading through her chest under her black knitted dress. Her head was a tad fuzzy but she felt strangely sober all the same, as though her eyes had suddenly been opened to something utterly important she couldn't yet explain. "I felt… felt that I finally belonged. Does that make any sense?" She turned her head to look up at Martin.

The dark threads of his chestnut hair were falling into his eyes, still sharp and burning with intelligence despite the amount of alcohol he had consumed. "It does. I thought you needed that. I heard your voice and—"

"Felt sorry for poor miserable publicity department girl?"

"It can't possibly be easy on you."

"It's all right. I like my job. It's just…" Libertas exhaled, searching for the right words. "I wish I had prospects. I had dreams when I came to Berlin. I wanted to create something. Didn't know what yet—plays, scripts, motion pictures. As long as I could say something with it. But after what I heard from Strengholt today..." A categorical shake of the head. "I'm only good for flirting with magazine editors on the phone and will never amount to anything. Just because I'm a woman and women have three things going for them: kitchen, church, and children." She rolled her eyes expressively.

"You're talking about that ridiculous speech Goebbels made recently? About bringing German women back into the fold of home and family, after Weimar Berlin had nearly turned them all into prostitutes?" Martin's tone was growing more taunting by the second. "The women's liberation of the 20s didn't sit well with him, I guess! An odd thing, too; most men were rather happy about such a turn of events, ha-ha!"

All of a sudden, Libertas was aware of the bartender polishing the glasses leisurely in close proximity. And of her Party member pin sitting on her left breast. She leaned toward Martin self-consciously. "Is it all right that we talk so freely about all of these things? I mean..." She shot a glance in the bartender's direction, who appeared to pay them no heed whatsoever. "It was so loud here before with the orchestra playing and now..."

"We were gossiping about old times." Martin shrugged nonchalantly. "There's no law against that."

"Goebbels' recent speech is not old times."

"It's still ridiculous. Much more ridiculous than Grosz and his cowboy spurs in the middle of Berlin." After a shared bout of laughter, Martin grew serious. "They only mind it when people start talking politics. Back in February, when the old, liberal papers still circulated, the editor of *Gegner*—an idealistic young man who grew up on Weimar's ideals and thought that everything could be decided by way of civil discussion—invited himself and his staff to an SA *Lokal*, where they usually gathered for beer and gossip. The owner expected a brawl, but rather, to everyone's astonishment, nothing transpired. The editor bought the SA fellows beer and sausage, talked to them in a very civil manner about politics and whatnot and even got the Brownshirts to agree to certain points he was making. I heard about it from one of his journalists, how they all walked out of there, unscathed."

"I'm expecting a however."

"However," Martin obliged.

Libertas smiled, but the smile didn't reach her eyes. She knew far too well what to expect from such stories. In this new Germany, they never had a happy ending.

"However, a few days after he and his assistant simply disappeared," Martin continued, blowing a cloud of smoke to the side. "No one knew what happened. They were just… gone. Only after the editor's lady friend contacted the poor sod's mother and the mother contacted her brother, who was an admiral or some such—a big shot, whose name carried certain weight—did the police tell her that her son was in the SS custody. They released him later. He could barely walk after what they'd done to him."

"And his assistant?"

"According to the SS's statement, he had committed suicide while in custody."

"But he didn't?"

"Of course not. The SS killed him in front of his best friend's eyes. After his release, they harassed that editor to sign a paper stating that his assistant's death was indeed a suicide, but he refused. And then vanished altogether."

"They killed him?"

"No, I don't think so. The Admiral's nephew, after all." Martin cringed slightly. "It wouldn't sit well with the uncle. Rumor had it, he moved somewhere far away. Broke it off with his lady friend, severed all of his political affiliations. I don't know what happened to him." He finished his drink in one gulp. "You're right though.

It's time to wrap this party up." He pulled out his wallet and asked for the bill.

"We'll split it." Libertas took out her purse as well.

"Never in my life."

"What happened to being one of the guys? Everyone paid for himself."

"I invited you out. Even when I invite my mates out, I always pay for them. You can pay for me when you invite me for drinks next, now how about that?"

"Next Friday?" Libertas suggested.

"I'm fairly certain that's Christmas Eve."

"Do you have anything better to do?"

After a few moments of consideration, Martin shook his head. "Now that I think of it, not a damned thing."

Chapter 5

The meeting dragged on for what felt like hours. Gathered in the conference room, MGM's staff sat in front of the radio listening to Goebbels' address to the nation. It was the usual business—race and blood and German greatness; only, what initially sounded inspiring to the young girl who'd never set foot in the capital and who knew of the Nazi Party from her uncle's words began to take an entirely different meaning now that Libertas was seeing all that blood and race propaganda from the inside.

"The Führer promised and the Führer delivered!" Goebbels declared to the cheers of the crowd gathered at the Sportpalast for the occasion. A carefully selected crowd, too—the translation was live; no one wished to risk any heckling from the dissidents the Gestapo hadn't shipped off to one concentration camp or another. "He promised to give jobs back to the German people and he did. He dealt swiftly with the Jewish dominance in press, culture, science, and law. We have taken back what rightfully belonged to us. We have appointed people to the leading positions who shall fight for the interests of the German people and not Jewish Wall Street bankers and their capitalist interests."

It took Libertas tremendous effort to contain her emotion and keep her face still instead of rolling her eyes at the hypocrisy of those words. She had recalled Uncle Wend laughing heartily at the "uneducated masses" who saw the "socialist" part in the NSDAP's name and not only ate it up with a spoon but asked for seconds.

"Playing on their ignorance is the most ingenious thing that fellow Hitler could have done!" Wend had declared, swirling his after-dinner cognac in his glass. "After realizing that he would never win the votes of the working masses against the Bolshevists and their KPD, he called himself a socialist, and voilà! Those muttonheads thought he'd be fighting for their 'simple man's' interests when, in fact, it's all of us, aristocracy and industrialists, who keep him and his feisty little Brownshirts in our pockets. Officially, he runs as a populist, gathers his rallies and talks about being the leader for all Germans. But right after, he gets into his Mercedes, drives to a dinner at one political donor's or another, where champagne and caviar flow in rivers, and has a good laugh at all of those muttons who head to the polls bleating his slogans like the good obedient herd that they are while we're getting richer and richer."

"…And everyone who disagrees with our policies should all get out of Germany right this instant!" Goebbels' screeching tore Libertas out of her brooding. "We don't want dissidents. We don't want liberals. We don't want Social-Democrats, Bolshevists, or anyone else for that matter who stands in the way of the new, great German Reich! They are the enemy of our people and shall be treated as such…"

Next to Libertas, Frits Strengholt stared at the loudspeaker in rapt attention, his eyes gleaming with a fanatical light about him.

Trying to tune out the Propaganda Minister's voice that was grating on her nerves more and more, Libertas shifted her gaze to the ceiling and began to study the plaster moldings adorning it.

At the end of the day, Strengholt's secretary handed every employee presents as the MGM head himself looked on with an official smile reserved specifically for such occasions and thanked his staff for their excellent service. The somewhat militaristic tone struck a false note with Libertas, but she accepted the gift with gratitude all the same. The workday was almost over, she would have a flute of champagne with everyone in the conference room and then head over to the Adlon to meet Martin, Libertas told herself as she was unwrapping the present in her office, a soft smile playing on her face. However, that smile was replaced by a scowl as soon as she extracted a book out of layers of rustling golden paper: *Mein Kampf* by Adolf Hitler. Limited edition. Inside, Propaganda Minister Goebbels' signature.

She leafed through it, her frown changing into a mask of utter disgust the further she read.

"It is the sacred mission of the German people to assemble and preserve the most valuable racial elements and raise them to the dominant position...

"...It is the press, above all, which wages a positively fanatical and slanderous struggle, tearing down everything which can be regarded as a support of national independence, cultural elevation, and the economic independence of the nation...

"...if, with the help of his Marxist creed, the Jew is victorious over the other peoples of the world, his crown will be the funeral wreath of humanity... Hence today I believe that I am acting in accordance with the will of the Almighty Creator: by defending myself against the Jew, I am fighting for the work of the Lord."

Her gaze fixed on the window, unseeing, glazed-over, Libertas didn't notice how the book slipped from her hand and spilled its hate-filled pages on the parquet floor. In her reverie, Libertas stood in front of the pyre once again. *That's what they should have been burning before it was too late. All this hatred, all this sheer lunacy, before it infected more minds and grew into something catastrophic.*

She felt her shoulders jerk at the shrill sound of the phone.

"Libertas Haas-Heye, MGM Publicity Department," she replied automatically.

"It's me."

Martin. In spite of herself, Libertas smiled.

"I'm almost done here—" she began to speak, but he interrupted her.

"I hope you will forgive me, but I can't make it today." Voices in the background made it difficult to hear what he was saying. "I found him. I'm waiting for him right now…" The noise drowned out the rest.

"Who?" Libertas pressed her hand to her other ear to shut out all the celebratory noises coming from the hallway behind her. "Martin? I can scarcely make out what you're saying. Who did you find?"

"The fellow from *Gegner*! The editor who disappeared!"

"Oh." She suddenly felt chilly.

"…if he agrees to an interview… such a story… trying to get hold of him when he leaves work…" Martin's excited voice was coming in and out in waves. "I'm in the lobby right now…"

Mechanical noise and silence.

"Martin?" Libertas called but heard nothing. "Call me on Monday, when you get back to work, will you?"

Silence.

Unsure whether he heard her or not, Libertas put the receiver down. Outside her window, the wind howled, tossing the snow in great white whirls. Hugging herself with both hands, Libertas stood for a while and watched the city disappear behind the impenetrable wall. Suddenly, she had nowhere to go and not a soul to talk to in the entire world.

Besides the *Mein Kampf* copies, the MGM staff were granted a short holiday "leave," as Herr Strengholt, who suddenly imagined himself a military leader, called it. Feeling lonely and nostalgic for some youthful innocence she had lost along the way, Libertas boarded the train heading for her native Schloss Liebenberg. Wrapped in silence and memories in her private compartment, she wondered why she hadn't visited earlier. It was not that the travel would have taken long, with her ancestral estate being only fifty kilometers north of Berlin. For some reason, she'd been avoiding her childhood home, replacing personal visits with a postcard, a short letter here and there and an occasional phone call, which she had invariably ended precisely fifteen minutes later with a "I have to go now, *Mutti*. Duty calls. Give everyone my love, please."

It was the calls she dreaded the most. Just a year ago, she would spend hours in a drawing room with her mother, immersed in local gossip and leafing through fashion magazines sent directly from Paris by her father, the fashion designer. Now, Libertas found herself twisting the phone cord in impatience as her mother recounted how fat Frieda's—the family cook's—geese had grown and how Scherzo, Libertas' horse, had lost his shoe when Johannes, Libertas' older brother, took him for a ride around the lake when he'd come to visit on those rare occasions his job in Sweden allowed it. It appeared inconceivable to her, how the tranquil world of Schloss Liebenberg remained unchanged and untouched when entire families had been uprooted and thrown into the violent political current of Hitler's new Germany. All around Libertas, books were burned, storefronts smashed, people harassed, political dissidents arrested and executed; all the while in Liebenberg, life went on without any change.

Her forehead pressed against the window, Libertas suddenly realized that she didn't belong to that old world any longer. She had outgrown it; it simply didn't fit her any more, much too small, much too stifling, much too set in its ways to care about anyone else as long as the geese were getting fatter and Scherzo had all of his four shoes about him.

At the station, Uncle Wend's uniformed driver was waiting for her with the car.

"No suitcases, madam?" he regarded her handbag doubtfully.

"I'm not staying for long."

They spent the rest of the short drive in silence. Warm and snug under the rug covering her lap, Libertas gazed out the window into the dark expanse and marveled at the softness of the night, at the starry sky and the moon that she hadn't seen for what felt like ages. In Berlin, dazzling advertisements lit the night sky, sparkling bright and colorful atop hotels, department stores, and cinemas. *Kakadu—best bar in Berlin. Chesterfields—a gentleman's choice. Wertheim: we have everything. SS, the elite troop: enlist here.*

At last, the familiar bend in the road; Schloss Liebenberg towering white and imposing against the black vastness of the lands—all theirs, as long as the eye could see. Wend's driver circled the fountain—a present from Kaiser Wilhelm to Libertas' grandfather Philipp—and pulled toward the entrance where Karl, the family's loyal butler, was already waiting, dressed in the uniform reserved only for special occasions.

The driver opened the door and Libertas stepped straight into the past.

"How goes it, Karl?"

She already knew the answer before he even uttered it in his usual monotone voice.

"Very well, Fräulein."

"Father is not visiting, I presume?"

"No, Fräulein."

He took her coat and gloves.

Libertas found her mother in the drawing room, as always wrapped in shawls, as always nursing a cold, as always stroking her Pomeranian absentmindedly as she complained about something to her brother, Wend, in her nasal, plaintive voice.

"Libertas!" Without rising, Tora Haas-Heye stretched her arm toward her daughter. "Come here, child, don't just stand there. Give your mother a kiss. How short you've cut your hair! I never understood that fashion… But just how pale and thin you've grown! Wend! Are you not looking after her over there?"

"She's not a child, Tora." Adjusting his uniform jacket, Wend put his aperitif glass down and advanced toward his niece to enclose her in a formal, somewhat stiff embrace. "Why didn't you tell me you were coming home for the holidays? We would have driven here together."

I wouldn't manage the drive.

"I didn't want to impose," Libertas said instead.

"What nonsense!"

"Has *Vati* called?"

"Your father is not coming," Tora announced chillily.

"I gathered as much already." The words came out sharper than Libertas had intended. "I was asking whether he called."

"He didn't," Tora responded without meeting Libertas' eyes. "He sent you presents from Paris though. I told Gerda to put them in your bedroom. He made up for his absence with the quantity—must have sent you his entire new collection."

Instead of a reply, Libertas went to the bar to fix herself a drink. Even if he did, whatever was *Mutti* complaining about? Her ex-husband's absence? His supposed neglect of his fatherly duties? But wasn't it Tora who had left young Johannes and little Libertas to Valerie's—their governess'—care, while she and her then-husband traveled all over Europe, spending three hundred days a year at different hotels and only fifty or so at home? Wasn't it Tora who shoved Libertas into one ridiculously overpriced boarding school after another so as not to be bothered with raising her daughter herself? Now, all of a sudden, after the marriage had fallen apart following Otto's opening a studio in Paris and Tora's refusal to move away permanently from Germany, she had a lot to say about Libertas' father neglecting his duties after she'd been neglecting hers for years.

Gin tasted bittersweet on her tongue. *Martin's drink.* The thought made her smile. *She was growing homesick for Berlin. How funny.*

"What are you mixing there?" Alarm was evident in Tora's voice.

"Gin and tonic," Libertas replied tonelessly, without turning around.

"Since when are you drinking?"

"Mother, you make it sound like I actually *drink*."

"Now, I don't mind some wine with dinner—" Tora began.

"And I don't mind some gin and tonic before," Libertas cut her short, not in the mood for lectures. "If you will excuse me…"

Already in the hallway, she heard Tora asking Wend what had happened to her daughter.

"Berlin."

Libertas imagined him shrugging in his usual nonchalant manner as he said it. Feeling strangely adult and rebellious, she began ascending the steps to the second floor.

Nothing had changed in Libertas' bedroom in her absence. It was still girlishly white and airy, tidied to immaculate perfection by the family maid Gerda, but otherwise preserved like a historical artefact: the room of a German aristocrat, early twentieth century. Previously belonging to Libertas Haas-Heye.

She sat on her childhood bed, a multicolored ocean of dresses, furs, hats, and silk shoes strewn around her, suddenly feeling like an intruder in her own bedroom. The old Libertas' ghost now haunted these quarters. The new Libertas didn't belong here any longer.

Her mind at war with itself, Libertas pulled the phone to her lap and begged the operator to connect her with Paris.

Yes, she was aware it was Christmas Eve. Yes, she realized that everyone was calling everyone else. She would pay money, whatever it is. Hell, she'd double the charges, just let her talk to the only person she felt close to.

The operator took pity on her.

"Libs! How's my little girl?"

Rather to her surprise, Libertas felt tears pricking her eyes when she heard her former governess' voice on the other end of the line. Valerie had left for Paris when both of her charges had grown up and Libertas' father had offered her a position at his fashion house. Yet, Libertas still missed her dearly—a stranger, really, who was more of a mother to her than Tora would ever be.

"I'm really great, Valerie." Her voice was bright, but the wrapping paper and hat boxes were swimming and dissolving before

Libertas' eyes. "Berlin is amazing. Not at all like when I was in a boarding school there. We weren't allowed to go anywhere, only to museums and only accompanied. But now the city is all mine."

"Are you taking it by storm?" The excitement was genuine in Valerie's voice.

Which made it even more painful to lie to her in such a despicable manner.

"Oh yes, I am! I work for MGM's publicity department."

"Otto told me. Your father's so proud of you! If he didn't have that dinner with the Prime Minister tonight—"

"It truly is all right, Valerie," Libertas interrupted her before the sympathy in the governess' tone grew too much to bear. "You don't have to explain, I understand completely."

As though catching on, Valerie changed the subject. "Well, *I* am here, so tell me all about your work! Are all the film stars kissing your perky little behind?"

Libertas discovered that she was laughing, through tears, but it was as genuine as it came. "I rarely deal with film stars, mostly with journalists. But that's even better."

"You've made new friends?"

"Oh yes! Martin and Willy and Carl and Norbert—"

"Wait, wait, these are all male names."

"Well, all of my new friends happen to be men."

"Just friends?"

Libertas imagined Valerie arching a mock-suspicious, lively brow.

"Just friends," she confirmed, chuckling in embarrassment. For some reason, Martin's wry grin appeared in her mind and she felt heat rising in her cheeks. They were indeed just friends, but who knew? Perhaps, it would eventually grow into something bigger…

Valerie's next question brought her out of her reverie. "No brooding handsome scriptwriters swept you off your feet yet?" She was all playfulness, as always.

"No. But I did meet Fritz Lang."

"Big deal! We dine with him every other weekend. He lives on the same floor with us at The Ritz."

"Oh no, you're lying!"

"I would never."

"I'm so jealous!"

"So, come here!"

"I can't... I work. Why don't you come here instead? You work with *Vati* as his assistant, he'll let you go for as long as you—" Libertas stopped herself abruptly.

There was a silence on the other end.

"Forgive me." Libertas exhaled. "I forgot."

Forgot that a Jewish woman who had raised her as her own was now a stateless person and would never be allowed to set foot in the new German Reich again. All at once, Libertas felt lonelier than ever.

Dinner was a somber affair. The conversation didn't stick, words and unfinished sentences falling apart like the pages of a book soaked in the rain, the familial glue unable to hold it all together. Wend talked politics to no one in particular. Tora made attempts to question her daughter about Berlin, but the questions were somehow all wrong, superficial, not deserving any further elaboration.

Yes, the landlady from whom Libertas is renting her apartment is nice.

Yes, the apartment is heated well. No, there is no fireplace. Just one bedroom.

She eats just well—MGM has its own canteen.

Yes, she does take the underground most of the times. No, it's not dangerous. No, no one gets robbed on the train.

The dining room was much too big for just three of them. The soft glow of the chandeliers couldn't even reach the other end of the long, oak table. Shadows gathered in the corners, quivering and shifting in the candlelight. When Libertas suggested that Karl, Frieda, Gerda, and Wend's driver join them—it was Christmas, after all—Tora just looked at her, positively mortified, as though her only daughter had completely gone off her head.

"But, *Schatz,* this is Schloss Liebenberg, not Berlin," Uncle Wend admonished her with a humoring smile. "We don't indulge in that liberal unification-of-the-classes sort of thing here."

Just behind his back, still as a statue, Karl stood, a white napkin wrapped around his bent arm. Libertas couldn't help but wonder what was going through his mind. He was a well-groomed sort though, coming from generations and generations of butlers. Outwardly, his expression hadn't betrayed a single emotion.

Dispirited, Libertas lowered her eyes back to her plate. Her mother didn't lie though—Frieda's goose was very fat indeed.

"I'm well aware, *Onkel.*" She stabbed at the bird's thigh with her fork. "It's very difficult to forget where I am."

Only fifty kilometers separating them, and yet, they might as well have been at different ends of the earth.

Libertas left early the next morning. As the train carried her back to the capital, she regretted she had taken it in the first place.

Chapter 6

The summons from the Gestapo waited for Libertas upon her return. The envelope was thick, official, with a stamp of the Führer's portrait and a return address of a new headquarters at Prinz-Albrechtstraße 8. Puzzled and faintly unnerved, Libertas turned it in her hand, searching her memory and failing to come up with a possible explanation for such an unexpected request.

Order, not a request; the failure to follow would result in a visitation from the Gestapo and her arrest, according to the last few lines, typed at the very bottom of the official document.

After the rush of nervous excitement had passed, Libertas found certain comfort in the fact that it was a summons. Summons meant they merely wished to talk. About what, that was anyone's guess, but Libertas thought ignoring it would be highly unwise all the same.

And so, after phoning work and explaining that she would be late due to an emergency, Libertas swiftly dressed, gulped down her coffee, leaving an untouched jam sandwich on the plate, her stomach too unsettled to eat, and ran down the steps, fastening the buttons on her coat as she went.

When she announced the address to the cabbie, he regarded her with silent horror through the rearview mirror.

"Good luck." Libertas heard him mutter just moments before he drove off, leaving her alone in front of the familiar entrance from which the bronze plaque—State School of Decorative Arts—had been pried off, leaving only a pale scar in the limestone façade.

It seemed only yesterday the Haas-Heye family car had delivered her and her brother Johannes straight into their beaming father's arms, whose fashion studio occupied almost the entire floor in this very building. It seemed only yesterday Libertas had watched her father's fashion students drape silk around headless, limbless mannequins as he looked on, nodding his approval or correcting them gently. It seemed only yesterday she had chased Johannes down the maze of carpeted hallways and hid from Valerie in the empty studios smelling of paint thinner, oil, and plaster dust.

Now, from the ground-floor window, a ghost of her past stared back at Libertas, transparent and featureless. Composing herself, she stepped toward the entrance, wondering how it was possible for the building to remain so unnervingly the same and yet house something so very sinister inside—a new German Reich in miniature. It was almost too much she could bear to think of.

Pushing the heavy doors open, Libertas came face to face with a young uniformed SS official sitting at a desk with three identical black phones on it. Obliging her with a typical clerk's smile, he asked if she had an appointment with someone. Libertas showed him the summons, somewhat reassured by the familiar surroundings.

While he was making the call, Libertas looked around, surprised to discover how cold it was inside. Was it because the new occupants of the former school of decorative arts had removed heavy velvet drapes from the tall windows, opening the way to drafts? Or because the thick carpets were no longer lining the stone floors… Why remove the carpets? So that the SS men's steel-lined boots echoed louder within its walls, turning the entire building into one insufferable parade ground?

Aware of the SS clerk's eyes on her as he waited for someone on the line to give him orders, Libertas cast her gaze about as subtly as possible. From across the vast hallway, a black bust of Hitler framed by two crimson banners was glaring at her with his empty sockets—a usurper of the short marble column where a bust of Beethoven used to stand, or was it Menzel? Or one of Franz Xavier Messerschmidt's surviving "character heads"? She'd been too young to pay attention to such trifles. She couldn't remember it now, with the best will in the world.

Libertas felt her breath hitch when, after an innocent glance over her shoulder, she suddenly discovered that there were no handles on the entrance doors from this side. An unsettling chill slipped down her spine. Her throat was dry, as though wiped with sandpaper.

"Second floor, room twelve." For some reason, Libertas felt herself jerk at the SS clerk's announcement.

Thanking him softly, she gathered her summons and headed for the staircase.

A wide flight of stairs she would never again associate with her childhood's carefree games. Bloody banners everywhere. Cool air tingling on her face—even the radiators strategically placed under every window couldn't warm the gothic palace that looked like a church with its arched ceilings and wooden benches—a grand inquisitor's lair, where heretics were tortured in the underground cellars; the same cellars in which sculptures used to come to life and geniuses had been born under the guidance of their bohemian professors.

Libertas hoped for a short wait to collect herself, but the secretary admitted her into a *Herr Sturmbannführer's* office without any delay. The secretary's "we've been expecting you," aimed to sound welcoming, struck an ominous note with Libertas. The secretary was smiling, but her eyes were ice-cold, glacial even.

Inhaling a lungful of air, as though before a dangerous dive, Libertas stepped inside the Gestapo official's office.

"*Ach*, Fräulein Haas-Heye." A stocky man in his early forties rose from his chair and indicated the one across from his desk. "Thank you for coming at such short notice."

As if she had a choice.

Still on guard, Libertas sat on the edge of the chair. "I admit, I'm rather confused, *Herr Sturmbannführer*…"

"Nothing to be confused about, Fräulein Haas-Heye. I assure you, it's a mere formality," he rushed to appease her. His disposition was most amicable so far. "I only need you to sign a document and you shall be free to go."

Libertas scowled as he leafed through a binder in front of him. "You summoned me here just for my signature? Couldn't you have sent it by mail? I'm missing work for this—"

"Again, I apologize for causing you such an inconvenience, Fräulein Haas-Heye. We shall give you an official paper stating that you were here on government business, Herr Strengholt shall never say a word to you against it."

They knew her boss's name. Libertas rubbed her forehead, almost chuckling at her own stupidity. Naturally, they did. They were the secret police of some sort, with seemingly unlimited powers. Most likely they knew what she had for breakfast this morning. Or *didn't* have, for that matter.

"Here, if you could just sign on the bottom." He moved a fountain pen and a typed-out statement bearing her name toward Libertas.

I, Libertas Haas-Heye, nationality German, residing at... have been acquainted with Martin Tressler, a journalist employed at Film Kurier, *and can attest to the fact that he established suicidal tendencies... during our last conversation, he admitted to me that he considered ending his life...*

Libertas' eyes widened in astonishment as she read the contents.

"Is this some sort of a joke?" she demanded, louder than she had intended.

"Not in the slightest."

"Martin has never been suicidal. He's perfectly fine. You ought to summon him here and you shall see for yourself."

The SS man regarded her strangely. The silence lasted so long, Libertas grew aware of the clock ticking on the wall to her left, louder and louder, measuring time till the drop of an ax.

"I'm afraid, it would be impossible given the circumstances, Fräulein Haas-Heye."

"Why is that?"

"Herr Tressler is dead."

"No, he's not!" Libertas protested, ice spreading through her veins with every frantic heartbeat. "I met with him just over a week ago. I spoke to him on the phone on Friday!"

The SS man inclined his head to one side in what was supposed to be sympathy. "And on Saturday, Herr Tressler unfortunately committed suicide."

"No, he didn't."

"Threw himself out of the window of his fifth-floor apartment."

"No, he didn't!"

"I'm afraid so."

"You're lying!"

"It's a fact. And I need you to sign this statement."

"I'm not signing anything." Now, instead of ice, wrathful fire radiated out of Libertas' eyes. With purpose, she pushed the pen and the official statement back toward the Gestapo officer. "Martin wasn't suicidal. If anything, he was excited. He had just—"

...discovered that editor from Gegner *and couldn't wait to uncover his true story.*

She stopped herself abruptly as the Gestapo man pulled forward, his gaze turning thoroughly hawkish.

"You were saying?" he said softly, searching her face, probing for the slightest slip of the tongue.

"He had just met a girl he liked very much," Libertas finished instead, keeping her face expressionless. "He was very excited about spending the holidays with her."

The Gestapo man looked slightly disappointed. Still, he recovered himself with impressive speed and tore a piece of paper out of the pad in front of him. "A girl, you're saying? Do you happen to know her name?"

"No, he didn't say. I'm sorry."

"Oh well." He gave a shrug and sighed. They had almost tied all the ends into a nice knot and now this nameless girl, this new witness, his expression seemed to say. "We'll find her sooner or later. Now, if you will please sign this, I won't hold you any longer."

A hint of a defiant sneer appeared on Libertas' face. She may have been young, pretty and blond, but stupid she was not. She saw right through the officer and his pitiful little charade.

"I'm not signing anything. Martin was not suicidal. Someone killed him."

The official flinched ever so slightly. "Fräulein Haas-Heye, I assure you, we have thoroughly investigated the case and it's pretty much open-and-shut. It was a suicide—"

"No, it wasn't. He wouldn't have done it. Someone must have helped him."

"You watch too many of your American murder pictures there at MGM." Gone was the friendly people's servant persona. The hawk was back, cold, predatory. "Don't be stubborn. Everyone else has already signed it. Herr Brandt. Herr Schwartz. Herr Henning… All testified to the same thing."

"After you dangled them by their ankles from their apartment windows too?" Libertas asked in a toneless voice.

The man chuckled softly. "No. They saw reason without such methods of persuasion."

"Well, I don't."

"That's unfortunate."

Libertas gathered her handbag and rose from her chair. "I'm leaving."

"Go ahead. I'm not holding you."

"If you get someone to falsify my signature—" she began.

He interrupted her with a raised hand. "It's unnecessary. We'll make do just fine without your statement." With a mocking grin, he waved a stack of signed papers in front of her.

Disgusted, Libertas swiftly turned on her heel and headed for the door.

She half-expected a secretary to call after her; for one orderly or another to intercept her on the stairs and order her to come back; for the clerk—or the sentry, whatever his official job description was—to prevent her from leaving. However, he only smiled at her once again, wished her a good day, pressed a buzzer that opened the door from the inside, and Libertas found herself back on the street, incensed, trembling with helpless ire, gasping for air that suddenly stuck in her throat and finally tore out of her in a series of sobs. For Martin, for the *Gegner* editor and his assistant who would never get justice, for Germany that was heading someplace very dark and from which there was no escape. Just as with the Gestapo's new headquarters, there were no handles on this side of the door. They were trapped good and fast. No one was coming to the rescue.

It rained on the day of the funeral. Cold, icy rivulets pelting down on the closed coffin containing the broken body of her friend. Libertas' face, streaked with tears, somber and pale; her eyes, unblinking and stern, boring holes through the wreath with a *Hakenkreuz* on it and two black ribbons—from the journalists' gild, the Propaganda Ministry. He wouldn't want it there, but they had placed it there all the same. Former bosses and colleagues, all with Party pins on their lapels, their expressions appropriately funereal. Only Martin's mother was crying openly, a handkerchief pressed to her mouth to stifle her silent scream.

In front of the coffin, the *Film Kurier* editor was giving the eulogy. No priests for sinners who took their own lives. They ought to be grateful the new Reich permitted to bury them in the family plots along with the others.

All thanks to our gracious Führer.

They lowered him right into the mud, washed away with the rain as though the skies themselves cried at the injustice.

Swallowing tears and anger, Libertas dropped white roses on the black shining wood. The pristine color of innocence, for the unjustly murdered martyrs.

The small crowd began to disperse. In the distance, by the parked car, two men in black leather coats stood, watching everyone closely. Libertas noticed them only after Willy Brandt motioned his head toward them, mortified, when she tried to approach him. Placing his sodden felt hat atop his head, he promptly swung round and went in the opposite direction—away from the coffin, from her, from the men in leather coats.

There would no longer be meetings at the Adlon, Libertas realized just then. Along with Martin, the last hope for a free press had been buried.

Chapter 7

January 1934

"Libertas?" Erich Tischendorf stuck his head through her office door. "I'm going to need you to promptly drop whatever you're doing and find us a new commercial artist."

"What happened to ours?"

Tischendorf grimaced. "He's gone."

"Just gone?"

"It appears to be the case."

"People don't just disappear."

Tischendorf cringed further, as though the entire conversation was making him rather uncomfortable. "He was a Social-Demo-crat," he whispered in a dramatic hushed voice, widening his eyes expressively.

"You're saying it like it's a contagious disease."

"Very contagious, indeed! He has caught it from somewhere. You know how it can happen with vulnerable minds. At any rate, he won't be coming back. A gentleman from…" Tischendorf rapidly snapped his fingers. "I'm forgetting which department he said he belonged to…" Annoyed at the memory failing him, he flicked his hand, surrendering. "The point is, he called Herr Strengholt personally to inform him that we ought to find a replacement for poor Herr Weber."

"How very thoughtful of him," Libertas uttered with great sarcasm.

"I thought so too." Apparently, the sarcasm was lost on Tisch-endorf. "Well, I won't hold you up any longer, you have a lot of work to do." With that, he disappeared behind the door so that she wouldn't torment him with any further interrogations he obviously tried to avoid at all costs.

Libertas spent the next hour on the phone in a frantic effort to secure the services of an artist in place of the one who, it was her profound conviction, would soon be grieved by his former colleagues for "committing suicide" by throwing himself out the window or into the freezing waters of the Spree. With a chilling lack of interest, Libertas wondered if the Gestapo leather coats were preparing his body at this very moment.

At last, after she had almost lost all hope, she tried Willy Brandt's number. He'd been avoiding her since Martin's funeral and she respected his keeping his distance but couldn't help but feel a pang of something painful in her stomach at the manner in which Willy's voice had tensed once he realized who it was on the other end of the line.

"I have a work-related question," Libertas said before he could find an excuse to slam the receiver down.

"Yes?" Willy was still on guard.

"Do you happen to know any commercial artist who isn't employed full-time?"

"A commercial artist?" Willy's tone relaxed a tad. "Let me think…"

Libertas waited patiently in the pause that followed. "Keep it between us, but we're rather desperate here at MGM. Ours has just—" She quickly bit her tongue. The memories were still too fresh for the both of them. "Never mind. It doesn't necessarily have to be a commercial artist, anyone with artistic abilities will do."

"I *do* know an advertising illustrator—"

"Perfect!" Libertas was already groping for a pencil among the paper mess littering her desk. "We'll take him. Do you have his contact information?"

"Only his landlord's number. He has just moved to Berlin from Hamburg and isn't employed anywhere yet. His name is Richard von Raffay. And, Libs?"

"Yes?"

"Better call him now before he goes bar-hopping. He's a bit on the wild side, that fellow."

A faint smile lit Libertas' face. The wild sort was just what she'd been craving in this new militaristic state where everyone tried their utmost to blend in.

Libertas met Richard von Raffay at the fashionable Café Kranzler onc of the few rare places on the Kurfürstendamm that hadn't yet lost its charm to Nazism. Its usual three long rows of tables under the bright awning just outside the restaurant had been removed for winter, but inside it was lively, as was always the case with places favored by bohemian Berliners. Outside, swastika flags may have been flying, but inside, the laughter of Absinthe-stained ghosts of the reckless past echoed around the walls, bounced from table to crowded table, reflected in the shining eyes of freethinkers exchanging illegally smuggled, prohibited editions under the table and quivered in the corners at the only sight of a uniform stopping by the bar to quickly gulp down his afternoon coffee.

A tall, exceedingly handsome man who couldn't have been a day older than thirty rose swiftly to his feet as Libertas approached his table by the window indicated by the maître-d, and enclosed her palm into both of his. Richard von Raffay did have the hands of an artist, she couldn't help but notice just then. Narrow white palms; long, sensitive fingers with neatly manicured nails, and telling callouses on his index and middle fingers from the pencil—or brush—he rarely parted with. In front of him, on the immaculately white tablecloth, lay an open portfolio, just a glimpse of which instantly told Libertas that she had discovered a true treasure.

"Thank you so much for meeting me on such short notice, Herr von Raffay—"

"Ricci." A warm, toothy grin, reaching his hazelnut eyes framed by long, dark lashes. There was something defiant in the manner in which he had offered that insolently non-German version of a nickname, a spark that Libertas recognized before anything else. "And it is I who ought to thank you for offering me this incredible opportunity, Fräulein Haas-Heye."

"Libertas," she offered and added, after a short moment of hesitation, "Libs."

Ricci's face brightened even more after a shadow of recognition of a fellow rebellious spirit passed through his eyes.

It was Libertas' turn to smile—not just from the triumph of securing an artist for MGM and saving her bosses from the impending disaster of having to release a new feature presentation without any promotional posters—but from the intuitive feeling deep inside her gut that was telling her that she had found a new friend who was just as free-spirited as she was and who wouldn't quit their friendship because of the threat of some leather coats.

As they were getting to know each other, Libertas discovered that Ricci laughed easily and loudly, throwing his head back to reveal two rows of enviously white teeth. Admitting to being jobless and almost destitute if it weren't for some loyal friends who had taken him in, he tipped waiters with the generosity of a count—"for good karma." Through the bold letters spelling Kranzler on the other side of the window, Ricci proudly and defiantly pointed to the Harley-Davidson motorcycle parked on the street outside, which was presently being admired by a small awestruck gang of *Hitlerjugend* boys.

"The best, most loyal ride I've had." Ricci smiled fondly at the gleaming chrome and gulped down his espresso in one shot. "Would you believe that I rode it all the way from Hamburg to here?"

Libertas did.

"Nothing but a single backpack on my shoulders and the wind in my face." He closed his eyes dreamily at the memory. "Freedom…"

His drawings were like him—angular and fearless, all bold strokes and unapologetic vision. But it was when Libertas began to interview him for the position that she realized she had indeed met a truly kindred spirit.

"I have to write your answers down to demonstrate to my superiors that you're not just qualified for the position, but a man of good moral character," she explained apologetically, extracting a notebook and a mechanical pencil.

A man of good moral character? Ricci pulled forward eagerly. *Now that should be interesting,* his very mischievous posture said.

"Are you a member of the Party?" Libertas began.

"I would have been…" Ricci looked appropriately grave, "only, I fear, I spend all my money on booze and girls and have nothing left to pay Party fees with."

Struggling to suppress her laughter, Libertas marked "no" under the question.

"What are your aspirations concerning your possible position at MGM?"

"I'll buy a boat with my first salary," Ricci replied just as solemnly. "After I pay off all my debts, of course."

"A boat?"

"Yes. A sailboat. To host wild Weimar-style parties on it." His earnest expression had not once wavered.

It took Libertas great effort not to burst out laughing. "You ought to elaborate on how you think your art shall help the Party and the German people."

Eyes drawn to the ornate ceiling, Ricci pretended to ponder. "I shall buy that boat and… invite Party members like yourself to partake in my wild parties?" He ended on a questioning note. "Will that do?"

"I'll just write that it's your utmost desire to serve the Party and the people by all appropriate means."

"Can I ask you something now?"

"Of course."

"Is MGM all nationalized as well now?" This time he was serious indeed.

Libertas grimaced and moved her shoulder in an evasive gesture. *What do you think?*

"I thought Berlin would be different." Ricci sighed, leaning back in his chair and locking his hands behind his head.

"Different from Hamburg?"

"Mhm. It was the only city that didn't vote for Hitler. A former multinational metropolis. A Babylon of Europe…"

"Don't lose your hope." After a quick check of her surroundings—no uniforms around this time, just the regular bohemian crowd drinking in the afternoon and indulging in the artistic world's gossip—Libertas pulled out an illegal copy of Remarque's latest book from inside her handbag to demonstrate it to her new friend and colleague. "My former governess sent it to me from Paris. The post office still closes its eyes to similar contraband ending up in Berlin. So, nothing is lost for the Babylon of Europe yet."

His eyes fastened onto the cover in an awestruck fascination, Ricci breathed, "Libs, you have just given me life."

"Welcome to Berlin." She grinned coyly.

"I'm beginning to think I shall rather enjoy my stay here."

June 1934

"So, you're quite certain you don't want to accompany me?" Wend asked Libertas as they stood in front of her apartment building. They had just had their obligatory Sunday family dinner and Wend's driver had given Libertas the obligatory ride home. The entire evening, he had gone on about Reichsmarschall Göring's invitation to the newly constructed Carinhall, named after Göring's late wife Carin, whose body was to be interred there during a pompous ceremony that upcoming weekend. "Even the Führer is going to be there."

Even more reason not to go, Libertas mused to herself but, as was her habit, only smiled sweetly at her uncle. "Are you quite certain you don't want to come with me and Ricci to the marina?"

In the course of the past few months, it had become a game of sorts between niece and uncle: Wend kept trying to get Libertas to tag along to one political function or another; Libertas, in turn, kept drowning him in invitations to the gatherings of the last surviving liberals in Berlin, starting at the Blau-Rot marina where Ricci now had his own dream boat ("small, but with all its sails about it; all business as it should be," according to Ricci himself) and ending at Rio-Rita swing club, still miraculously functioning in the new, freedom-rejecting Reich.

"Ricci is that Dadaist fellow with long hair?" Wend asked with a grimace of faint distaste.

Despite seeing Libertas' new friend several times and even sharing a lunch with them on one rare occasion, Wend positively refused to acknowledge Ricci for anything but "the Dadaist with long hair," which amused Libertas greatly.

"Not all artists are Dadaists, *Onkel.*"

"I saw his sketches. They're all angular and strangely distorted."

"And that's precisely what MGM wants. It's the latest fashion in Hollywood, haven't you heard?"

Wend grimaced further. "That's not real art."

"What's real art to you?"

"Portraits and paintings in picture galleries, where people look like people. Now, it's all shapeless figures and you can't even tell whether it's a man or a woman, breasts or murder. Everything is either sexualized or sensationalized. And all of it comes from your beloved Hollywood. Good thing Minister Goebbels banned their degenerate art and literature. As though we don't have our own great writers and artists."

"We do—Erich Maria Remarque." Libertas began to bend her fingers. "Oh, beg pardon, he's banned too. Thomas Mann—now, that's a true literary genius. Apologies, he's also banned. Brecht! Oh. Never mind him as well. What about—?"

"You've made your point." Wend sighed, growing serious. "Libertas, you don't have to like all of their policies. As with every regime, there will always be certain…" He appeared to be searching for the suitable word. "Extremes," he finally offered, throwing a probing glance at his niece and looking away, seeing that she didn't buy it. "We're aristocracy, Libby. Would you have truly rather preferred it if the Bolshevists were in power? Have you forgotten what they did to their upper classes in the former Tsarist Russia?"

Libertas broke into mirthless laugher, shaking her head. "Straight out of Goebbels' propaganda book," she muttered under her breath. "*Onkel*, I'm not a 'clueless member' of the 'uneducated masses' he loves so much. It's them, who swallowed his concept of NSDAP against the Bolshevists as if there were never any other options. How conveniently he erased the entire history of Weimar and Social Democrats running it just fine. Yes, there were times of turmoil, but we overcame; we were moving in the right direction, toward democracy—"

"Libertas." Wend regarded her sternly and wistfully. "They were going to break up our familial lands. Social Democrats were too weak to resist the demands of the people, giving in more and more to their outrageous calls for equality and all that rot. Schloss Liebenberg, the estate that we've owned for centuries, broken into plotlands for some farmers! Over my dead body would I have allowed it to happen. Yes, Hitler says some cringeworthy things about Jews and homosexuals and communists, but he's the one who shall keep our lands intact, and that's all that matters to me.

And what should matter to you, as my heiress. We, the aristocracy and the industrialists, are the ones who pump the money into the Party's veins. They will stand by us and pass laws that shall be in our interests."

"What of the *socialist* part in that Party of yours?"

"That?" He laughed heartily. "That nonsense shall be taken care of shortly."

Libertas scowled, but Wend had already switched the subject as though sensing he'd let on more than he was supposed to.

Only two short weeks later did Libertas comprehend the true meaning of his ominous prediction, when she opened a fresh newspaper in her office and came across the front-page article, aptly titled, *"The Führer's security forces suppress the SA putsch. SA Leader Ernst Röhm found in bed with his driver and executed for treason shortly after being taken into custody and confessing to his crimes against the state and the Führer."*

The sun was blazing brightly, and the water was splashing softly against the boat, but Libertas' mood was far from carefree.

"I still can't wrap my mind over what's happened," Ricci declared, his bronze arms tensing as he flipped another page of a London newspaper. "Foreign correspondents don't seem to know either. What in the blue hell did that fellow Röhm do to Hitler that he'd butcher him and his cronies in such cold blood?"

"Nothing." Her eyes still closed, as though facing the gloriously blue sky was physically painful, Libertas pulled dark shades from her forehead onto her face. "The aristocracy and industrialists weren't happy with Röhm's demands for socialist reforms and so Hitler went and chopped off that socialist part of the Party's body. Now, it's just the Nazi Party. No more socialistic pretenses. The workers aren't going anywhere anyway; all of their leaders have been arrested, unions dismissed and pronounced illegal. He keeps them occupied working on his autobahns and happy with the promises that as soon as the last Jew disappears across the border, they'll be sitting nice and dandy on all those Jews' confiscated money. All paid by the likes of the uncles of yours truly, for whom it's much more important that their servants know their place than the fates of hundreds of thousands of people who shall suffer just to pay for keeping him in power. And I'm an accomplice in all this, just by association. How utterly, utterly disgusting," she whispered, her voice betraying herself with a wrathful tremor.

"Don't blame yourself, Libs." Ricci reached out and patted her knee with a friendly affection. "You're not your family. You're your own person. You make your own decisions."

"How am I any better than them? I do nothing at all to help anyone. And standing silently by when the oppressed suffer is the same damned thing as approving of the oppressors' methods."

"Not the same in the slightest," Ricci argued stubbornly. "Protest doesn't necessarily mean a physical march toward the Reichstag, waving flags and whatnot. Reading banned authors and sharing them with your friends is a form of protest. Speaking of which, you were right—Remarque's new book is brilliant."

Libertas smiled through gathering tears.

"Shaking hands with your Jewish friend and inviting him over for tea is a protest. Supporting a struggling artist, who nobody wanted to hire because of his leftist leanings is protest." He looked at her with gratitude. "If we march toward the Reichstag, they will slaughter us all, plain and simple. But we can still protest in small ways. And, Libs, trust me, it will make a difference. Perhaps not in the grand scheme of things, but for that one Jew, for that one artist, it will. And that's all that matters."

Chapter 8

"I'm thinking of quitting my job."

"You're not serious, are you?" Valerie sounded genuinely upset.

For an instant, Libertas wondered why it was always her former governess she called and not her own mother.

"I am." It was Sunday, the evening of Sunday—the most miserable time of the week, according to Libertas herself—good only for drinking cognac alone and writing grim poems about all things dark in her journal. "There are no prospects for me there. Strengholt laughed in my face when I asked him for an assistant director's position. Onkel Wend suggested that I transfer to the Propaganda Ministry to some administrative position, but working at that vipers' nest, no. That, I couldn't do."

"Of course not."

In the pause that followed, Libertas heard Valerie tap the receiver with her nail as she was working things out in her mind.

"Libs, I know you shall say I've gone mad, but hear me out: why don't you come here?"

"Here? As in, Paris?"

"*Bien sûr.*"

Valerie's confident, French "*naturally*" made Libertas break into a fond smile. "And just what shall I be doing there, in Paris?"

"A thousand things! Your father will be delighted to hire you. You can become a publicist for our fashion house. Or a model; and why not? You're tall, slender, pretty as a china doll and—"

"Well? Why have you stopped so abruptly? Continue, by all means. Remind me how I have no breasts or any remarkable behind for that matter." Libertas laughed, in spite of herself, when she heard Valerie snort on the other end of the line.

"Well, you may not be perfect German woman material with two melons for a bosom or childbearing hips, but Paris fashion houses will welcome you with open arms."

After another bout of laughter had passed, Libertas grew wistful again. "That's not what I want to do though."

"What *do* you want to do? Because, you know, as I've always told you, you can do anything. Anything you set your mind to."

A warm feeling spread through Libertas' chest at those words. "Something remarkable. Something that people shall be talking about for years. Something that will inspire others and pave the way for them. Sounds idiotic and naïve, I'm well aware—"

"Not in the slightest!" her former governess protested at once. "And, Libs? You *will* do something remarkable, mark my words. Chin up, girl. Promise me you'll make plans for next weekend. You deserve a little vacation after working yourself to the bone. Speaking of, have you received my latest parcel?"

"With the two-piece bathing suit? Yes. I was going to ask you if that was your idea of a bad joke. You know they've been banned in Germany. Unsuitable for German women. Just like pants. Just like high heels. Just like makeup. Just like the perm. Just like trying to get an education or a career, instead of popping out a soldier for the Reich each year." Even though Valerie couldn't see her, Libertas couldn't help but roll her eyes.

"And that's precisely why I sent you one." Valerie wasn't one to surrender. "That marina where you occasionally go with your new friends, it's private, isn't it?"

"More or less."

"Well then? Are they going to call the Gestapo on you for scandalizing them with your bare stomach?"

"I'm rather certain they'll welcome it."

"Well, then? Go and live a little. Find yourself a young man. When was the last time you were on a date?"

"Young men are not quite on the list of my priorities right now, Valerie."

The wound which Martin's death had left was still too fresh. She felt his absence sharply, like a phantom limb that was no longer there but which still hurt from time to time, especially when the weather turned gloomy and her thoughts grew dark.

Valerie scoffed in mock desperation. "I'm not telling you to get married and start popping babies out right away. I'm telling you to take advantage of your youth while you still can. Have some fun, go to dance clubs, kiss handsome boys, take a couple of rolls in the hay with them when the sun sets."

"Valerie!" Libertas broke into incredulous laughter, feeling her cheeks heat up. "Whatever happened to exercising good influence on me?"

"I am. In fact, I'm the best influence you've ever had," Valerie replied in all seriousness.

Libertas didn't argue this time. That much was true.

July 14 dawned humid and balmy, sending Berliners—those who could afford it, that was—out of the city and back into nature's cooling embrace. Her skin generously lathered with sun lotion, Libertas sprawled on a soft duvet Ricci had placed on the bottom of his small boat, *Haizuru*, specifically for his friend's comfort. Under the lazy strokes of his oars, the water splashed gently, rocking Libertas further into that relaxed state between slumber and wakefulness where the line between dream and reality was awash and where time itself appeared to have come to a stop.

At noon, when the sun blazed the hottest and cold beer from the portable icebox tasted the best, Ricci abandoned his oars and reclined at the opposite end of the boat, his eyes shaded by sunglasses.

"What a perfect day," Libertas mumbled through the haze, her words melting as soon as they slipped off her lips. "I wish it would never end."

Ricci made no reply. He was already sleeping.

Following his example, Libertas also closed her eyes and let the water carry them into infinity.

"...You old fox! Wherever did you disappear that night?"

"Just wanted to go for a stroll."

"In the middle of the night?"

Hushed voices, breaking through the tender matter of her dream, awakened Libertas from her afternoon nap. Her eyelids still heavy with sleep, she lifted herself on one elbow, her palm against her brow to shield it from the sun.

It was then that he noticed her, Ricci's acquaintance in his paddleboat, with a golden halo of light shining around him as though he, himself, was a part of her dream, or had stepped straight from it and into her life.

"Have we awakened you, Fräulein?" he asked. "I hope you shall forgive us..."

"Oh, what nonsense." Libertas waved him off, sitting up, alert all of a sudden. "It's the sun."

"Yes, the sun."

In its light, his skin appeared almost bronze, in stark contrast with the white shirt he was wearing. Strong, muscular arms under rolled-up sleeves; windblown golden threads of hair falling onto his high forehead; eyes, ice-blue and sharp, alert with intelligence and something else she couldn't quite identify.

The stranger also appeared to be studying her with apparent interest; though, he made sure not to let his gaze wander anywhere beyond her exposed collarbones despite the enticement of her revealing two-piece bathing suit—Valerie's present, illegal, as most of them.

Their eyes fixed on each other, they never noticed the knowing grin growing wider and wider on their mutual friend's face.

"What a mutton I am!" Ricci slapped his forehead intentionally loudly, calling the attention back to himself. "Libertas, this is my good friend, Harro. Harro, this is Libertas, my even better friend, for she was raised better than certain people and has never abandoned me in the middle of the night because she fancied a stroll in the city where no one in their right mind would walk after midnight."

The timely introduction broke the embarrassed silence, and, as though on cue, both Libertas and Harro reached for each other's hands simultaneously, sending both boats rocking slightly in the calm waters.

"Libertas. Friends call me Libs."

"Harro. Friends, if they can be called so," a dirty glance in Ricci's direction, "call me Old Fox."

Even Harro's smile was dazzling, frank and open; only something wistful still remained in the corners of his cornflower blue eyes. How was it possible for all the stars to come together and settle in one human being whose face belonged on movie posters, Libertas mused, staring at him with eyes full of wonder. But then he turned to Ricci, and she noticed a still-fresh, ugly scar nearly splitting his ear in two and felt a pang in her stomach. It wasn't a clean, dueling mark some of the fraternity types wore proudly on their faces, it was something he was obviously conscious of, judging by the manner in which he swiped his longish hair to that side as though to cover it from curious eyes. For some reason, it only made Libertas want to get to know him better, to hear all of the stories he had to tell.

"What a numbskull I am!" Ricci laughed once again, his gaze shifting from Harro to Libertas and back. "I entirely forgot that I have an assignment that is due tomorrow morning and I haven't started sketching it yet, so..."

"Oh, no!" Libertas regarded him pleadingly. "Do we truly have to go then?"

"*We* don't." Carefully balancing himself, Ricci rose to full height, suddenly looking very crafty indeed. "*I* do. So, why don't you, Old Fox," he said, gesturing to Harro, "be a good sport and lend me your paddleboat to get to the shore? And you, children, sail my *Haizuru* for as long as you want. Just don't forget to tie her up nice and tight when you get back to the marina."

And just like that, the two of them were left alone, in the middle of a silver river shifting around them serenely as an unhurried current carried them toward the horizon.

"How do you know Ricci?" Libertas asked first, her palms suddenly wet with perspiration—and not due to the heat this time.

"He picked me up when I was wandering the city in one of my brooding states and adopted me into his clique, for which I'm immensely grateful."

"You're a traveling artist then?"

"Something of that sort," Harro replied evasively, as though not quite keen on revealing his true occupation.

"That's quite all right. I'm sort of an artist too, only not traveling. I work at MGM."

"Don't tell me you're an actress."

"Why? You'd be disappointed?"

"Immensely."

Libertas discovered that she was grinning. "What do you think I am?"

For some time, Harro studied her with his head inclined to one side and his eyes slightly narrowed. "You're a writer. A scriptwriter, perhaps?" He kept guessing as Libertas remained silent, smiling enigmatically. "It has to be something creative. Or perhaps you're a set designer?"

"You realize that you're enumerating all male professions, don't you?"

"What do you mean?" he asked, genuinely confused.

"No one would hire a woman to do any of these things."

"I would," he replied, unperturbed, and Libertas felt her heart beating its wings like a caged butterfly under the silk of her skin, barely covered by the thin bikini top.

"Are you not hot?" She changed the subject self-consciously. "You can remove that shirt, you know. I promise, I won't stare."

Harro appeared to hesitate, his expression losing its carefree beauty for the first time as something dark passed through his eyes. "I don't want to frighten you," he said at last, his tone oddly detached, almost hollow.

"I have seen my share of male torsos in my short life," Libertas joked as she searched his face carefully, trying to decipher the secrets he harbored in those two reflective pools of blue.

Without another word, Harro undid one button after another until he pulled the shirt off himself and dropped it onto the boat's seat next to him.

A lump rose in Libertas' throat at the sight of several long, raised scars marring his otherwise perfect physique. Whip marks, she realized just then, the exact same ones she saw in history books, forever imprinted into enslaved people's skins—a map of their endless suffering.

Harro still stared at her, his eyes hard and cool, as though daring her to avert her gaze in disgust or fear. Instead, Libertas only leaned closer and gently traced the jagged lines with utmost tenderness.

"Who did this to you?" she whispered, not recognizing her own voice. "And why?"

"I'll give you three guesses. If you guess correctly, I'll buy you dinner."

When she looked at his face, washed out in a film of her tears, Libertas saw that Harro was grinning again, as though she had just passed a test everyone else had failed.

"The Gestapo?" she asked, swallowing hard—a lump of memories of Martin and the grim halls of the Prinz-Albrechtstraße, Germany's grand inquisition palace.

"It wasn't the Gestapo back then. Just the newly formed SS," he said and added quietly as though an afterthought, "they killed my best friend in front of my eyes."

Libertas looked up at him, her eyes widening slightly, wondering if it was fate that had brought them together to share their suffering and help each other heal from their wounds.

"They killed mine too. He was a journalist."

It was Harro's turn to stare. "So was mine. What was his name?"

"Martin."

"My friend's name was Henry."

"I'm very sorry for your loss."

"And I'm sorry for yours."

"They tried to make it look like a suicide," Libertas continued, a rush of words suddenly pouring out of her to this kindred soul she had just met and yet felt like she'd known her entire life. "Threw him out the window and made all of his colleagues and friends sign papers in which they stated that he was insane and expressed a desire to take his own life on numerous occasions."

"It appears they don't suffer from an overly vivid imagination." Harro sneered with disdain. "They tried to force me to sign a paper which stated that Henry had committed suicide as well, even though it was murder, pure and simple. I saw it happen." Harro's voice rose, a carefully contained anger breaking through his tense jaws.

"Did you sign it?" For some reason, it was of utmost importance for Libertas to hear his answer.

"No." He tossed his golden head, as though the very idea of such a betrayal disgusted him. "Did you?"

She shook her head and saw a smile blossom on his face once again.

He reached out and grasped her hand. "Ricci would be infuriated if he heard us right now." His voice was soft once again, almost caressing, just like the rays of the sun that were rolling slowly westward. "We ought to be flirting with each other and talking about film stars, swing, theater, and whatnot and, instead, we talk about blood and murder."

"You still owe me dinner."

"I'm afraid to think what our first date will be like, if this is what we discuss during our very first meeting."

"Something tells me that it won't be boring." Libertas grinned.

"Oh, I can promise you that," Harro replied confidently.

Chapter 9

Summer exploded around them into myriad lights, sweeping them off their feet and into each other's arms. Each day spent together only pulled them closer, making a separation, even for a few hours, full of torment and longing. They lost themselves to their summer affair and grew inseparable and dependent on each other's company as if it were opium and one would surely die without inhaling the other's scent—the most exquisite drug on earth.

Friends teased them unmercifully, but for Libertas and Harro their summer fling had evolved into something far more serious long before anyone could have noticed. At first, it was just maddening attraction, insatiable desire to consume each other for hours on end, drifting and forgotten on the bottom of Ricci's boat that could very well have been called theirs now; making love; talking until the moonlight lulled them to sleep; waking up in each other's arms and finding each other's lips just as the dawn was breaking.

But then, on the last day of July, a familiar name—*Martin Tressler*—sprang out at Libertas from an old issue of *Film Kurier* into which Harro had had the misfortune of wrapping grapes. The old festering wound in her chest began pulsing once more, resulting in a conversation that soon brought them closer than any simple summer affair could.

"I'm still thinking about my murdered friend," she confessed to Harro as they lay side by side on the sandy beach of the Wannsee, a picnic basket in front of them. "He was investigating something important... just before they got to him."

Lifting himself onto one arm, Harro searched her pensive face. "You can tell me, if you want to."

"I want to."

Only, the unspoken "but" hung between them in the sultry air.

"I will never betray your trust."

"I know," Libertas said softly and reached for the pale raised scar on Harro's chest that stood out against his bronze skin in the rays of the setting sun. "It's just, you have already gotten your share of trouble from them. I don't want you to get involved with this also."

"I may know something. We come from the same circles. Well, at least before…"

Another swallowed truth, still too uncomfortable to utter. He still hadn't told her where he worked after dropping out of journalism on the Gestapo's insistence. She never rushed him. His secrets were his to keep, until he decided to share them with her. Just as hers were hers, only until that day, that was.

"Martin told me about this newspaper—or was it a magazine?" Libertas tossed her head impatiently. "No matter. I tried to find it, but after that book burning, it's as if all of those banned publications had never existed. Not a single issue could have been had and everyone I asked either thoroughly pretended to have never heard of it or advised me to leave it alone for my own sake."

"Was it local? A Berlin publication?" Harro straightened further, interested.

"Yes. A small circulation, but very popular among certain liberal circles, from what Martin told me."

"Do you remember the name?"

Libertas nodded. It was emblazoned in her mind forever, like an engraving on Martin's headstone. "*Gegner.*"

Never in her life had she expected the effect that one simple word would produce. White as ash, his eyes shining wildly, Harro sat bolt upright as though hit by an electric shock. "Are you quite certain it was *Gegner?*" His voice was a mere whisper, drowned, disbelieving.

"I would never forget that name." Libertas stared at him with concern. "What? Harro, tell me. Do you know anything about it?"

But Harro said nothing, just sat there and trembled, his entire body in some wild agitation.

"Do you know its editor perhaps?" Libertas probed, afraid to ask and even more afraid to bury the matter altogether, condemning Martin forever to silence. "Martin said the Gestapo killed the editor's assistant but the editor himself had disappeared. But on that very last day I spoke with Martin on the phone, he said that he had found the missing editor and that he was going to meet with him... Harro?"

Harro's eyes were the color of the sea at storm now, gazing somewhere through her without quite seeing her, lost in memories—or nightmares—of the past. He swallowed hard once, twice; licked his suddenly parched lips as though searching for the voice somewhere deep inside where he had buried it. "I was the editor of the *Gegner*. And it was my best friend whom they murdered. Henry. Henry Erlanger."

Speechless and suddenly cold, Libertas stared at Harro and wondered if fate had brought them together with some other purpose than just to unite two kindred souls. She had always been a skeptic, always scoffed at superstitions and mocked her mother's fondness of horoscopes and all that sort of cosmical nonsense, but that July afternoon her faith had awoken all at once, if not in something higher, but in Harro and his scars that were now hers as well.

Struggling with words that had been locked up for far too long, stumbling over memories that still visibly stung, he told her all about loyal Henry, who was beaten to death in front of his eyes in the SS prison courtyard; showed her a swastika they'd carved into his thigh with their daggers—a mocking farewell present to a liberal fellow, who, unfortunately for them, had an uncle who happened to be an admiral in the Navy and who had demanded his nephew's release. Swiping at the unwelcome tears in annoyance, Harro confessed that he had run like a damned coward, marked for life and haunted both by the memories and leather coats who weren't quite through with him. Ran all the way to the Baltic Sea, away from his family, away from his then-girlfriend, away from former friends and political beliefs, and donned an Air Force uniform just to become indistinguishable from them, just to create an image of someone who had learned his lesson and swore to comply, just not to give them a reason to get their hands on him and torture him again for days on end... Just not to see anyone else he cared about die in front of his eyes.

"If you don't want to see me again for lying to you, I'll understand," Harro concluded his speech, his eyes downcast—already pulling away, already reconciling himself to the fact that she would gather her things and walk away, out of his life—forever.

"You never lied to me."

"I did. You asked me if I was a traveling artist and I said that I was."

"You still are."

"I'm wearing a uniform that I loathe with all my being."

"And I'm a member of the Party."

For the first time, he looked up in surprise. Apparently, imagining this golden-haired free spirit in front of him belonging to the NSDAP was far too wild a concept to grasp.

"See?" Libertas smiled at him gingerly. "We're both not perfect."

"Why?" Harro managed at last, still visibly confused.

"I wanted a job at MGM. Needed to persuade them that I was politically reliable. Just like you, with your uniform."

At last, the faintest hint of a smile brightened Harro's face as well.

Pulling closer, Libertas wrapped her arms around his neck and promised that she'd never let go. From that moment on, there was a different sort of intimacy between them, far more profound and intense than any physical attraction; something that united them against the entire hostile regime, against the iron fist that kept tightening its grip on the nation, against the uniforms that threatened to reduce them to ash for just one carelessly uttered word.

"We are still traveling artists, Harro. We're just in hiding."

"For now."

"Yes. For now."

*

Something transformed in Harro after that day. Some inner, invisible force unraveled its wings, lit up his eyes from the inside with unmistakable defiance. Instead of solitary walks alone, he craved like-minded people's company once more. Instead of hiding out in a dingy rented room, he moved in with Ricci and his friends and once again learned to laugh and drink good wine and sing along as Libertas played her accordion—a concoction of American jazz and dirty French songs picked up at her Paris boarding school and German swing as well, of which Harro had never heard before.

Shortly after Harro turned twenty-five in September, Ricci and his mates quietly gathered their suitcases and moved out, knowing grins in place, and Libertas moved in the very next day. Nothing much changed, aside from Ricci being the visitor now and Libertas the hostess and the mistress of the place, where all the traveling artists were welcome and where German swing was the national anthem and where warm embraces were exchanged instead of stiff-armed salutes.

Their apartment turned into an oasis of freedom amid the sea of black uniforms and crimson *Hakenkreuz* banners; a safe harbor for everyone who still hadn't forgotten how to speak one's mind and to believe in things bigger than blood and race and all the other garbage the Propaganda Ministry poured through its mouthpieces and loudspeakers straight into the Germans' throats.

*

October 1934

"I'm thinking of buying a car."

Harro looked up from his desk, swamped with the paperwork he often took home from the Air Ministry.

Sprawled on the carpet in the middle of the living room, Libertas was leafing through a magazine, her bare, slim ankles crossed in the air. Knowing that she had his undivided attention, Libertas lifted her lashes in a seductive sideways glance.

"A convertible. So we can drive it, sans roof, through Grunewald in summer. I'll wear sunglasses and a silk scarf over my hair and you'll sit shirtless next to me and all the women we meet along the road will fall over with jealousy."

She loved his laughter, this new version of it, carefree and boyish.

"If that's what you want." Harro looked at her over the desk with infinite affection. "How much is it?"

"I'll buy a used one. Around a thousand, I think. I already have more than that in the bank. Don't worry your handsome head about it."

"You're the boss," he conceded with ease.

What a breath of fresh air his view on such things was, Libertas mused, watching him work on his papers with a look of concentration about him. And how delightful it was to feel as though she were in charge after constantly being told that all she was good for was birthing children for the Führer and tending to all of her husband's wishes.

No, she wasn't the boss in their relationship and nor did she want to be. No one was. They were equal partners, switching roles with ease and never arguing over any gender-related matters. Whoever rose first made breakfast, which they shared in their bedroom; whoever left later for work washed the dishes. They spent their Saturdays cleaning the apartment together before making dinner—or what passed for such—for their friends who came over at six sharp. And on days they felt lazy, they took a train to a newly opened Chinese *Lokal* on Kantstraße, where they indulged in sampling fish spiced with exotic sauces and pork dumplings with mushrooms and rice.

In contrast with self-important Air Ministry martinets who never spoke about work with their wives, Harro entrusted Libertas even with his documents, dictating memos and reports and always marveling out loud at her typing speed and the fact that Libertas scarcely ever made a typo.

A few times Libertas overheard him arguing in hushed tones with his parents on the phone when they complained about such unorthodox living arrangements and weddings and grandchildren—as was her suspicion, as Harro never related his parents' concerns to her, most likely in the desire to spare her feelings. He always took her side, sweeping aside all of their arguments in one simple, "we love each other and we're happy together as we are. Why don't you mind your own affairs and let us worry about ours?"

They had each other and that was all that mattered. Libertas only wished such an idyll would last for as long as possible. For the first time in her life, she was unspeakably, unconditionally happy. And each night, as she fell asleep wrapped in Harro's arms, his lips caressing her hair lightly, she knew that so was he.

Chapter 10

Summer 1935

The streets were still light when Libertas and Harro, accompanied by Ricci and his clique, poured from the darkened hall of the cinema on the Kurfürstendamm and into the welcoming cool air of the street. Above their heads, the film title *Pettersson & Bendel* flashed in multicolored lights, somewhat washed out and dimmed in the early-evening shadow. It wasn't Libertas' first choice, just as it wasn't Harro's, but the management at MGM were quite adamant in promoting the Swedish motion picture to all its employees, heaping praise on its "ideological value" and Propaganda Minister Goebbels' personal approval of the film, to the point where not watching it would equal a crime against the German nation, no less.

"It wasn't that bad." Invariably optimistic, Ricci was the first one to speak when no one else did. Ordinarily, the position of the group's leading film critic was reserved for Libertas, but that evening, for the first time, she came out of the theater silent and grim. "The humor was rather primitive for my personal taste, but the actors didn't do that bad a show of it."

Ricci looked at Libertas almost imploringly. She saw the silent plea in his eyes—*yes, an hour and a half of badly filmed and even worse acted anti-Semitic garbage, I'm well aware, but can we perhaps just forget it like a bad dream and head for a drink?*—tried to force a smile to humor him… and discovered that she couldn't.

"I've never felt so disgusted in my life," she said softly and viciously, her entire body trembling with a suppressed emotion under the layers of her light silk dress.

Aware of the crowd around them, lively and exchanging favorite lines from the film, Harro took Libertas' hand in his and gave it a warning pressure. He knew how protective she was of the Jewish after being raised by a Jewish governess whom he'd met on the phone and grew to love like his unofficial mother-in-law. He, too, took the film personally, on account of his murdered friend Henry, who had the misfortune of being born Jewish and had to pay with his life for such an unforgivable—in the eyes of the SS—crime. But it was not the time nor the place to express their disgust openly. Their apartment may have still been a safe harbor for free speech; the streets of Berlin were an entirely different matter altogether.

"But just how accurately they portrayed those Jewish crooks!" a young woman with a beautifully made-up face exclaimed as she and her group leveled with Libertas. "I had a landlord who was precisely the same sly type, I tell you. Every two weeks, he would come round with a little black book of his to collect money for the gas. My mother tells him, *Herr Rosenblatt, we're supposed to pay for gas once a month.* And he makes such an honest face at her and puts his notebook under her nose: *But, my good woman, it's been a month! Look, I have it all written down.* And, naturally, he had a new black book for each occasion that he would show to his tenants. And one couldn't argue with him—his son knew how to falsify our signatures!"

"They're all crooks and liars," her escort, a tall blond fellow who looked like he'd just stepped from the SS recruitment poster, proclaimed, challenging everyone with a sharp look. "The entire rotten nation."

"We had a family dentist who was Jewish," another girl chimed in. Unlike her well-dressed friend, she appeared much more confused and even upset. "He was always very kind to us. The one that we're going to now is horrible compared to Dr. Wasserman. Dr. Wasserman was a pain-free dentist, even had a little sign above his office that said so." A small, unsure smile began to play on her lips. "I used to loathe dentists when I was a little girl. My mother couldn't drag me to one even by force. But Dr. Wasserman promised me that I wouldn't feel a thing and he didn't lie. I truly didn't! He gave me some numbing shot—"

"That's the very thing!" the tall blond fellow roared, his eyes growing wide and wild. "That's precisely what they do: pump young German girls with drugs and molest them!"

"What? No," the girl protested feebly, blinking at him. "He never did anything of the sort..."

"He would have, if he had more time! They're all pedophiles and child molesters!" The blond girl's escort bared his teeth in a snarl. "He was grooming you, ensuring you were good and compliant. And then, when the moment was right, you'd see what he would have done to you! Have you not read *Der Stürmer*? They have just the articles about that sort of thing. I'll bring you a few copies next time."

Unable to take such vicious slander any longer, Libertas pulled on Harro's hand. Compliantly, he slowed his step to let the film crowd pass. Surrounded by Ricci and his friends, they stood in the middle of the excited current, words full of hatred washing over them and spreading further and further.

"...Never even knew a single Jew personally. But now I'll make it my business to warn everyone of their deceitful nature..."

"...Shameless profiteers feeding on our good nature..."

"...Now that was hilarious! One has to admire them: only a Jewish crook could pull something of that sort off! I shall tell my brother to go see it with his whole family. His wife is still much too soft on their account and..."

"...Remember Weiss? He lived on the same floor with us. He acted just as suspiciously as Bendel! I told you he was a bookie and you didn't believe me then..."

Over the gilded rooftops, the sun was slowly setting. The darkness was coming to Berlin, creeping through the streets slowly and deliberately on its silent, spidery feet.

As though in an effort to protect his friends from it, Ricci stepped in front of Libertas and Harro, shielding them from the shadows with his body.

"It's just an idiotic motion picture," he said quietly, with a confidence he didn't feel. "They'll forget about it as soon as the new one comes out. Libs, what's the next one on MGM's schedule?"

With a tremendous effort, she brought a smile to her face and told him the title and how the leading actress was a thorn in everyone's side, but how the director was a sheer delight, even though he was flirting with her terribly...

For the rest of the evening, they all thoroughly pretended that the film had never happened, and that half of the city didn't discuss it on every corner and even at the bar where they'd stopped for drinks and wurst. Only when they were back in their apartment did Libertas let it all out, in hushed, incensed whispers and torrents of protest, and only felt her shoulders relax when Harro enclosed her in his embrace and promised that they would do something. He didn't know what yet, but they would. That much he promised her.

Libertas couldn't quite pinpoint the exact moment when it all started. At first, it was just a baseless rumor that MGM's biggest gossip, Marlene, was telling at the canteen "on the most reliable authority": Jews had been protesting *Pettersson & Bendel* and heckled the six o'clock showing at the UFA Palace cinema. Next, it was Strengholt's secretary who repeated it during lunch. The following morning, Tischendorf mentioned it at the publicity department's meeting, but it was when Libertas saw it on the first page of the *Berliner Tageszeitung* that concern began to prick at her mind like some demented alarm bell.

She swore to herself that this time she wouldn't just ignore the gossip that threatened to get out of control and wouldn't remain silent; after all, she had been at that exact showing and heard nothing close to any heckling. Only laughter and cheers at the Jewish crooks' antics. But her speaking out—loudly and defiantly, in the middle of MGM's weekly assembly—failed to produce the effect that she'd hoped it would.

"What do you mean, the story is a lie?" It was Strengholt himself who regarded Libertas closely and with a warning in his cool, gray eyes. "*Berliner Tageszeitung* is a respectable daily edition. They wouldn't publish it without verifying the facts first."

"Then it's worse than a lie." Her arms crossed over her chest, Libertas refused to surrender. "It's deliberate misleading of the public. I was there, *Herr Direktor*. At that very showing, at that very theater. There was no heckling and certainly no Jews. I mean, why would they even go and watch a motion picture that mocks them in the first place?"

"To protest it and to ruin it for the others. They play the victim. That's what they always do and that's how they get their way."

"But there wasn't any heckling!" Libertas' temper was getting the better of her, but for the life of her, she couldn't stop herself.

Strengholt remained oddly calm. "Minister Goebbels said there were Jewish protests. You're saying that he's purposely misleading the public too?"

Be very careful what you say next, his expression read.

The truth was bursting from Libertas' very chest; she bit her bottom lip—hard—to prevent it from escaping. She'd been fortunate to escape the Gestapo once. It was her profound conviction that the second time she wouldn't be so lucky.

"No, *Herr Direktor*. Of course not," she forced the words through gritted teeth. "*Herr* Minister would never lie to the German people. I must have somehow missed it then. The heckling, that is. Or perhaps I'm confused about the date. Or the time. It's my mistake. I apologize."

"No need to." He was all benevolence now. "We all can get confused from time to time. What's important is that we acknowledge our mistakes in time, when faced with facts."

"Yes, *Herr Direktor*. You are correct, as always." Libertas swallowed her pride and, along with it, her conscience, it seemed.

When she arrived home that evening, even Harro's welcoming kiss failed to calm her rattled nerves. It was her own fault perhaps, Libertas thought just then; she'd been agitated all day and gotten herself into quite a state by the time she left work. But she couldn't help it; it suddenly terrified her, the power of that great propaganda machine that Goebbels kept winding further and further.

"You should have seen them today, Harro!" Libertas kept saying, pacing the carpet in the living room, still unchanged from her work clothes.

As always perfectly attuned to his lady friend's moods, Harro made Libertas a drink, but even her favorite gin failed to take the edge off things.

"I've been working with these people for over a year. They're not a stupid bunch, but educated, intelligent people. But the fact that they would rather believe their propaganda minister than take the word of someone who'd actually been there..." Pale and distressed, Libertas stopped in her tracks and turned to Harro. "I kept telling them that I was there. And they... they just kept looking at me like I was the enemy of the people, simply for speaking the truth that contradicted the official version of the Propaganda Ministry."

For some time, Harro remained silent, brooding over his own drink as he sat on the sofa. "I fear that was all concocted a long time ago," he spoke at last, his sorrowful gaze trained on the carpet. "In fact, it is my conviction that Goebbels thought of it when he saw the film." Seeing Libertas' disbelief, he smiled wistfully. "That's how propaganda works. He said it himself: if you repeat the same lie enough times, no matter how outrageous, people will start believing it. He keeps repeating that Jews are drinking newborns' blood and practice human sacrifice to remain in power. *Der Stürmer* is already publishing caricatures to that effect. Now, the center-leaning, more or less independent press begins to publish similar nonsense, that heckling story being the latest. They're going somewhere with this, mark my word."

"I'm not sure I want to imagine where," Libertas whispered and felt a shudder run through her tense muscles.

They didn't have to wait long. On July 15, mere days after that conversation, crowds gathered on the Kurfürstendamm demanding that Jews pay for their insolence. They grabbed whoever looked much too dark for their taste and gave them a thrashing as the police watched on, indifferent and compliant with the higher orders to stand down and not interfere with the public's righteous outrage.

In the evening, when the masses swelled in number and fueled themselves with schnapps and beer, they took to the streets again, this time smashing the windows of the remaining Jewish-owned businesses and harassing their fellow Germans enjoying their evening in the Jewish-owned cafés.

Encouraged by Minister Goebbels himself, the madness continued for several days. When Libertas and Harro drove through Charlottenburg to check on Henry's surviving parents, they didn't recognize half of the streets. Smashed windows, torn signs, swastikas painted everywhere, along with crude caricatures depicting "the eternal Jew," defaced beautiful façades and storefronts. It was as though an army had marched through it, a drunken army of debauchers and savages, who didn't fight for their principles or freedom, but out of sheer desire to smash things they couldn't afford and destroy what they couldn't understand.

"Make no mistake," Goebbels' voice poured out of state radios, repeating the same message ostentatiously, "the Jews did most of the damage to our beautiful Charlottenburg. When good German patriots took to the streets to peacefully protest, the Jewish scum took to their tricks once again and, under the cover of the night, smashed their own windows and looted their own stores just to blame us and claim insurance money."

Libertas switched it off.

Two days later, Harro and Ricci brought a foreign-made radio they had purchased from someone who could arrange such things, and from that day on, they only listened to the BBC, marveling at how different the truth was compared to what they were forced to listen to in their homeland.

Chapter 11

Winter 1935

"Do we have any plans for Christmas yet?"

Libertas' innocent question seemed to startle Harro. He froze for an instant, his pen hovering over a paper he was working on, his flushed cheeks betraying his state.

"I'm only asking because Ricci wants to rent a cabin in Austria. He was asking if we're coming or not. If we are, he'll rent a bigger one."

Waiting for his answer, Libertas was playing with a tassel on her woolen cardigan's belt.

"Do you want to go?" Harro probed gently.

Libertas wondered if he had one surprise or another planned for them; he was a romantic type and loved that sort of thing. Not wishing to ruin it for him if that was indeed the case, she shrugged her shoulders evasively. "It's all the same to me. Austria won't be that bad, with skiing and all of their quaint little inns. But if you want to stay here in Berlin, it's fine with me too, if that's—"

"My parents want us to celebrate with them," Harro blurted out before she could finish. "If you want to meet them, that is," he quickly added, reddening even further.

It amused Libertas greatly, his agitation concerning all matters of German tradition. They were anything but a traditional couple, living together openly without being married or even engaged. Just like Libertas, Harro rejected typical gender roles, which were growing more and more rigid and pronounced in the new German Reich. Even when he met Libertas' mother and uncle, it was casual and nonchalant—*Mutti, Onkel, this is Harro; Harro, this is my mother, Gräfin Tora zu Eulenburg and my uncle Wend.* Right after they shook hands, Libertas informed her relatives that she and Harro would be heading to the lake now and wouldn't see them until the evening, when they all had dinner together.

Judging by the manner in which they'd welcomed him, with well-bred smiles but a certain lack of interest, Libertas suspected that Harro must have gathered that he wasn't the first young man she'd brought home and who had spent the nights not in a separate bedroom, but her own. Yet, he said nothing and only appeared to heave a sigh of relief, if anything.

Libertas knew of his first serious lady friend out of many, Regine, with whom he'd broken it off right before he took flight to the Baltics from the Gestapo. Harro, too, had that inexplicable fear of forming attachments; he, too, preferred their present, bohemian lifestyle. Perhaps that was the reason why they fitted together so well, like two broken pieces of a puzzle, which, together, formed a beautiful union some bigger picture that they were still trying to see.

"Why would I not want to meet them?" Libertas struggled not to smile, but the mirth was evident in her eyes.

"Their home is rather modest, I'm afraid."

"So you're just now telling me you're not a prince?" Libertas arched her brow in mock astonishment. "How dare you deceive me and take advantage of me in such a despicable manner! It's over between us."

In spite of himself, Harro snorted, rose from his chair, and went to hug his beloved tightly. "I know how much you love our bohemian apartment but I fear once you see my parents' bourgeois abode and realize that this is the future, this is how it may be in years to come, when you see how they sleep in separate bedrooms after losing interest in each other after all the small squabbles over the most minute things, you'll run for the hills and I'll never see you again."

Nuzzling his neck, her eyes closed against the faint traces of his aftershave, deliciously citrusy with just a hint of musk, Libertas shook her head slowly. "It takes more than that to frighten me away."

"Oh, I'm well aware. If my scars and the Gestapo watching my back didn't…"

"And we'll never lose interest in each other and we certainly won't be sleeping in different bedrooms, no matter how many years we spend together. Because we don't fight over anything. We talk it through and we come to a mutually beneficial solution."

"Or I just surrender when I look into your beautiful blue eyes. It's always all over for me when you give me that look."

"Like this?" Lifting her head, Libertas looked up at her beloved with eyes full of the most profound adoration.

"*Gott im Himmel*," Harro whispered, caressing her short platinum locks. "My heart melts when you look at me like this."

"And mine beats faster and faster. Here…" Libertas took his hand and put it atop her left breast. "Feel it?"

"No. Your sweater is in the way."

"Well then, take it off." Libertas' smile turned outright seductive as she pulled the ties of her belt, offering her body to him as she had done countless times before.

They made love right on the carpet in the middle of the living room and, later, fell asleep there, covering themselves with a throw Harro had pulled off the narrow sofa.

Cradled in his arms, bright advertisement lights from the department store across the street playing on her serene face, Libertas lost herself to a world of dreams where only love existed and where their ridiculous, gypsy happiness would never end.

On Libertas' suggestion, they drove all the way to Mülheim, the small town in North Rhine-Westphalia where Harro's parents presently resided. With Harro as her guide, she carefully navigated the road that was growing progressively narrower and bumpier the further they were from Berlin. In place of busy streets, a vast expanse of snowy fields and woods surrounded them, a sleepy terrain with not a person in sight for miles on end. On rare occasions, a farmer in a horse-drawn wagon appeared as though from another age, dressed in traditional garb and holding the reins in work-hardened, bare hands, lying relaxed in his lap.

"His horse does much better on this pitiful excuse of a road than our poor Spengler," Libertas remarked, addressing their second-hand Opel by its nickname. The autobahn construction, which had employed thousands of workers all over the country, hadn't reached those provincial parts yet. For the past hour, Libertas felt every bump in her very bones. Her back had begun to ache, just like her shoulders. "Next time you have a meeting with your bosses, make sure to give them a formal complaint about the present state of affairs here."

Harro chuckled. "I'm Air Ministry. We have nothing to do with the autobahn construction."

"It is my conviction that your superior Göring does. He holds fifteen different titles—one of them must be something to do with the road construction."

Throwing his head back, Harro laughed—freely this time. Libertas suspected it was liberating for him to mock government officials so openly without having to constantly look over his shoulder and mind the level of his voice. More and more of such outspoken types were being arrested all over the country for voicing their thoughts—a crime now punishable by re-education in a new complex of camps people mentioned in hushed, anxious whispers.

"All jokes aside, it is strange—their construction plans, that is," Libertas continued in the meantime, her gloved hands clasping the steering wheel tightly. It was a tricky part of the road, uncleared, with ice under the fresh snow. After Berlin's cobbled streets, something not to take lightly. "I saw the maps in the *Beobachter*. Whoever planned the entire affair must have been drunk."

"Not drunk," Harro said softly, his gaze growing pensive. "A military man, most likely."

"Why's that?"

Next to her, Harro shrugged. The gesture came out somewhat dejected, resigned. "They aren't building those highways for people to drive smoothly on."

For the first time, Libertas tore her gaze, full of concentration, off the road and looked at him in surprise. "For whom are they building them then?"

"For the Army to travel toward the borders of the enemy nations in mere hours."

Harro's words were so quiet, Libertas could barely make out what he'd said. Or was it the message behind those words that her mind simply refused to process?

"Army?" She tossed her head in denial. "We're not allowed to have an army. The Versailles Treaty expressly prohibits it."

"And what does your uncle Wend say about it?"

For some time, Libertas remained silent. "We don't really talk about politics anymore," she said at last. "We don't agree on most things, so…" She released a sigh. "It's best to ignore it altogether than quarrel about it. Now, we only talk about theater, motion pictures, the family estate, and horse races. And all is fine between us again." After another pause, she added quietly, "It's unfortunate that one can't just wish it all away by ignoring it, isn't it?"

Harro nodded sagely and placed his palm atop the warm rug covering her thigh in a silent gesture of support. "Are you tired? Do you want me to drive for a while?"

"Harro, you would tell me if you knew something concrete about it, wouldn't you?"

"Yes. Of course, I would."

"But you don't?"

"No. It's just my guess, that's all. Hitler promised to do away with the Treaty. When he was just running for the Reichstag elections, I wrote his words off as the ravings of the lunatic that he is. In fact, even when the Nazis were already in power, I wrote in the *Gegner* that the NSDAP still didn't persuade us… Thought that they wouldn't go through with everything they declared from the podiums during their rallies. And then they proved me wrong. Arrested me and Henry and since then on, I'm a believer. They promised to make Germany great again and they will. Only, their understanding of greatness is that of savages and criminals. It began with murder and it will end in total annihilation. Mark my words, it won't end well for any of us."

When Libertas glanced at him once again, she saw pain in his eyes that stared directly ahead, as though he was already seeing their common future written somewhere past the white expanse by an invisible, almighty hand.

"Harro! Harro is here!" An adolescent boy bearing an astonishing similarity to Harro charged out of the house in shorts and a smart pullover atop an ironed shirt, seemingly ignorant of the gusts of wind that threatened to carry Libertas away as soon as she exited the car.

Harro's parents—a tall man with a military bearing and a blond woman with an anxious expression, a bit too overdressed for the occasion—stood in the door, basking in the warm light pouring from the hallway.

Despite her nerves, Libertas raised her hand in a friendly wave as her well-practiced, beautiful smile blossomed on her face. It was a defense mechanism of sorts, charming her way into any new group of people, smiling until her cheeks hurt and throwing timely jests around just to ensure that she was well-liked and accepted. Not that she cared one whit about what people thought of her; it was a sad remnant of her lonely childhood when she, abandoned by her parents and tossed from one ridiculously overpriced European boarding school to another, had to fight twice as hard to make friends out of mere strangers, to squeeze affection out of them at least, if her own mother refused to provide it.

"Is this yours?" the boy pointed at the Opel after nearly knocking his older brother down with his bear hug.

"No, Hartmut. It's Libertas'," Harro replied, ruffling his brother's hair and giving his girlfriend a conspiratorial smile over the car's roof. A shadow passing over Harro's mother's face at those words didn't escape Libertas when she turned to the couple once again. "Now, where are your manners, young man? Have you greeted the love of your brother's life properly?"

Something dropped and instantly jumped back into Libertas' throat at those seemingly playful words. Despite his grin, Harro's eyes on her were deadly serious and suddenly, she found it hard to breathe.

The love of your brother's life.

Hartmut, giggling with embarrassment, was already circling the car, his light blue eyes studying Libertas with unconcealed interest. She had expected a shy handshake or another hug—the boy was still young enough to express his affection openly—but instead, he clicked his heels and snapped to an exemplary salute, his arm stiff and straight like an arrow.

"Heil Hitler!" Hartmut bellowed, most certainly as he'd been trained, and right after that harsh bellow broke into that innocent, sweet smile again.

Rather at a loss, Libertas turned to Harro and saw his own surprise and disappointment reflected on his face as though she looked into some demented mirror. Harro had forever taken pride in his family being a liberal bunch, where discussions were always welcome and where freedom of thought was valued the most. It was due to their influence that he'd decided to pursue a career as a journalist and a newspaper editor, until the Gestapo put an end to that dream. And now, this despicable Heil Hitler business and from whom? His own little brother, whom he loved to bits; the most impressionable mind, already corrupted by ideas he didn't even comprehend.

Libertas gave Harro a sympathetic look and decided to smooth it the best she could before Harro said something harsh he'd later regret. "Hello, Hartmut," she said, offering the boy her gloved hand. "I'm Libertas, but you can call me Libs."

Hartmut's grin widened, displaying two adorable dimples in his round, rosy cheeks. He readily seized her hand, obviously excited at the prospect of greeting someone with a proper, adult handshake and particularly in front of his parents.

"Your brother told me you like to sing?" Libertas asked. After getting an affirmative nod out of the boy, she tossed her head toward the boot of their Opel. "That's a relief. I was beginning to fear that I'd dragged my accordion here for nothing."

With Hartmut now holding onto her hand and with Harro's arm wrapped around her waist, Libertas finally made her way toward Harro's parents. There was a nervousness to her fixed smile, which she couldn't even explain to herself. All of a sudden, it was a matter of paramount importance that these two people find her agreeable. Not because it would in any way change Harro's feelings toward her if they didn't, but because Libertas didn't want him to suffer and sulk after every phone call home or avoid such calls altogether, as he was doing of late.

Erich and Marie Luise welcomed her into their home with reserved, somewhat stiff enthusiasm. Harro's mother in particular kept a watchful gaze on the young woman's every movement, scrutinizing her with attention that made Libertas more self-conscious than usual. And so, instead of laughing openly and loudly at Harro's jokes as she ordinarily would do when they were alone or with Ricci and their friends present, Libertas hid her white teeth behind a close-lipped, aristocratic smile and graciously raised the crystal glass by its stem and spoke in a well-regulated voice and sat just as she used to at boarding school, with an unnaturally straight back and head held high and proud.

Only, instead of approving of her son's beloved, Marie Luise appeared to be more and more nervous and almost intimidated by *Gräfin* Haas-Heye—a countess!—under her modest, bourgeois roof. Harro's mother wouldn't stop apologizing for her poor cooking skills, even though Libertas made a point of eating everything that had been put before her on the plate.

"I've never been much of a cook, and we don't have servants, you see..." Marie Luise's voice trailed off as she dropped her fork onto her plate as though in hopeless surrender. *Why did Harro have to go and find himself a princess from a castle instead of marrying a good, modest girl from a good, modest bourgeois family like theirs,* Marie Luise's very expression seemed to read.

Libertas saw that Harro was already pulling himself up, ready to throw a napkin on top of his plate and demand *what was the issue now and wasn't it her, his mother herself, who'd asked them to come and celebrate Christmas with them and if she continued in the same manner, wouldn't it be better if Libertas and he left right after dinner—*

It amazed Libertas how well she had grown to know Harro that by now she could read the emotions in his eyes like an open book. Desperate to save the situation, Libertas broke into laughter and reached out to grasp Marie Luise's hand. Enough with this aristocratic rot. This was not who she, Libertas, was; not any longer in any case.

"I'm not much of a cook either," she confessed with yet another disarming grin, this time all her teeth on display. "Compared to the feast that you have prepared, my skills are rather nonexistent. It's a miracle I haven't starved your poor son to death. Sometimes I think he only eats my miserable attempts at meals because he wants to humor me."

Across the table, Harro looked at her with eyes brimming with love and gratitude.

"My cooking is no better," he said, his shoulders visibly relaxing. "Thank God for the dives that spring up around our street like mushrooms after the rain."

"Have you any Chinese restaurants here?" Libertas turned back to Marie Luise, encouraged by the fact that Harro's mother hadn't made any attempts to pull her hand away. "No? Oh, next time you're in Berlin, we'll take you to our favorite place. It takes some getting used to, but after a while you will discover yourself craving those spices as though you grew up in the Orient, no less!"

"You wouldn't mind us coming?" Marie Luise probed. The invitation was clearly never extended from her son.

"Of course not!" Libertas livened up even more. "We'd love to have you with us in Berlin, for as long as you want. We would go to the opera and to the Linden and..."

Fully in her element now, Libertas was chirping and gesticulating wildly, her eyes shining with the sincerest enthusiasm. Even Erich, Harro's father, began to crack one smile after another as he smoked his pipe, finding his son's lady friend more and more amusing and endearingly charming. By the time the after-dinner drinks were served, with Libertas gladly offering to help Marie Luise with the tray, Erich warmed up to his guest so much that he offered her a tour around his study—something that surprised even Harro.

"You never allow anyone into your study. What happened?" he asked his father teasingly.

"What happened is you finally brought a girl home who knows about these things," Erich grumbled good-naturally.

Behind his retreating back, Harro offered Libertas a mock-stunned expression, to which she giggled silently. Seeing Harro so happy made her mood soar. And Erich Edgar was already demonstrating the antique furniture he'd collected from every country he'd visited as a ship captain: exotic masks, drums, and carpets he'd brought from his voyages to the Orient and the Middle East; and books, shelves and shelves of them, leather-bound, antique tomes lining the walls from floor to ceiling, leaving Libertas breathless with wonder.

"Books are my obsession," Erich admitted, as though confessing to a secret unbefitting to a man of his profession. "And art too. I've always said, through art we learn of the world." Leaning toward Libertas, he lowered his voice even more, "I did eat Chinese food when I traveled there. You are quite right, it is quite a delicacy. My mouth was watering when you were describing your restaurant's menu to Marie Luise. But don't tell my wife, she shall never forgive me for trying something and not sharing that experience with her."

"Herr Schulze-Boysen, my lips are forever sealed."

After a moment's hesitation, during which he struggled to conceal a grin, he finally said, "Call me Erich, please."

Inside Libertas' chest, warmth spread and filled her with exhilaration. She'd won over one parent at least. For some reason, she was certain that Marie Luise would come round as well. It always took longer with mothers.

It was not long after midnight when Harro climbed out of their bed, careful not to disturb Libertas. She wasn't sleeping yet, only floating on that delicious verge between dreaming and wakefulness that made her too lazy to stir. Only after she heard hushed voices coming from the living room did she open her eyes, listening to Harro and his father behind the rustling of wrapping paper. She grinned; they'd already exchanged presents on Christmas Eve, but the men of the house were putting more under the tree to surprise their women in the morning. *Such a sweet gesture*, Libertas thought dreamily.

"Whatever is there to consider?" Erich demanded in an undertone. "I've seen how you look at her. You've never looked at any of your lady friends with such eyes."

"What eyes?" Harro sounded tired, as though the conversation had taken place far too many times.

"You love her," Erich stated calmly.

"Of course I do."

A sigh, full of torment for some inexplicable reason. Libertas raised her head off the pillow to hear better. Inside her chest, her heart was gathering speed.

"Well then?" Erich pressed. "Why not marry her?"

"Have you forgotten what happened with Regine?" Harro hissed back. "How the Gestapo turned her on me and tried to use her to make me sign that paper stating that Henry committed suicide?"

After a pause, Erich exhaled audibly. "No, I haven't forgotten. Do you think Libertas would do something of that sort to you?"

This time, Harro replied without hesitation and with passion audible in his voice. "No. Libs would never."

"I don't think she would either. Hence my question, what are you so afraid of? Commitment?"

"No, of course not. That's ridiculous. I love Libs more than anything. I can't imagine my life without her."

"I'm even more puzzled than ever."

Silence. Only the old antique clock ticking loudly, much slower than Libertas' heart.

"I'm still a hunted person, father. You know it as well as I do. They left off when I began working in the Air Ministry and cut all old contacts, but make no mistake, they will never strike me off their lists. They will always watch me. And I know myself too; if *this*," Harro stressed the word and Libertas imagined him gesturing vaguely around himself, indicating bloody banners in the streets, benches with plates *For Aryans Only*, his own brother throwing Hitler salutes, "if this gets any worse, I *will* do something stupid once again that will put me and everyone around me in danger. And only the thought of Libs suffering for my mistakes instills mortal fear in me. So, no, Father, I'm not afraid she'd turn on me. I'm terrified of what they could do to her to press me into submission."

"Then break it off with her now, son. Because a girl like her, she would not leave you voluntarily. You and your idiotic mistakes. She'll be with you till the end, married or not; you know it and I know it."

Another pause, longer than the first one. Around Libertas, the air itself was tingling with tension. She didn't care all that much for marriage. Neither of them wanted children—at least, not yet—and their bohemian lifestyle suited her much more than any traditional union would. But when, later that night, Harro slid under the blankets with her, wrapped his arm tightly around her waist, kissed her as though he was heading for the gallows, and asked if she would marry him, Libertas said yes without hesitation.

Chapter 12

Schloss Liebenberg. Easter 1936

It must have been strange for Tora to be the one to give her blessing to this young man in a smart uniform who was regarding her expectantly until Libertas cleared her throat loudly and called her mother out of her stunned state.

"You will have to forgive me," Tora muttered, offering Harro an apologetic smile. "I didn't expect it… Ordinarily, it's a father's duty, to give his consent to a couple—"

"He has already asked *Vati*," Libertas inserted at once, her hand resting atop Harro's. "But Harro insisted on asking you in person. After all, it was you who took care of me after *Vati* left for Paris."

She permitted herself this little lie for her mother's sake.

It produced the desired effect: a slight blush of pleasure warmed Tora's pale cheeks. She was studying Harro with some newfound respect and interest, for the first time.

"That's most thoughtful of you," Tora said, inclining her head in a slight acknowledgment of gratitude. "Of course, you have my blessing. If Libertas is happy, so am I." Once again, her gaze slid to Harro's starched uniform. "And Wend will be most pleased. For quite some time he feared that his niece might marry some artistic type with an aptitude for words but no job and not a *Pfennig* to his soul."

While Tora was busy ordering Karl to fetch champagne, Libertas and Harro exchanged conspiratorial grins. Countess zu Eulenburg had not the faintest idea how close she'd come to the truth.

Wend was indeed bursting with enthusiasm at the prospect of his only niece getting married to an officer. All at once, the young man whom he had for the most part ignored became the sole object of his undivided attention.

"Why didn't you tell me you were in the military before?" Wend boomed, personally pouring cognac into Harro's glass and clapping him amicably on his back. "I have connections with the top brass in every branch. I can bring your name to Reichsmarschall Göring's attention."

Despite all of Harro's assurances that this was not necessary, Wend was already lost in his own fantasies where his new nephew was Reichsmarschall Göring's personal adjutant and where Liebenberg was the Reich's top brass's favorite hunting estate.

Libertas and Harro let him indulge in those dreams, as long as he didn't put any obstacles in their future. But Wend not only seemed to approve of Harro greatly, he even promised an additional sum of five hundred marks to be added to Libertas' official dowry of ten thousand.

"And the wedding expenses—that shall all be taken care of by me," he declared later that evening, with a sweeping gesture around him. "Have the most extravagant one; I'll pay for everything."

"Do you want an extravagant wedding?" Harro asked Libertas when they were back home, in Berlin. The night was warm and velvet; the moonlight caressed their bare bodies lying on the tangled sheets with a silvery touch. "With Reichsmarschall Göring attending?"

Her head nestled in the crook of Harro's arm, Libertas snorted with amusement. "I suppose, we'll have to extend invitations to Hitler, Himmler, and Goebbels as well, so they don't feel snubbed."

It was Harro's turn to chortle. "That's just the very company we need. Shall I invite the Gestapo as well?"

"I imagine you ought to," Libertas replied in mock seriousness. "If you're inviting their boss Himmler, you might as well invite the entire staff of Prinz-Albrechtstraße 8."

But the jokes soon died down, replaced by thoughtfulness and silence.

"Perhaps they will leave off after that," Harro mused out loud, all mirth gone out of his voice.

"Leather coats?"

"Yes. I shall be a married man, with a wife from an exemplary family. An officer, who wears their Reich eagle on his sleeve. Suppose I came to my senses, there's no more need to watch me, right?"

"No. I don't think there will be," Libertas replied with a certainty she didn't feel. "We'll be fine, love. Together, we'll pull through."

"But only together."

"Together forever, like in the cheesiest Hollywood film."

"Yes. Together forever, until death do us part."

An odd feeling stirred in Libertas' chest at those seemingly innocent words that had taken an ominous meaning for some inexplicable reason. The chilly wind tore into the sheer curtain, blowing it like a sail of a great ship. Watching it from the side of her eye, Libertas shivered as though touched by a bad premonition. But then Harro sensed her discomfort, rose from the bed and pulled the window closed, and all was well again. At least, so Libertas told herself when she closed her eyes, safe and warm once again in her fiancé's loving arms.

Schloss Liebenberg. July 26, 1936

Looking into the tall, ornate mirror in her former childhood bedroom, Libertas kept passing a nervous hand over the luxurious material of her dress just to ensure that this was not a dream. It was one of her father's presents, this simple and yet stunningly elegant wedding gown he'd created personally for his only daughter.

"The veil is from Valerie," Otto Haas-Heye had said after presenting Libertas with the box in which the cloud of silk and lace floated on layers of the thinnest, rustling paper—a cloudlike perfection that took Libertas' breath away.

But it was the veil that turned her eyes misty and wistful once Otto had placed it on her golden head. She sensed her former governess' absence particularly sharply that day—a mother figure who should have been there on her special day but couldn't, all due to Hitler's hateful laws.

"I know, Libs," her father had said quietly, adjusting the veil with his skillful designer's hands. "She wishes she were here too. I promised to take plenty of photos for her though, so—chin up, girl, and no tears. You'll ruin the makeup and all my efforts will be in vain."

Now, alone in her room, minutes away from the ceremony, Libertas studied her reflection and wondered what the future held for her and Harro. They were only in their twenties, but they had seen their share of terrors already, tasted the bitter pill of the Gestapo's brutal injustice, lost people dear to them and mourned the lives they dreamt of living but never would, not in the Führer's Reich at least.

But once Otto took her hand, patted it after placing it in the crook of his arm and smiled at her in that special way that reassured Libertas that he loved her, his little girl, despite living hundreds of kilometers away; once the small orchestra, positioned in the corner of the castle's quaint chapel, began to play and the guests rose from their seats; once she laid eyes on her impossibly handsome groom, beaming at her with endless love and adoration, Libertas felt strangely at peace, as though these moments of happiness were enough to erase years of sadness, wipe out all the tears once and for all.

In the front row, Wend stood to attention, much too overdressed with all of his dress uniform cords and a sword, still looking a tad at a loss at the couple's decision to keep the ceremony simple and invite only close family and friends. Neither did he understand

Harro's desire to wear an elegant tailcoat instead of his Luftwaffe dress uniform and forgo the military tradition of a bride and a groom walking out of the chapel under the arch of daggers formed by Harro's comrades.

Only Libertas knew of Harro's reasons; it was his personal rebellion against the Reich, against what he was forced to turn into—this tuxedo and his best man Ricci instead of a uniformed comrade, and a barely noticeable twist of his mouth that had disappeared before anyone could notice when, in conclusion of the civil ceremony, a representative of civil authorities presented them with an obligatory copy of Hitler's *Mein Kampf.* Libertas quickly took the book from Harro's hands and passed it to his young brother Hartmut—"for safekeeping," she'd explained with a bright, false smile. Deep inside, she hoped the boy would lose it somewhere and they would never have to see the hateful thing again, much as she'd "lost" the copy Strengholt had presented her with on behalf of MGM.

With a radiant smile, Libertas signed her new last name on the marriage certificate and offered her glowing face to Harro for their first official kiss as a married couple. They had kissed a thousand times before and yet her breath hitched as her new husband's lips covered hers, making her head light and body weightless with excitement. The wedding photographer blinded her momentarily with the flash of his camera, sealing the moment in time, but it suddenly occurred to Libertas that even without any photographs, the memory of ridiculous, blissful happiness would stay with her forever because Harro shared it with her, just as she'd share her entire life with him, come what may.

"Schulze-Boysen." Back in Berlin, Libertas kept tasting her new last name on the tip of her tongue as she passed her finger over the embroidered initials on their towels and sheets—Marie Luise's personal touch that moved Libertas to tears.

Next to her, Harro was carefully unpacking intricate silverware and expensive porcelain that had come from Libertas' uncle and mother. "Look!" he exclaimed, turning the plate to his new wife. "Your mother and Wend initialized these as well."

Their train for Sweden was leaving soon. In the hallway stood the suitcases they'd packed before setting off to Liebenberg for the wedding. And in Libertas' mind, the civil servant's question kept repeating itself like some demented bell: *Do you swear that you are Aryan and have no alien blood in you?*

Alien blood.

A crime against the Reich according to the newly passed Nuremberg Laws.

"Harro?" she called to her new husband, picturing anew all of his scars under his light summer short-sleeved shirt.

"Yes?" He looked up from the card he'd been perusing.

"Sweden is a nice country, isn't it?"

Harro hesitated, puzzled by her question, before breaking into a grin. "That's why we chose it as our honeymoon destination, no?"

"That, and because I have relatives there." Libertas paused before adding in a probing tone, "And you have friends."

Hands thrust in pockets of his flannel pants, Harro searched her face for clues. "Yes?"

"Have you ever..." Libertas wetted her lips nervously before asking, "have you ever thought of leaving, just like your friends have left?"

"You mean... leave Germany?" His voice was a mere whisper.

"Just a thought that sprang into my head. I haven't thought of it myself before. Just now."

"Why now?"

Libertas couldn't quite answer; she only gestured vaguely toward the copy of *Mein Kampf* that Hartmut, just their misfortune, had preserved for them and even wrapped carefully in paper; toward the red banners out in the street; toward the box with the veil created by her governess whom she loved like a second mother and who couldn't even attend their wedding because her blood was "alien" and her very presence in the Reich was now a crime against its citizens.

Harro nodded slowly and gravely. He understood her without any words. "Sweden *is* a nice country," he said, circling Libertas' shoulders with his arm. "Let's see what we decide once we're there."

Chapter 13

Berlin. August 1936

Their honeymoon had come and gone, dreamlike, a fond memory to cherish forever. Libertas and Harro had been inseparable and madly in love, wandering historic avenues but only seeing each other; visiting medieval cathedrals and modern art galleries during the day and making love through the night as the hotel-supplied complimentary champagne was sweating in a silver bucket by their four-poster bed. They'd entertained the thought of staying, toyed with it as they fed each other fresh shrimp sold in an open café, but abandoned it eventually. Stockholm was lovely, but it was no Berlin, and besides, according to the local German papers, things were improving in the Reich. Not that they believed it all that much, but they had gathered their suitcases and headed back to the city they loved and loathed in equal measure.

Back home, seated on a park bench, from which a recent plaque "For Aryans Only" had been pried off, Libertas gratefully accepted a strawberry ice cream cone from her husband. It was wrapped in a paper depicting Olympic rings and a German eagle holding a leafy wreath. Even the *Hakenkreuz* inside the wreath was green instead of the traditional black, but neither Libertas nor Harro were deceived.

Upon their return from Sweden, they had found themselves mystified by a sudden change in the lead-up to the Olympics, as though they'd been dropped from the Anhalter Bahnhof into some parallel reality where Coca-Cola posters with smiling women on them hung right next to the newsstands from which all anti-Semitic editions had magically disappeared. In their place, the Games' official paper, *Olympia Zeitung*, featured German athletes shaking hands and even hugging their international counterparts, suddenly color- and race-blind. Fingers smudged with fresh ink, young men read of their compatriots' athletic prowess as they waited for their dates next to the entrances to the cinemas, which, together with swimming pools and public beaches, welcomed Jews with open arms once again. The entire city of Berlin screamed internationalism and acceptance with its advertisements in English and French, and even previously banned "degenerate" jazz and swing music poured out of the Tiergarten's loudspeakers.

A spark of hope had ignited in Libertas' and Harro's hearts on that very first day when they had wandered the streets of their beloved city, swamped with tourists and thoroughly devoid of any semblance of the SS or their SA counterparts, and breathed the air of freedom greedily, fingers entwined, hoping for a miracle.

"Perhaps, we did the right thing when we returned," Harro had told Libertas. "Perhaps, they have come to their senses in our absence."

But then he had re-entered the new, expanded Air Ministry and his new office—"fifth floor, I nearly lost myself in that labyrinth!"—and gulped the entire martini glass Libertas always prepared for his return and dropped into a chair, head in his hands.

"It was idiotic to hope that Hitler would change course," he'd told her grimly, fingers clawing at the stiff collar of his uniform as though it was suffocating him. He'd just met an old comrade from the *Gegner* days and he'd revealed to Harro that the Nazis were actively sending saboteurs to Spain; organizing their travel through legal means, sponsoring their trips via the "Strength through Joy" program and then, upon their arrival, dressing them in unmarked brown uniforms—no insignia, no rank—and arming them with weapons to fight the fascist Franco's war against the democratically elected government.

"My friend—Werner Dissel is his name—is stationed near Neuruppin with his regiment. They let him go on leave, but he already has marching orders for Spain. It's a matter of a couple of weeks. Days maybe..." Harro's voice had broken, trailed off as his eyes stared wildly at his clasped hands. "We have to warn the republican government in Barcelona somehow."

But how, that was another matter entirely. Until that day in the Tiergarten, when they sat on the bench eating ice cream and feverishly thinking of the same unspoken matter, when Libertas' eyes suddenly widened and she nearly dropped her cone onto the immaculately swept ground.

"Evan!" she screamed, waving wildly at a young man with a professional camera hanging off his neck. His chestnut hair was neatly styled, and his vest, slacks, and Oxfords screamed London before Libertas had a chance to reveal his nationality to Harro. "Evan James! It's me, Libs!" she called to him in English.

The young man's face instantly brightened in recognition. "Libs from Berlin!" Hand outstretched, he was already heading in the couple's direction. "Fancy meeting you here. It's been forever."

"A few years at least." Swiftly ridding herself of the melting, half-finished cone, Libertas grasped his hand and gave it a thorough shake. "I was still at boarding school."

"So was I." Evan laughed, somewhat embarrassed, and looked at Harro with curiosity.

"Meet Harro, my husband," Libertas announced with audible pride in her voice. "Harro, this is Evan. We became friends when I studied in London. He was in the all-boys' boarding school and I was in the all-girls'. Both buildings were right opposite each other, so we were allowed to visit sometimes."

After the men exchanged handshakes, Libertas gestured toward Evan's camera.

"I see you have finally decided to visit our beautiful capital."

"Not visiting. Working." Evan cringed slightly. "I'm a reporter."

"A reporter?" A light ignited in Libertas' gaze. She grasped her friend's elbow tighter. "But that's absolutely splendid! Where are you staying? The Adlon?"

"I wish." Evan gave her a self-conscious grin. "I don't work for *The Times* as of yet; unfortunately, my little newspaper could only afford some run-down place in Pankow, where you can rent a room by the hour. I need hardly explain what sort of guests usually visit there." The young man from a good family cringed even further.

Libertas supplied a well-timed sympathetic look. "Oh, you poor thing! That's not how you should be seeing Berlin for the first time. It's decided, you're staying with us, starting this very night. Go pack your suitcase and tell them to deliver it to—" She was already digging in her bag for a notebook to write down the address under Harro's uncomprehending gaze.

"It's really not necessary," Evan protested faintly. "I wouldn't want to impose—"

"Nonsense." Libertas cut him off, nearly pushing the note into his limp hands. "We'll be happy to be your hosts. Right, Harro?"

Thankfully, her husband had the good sense to nod dutifully in response to her meaningful look.

"He seems nice," Harro said, looking at Evan's back after they had parted ways.

A triumphant grin on her face, Libertas was watching for her husband's reaction.

He scowled slightly. "What? Libs, what?"

"Harro, my love, you're disappointing me."

Positively puzzled, Harro only blinked at her once again.

Leaning closer to him as if to adjust his tie, Libertas lowered her voice, "We have been speaking of warning the Spanish against our German spies. Evan is an international reporter. *International*, Harro."

At last, recognition transformed his entire expression. Wide-eyed and unbelieving that such good fortune could have possibly landed in their laps, Harro grasped his wife's face in his hands and kissed her ardently on her lips. "Libs, you're a genius! A veritable genius! How did I get myself such a smart wife?"

"I blame it on Valerie and her two-piece bathing suit," Libertas said with mock seriousness. "It has completely turned your head and you haven't been the same since."

Still holding her rosy cheeks in his palms, Harro smiled tenderly at his wife. "No. I haven't, and I never will. And thank God for that."

"So, how are you finding Berlin so far?" Ricci asked Evan, playing with his cognac glass.

The welcome dinner had long been over; they'd been drinking and listening to a BBC music program—another intimate touch to make Evan feel more at home—for at least a couple of hours now. The English journalist kept protesting, but both Harro and Ricci (who was well aware of his best friend's predicament) kept refilling Evan's glass and raising toasts to everything that was sacred in the British man's life, the King and the entire royal family included.

"It's a beautiful, cosmopolitan city." Evan's speech was slightly slurred, his eyes growing more bloodshot and less alert with every glass. From her chair, cradling the accordion on her lap, Libertas was watching him closely. "I never expected it to be so… European?" he probed at the word, unsure of it in his alcoholic haze. "Very elegant; a true metropolis. I didn't anticipate seeing so many smiling faces, to be completely frank with you."

"You see what they want you to see," Ricci grumbled under his breath.

"How are you planning to cover the story?" Harro asked Evan, his sharp gaze trained on him over the cognac glass. Unlike Evan, he wasn't a lightweight drinker. Just like many of his fellow Germans, he was used to drinking beer since his teens, in quantities that could easily put any horse to death. On him, an entire bottle of cognac scarcely produced any effect. "Just the Olympics or will you write about Germans, in general? Good and bad? All shades of gray, instead of just black and white?"

A wrinkle creased Evan's brow. He didn't quite understand, even though Harro expressed himself perfectly in English.

"The Jews, for instance." Seeing that the reporter was too drunk, Ricci decided to press harder. "Will you be writing about what the people do to them here?"

But before Ricci could even finish the sentence, Evan was waving a hand in front of his face.

"No, no, no; no Jews. The editor said explicitly, nothing of that sort. I'm not that type of a journalist. I only write about sports and international fairs, theater, museum, opera, car races—that sort of thing. No Jews. Jews, that's… a rather sensitive subject nowadays. We prefer to steer clear of it."

"What about arrested communists? Persecuted Social-Democrats?" Harro asked quietly, a hidden emotion in his voice. "Journalists, like yourself, tortured and murdered by the Gestapo?"

Evan paled visibly at the mention of the German secret police. "No!" he almost cried in horror. "Certainly, no Gestapo. We don't want any such sensationalism—"

"It's not 'sensations,' it's the truth." It was Libertas who gave her voice this time. She wasn't looking at Evan, but at her husband's body, which still bore the marks of such inconvenient, uncomfortable truths no one wished to write about.

"People in London don't want to hear that," Evan was mumbling now, growing more and more uncomfortable. It occurred to Libertas that he was missing his motel, teeming with prostitutes and their clients, sorely now. At least German ladies of the night didn't pester him with such interrogations. "They want entertainment… Sports…" He gestured vaguely in the direction of the grand Olympic stadium, invisible from the window. "They don't want tortures and murder. And besides, look around yourselves.

Berlin is so beautiful! Germany is such a marvelous country… So European… cosmopolitan. I'll write about that. Show you all in the best light. Tell everyone how nice everyone is…"

"Nice Germans will be going to war soon." Harro looked at him pointedly, cards out in the open. Too much was at stake. He couldn't tiptoe around the issue anymore.

Evan was already shaking his head. "No, you're wrong, you're so very wrong. Just the day before, Hitler said it himself. He doesn't want a war. No one wants a war. He wants peace. Why write such things about him and poke the bear? It's best to praise what he did for his people, for the nation, and leave it alone."

A sneer twisted Harro's mouth. "Only, appeasement doesn't work much with Hitler and the Gestapo and the SS. They're savages. Butchers and merciless killers. They don't speak a diplomatic language."

Later that night, when Evan was snoring loudly in his room, Libertas spoke quietly to Harro as he dried the dishes she was washing.

"He won't do it."

"I gathered as much myself." His eyes stared at the wall, unblinking, but deep inside, Libertas could almost see a thousand thoughts churning, working. "I'll still ask him tomorrow morning. Openly. See what he says."

"He'll say no." Libertas sighed. "He's not like you, Harro. He's a coward. Too bad. I had hopes for him."

"Don't sulk, Libs. You did what you could. We'll figure something out." This time, he looked at her with utmost seriousness. "We have to."

"Yes. We do." She gazed pensively ahead. "The good news is, you're at the center of it all."

Harro laughed mirthlessly. "What use is it, if I'm only a cog whom no half-sane higher-up will promote due to my former 'political unreliability'? Only high-ranking officers have access to all of the top-secret information. I can only gather rumors from former comrades like Dissel."

But a familiar spark ignited in Libertas' eyes. "My dear husband, you're forgetting who you're married to," she said playfully, handing Harro a freshly washed glass.

"The most beautiful and intelligent woman on earth?"

"There's that," she responded with mock seriousness, causing Harro to burst into chuckles, "but also, your wife happens to be the niece of a certain Wend zu Eulenburg. And a certain Wend zu Eulenburg and his sister Tora are neighbors with a certain Reichsmarschall Göring, who just happens to be your boss."

Harro forgot all about the glass he was drying, sensing that Libertas was onto something.

"What if your wife asks her uncle very nicely to invite the said Reichsmarschall to their familial estate for a hunt?" Libertas continued, lathering another glass with soap with purposeful nonchalance. "And then, following the hunt, when *Herr Reichsmarschall* is in the best of spirits, what if your beautiful and intelligent wife asks him very nicely to look personally into her poor husband's case?"

Harro looked at her, smiling, with unconcealed delight at such ingenuity.

Chapter 14

Schloss Liebenberg. September 1936

"It was all one big misunderstanding, as you can clearly see," Libertas concluded her carefully prepared speech, watching Hermann Göring's reaction from the side of her eyes.

Harro and she had been preparing for this day with the seriousness and calculation ordinarily directed at military operations. After gracefully accepting Evan's formal refusal to pass the information to his government, they had set to devising a cunning plan which would ultimately allow them to put Harro in the position of if not active power, something close enough; something which would allow him to gather government secrets and pass them through a source they were yet to uncover to the governments of European countries. Undoubtedly, those allied governments would find the German involvement with the Spanish Civil War extremely interesting, considering the fact that, according to the Versailles Treaty, Germany wasn't allowed to rearm or involve itself in any manner in any conflicts.

The German war machine had to be stopped before it gained its full power. Libertas and Harro were ready to go to great lengths to prevent the spread of fascism's cancerous growth that kept penetrating the tissue of their homeland deeper and deeper, poisoning everything and leading someplace very dark they didn't wish to imagine.

"I'll take care of Göring," Libertas had said, marking the possible dates in the calendar that would allow them enough time to carefully plan and execute their plot. "But in order for me to do that, you'll need to become one of the most rabid Nazis in the Air Ministry, so when he asks about you, no one will be able to say that you're politically unreliable."

His brow creased with a painful scowl, Harro had exhaled expressively. *That was the last thing he wanted*, his expression read, *pretending to be the very person he loathed.*

Sensing his reluctance, Libertas had placed a tender palm on his clean-shaven cheek. "I know how much it disgusts you, even if it's just for their eyes—"

Harro had tossed his head, pulling himself together. "No, you're right. That's precisely what we need—my enthusiasm for their blasted *cause*." He had spat out the last word as though it tasted vile on his tongue. "I can do it. I'll become one of them."

"Not just one of them." Libertas had caressed his face pityingly. "The most rabid of them. Someone they'd want to set as an example."

Harro had done just that. He had groaned and wiped his hands down his face each morning as he stared in the mirror, loathing his own reflection, loathing the blue-gray of his uniform. But he had gritted his teeth all the same, picked up his valise, and set off in the direction of the Air Ministry, where he had clapped the backs of men he couldn't tolerate, laughed at racist jokes they uttered in the haze of cigarette smoke, and submitted articles to the Luftwaffe newspaper glorifying the Reich, Hitler, Göring, and everything he despised with every fiber of his soul.

Libertas' heart had broken each time he'd returned from work, much later than she returned from hers—*forgive me, my love, another invitation for cognac at the officers' lounge I couldn't refuse*—and gulped down his self-loathing and guilt along with the martini she mixed for him.

The strategy had soon bore fruit: one commendation had followed the other, fellow Air Ministry staffers had begun to stop by his office; invitations to weddings, birthday parties, and baptisms had started to pour in from the men who had eyed Harro suspiciously just months ago.

And Libertas had gathered more and more articles bearing the Schulze-Boysen name; learned the words Harro's superiors used to describe him by heart—"a fundamentally reputable attitude," "friendly, helpful manner," "straightforwardness," "undoubtedly a good upbringing," "the son of a Navy officer," "reliable and trustworthy comrade"—and repeated them at every chance she got during conversations with her uncle Wend as they planned the hunt, much to Wend's delight.

By the time Reichsmarschall Göring had arrived in his Mercedes with an escort of three other cars, Libertas was more than ready to meet him. Attired in a white, elegant dress, her neck and wrists wrapped in pearls, she had smiled graciously at the men at the feet of her family manor, "a perfect Reich girl"—as Göring himself had remarked to Wend with an approving nod—with very anti-Reich thoughts hidden in her platinum head.

Now, as she sat across from the second most powerful man in Germany, Libertas felt comfortable and almost at ease, like an actress who was born to perform and couldn't botch the part even if she wanted to.

"A misunderstanding," Göring repeated, regarding Libertas closely over the rim of his glass.

They sat in the room Libertas had personally selected for him—her father's former one, with a grand four-poster bed of rare oak, heavy velvet burgundy drapes pooling atop the rich Persian rugs, and a fireplace of marble and gold. The room that her father had always detested for its opulence, but which oddly fitted Hermann Göring, whose very belt buckle, imitating a stag, was made out of diamonds.

"A very silly one." Libertas smiled in the most disarming manner she ordinarily reserved for the most stubborn film stars. "Harro has always been such an idealistic young man. He believed in the most utopian things and particularly after getting influenced by all of those…" She lowered her eyes as though uncomfortable to utter a certain word. "Those *types*; surely, you understand?" Another look from under the long, lightly mascaraed eyelashes.

"The Jews, you mean." Göring nodded sagely and gravely. "They can confuse anyone, you're quite right. But fortunately for our youth, we rid ourselves of their parasitic influence. They won't be able to cloud our German youth's minds with their poisonous ideas any longer."

Libertas understood then just how disgusted Harro must have been with himself for having to spew such hateful nonsense. But for the others' sake, her own discomfort was something to disregard for the time being.

"Quite so. And I can't express how grateful I am for your officers' influence that finally set him on the right path and brought Harro back to the bosom of the Reich."

Göring couldn't conceal his self-satisfied grin. "I'm pleased to hear that your husband is doing so well."

From Libertas, a strategically placed sigh full of dejection and unspoken sadness.

At once, Göring pulled forward, searching her face. "What is it, dear? You may tell me. Is he not treated well in the Ministry?"

"Oh no, he is!" Libertas rushed to assure him, her cheeks assuming a slight blush. "He's very well-liked there and even his superiors won't stop singing praises of his character and his professional manner. It's just…" Her voice trailed off once again.

"Dear child, whatever it is that is bothering you, you are obliged to confide in me. There is nothing that I can't help you with."

Here it was. Now, it was of the utmost importance not to rush things.

"That old case with his arrest…" Her words were scarcely audible, full of tremor and tears. "No matter how hard Harro works, he'll never rise through the ranks because of that idiotic—" Libertas made a point of breaking down here, hiding her face behind her pale narrow palm.

When the Reichsmarschall swiftly produced a monogramed silk handkerchief, she accepted it with gratitude and dabbed at the corners of her misty eyes.

"All Harro wishes is to prove himself to his superiors, to his country, to his Führer, and to his family. But it will never be, because he shall never be trusted and has brought shame on his family for the rest of his life—"

"What nonsense!" Göring cried in indignation. His fleshy face grew quite red. "Because some University Zionists led him astray, a good, honest German man shall remain a pariah? Not with me in charge." He banged a fist on the polished table to emphasize his point. "I shall speak to his superiors directly, you have my word. Your husband will get his promotion, even if he gets it out of my hands personally."

"I don't know how to thank you, *Herr Reichsmarschall.*"

Göring's expression softened as he saw a smile on Libertas' face. "Dear child, we are practically family. Your forester's son is my forester. We live next to each other. Your uncle is one of my closest friends. Now, what would it make me, if I refused to help my family member's case? I'll tell you what—a most dishonorable bastard, forgive my language, that's what."

Libertas released a well-timed, girlish giggle she had discovered Göring found particularly charming.

"Good. It's all settled then." He slapped his thighs with great enthusiasm. "And now, let's go eat that delicious venison we shot ourselves today. It must be ready by now. Your husband is coming for dinner, isn't he?"

"Of course, *Herr Reichsmarschall.* He wouldn't miss it for anything."

"Splendid. I truly can't wait to make this young man's acquaintance."

*

The following day, after Göring's party departed, Wend invited Libertas to share a glass of brandy with him.

"Well? It wasn't such bad fun, was it?" he teased her good-naturedly.

"No, it wasn't. I never expected that *Herr Reichsmarschall* would show such kindness to Harro." Carefully hiding her eyes from Wend, Libertas toasted glasses with her uncle. It was important to persuade him too, but he was no Göring, who had ended up taking great delight in making Harro's acquaintance. Uncle Wend was family and not just family, but the family member that knew her all too well. "Thank you for inviting him, *Onkel.*"

"I'm pleased you finally asked me to."

"I should have done it a long time ago." The lie didn't come easily, but Libertas carefully concealed it by a healthy gulp.

"I told you they're not such bad fellows."

"No, they're not."

"And now, Harro will get his promotion that is long overdue."

"Yes, *Onkel.* Thank you."

"Thank Onkel Hermann, not Onkel Wend," he joked, but his eyes remained serious, searching his niece's face for clues.

Libertas was aware that he sensed a falseness about her, even if he couldn't quite put his finger on her motives.

"So, no more political arguments between us then?" Wend asked, suspicion audible in his voice.

"No more."

In the pause that followed, Wend seemed to chew on his next question. "Is it Harro? Is he really such a good influence on you?"

"He must be, *Onkel.*"

Wend kept staring at his niece closely, but in the end must have come up blank. "I'm glad you're coming around then."

For the first time, Libertas raised her gaze at him. In her eyes, there was a shadow of something that made Wend pull back ever so slightly.

"I suppose I grew up, *Onkel*. Became wiser," she said slowly, amber liquid swirling gently in the glass she was playing with.

"No more childish idealism?" Now, he was outright incredulous.

"No more," Libertas promised gravely. "From now on, only serious business, *Onkel*."

If something in those words had caught his attention, Wend decided to dismiss it for now. The evening was much too warm and pleasant; the hunt too successful; the cognac in his glass tasted too good.

"Good. Well," he said, finishing his glass, "I'll be off now. The fun and games are over. Tomorrow, hard work begins anew."

He had already left the room when Libertas repeated slowly under her breath, "Yes. Hard work begins."

Chapter 15

Berlin. October 1936

A suitcase still in hand, Libertas stopped in front of the window of the four-and-a-half-room apartment and felt her breath catch at the view of Berlin that opened to her eyes. Their new residence at Waitzstraße 2 was on the top floor—their personal perch from which the entire capital lay at their feet. Nothing was impossible for them now, the masters of the world; free spirits whose words would soar above the streets of Berlin and call to more like-minded people for resistance.

"I take it, you like it?" Harro's lips found the curve of her neck just above her silk scarf.

Eyes closed with pleasure, Libertas turned her head to meet his mouth.

"I love it," she whispered after pulling away. "This shall be our new headquarters. The place where everything begins."

"Yes." Harro nodded, eyes gleaming with fiery force. "The place where everything begins."

They began their resistance work subtly. First, it showed itself in touches only a trained Gestapo eye would spot: a room furnished into a salon instead of a nursery; a powerful, four-tube radio that could pick up broadcasts from any city in the world; modern furniture in place of German traditional one; a frowned-upon Picasso reproduction—degenerate art, according to the Nazis—in the center of the living room rather than the obligatory Führer's portrait; a roll-front cabinet with hidden sections in it and a suspicious variety of foreign magazines and newspapers spread over the coffee table where the couple would receive their guests.

It didn't take long for the old comrades to flock into Libertas' and Harro's new residence. Naturally, it was Ricci who paid the couple their first unofficial visit while they were still unpacking and covered with paint splatters—the result of bathroom renovations.

Dressed in leather from head to toe, Ricci whistled his approval as he strode into their spacious, airy apartment. His blond lady friend, who must have arrived on the back of his Harley, Libertas had assumed, and who was also dressed somewhat scandalously in slacks and a black leather jacket, headed straight for the window Libertas and Harro had left open to air out the smell of the paint.

"Well, I'm blown!" she exclaimed, acting just as at ease as Ricci, rather to Libertas' amusement. "It's some penthouse you got yourselves here, if I do say so myself!"

To get a better view of the bohemian Kurfürstendamm lined with countless shops, cafés, and artists' dives, she leaned further out of the window, offering her perky behind to Ricci's openly admiring gaze.

"Libs, Harro—meet Gisela." Ricci's voice betrayed his feelings for the vivacious, slim blond at once.

Suddenly remembering her manners, the young woman swung round and headed for the couple, her hand outstretched and both rows of teeth bared in a mischievous, open grin.

"Gisela von Pöllnitz." She grasped Libertas' hand with great enthusiasm. "Ricci has told me so much about you two."

Before too long, she was wringing Harro's palm, ignoring his comments about having paint on it with admirable nonchalance about her.

In the opalescent light of mid-October, there was a paleness to Gisela's complexion, some haunting, specter-like quality that couldn't possibly have come from the overuse of rice powder.

Libertas had always been self-conscious about being called too bony far too many times in her boarding-school years, but even next to her, Gisela appeared much too thin, sickly, almost starved. She was all sharp angles under that unnaturally pallid skin, against which the telltale red patches of her sunken cheeks stood out even further. The crimson blemishes were uncovered by cosmetics and displayed like a badge of honor by the woman who clearly had no fear of her approaching death and refused to conceal the evidence of her diagnosis to spare anyone's feelings. But Gisela's most prominent feature was certainly her eyes: bright and lucid, they shone with a feverish power about them, as though her entire life force was concentrated in their gray steel.

"Mine is not a contagious type," Gisela announced without any further ado and, as if in a desire to spit in the face of the Grim Reaper, extracted a pack of Chesterfields and lit up one.

"Is your type curable though?" Harro probed gently, not wishing to offend his guest.

"Tuberculosis?" Looking at Harro as though she was finding him positively hilarious just then, Gisela broke into husky laughter. "Ha! Of course not. The best those self-important ravens in white coats can offer is to stick you into one sanatorium or another and 'prolong your life' for as long as possible, but what sort of life is that, I ask you?" She snorted with great scorn. "Spend whatever precious time I have surrounded by nurses, doctors, and their patients already lined up for heaven? Much obliged, but I can think of better things to do. I've already crossed off learning how to ride an American motorcycle from my list, thanks to this handsome stud," she said with a playful pinch at Ricci's waistline, to which he broke into another adoring grin, "but I still have quite a few things I'd like to try before I'm off to meet my maker. Or that horned gentleman he had expelled from heaven—whoever shall have me first," she finished with such lightness in her voice that Libertas instantly felt a kinship to this reckless, fearless creature.

Soon, the two couples were seated together around the coffee table overflowing with drinks and weighed down by a hookah Harro had fetched for the occasion from one of the still-unpacked suitcases.

"You should have told me you indulge in the oldest Oriental tradition," Gisela spoke in her slightly hoarse voice, blowing out a cloud of aromatic smoke toward the ceiling with its past century's distinctive plasterwork. "I would have brought you something more interesting to smoke instead of regular flavored tobacco."

Libertas nearly choked on her gin, caught between sheer delight and stunned amazement.

In response, Gisela only arched an expressive brow, passing the hose to Ricci. "If you tell me it'll kill me, I shall walk out and never come back."

"No, it's not that." Still struggling between coughing and chuckling, Libertas wiped tears gathered in the corners of her eyes. "I was just wondering how you came by such connections with the present administration in charge."

"Much like everyone else comes by them." Gisela shrugged, unconcerned. "I met them in jail."

It was Harro's turn to break into astonished, somewhat embarrassed laughter. "Now, we shall need to hear a little more of that story!"

From his seat on the Ottoman pillow, Ricci kept shifting his delighted gaze from Harro to Libertas and back, his entire countenance beaming with pride for his lady friend.

"There's not much to tell, it's all rather familiar business," Gisela said, reaching for her glass. "The Gestapo first arrested me back in 1933. Didn't even tell me why. I must have said something about Hitler's lack of genitals to someone who had reported it, who knows? So, they simply threw me in jail like a dog and released me after two months." Her words rolled off her tongue smoothly, without much emotion, but one look into the depths of her steely gray eyes instantly made one aware of all the horror she had lived through and returned to tell about it. "The second time I decided to give them a real reason to arrest me. They seized me after I left one of the communist meetings and discovered a booklet for *Rote Hilfe*—Red Aid, a political prisoner support group in case you don't know—that I stuffed in my underwear."

Libertas couldn't help but snort with amusement at such an ingenious idea of concealing compromising documents. She would have done the same. The more Gisela spoke, the more kinship she felt for the young woman. She couldn't shake the feeling that it was the same rebellious blood that ran through their veins.

"You know they don't have women staffers in the Gestapo, right?" Gisela continued, popping a grape in her mouth. "So, it was a pimply-faced, red-haired weasel who pawed at me in that interrogation cell. Well, the offending woman that I was, I punched him in his ugly mug, tore up the booklet, and ate the pieces. By the time his superiors poured into the cell following his cries for help, all evidence was gone. But they still gave me a good thrashing and threw me in jail for another two months."

"They also permanently banned her from owning a driver's permit," Ricci added, oddly proud of the fact. "Said if they allowed her more mobility, she'd definitely go round and agitate more people by her reckless speeches."

"As if I need a permit to drive!" Gisela scoffed and rolled her beautiful eyes expressively. "Ricci has already taught me how to ride his motorcycle."

"That's true." Ricci beamed, his gaze riveted to his lady friend. "When I'm too incapacitated, it's Gisela who takes me home from one haunt or the other. And let me tell you, she can give that American fellow downstairs real hell!"

He went on singing more praises for his lover, but Gisela had concentrated all of her attention on Libertas, studying her with the same curiosity with which Libertas was examining her.

"You know, you look awfully familiar," Gisela finally declared, her index finger aimed at her hostess. "Have we met before?"

"I was just wondering the same!" Libertas pulled forward as well, peering closely at Gisela through the haze of the scented smoke. "You said your last name was…"

"…von Pöllnitz," Gisela supplied readily. "And what is your maiden name, if you don't mind me asking?"

"Haas-Heye," Libertas replied, to which Gisela shook her head pensively. "But that's my father's name. My familial name is zu Eulenburg."

"No!" Gisela exclaimed, her eyes gleaming brighter. "You have lands nearby, don't you?"

"Schloss Liebenberg, yes!"

"Who is Fürst Philipp zu Eulenburg to you?"

"My maternal grandfather!"

"And do you know whom his sister married?"

Libertas admitted that she didn't.

"Friedrich von Pöllnitz. My paternal grandfather," Gisela announced triumphantly.

Instantly, Ricci leapt to his feet. "You're telling us you two are related?" he cried in excitement. "Harro, old fox, this calls for champagne!"

"We don't have any!" Harro shouted, laughing over everyone's overlapping voices.

"Then what are we waiting for?" Ricci was already groping for his leather jacket on the sofa. "Let's go get it!"

When later that evening, as they staggered drunkenly along the Kurfürstendamm and Ricci mentioned that Gisela was looking for a room to rent, it took Libertas and Harro a mere instant of exchanging glances before they both turned to the blond.

"We have four and we only need two. If you liked our 'penthouse' so much, you are more than welcome to join us."

It didn't take Gisela long to make a decision: "When do I move in?"

By the time the first snow covered the silver roofs of the Kurfürstendamm, Gisela had become a permanent fixture in the Schulze-Boysen household, a shrewd fellow resistance fighter and the sharp-tongued sister they both could no longer imagine their lives without.

The secret compartments of Harro's desk began to swell with copied documents smuggled from the Air Ministry. Citing her new position as a wife whose main obligation was to her husband, Libertas returned her NSDAP membership book. Even the stunned Nazi Party official couldn't quite say anything against her innocent claim that the Führer himself told German women that their husbands came first. *She belonged in the kitchen and ironing her husband's uniforms, not in political meetings.*

With a triumphant smile, she left the Party quarters never to return. The New Year was coming. They were ready to face it, together.

Chapter 16

Berlin. January 21, 1937

It was difficult to hear through the loud swing pouring from the record player, but the small inconvenience served its purpose: one could speak freely of all things illegal in a tight circle of friends.

The group had swollen, growing from its original nucleus of four. Werner Dissel—the Wehrmacht fellow who had informed Harro of Germany's involvement with the Spanish Civil War—stopped by whenever he was on leave, invariably supplying Harro and Libertas with more information "in exchange for their excellent cognac and imported cigarettes," as he loved to jest. It never ceased to amaze Libertas to enter her own living room and discover two uniformed men plotting against the Reich in between sips of brandy, the tips of their polished tall boots swinging in time with "degenerate" American jazz.

Then one day, by sheer accident, Harro stumbled into Walter Küchenmeister, an old comrade from the *Gegner* days, as he was waiting for his U-Bahn train. Before too long, the former disgraced journalist had not only made himself at home in Libertas' library, where he pored greedily over illegal literature sent to Germany by Libertas' former governess, but soon he began to bring along his lady friend, Dr. Elfriede Paul.

To Libertas, the woman with penetrating eyes and dark blond hair twisted into a severe bun at the nape of her neck first appeared somewhat cold and standoffish. Never indulging in drink or dancing, Elfriede preferred to remain alone, studying everyone present from her chair in the corner with such a hawkish expression about her that it positively unnerved Libertas. However, as soon as Walter confided to her that Elfriede simply didn't trust people easily due to her activities ("she travels to Paris and London every other month, helping Jewish people with visas and whatnot," Walt whispered with a measure of respect and almost reverence in his voice), Libertas warmed to the cautious doctor.

One evening, when the opportunity had presented itself at last, Libertas had approached Elfriede and placed a hand on her shoulder. "You have nothing to fear here," Libertas had told her in an undertone, despite the fact that everyone was much too drunk to pay any heed to their conversation. "Here, we're all friends."

Elfriede had given her a long look before uttering softly, "It's not my life I fear for, it's the others."

"Well, their secrets are safe with us." Libertas had looked across the room at her husband, who was loudly discussing recent Spanish affairs with Ricci, Gisela, and Walt. "Harro also suffered at the Gestapo's hands. And so did Gisela, my distant cousin. Trust me, we don't harbor any warm feelings toward the Nazis any more than you do."

"It's not that I don't trust you," Elfriede had released a sigh, suddenly appearing very tired. "I know you're good people. It's all this business." She had gestured vaguely around. "All these bohemian parties, all of these new faces you scarcely know. Your husband speaks so freely around them."

"They're all friends of our friends," Libertas had tried to argue, but Elfriede had only regarded her with the sympathy of an adult pitying a child's innocent logic.

"You ought to be more careful who you allow into your immediate circle, if you wish to live long enough to keep helping people, that is. What use are you to them dead?"

That was Elfriede in essence: maddeningly practical, logical to the point of annoyance, and ready to drop everything—her flourishing practice and her lover she adored—just to travel to a foreign country to aid people she had never met in person.

Gisela disapproved of her something fierce, not due to Dr. Paul's underground activities, but solely because she was a thoroughly careful type and reminded Gisela too much of her own mother.

"*Mutti* sheltered me something terrible as well when I was a child," Gisela grumbled one morning, rummaging through the cabinets in the kitchen in search of aspirin after yet another wild party, while Libertas nursed her own hangover in her bed. "Fat lot of good her sheltering did. I'm only twenty-five and I'm dying." Another cabinet door slammed, followed by indistinct cursing. "I wish she let me live while I still could; run until I dropped like children ought to; dive into the lake at night with the boys and dance until the sun would rise."

At the sound of the water pouring into a glass, it occurred to Libertas that her cousin must have discovered the pills after all. With a weak voice, she called to her to save her a couple as well.

"The point is, when your time is up, you shall drop dead no matter how careful you are about it," Gisela continued without acknowledging her. "It's pointless, what she's doing. All that fretting and secrecy and disapproving glares... If the Gestapo come, all of our heads shall roll. If she's so adamant about keeping hers, she should just piss off and stay away."

With that, Gisela slammed the glass on the countertop with a finality to her speech that made Libertas grin under her covers, where she was hiding her splitting head from the piercing rays of the sun. Suddenly, a hand peeled them off, causing Libertas to shut her eyes and groan.

"You look like a Nosferatu." Before Libertas could protest, Gisela pushed two pills into her mouth in her no-nonsense manner. "And that says a lot coming from me."

"Elfriede has a point, you know," Libertas said hoarsely, groping blindly for the water Gisela was holding out for her.

"So do I, but I'm not acting like a stuck-up bitch about it."

And thus, their ranks continued to recruit new members—bickering, exchanging sarcastic retorts, arguing about methods and final goals, but united by the same purpose: free Germany and Hitler's head on a spike.

Besides Elfriede, Walt invited another old friend from his and Harro's university days.

"Kurt Schumacher," a soft-spoken, mild-featured Swabian announced, carefully shaking Libertas' hand.

Just like Ricci, he had an artist's hands—narrow palms with long, sensitive fingers and skin soft as a woman's.

"Tell Libs whose doors you have just finished carving?" Walt nudged his friend playfully with his elbow.

Kurt grimaced a little, visibly. "Why do you have to bring him into this?"

"Hermann Göring's," Walt announced triumphantly, paying no attention whatsoever to his friend's discomfort. According to Harro, Walt had delighted in sensationalist news back in the *Gegner* days and missed it terribly. It was only natural that now, robbed of the *Gegner* as his mouthpiece, Walt never missed a chance to impart some juicy rumor to anyone who agreed to listen. "Kurt hates that fat goat's guts, but his Swabian dutifulness wouldn't allow him to say no to work offered."

"Göring? He visited us in Liebenberg in September," Libertas said, and grinned when Kurt stared at her in alarm. "Don't fret, we hate his guts too. But Harro needed a promotion."

After the laughter died down a tad, Kurt turned to Harro with the most earnest expression. "Walt told me about the things you've been discussing. Just so you know, as an artist, I have an almost unlimited access to paper. I buy it in bulk from different merchants, so it'll be nearly impossible to trace. Ink, paint, glue—that, too. Whatever you need. Just let me know."

"Oh, we certainly will," Harro promised, his gaze darkening with new prospects unraveling right before him.

How liberating it was to speak so freely and without restraint with all of these old friends and new acquaintances while American swing played in the background. How remarkable the atmosphere was inside, warm and inviting, despite the freezing temperatures outside.

For their next weekly party, Kurt brought his wife along.

"Elisabeth also suffered from the regime," he explained to Libertas quietly while Harro and Elisabeth were exchanging obligatory pleasantries. Kurt's wife was a woman of rare beauty, more Italian than German, with smooth olive skin and glossy dark locks framing her beautifully sculptured face, in which her liquid black eyes radiated calm intelligence. "Her father was Jewish. A Jewish hero, one ought to say, who fell for his country on the front during the Great War. But that mattered not to the present government. They still banned her from working as an independent artist and only permitted her to be employed as a simple graphic designer. But she's a master of photography, so..." He let a meaningful pause hang. "If you need anything reproduced or reduced in size for, say, safe transportation abroad..."

Libertas merely nodded, instantly filing the information away in her mind. They *did* need something of that sort. With unconcealed enthusiasm, she grasped Elisabeth's hand and shook it thoroughly.

"Welcome to our house, Elisabeth."

"Please, call me Lisl."

"Lisl." Libertas grinned wider. "I'm Libs. It's my utmost pleasure to make your acquaintance."

Kurt must have already uncovered certain details to his wife, for the light of defiance in Libertas' eyes reflected in hers as well.

"The pleasure is all mine, Libs. I was looking forward to meeting you two."

In the streets below, BDM girls with long blond braids shook their collection boxes at the passers-by. SS men in long overcoats patted their cheeks whenever they dropped a coin in the slot. Bloody banners, soaked by the snow, dripped red onto the pavement. And in the top-floor apartment facing the Kurfürstendamm, Lisl was already looking through the pink and blue sheets smuggled by Harro from the Air Ministry, explaining to him how their size could be reduced to that of a postage stamp.

In the streets below, unsuspecting Berliners went about their business. In the apartment above, rebels congregated well into the night, forming connections that were stronger than blood, taking an oath more important than life.

Free Germany or nothing.

There was no other way around it now.

Chapter 17

Berlin. August 1937

August hung over Berlin in stagnant, suffocating heat. Even with all the windows thrown open, it was impossible to find relief from its clammy, sluggish grip. In Tiergarten park, all the shadowy spots had been occupied by mothers with babies that wailed piercingly and incessantly, cranky due to the heat; Gisela announced that either Libertas drove them to the Wannsee, where at least the water was cold and one could rent a boat to get far enough away from the screaming children, or she would throw herself under the first tram to put herself out of her misery.

But even the Wannsee lake was swarmed with restless Berliners that day. After parking their overheating car and walking for an intolerably long time on the melting asphalt toward the beach, Gisela and Libertas began to pick their way among towels and blankets which were almost invisible under picnic baskets, sandals, and stacks of neatly folded clothes. Whoever wasn't fortunate enough to secure a cool spot under one of the leafy trees was hiding from the blazing sun under colorful striped umbrellas, which Gisela kept eyeing enviously. The air itself was a mixture of sweat, perfume, suntan lotion, warm spilled beer, and ice cream sold by vendors from silver metallic iceboxes.

"Quit your moaning," Libertas noted snidely with a sideways glance from under her sunglasses that kept sliding down her nose, which was dripping with sweat. "Sun is good for your lungs."

Gisela glared at her cousin murderously. "You won't be able to see that sun ever again if you don't shut your trap right this instant."

Libertas exploded in laughter and, ducking Gisela's swatting palm, nearly stumbled upon a distinguished-looking gentleman's folding chair, in which he was taking the sun with a somber air about him.

The sandy strip of the beach wasn't an option either; far too many bare, cherubic-looking children were busy burying one another in the wet sand when they weren't waging wars on each other's sandcastles, fortified with walls and even ditches, to which their elder siblings were directing water from the lake with the look of sage engineers working for Krupp factories, no less.

After studying the terrain in a Prussian *Feldmarschall*'s stance, her fists butting her narrow hips, Gisela finally thrust her chin in the direction of a restaurant with its open terrace. "Let's go get a couple of cold beers. It's Sunday; workday tomorrow. The families shall start packing up soon. Then we'll get ourselves a nice spot under a tree."

Libertas didn't argue, only groaned and asked not to be reminded about work. Her summer dress was sticking to her back and thighs like a second skin and she didn't see how a couple of cold beers wouldn't remedy the situation.

"You are officially mad, my good woman!" Gisela declared as soon as they settled down under the thick striped awning and took the first few blissful gulps of refreshing ice-cold beer. "How many years have you been on that job?" she asked incredulously, pressing the sweating glass to her temple, where a small pale-blue vein was pulsing under the translucent, clammy skin.

Libertas grimaced, already expecting a dressing-down from her cousin. "A little over four years."

"A little over four years!" Gisela repeated. It sounded worse coming from her. "In the same position. If you were a man, you would have been leading the department now."

Libertas didn't argue the point. "It was through my contacts that I helped you get that position as a stenographer at the United

Press though," she said instead, with a sideways glance at Gisela, clearly hoping for a break.

"Thank you kindly." Gisela imitated a sarcastic bow. "Now we're both chained to our desks."

In spite of herself, Libertas broke into laughter. She had always considered herself a free spirit and an adventure seeker, but it wasn't until she'd met Gisela that the true meaning of a free spirit occurred to her.

Having only four years on her younger distant cousin, Gisela could have had a book written about her adventures. Escaping from a traditional aristocratic household and diving into bohemian life where nothing was forbidden and everything could have been paid for, Gisela had grown into a reckless thrill-seeker, a fearless rebel who refused to acknowledge danger and laughed at those who feared death.

"We'll all die one day or another," was her motto. She always announced it with a carefree shrug, chased by a shot of something throat-burning. "I'd rather die without regrets."

That attitude of hers drove her across the Channel because she fancied picking raspberries in Scotland instead of the garden of her own familial estate. It was the same attitude that sent her on a voyage to the Balkans and Greece—scandalously unaccompanied—because feta tasted better there and because a friend had bragged about her new Balkan lover and Gisela refused to be upstaged and wished to see for herself what all the fuss was about. It was that same reckless nature that got Gisela arrested for participating in highly illegal activities and for assaulting a Gestapo official, "for putting his hands where they didn't belong" during the search, according to her own words.

Libertas was aware that it was Gisela's lung condition that drove her to treat each day as if it was her last, but instead of pitying her, Libertas openly admired her distant relative, so alike her in appearance with her boyishly thin limbs and fine, aristocratic features, but so different inside, with something dark and dangerous brewing behind those steely eyes of hers.

Even now, as she was lathering her skin with suntan lotion after they'd moved from the restaurant to the grassy spot under the nearest tree, Gisela reminded Libertas of a feral cat, with her lazy, graceful movements, seemingly relaxed in the shadow of the tree, sprawled on their beach towels, but still alert, tense like a spring ready to be released at the first sign of danger.

"A little over four years and what do you have to show for it?" Gisela continued, motioning for Libertas to turn toward her so she could lather her back. "Besides getting me that position at the United Press?" she added before Libertas had a chance to open her mouth.

Libertas exploded once again. Even after their laughter subsided, a smile kept passing over her lips at the thought of having Gisela so near—the longed-for sister she never had, the best friend, the woman with whom she could discuss anything, beginning with Harro's problems with kidney stones—a grim reminder of the SS tortures—and ending with plans of taking down Hitler's regime.

"What do I have to show for it? A convertible Opel and a dead friend." The words flew from Libertas' lips before she could think them over.

At once, she froze under Gisela's palm, wondering wherever that came from, that grim humor and bitterness in her voice. She had thought that she'd forgotten. It appeared, she had not.

Behind her, Gisela coughed softly, covering her mouth with the back of her hand. "More than a friend, perhaps?"

They never spoke about Martin, only in very general terms.

Libertas considered for a while. "No." She shook her head after all. "Just a friend. It never got further than that."

"But it was heading there?"

Libertas was glad that Gisela couldn't see her eyes just then. "Does it matter now?"

"No, I suppose it doesn't. Still," Gisela abruptly changed the tone and the subject along with it, "you ought to apply your talents elsewhere. To hell with MGM, if they don't value you as their asset."

"And just what am I supposed to be then? You see how it is now. A woman's place is in the kitchen. Our main purpose is to birth more soldiers for the Reich. They virtually closed all the possible paths for us to pursue."

"Then do something the government has no control of." Gisela shrugged it off as though the matter couldn't have been simpler.

"Like what?"

"Become a musician. Or an artist. Or a writer. Sell your works abroad. No one shall stop you from doing that. Just don't confine yourself to that desk and that office where your talents will rot and die."

"First comes death, then comes rot."

Gisela didn't laugh this time. "Libs, you need to go away for a few weeks."

"Go away?"

"Yes."

"As in on a trip?"

"I was thinking a voyage. But it's of utmost importance that you go by yourself, without Harro. I know how much you love him, but some time alone will do you good so you can figure out what you want to do with your life. You need to find yourself. Your *true* self. You will—" Gisela broke off abruptly and glared at two young men who had stopped much too close to their blanket for her liking.

Libertas was also familiar with the type: tall, blond, athletically built—SS or the Wehrmacht, most likely. The Olympics had come and gone and now the fashion to wear the Party pins on one's bathing suit had returned. Both men had theirs pinned to the opened shirts they wore over their swim trunks.

Libertas had already prepared a lengthy explanation about having a husband in the Air Ministry, but, as always, Gisela threw herself at the offending intruders before she even had the chance to open her mouth.

"Move along, *Herren*. Nothing for you here. We're here together, if you know what I mean." A seductive look purposely thrown at Libertas and a possessive arm sliding over her shoulders. "Not interested in whatever knackwurst you're offering, but thank you all the same."

After the men beat a hasty retreat, visibly embarrassed, Libertas gave her cousin a look of reproach she didn't actually feel. "Now, what possessed you to go and say something of that sort?"

"Why? It's the male homosexuals they persecute. There's nothing in the law against ladies who prefer the company of other ladies." Gisela wiggled her brows suggestively.

"They may still return and write us up."

"What are you afraid of?" Gisela asked, her nonchalance back. "Your husband is getting a promotion on a personal request from Göring. I doubt anyone will give you any trouble for an innocent joke your idiot cousin made. And if they do, I'll just explain to their superiors how they should teach their soldiers manners so that they don't pester women who are trying to mind their business and catch some sun instead of watching them flex their muscles and having to listen to their pitiful attempts at jokes."

Libertas snorted with laughter. "I wish I were more like you," she said, suddenly serious.

Gisela only grinned in that catlike manner of hers and winked. "Then, be, little sister."

"Perhaps I don't have what it takes."

"Oh yes, you do. Don't forget, we share the same blood. When the time comes, you'll be even braver than me. You're just more careful, not as impulsive as I am. You have some of that Elfriede in you. But even that's good. Especially now."

Over the Wannsee, the sun was slowly dipping its toes into the lake. Sharp, golden knees bent, Libertas and Gisela gazed at it from under their lowered eyelashes, too warm and lazy to talk. The darkness was descending on Berlin, but they were ready to meet it face to face.

"Dissel is under arrest."

Libertas and Gisela were in the middle of setting the table when Harro burst into the living room, wild-eyed and disheveled. He stood there a while, breathing heavily—he must have run up the stairs, it occurred to Libertas, an oddly and disproportionately stupid thought given the circumstances—and stared at the women with the same mute horror with which they stared at him.

The announcement registered with Libertas fast and hard, like a punch in a gut that left one breathless. Werner Dissel's face swam before her eyes, noble and mischievous; from the folds of her memory, his laughter arose, contagious and almost musical.

Werner Dissel. The man who had propelled Harro to action by revealing the German High Command's plans concerning the civil war in Spain.

The terror in Libertas' eyes was reflected in her husband's.

In the next instant, he threw his valise on the floor, charging past them and into his study, where he kept all of the compromising materials copied and stolen from the Air Ministry.

Recovering themselves swiftly, the women followed him, fast on their heels, after dropping the utensils on the dining table.

His breathing labored and tense, Harro pulled the secret compartments of his desk open and began tearing stacks and stacks of documents and blueprints from them.

"Do you know the charges?" Libertas asked, fearing the answer. Her hands, catching the papers from Harro's, turned cold and clammy.

"Cultural Bolshevist activities, communist subversion of the Wehrmacht—"

"That's not so bad," Gisela interrupted, a hopeful smile creasing her lips.

Pausing, Harro turned to her. It wasn't so much his silence, but the doomed look in his gaze that turned Libertas' heart to ice.

"Negligent betrayal of military secrets," he finished softly.

To Libertas, the stillness of the moment that followed sounded like the aftermath of an ax dropping on someone's neck.

"Do they know…" she stumbled upon the word, lips trembling, fingers clawing at the coarse sleeve of his uniform, "…know about him… coming here? About you?" She pulled the words out of herself with torment.

Harro. Her Harro. The love of her life; the man she would die for.

Her grip on his sleeve was like steel now. They'd need regiments of the strongest SS men to tear her away from him. She wouldn't let go, not until her heart had stopped beating.

Her brave, brave Harro. They had already broken his body once, just for being in charge of a liberal newspaper. What they would do to him for treason and espionage, Libertas didn't wish to imagine.

He saw it all in her eyes—the mortal fear, the infinite love—and managed an ashen smile just for her sake. "I don't know, Libs."

She barely noticed when Gisela gently took the papers out of her hands.

"I'll start the fire."

"Thank you," Harro nodded his acknowledgment. "The coal is—"

"Under the stairs." Gisela had lived here long enough. She knew everything. She was a good comrade. They could trust her with their lives.

Harro's hand found Libertas' over the disarray of blueprints and lists of German saboteurs. He stared at them tragically, caressing the corners of the papers gathered with such difficulty and kept with such diligence until they could be passed into capable hands; hands that could actually do something about their contents. Contents that could turn entire countries against Germany before it was too late. Contents that could bring down Hitler's regime, if applied in time.

In the living room, the coals began to crackle.

A mask of terror set Harro's features before he broke into a scream. "Gisela! Stop!!"

In a few seconds, he crossed the room, dropped to his knees before the open stove, and with his bare hands began pulling the burning papers out of the fire.

Next to him, Libertas was tapping them with her own palms, beating down the dying flames, and singeing her own flesh in the process. She scarcely noticed, only breathed in relief when she saw that just a small stack of them was charred.

"It's all right," Harro kept saying, smoothing them out and inspecting the damage, "I remember most of their contents by heart. I'll retype them. It's all right."

At first puzzled, Gisela's expression softened as understanding dawned on her. "Couldn't burn them?" she asked Harro sympathetically.

"No."

"They could cost you your life."

"They're bigger than my life," he replied without looking up at her.

"We can't keep them here," Libertas whispered, noticing only now the superficial burns on her palms.

"Out of the question," Gisela agreed at once.

For a few excruciatingly long minutes, the three of them sat in a circle with a few singed sheets at its heart, eyes riveted to the inky lines that could just as easily turn into their death sentence as they could turn into a death sentence for millions of Germans... or any other nationals, depending on how they were applied.

The Gestapo could very well be on their way here now; they all were aware of the possibility.

"Do you think Dissel would tell?" Gisela asked, all business as usual.

Harro slowly shook his head. "I don't think he would. But he could have written my name in his appointment book or something of that sort…"

"People know he always comes here when he's on leave," Libertas supplied, her bottom lip pressed hard under her teeth.

"Then it's possible they'll search the place." Gisela rose swiftly to her feet. "Harro, be a lamb, gather all of the papers for me into a bread bag."

He looked at her, mystified. "Where are you going to take them?"

A sly grin appeared on her face. "Ricci has just the place to hide them. He still has a cabin near the marina; he kept it even after he sold his boat. It's registered with the boat's new owner, but, technically, he's the one who lives there in summer as the owner travels during those months. No one will think to look there."

Chapter 18

The next few days dragged torturously minute by minute, interminably long and full of silent anguish. It came almost as a relief when the postman delivered the summons one morning, excruciatingly familiar to all three of them.

"At least they didn't barge in here and arrest me," Harro said with an uneasy bark of laughter, passing a hand over his forehead. "That's good news. They only want to talk."

"Which means Dissel didn't betray us." Libertas' face brightened as well.

"Yes." Gisela nodded with the look of someone who had more experience in such grim matters than she wished to admit to. "It means they have nothing solid; perhaps they only want to ask you how often he came here and what he was generally saying to the others."

Both women helped Harro with his dress uniform. While Libertas adjusted a rapier on his belt, Gisela finished oiling his holster, in which his service Haenel Schmeisser pistol sat.

"At least this time I'll be armed," Harro jested darkly.

No one laughed.

"Planning to shoot your way out of there?" Gisela handed him the holster.

"I hope it won't come to that," Harro said.

It suddenly occurred to Libertas that she wasn't sure whether it was a joke or not.

She drove Harro to the Gestapo headquarters; kissed him in front of the entrance with all the love and passion she felt for him; wiped the lipstick from his mouth with her thumb and nearly pushed him toward the heavy double doors—no handles inside. That much she remembered.

"Go. The sooner this matter is dealt with, the better."

Harro threw a glance at their car, as if he thought of asking something, but Libertas already had the answer to the unspoken question in his eyes.

"I'll be waiting for you. Right here, for as long as needed. I won't budge until you come out of here."

"What if I don't come out of here for a few days?" His words were a mere whisper.

"Then I'll stay here for a few days." Libertas shrugged, ashen-faced but so very brave. "For a few weeks. For a few months if needed. And now, go. I can't bear this wait any longer."

A last glance passed between them—silent, full of tenderness, and infinite longing—and Harro disappeared behind the doors of the limestone castle that had swallowed countless victims before him.

With a ragged breath, Libertas turned on her heel and headed back to her car.

She remained there, leaning against its hood, a vigilant little sentry with her eyes trained on the entrance, sharp as a hawk's. Around her, life went on as though nothing had happened, all the while Libertas' nerves were ready to snap any moment now. Cars with SS numbers pulled up, spilling out uniformed drivers and their black-clad superiors. Passers-by inconspicuously but purposely crossed the street—a superstitious school of fish shying away from the lair of a great white shark. Only a small troop of the *Hitlerjugend* boys, all white hair, brown shirts, and skinny legs, marched proudly right by it, eyes riveted to the coveted place where enemies of the state paid for their mistakes; where they hoped to rise through the ranks by beating the truth out of traitors and spilling confessions along with blood. The daggers hanging at their hips were there for a purpose, it occurred to Libertas; so that Germany's ideological youth would get used to their weight and to the idea of slashing throats with their sharp, short blades. When they grew up, they'd get longer ones. Perhaps an SS sword as well. Libertas couldn't bear to think what they would do with those.

And then, after what had seemed like an infinity but was in fact less than one pitiful hour, suddenly came a burst of light in a day filled with darkness—Harro's blue uniform, golden hair, and white teeth bared in a delighted grin. He scooped her off the ground and twirled her until she was laughing along with him, through tears and fried nerves, lips pressed against each other once again—reunited, at last.

"Everything's all right," Harro whispered to her. "Dissel came through. He didn't tell them anything, the good, honest fellow."

"What of our parties?"

"I told the interrogator that we have a rule—no politics inside our walls. He seems to have swallowed it."

That evening, they went to dance at the *Lokal* and drank themselves almost stupid, euphoric with relief and more in love with each other than ever. But the next morning, wrapped in sheets, smoking on the windowsill, and gazing at the sunlight-gilded roofs, they began their scheming and plotting, despite the still-fresh burns, despite the danger still lurking dangerously near.

"I was thinking…" Eyes narrowed at something in the distance, Harro exhaled a wreath of gray smoke. "The British, or at least the ones we know, are out of the question. They don't want to meddle with our German affairs, which is fair, I suppose…" Once again, his voice trailed off.

"But?" Libertas searched his face, under the façade of which thought was feverishly at work.

"But we can't just sit on this information. We don't have the moral right to." On his bare torso, old scars stood out, pale and razor-thin. "The German Condor Legion has just leveled the

Spanish city of Guernica to the ground—the city, to which refugees running from the Franco's troops flocked, seeking protection. Our own German troops are guilty of annihilating innocent civilians." Wrath shone in his eyes, along with fiery determination. "This cannot go unpunished, unaddressed."

"But who shall stop them? The French?"

"The French don't care one way or the other. They're building their own wall in the hope that this time the Germans won't get to them. The memories of the Great War are too fresh in their minds. They will try to avoid any new conflict as long as they can help it."

"The Americans?" Libertas probed.

Harro only snorted with disdain. "Americans are far away. They care even less than the French what we do here, in Europe."

"Who's left then?"

There was a long pause, filled with smoke and uncertainty.

"The Soviets," Harro said at last, slowly and carefully, as though tasting his own words.

Libertas regarded him with doubt. "Stalinists? Aren't they too busy with their own purges?"

"They may be, but they're the only ones left. They're the ones ideologically opposed to Germany. They're the ones who fight them and Franco in Spain as part of the International Brigades." Slowly, Harro's words gathered conviction. "They have a rather impressive espionage network and are well-versed in it. They certainly want to bring any fascist regime down as it goes against their communist doctrine. You know, the more I think of it, the more I grow confident that the Soviets may just be our only choice."

"I see your point. But how are you going to pass the information to them? You can't just walk into a Soviet embassy; it's watched the whole time by the Gestapo leather-coats."

Somewhere within the depth of their apartment, the door opened and closed. A knowing grin appeared on Libertas' face.

"Looks like our harlot Gisela had a late one again."

"An early one, more like it," Harro noted, throwing a glance at his wristwatch.

As though on cue, Gisela materialized in the doorframe of their bedroom, rosy-cheeked and bright-eyed. "Good morning, lovebirds. Had a good night?"

"Looks like we aren't the only ones who did," Libertas said, giving her cousin's yesterday's attire an expressive up and down.

Gisela only laughed, not bothered in the slightest. "Ricci sends his love."

"I'm sure he does." Harro tried to hide a grin.

"Mind your own affairs, Schulze-Boysen," Gisela retorted with mock disdain. "I'm leaving for Paris in two weeks and I'll miss that bastard."

"Thank you for informing us." It was Libertas' turn to sound theatrically offended.

"I only got the call from the office while you two were out."

"United Press sending you?" Libertas asked.

"Mhm." Gisela approached her and took an unfinished cigarette from her cousin's fingers, ignoring the couple's state of undress with her usual nonchalance. "I'm a stenographer, aren't I?"

At once, Harro and Libertas locked eyes; a silent exchange without a word being said and everything understood.

"Gisela?" Harro turned to her, a smile on his lips.

"Yes?" She narrowed her eyes doubtfully. "I don't know what you're about to say, but I don't like that look of yours."

"Since you're going to Paris—"

"You want me to buy your beautiful wife some French perfume? Please, say that's all you want." Gisela groaned.

"I would be much obliged if you could do that." Harro's grin grew wider. "But could you also drop something off for us?"

"What?" She moaned louder, resigned to the fact that it most likely would be something very illegal.

"Just one little envelope."

"Well, it won't be that little, given how much we have," Libertas inserted.

"I stand corrected." Harro inclined his head. "One *big* envelope."

Gisela released a tremendous breath. "Let me guess, you want me to stuff everything I took to Ricci into it?"

"That's the very thing we want you to do," Harro acknowledged with a slight grimace. "I truly am sorry for burdening you with this—"

Gisela swept his apologies aside with a negligent sweep of her hand. "Save your breath. You're well aware I'm only pretending to be upset. You know I live for these things. Now, whom do you want me to take it to?"

"The Soviet Embassy," Harro said and pulled slightly away as though fearing a slap for suggesting such a thing.

Gisela snorted, waited for a punchline to the joke, and then paled as soon as she realized that it wouldn't follow. "You're serious, aren't you?"

"As a heart attack."

Libertas' guilty expression mirrored her husband as he said it.

"Harro, why?" Gisela was still puzzled.

"Because no one else wants to get involved." Harro grew serious once again. "And I can't, in all good conscience, wait for someone to do something while innocent civilians are being slaughtered by our own troops."

"Bolshevists then, eh?" Gisela took another long drag and burst into a coughing fit.

"You really ought to quit it," Libertas shook her head, taking the cigarette out of her cousin's hand.

"It's the Gestapo that will kill me in the end, not cigarettes," she declared with a certain mischievous pride in her voice as soon as she'd caught her breath. "And particularly with all the errands your husband is sending me on."

"Gisela, you don't have to do it if you don't want to," Harro rushed to assure her. "I would never dream of forcing you into anything against your will—"

"I said, save it, Blue Eyes. I'll take your damned contraband to the Soviet Embassy. Hey, maybe they'll offer me to defect while I'm there. After all, it's because I was helping the local Bolshevists that I got arrested the second time."

Gisela had gone to take her morning bath and Libertas and Harro sat on the windowsill, her feet resting on his lap.

"I could go instead," Libertas mused out loud.

"No. Too suspicious. With Gisela, it's all perfectly innocent. Her office sent her there. Nothing to question."

"I'm afraid something will happen to her."

"She's an incredibly intelligent woman, Libs. She knows what she's doing."

"You're an incredibly intelligent man too, Harro. And look what they did to you." She pressed her toes ever so gently into a map of scars crossing his flat stomach.

"I'm still alive, aren't I?"

Libertas looked at him and wondered for how long; for how long any of them would be.

Chapter 19

September 1937

Without Gisela, their apartment was more silent that usual. Out of caution, Harro had warned their friends against visiting for a few weeks—until the matter with Dissel was cleared; until they'd heard from Gisela; until he and Libertas were certain that a mere association with the couple wouldn't land their comrades-in-arms in jail.

For the past few years, they were always surrounded by people, conversations, loud music, and laughter. However, confined to their rooms and having only each other as company, Libertas and Harro discovered that they enjoyed their involuntary seclusion immensely. Instead of loud parties, they read in companionable silence and later discussed whatever books they had devoured. Eyes sparkling, hands gesticulating, they were getting to know one another anew, and, somewhere along the way, had fallen in love with each other even harder than before. By the second half of September, when the leaves turned golden in the Tiergarten, they had grown quite inseparable and shed the last pretense of former independence from each other that was in fashion among the remaining bohemians in Berlin.

Without guests keeping them up late at night, they made love more often than before; sometimes right on the sofa in the living room—the absence of a roommate offering them freedom they hadn't been accustomed to before. Some evenings, they took a bath together, legs framing each other, candles dripping wax onto the tiled floor, wine sweating in a silver bucket by the tub.

"I feel like we're on our second honeymoon." Libertas regarded Harro lovingly. In her hand, a crystal glass of merlot gleamed soft ruby-red, just like her lips, stained with imported cherries only high-ranking officers had access to. As Göring's protégé, Harro had bought them for his wife for an exuberant price just to watch her eat them with her eyes closed and moan in that seductive manner of hers that turned his blood to molten lava.

"I feel like my entire marriage to you has been one never-ending honeymoon," Harro replied, caressing her thigh, that silky-soft skin. "I love you more than life. You know that, don't you?"

Of course she did. He showed it to her every night when she craved his affection and he hadn't once pushed her away despite paying the price afterward. Too proud to complain, Harro held her in his embrace until Libertas fell asleep and only then tiptoed into the bathroom, where he would lie on the cold tiles until the stones in his kidneys settled at last. He must have loved her more than life if he made love to her through the stabbing pain just to show her how much he desired her.

Loathing herself for hurting him, Libertas tried to fake indifference and assure Harro that it was truly all right if they just went to sleep early—"no amorous affairs, tonight; we both ought to be up early tomorrow"—but her husband knew her too well to buy into the lie for his sake. And so, once again she would awake alone and find a thin pale strip of light under the bathroom door and Harro's strained breathing tearing her heart to shreds.

At last, she couldn't take it any longer.

"What is it?" Confused, Harro turned the leaflet in his hand this way and that.

"It's a sanatorium in Bad Wildungen, in Hesse. An excellent one from what I've heard. For your kidneys," Libertas clarified.

Harro looked at her with a miserable smile. "Do I keep you up at night? I thought you were a heavy sleeper."

"I used to be. I am. Only not with you. You'll think it odd, but…" Libertas sighed. "I've grown so attuned to you, I instantly feel when something is wrong. When you hurt, I wake up as though it's me who's hurting."

Harro made no reply, only looked at her with understanding. No, he didn't think it odd. He felt the same about her, and Libertas knew it.

"You haven't taken leave in a while," she proceeded, opening the pages of the leaflet for Harro to see.

The sanatorium was indeed one of the best in Germany she could find through recommendations coming from the very top. In the pictures, smiling patients dressed in expensive robes and pajamas relaxed by the pool served by medical personnel. In the background was a flag with a swastika. Libertas covered it with her hand.

"And I have nothing holding me at work either. As a matter of fact, I have submitted my resignation letter today. Explained that I have a duty to my husband and all that business and they signed it even faster than my resignation from the Party." She beamed at her husband brightly. "From today on, my full-time job will be taking care of you. Are you happy?"

Harro wasn't; Libertas saw it right away.

"No, Libs, that's not—" Stopping himself abruptly, Harro was already shaking his head. "You haven't even discussed it with me."

"The sanatorium?"

"Leaving your job."

"But how else would I go with you to Hesse? The treatment may take a few weeks, perhaps a month or two. They wouldn't hold my position for me for so long at any rate."

"That's not what I'm—" Harro sighed once again, looking annoyed. Not with her, Libertas knew that much, but most likely with himself for not being able to express himself properly, for causing all this trouble for the woman he loved more than anything. Libertas felt a sharp stab like a knife to her gut when she saw all the pain he was desperately trying to hide from her. "I would never have asked you to quit your job for me. You don't have to come with me to Hesse. There are ten nurses and five doctors to one patient there, judging by this brochure." He waved the leaflet in the air before dropping it on the table. "I wish you had discussed it with me first."

"I wanted to surprise you." Libertas' voice was small with disappointment.

After another deep breath, Harro dragged his palms down his face and then took Libertas' hands in his, kissing them, first left, then right. "Forgive me."

"For what?"

"For being an ungrateful mutton."

"You're not being an ungrateful mutton. You're right. I should have asked you first."

"No!" Harro cried again in exasperation. "Libs, *Liebchen*, I don't want you to ask me for permission to do anything."

"But you just said I should have discussed it with you."

"Yes. *Discussed* it. Like we always discuss everything. Not *asked*. I wish we'd sat down and spoken about it and I would have thanked you properly for your care and talked you out of quitting your job for me. That's all I meant." He was looking at her with infinite tenderness. "I don't want you to throw away your ambitions for your sick husband's sake. I don't know what I did to deserve you in the first place. I can't even satisfy you properly—"

"Don't be ridiculous." Libertas tossed her head, a sharp crease between her brows. "That's not why I got this brochure for you. I can't stand seeing you in pain, that's all. You satisfy me just fine and don't you ever even imply anything to the contrary. And my job—big deal! Gisela was right when she said that I was stuck at the same place for years with no prospects whatsoever. What sort of ambition is that?" She snorted with contempt. "Harro, love, trust me, quitting was not difficult at all. What are you grinning at?"

"You."

"Happy that we're discussing things?" She mocked him with her fists butting her hips in good-natured contempt.

"I wouldn't call that a discussion; you're standing there explaining to me why I'm an idiot." Harro was barely containing his chuckles. "But taking into consideration the fact that most of our discussions go the same way—"

Libertas' play-swatting him drew his speech to an abrupt stop. Simultaneously, they exploded in laughter and then, Harro scooped her into his embrace and closed his eyes, while Libertas covered his face in kisses and all was well once again.

"A sanatorium?" Wend looked at his son-in-law with interest. "That's a grand idea."

"Libertas' idea." Harro smiled warmly at his wife.

They sat in a restaurant frequented by the top military brass, where the orchestra was attired in tails and the waiters wore Party members badges. Libertas had offered Harro to politely decline her uncle's invitation, but Harro suggested they trooped through it. Wend had implied that Göring could attend. Who knew what military secrets *Herr Reichsmarschall* would blurt out if well-lubricated with imported brandy?

But Göring had other affairs that required his attention, and so, it was his replacement, Nicolaus von Below—Hitler's Luftwaffe adjutant and Harro's superior—who stared daggers through the newly promoted officer as he sat framed by Wend on one side and a rosy-cheeked pilot from the Condor Legion on the other. It was von Below, a dedicated Nazi, who was behind Harro's trouble getting a promotion. He didn't trust the former editor of a liberal newspaper and didn't conceal that fact. Only Göring's personal intervention had made Harro's career move forward. As far as von Below was concerned, Harro belonged in a concentration camp, not in the Air Ministry, and certainly not in its Foreign Air Forces recently combined with the Operations department with too much sensitive information exchanged freely among its officers.

Wend had informed Harro about his superior's attitude, chuckling in a conspiratorial manner as though he found the matter positively amusing.

"Ignore that Pale Templar," he had advised Harro with a nonchalant sweep of the hand as they drove to the restaurant. "He sees conspiracies everywhere. I won't be surprised if he accuses me of being a foreign spy one day."

To Libertas, however, such a dismissive attitude spelled danger. She remembered far too well how things ended for the SA leader Röhm after someone had whispered a similar conspiracy into Hitler's ear, implying that Röhm was plotting against him when it was very much not the case. To Libertas, no conspiracies were harmless, and particularly those spread by people like von Below, who had Hitler's ear.

She poked her crab cake without much appetite, her back stiff with tension and a charming smile plastered onto her face, ready to come to her husband's aid at any moment.

"You have troubles with kidney stones too?" the pilot, whose name kept escaping Libertas, straightened in his chair, a piece of asparagus forgotten on his fork. "Please, do let me know if the treatment helps you on your return. I have developed quite a few stones myself after drinking bad water in Spain. Too much calcium, the garrison physician said. And the black pepper those bastards put on everything—excuse my language, please," he quickly apologized to Libertas, his hand pressed to his chest. "That did a number on my kidneys too."

"I ought to thank the SS for awarding me with mine," Harro replied casually, eyes trained on a veal cutlet he was presently cutting.

In his seat, von Below pulled himself up visibly.

Under the table, Libertas nudged Harro's boot with the tip of her shoe. *Don't poke the bear.*

"The SS?" the pilot's eyes widened in surprise.

"Mhm," Harro confirmed, ignoring his wife's warning nudge. "They arrested me in 1933."

"On what charges?" The pilot looked as though he couldn't quite take it in, how this upstanding officer in full regalia could have been mistaken for a common scoundrel.

"They took him for a communist." Wend laughed, positively delighted, and dealt his relative an amicable clap on his back. "Imagine that?"

"Perhaps it was the SA?" the pilot suggested doubtfully. "They were infamous for getting drunk and harassing honest folk..."

"No. It was the SS," Harro countered with the same fascinating calmness. "Black uniforms. Not brown."

"Even the SS were much too enthusiastic concerning their methods at the very beginning." Wend waved him off as though the matter was a mere anecdote, water under the bridge, good only to mention at the dinner table as a joke among friends.

Neither Libertas nor Harro laughed.

"I can see how they could have been confused," von Below said, his pale eyes fixed on Harro without blinking. "You were in charge of that leftist newspaper. What was it called?"

"*Gegner.*" Harro met his gaze without a trace of fear. "It wasn't leftist, though I can see how you may consider it such," he said, subtly mocking his superior's manner. "It was a paper that was not censored by the government and which promoted free speech. We had news and opinion columns in it, which offered different views on nationalism, fascism, communism, democracy, and all other political matters, but we never pushed our views on our readers. The entire point of the paper was to let them decide what to think, how to think for themselves."

"Do you still hold those views?"

A tense pause hung over the table after von Below's question.

"Of course, not," Harro responded at last, looking his superior directly in the eye. "You know that well enough. I write for the Air Ministry paper now." After those words, he smiled with such charm it was impossible not to believe him.

"Just as well that you do," von Below said coolly. "The Gestapo aren't as lenient on enemies of the Reich as they used to be. In fact, they had to abandon the ax and employ a guillotine in its place—executioners couldn't cope with the numbers."

"Poor fellows," Harro shook his head, full of sarcastic sympathy. "Must be a tough job."

"It is," von Below hissed through his teeth. "Cleaning the Reich of its cancerous elements always is. In any case, one such 'hero,' a Bolshevist of the brightest crimson it goes without saying, had just been caught smuggling information to the Soviets. Got executed, like he deserved, but the real tragedy is that his beautiful wife, who had already gifted four beautiful children to the Reich, poisoned those beautiful children so that 'the government wouldn't get hold of them,' according to the note she'd left, and then poisoned herself because she didn't want to live without her lousy criminal husband." He looked at Harro pointedly. "We loathe to see such things happening. So, I'm twice as pleased that you have abandoned your dangerous leftist views and returned to the fold of the Reich." After taking a sip of his wine, he added, "You're a married man now, Schulze-Boysen. You have responsibilities."

For the first time, Harro looked serious.

"Yes, I do." Libertas heard him mutter.

Harro was unusually silent on the way home. Even after they parted ways with Wend and were left alone, he still hadn't come out from under his brooding spell.

"He's right, Libs." He sighed after Libertas demanded what was the matter with him. "It's dangerous that we're so dependent on each other."

"Whatever nonsense are you saying now?"

"Not nonsense. Think about it. What if I get discovered?" He looked at her firmly, as though searching for the truth in her eyes. "What would you do?"

"I would want to die with you." Libertas didn't need to think over the answer.

"That's precisely the matter."

"Wouldn't you want to die with me?"

"I would. That's why it's not good."

"Not good for whom?"

"For the people we're trying to help. We're very selfish in our love for each other. Yes, it's all fine and well to die holding hands, but what of them? Who's going to continue our work if we all commit mass suicide, you and I, Gisela and Ricci because they love each other as well? Who shall be left to fight?"

For a long time, they sat side by side on their bed, still in their evening clothes, painfully beautiful and already doomed.

"We have to learn how to function without each other," Harro said.

"Yes. You're right." It went against all of her instincts, but Libertas knew it was so.

"Perhaps you ought to go on a trip while I'm undergoing treatment. By yourself."

"All alone?"

"Yes."

In the darkness, his hand found hers. He wasn't rejecting her; if anything, he longed for her more than ever; she sensed it through that silent gesture.

"You're right," Libertas repeated, swallowing back tears. "We need to learn how to be apart... How to be strong on our own."

"How to survive."

"Yes, how to survive."

"Because we owe it to them, the people."

"Yes."

"We can't be selfish."

"No."

"No matter how much I love you."

"No matter how much—" She choked on the last words in spite of herself; felt them wrap themselves hard around her neck, like barbed wire.

"It will be tough, but we can do it, little freedom fighter."

Libertas nodded through the mist in her eyes. *Little freedom fighter*. She had almost forgotten about the note Fritz Lang wrote to her, on that platform shrouded in darkness, when it felt as though there were only two of them left in the entire world—the one who ran and the one who had stayed to fight.

Recovering herself, she straightened her shoulders and was brave once again. "Yes. We can do it. For them. For the people."

"For freedom."

"And for each other."

Chapter 20

Black Sea. October 1937

Waves lapped softly at the sides of the ship heading for the Crimean coast. The *Ilona* was a coal transport manned by coarse-tongued, bronze-skinned sailors, but frankly speaking, Libertas wouldn't trade their company for any well-trained army of white-gloved lackeys that would have served her, had she chosen to travel first class.

At first, the sailors had regarded her with visible apprehension, the blond slip of a girl who had climbed aboard their vessel armed with an accordion, a suitcase full of books and notebooks, and a Leica camera hanging off her neck. But as soon as she had sat down with them at the same communal table instead of taking her dinner in her cabin and downed the first *Stein* of beer without blinking an eye, their apprehension had eased. It vanished entirely after Libertas picked up her accordion and sang for them in her high, clear voice—frank songs of the sailors Ricci had taught her during one of their parties when they were drunk and prone to mischief.

As they sailed the waters of the Black Sea, Libertas snapped their photos and scribbled their stories of hardships and simple joys as she sat, cross-legged and generously lathered with suntan lotion, right on the sun-warmed, thoroughly mopped deck of the ship. She wrote to Harro religiously and at every chance, sending her letters in bulk whenever they docked in a new coastal town. In her letters, her days were summarized, filled with adventures and anecdotes she knew he would find amusing, and also the nights filled with longing and infinite love for her only one, her dearest one, whose embraces she so sorely missed and so feverishly craved.

"One thing became clear to me during this journey," Libertas wrote to Harro during a stormy October night, when the waves were too rough and sleep wouldn't come. "I hate to be apart from you. Yes, to be sure I can survive on my own; you would be immensely proud to learn that your little kitty has mastered all sorts of knots by now and can become a first-rate sailor. But this is precisely what this is, without you—surviving, not living. And I desperately want to live, Harro. With you by my side, or not at all. Forgive the morbid mood; the weather is so melancholy tonight and I have drunk too much brandy. At any rate, I've had enough of this. I'm coming home. See you on the other side. Eternally and irrevocably yours, Libertas."

She hadn't expected to receive an answer; due to the *Ilona*'s travel schedule, they had decided that it would have been useless for Harro to write as his letters would miss Libertas. However, when she stepped onto Hamburg's dock, it was Harro himself who was waiting for her with the brilliant smile she loved so much, an open embrace and eyes shining with eternal devotion. A few weeks of rest and medical treatments had done wonders for him: gone were the bags from under his eyes and the sickly, yellowish undertone to his skin. He was a picture of health, much to Libertas' joy and relief.

"Never send me away again," Libertas muttered through the mist in her eyes, hiding her face in the folds of his uniform overcoat.

"I won't," Harro said and meant it. "I swear."

Berlin. January 1938

Christmas came and went, a sad affair at the Schloss Liebenberg estate, for the traditional festive songs were now frowned upon and all but banned by the recent decrees of the Secretary of Culture and Propaganda in favor of an "Aryan" pagan tradition of the solstice celebration. Back in the capital, January was dragging its feet along the calendar, a typical Berlin one—muddy, snowless, and with the sky the color of lead. After Gisela's report about her successful carrying out of their mission and leaving the envelope with some stern-looking Soviet official, there was no news once again and no Gisela herself. Just like Libertas, her cousin had realized that she had missed Ricci more than she cared to admit while alone in Paris and moved her meager belongings from her room at Harro and Libertas' apartment to Ricci's boathouse, where they now lived like two vagabonds, in a shack but madly in love.

Restless without a job, Libertas took to vigorous exercise and began taking trains to the Tiergarten, where she ran in her training suit until the beehive of her thoughts would somewhat settle and exhaustion would replace some vague anxiety plaguing her mind. Alone at home, she organized her diaries from the ship into some semblance of order, typing them out into separate entities, crumpling pages and throwing them, annoyed, into a wastebasket standing under her desk, and retyping them anew, just so in the evening Harro could have something new to read besides the Air Ministry reports he detested and the popular German novels full of blood and race he equally despised.

One evening, while Libertas was listening to the BBC on the lowest volume, Harro suddenly looked up from the notes he was reading.

"Have I told you that I met an old friend of mine at the bus stop?" he asked.

"No. Is he one of your *Gegner* friends?" Libertas turned the radio off.

"Yes. Günther Weisenborn. I haven't the faintest idea how he has managed to escape the Nazis so far, but…" Harro chuckled, his gaze full of wonder and memories. "He used to be a dramaturg at the Volksbühne theater and a good friend of Bertolt Brecht, that mad communist fellow who called himself the People's Director.

In fact, one of Weisenborn's novels was burned during that book burning event in May of 1933; you remember?"

Libertas remembered it far too well. The smell of burning freedom, the ash on her skin, like tears.

"At any rate," Harro continued, "I'm thinking of showing your notes to him."

Libertas stared at him in stunned amazement. "To Weisenborn?"

"Why? Do you mind?"

"No, it's just… Why would you want to?"

"Because I think they're really good and that he may help you turn them into a book or submit them to a magazine or something of that sort."

Libertas began to laugh, but seeing Harro's expression, receded. "You're serious, aren't you?"

"Of course I am."

"But these are just my personal notes. They aren't any good. I wrote them for myself and for you, maybe for Gisela and Ricci, but not for the public to read."

"And just why not?"

"Because I'm not a writer."

A grin appeared on Harro's face. "And just who decides these things?"

On January 12, Günther Weisenborn knocked on their door—black overcoat, black eyes behind horn-rimmed glasses, black leather gloves holding a bouquet of roses for Libertas—not what she had imagined him to be at all. Without further ado, he demanded to see "the manuscript," which Libertas handed to him with great hesitation; leafed through it while she, embarrassed and anxious to the point of lightheadedness, retreated to the kitchen to fuss about the tea and dessert. By the time she returned with a tray that was shaking slightly in her hands, Harro and their guest were already discussing the format that would best suit the diaries.

"Marvelous!" Günther greeted Libertas, holding her typed notes in the air like a trophy. "Simply marvelous! Such attention to detail, such a distinctive voice. From the few pages I've read, I feel I'm right there with you, on that ship. And your wonderful sense of humor, your dry, sarcastic remarks, your wit, sharp as a whip—I'm in love. I shall be a criminal if I don't show it to my publisher, Ernst Rowohlt."

A blush creeping up her cheeks, Libertas shifted her gaze from Günther to Harro and back, the entire colony of butterflies exploding in her chest at the hope that perhaps not all was lost yet, and she would leave her mark after all. Even though she was born a woman. Thankfully, she had a man by her side who believed in her and was her biggest supporter. How much she loved him just then.

February 1938

It was late evening, long past dinner, when Ricci burst into Libertas' and Harro's apartment, pale as death, and uttered in a voice of a man who had just been mortally wounded: "Gisela is arrested."

All color drained from Harro's face as well, while Libertas stared at Ricci, a hundred scenarios, each more dreadful than the other, already forming in her mind.

"When?" Harro demanded in a hoarse voice, recollecting himself with visible effort.

"Just today." Ricci's face was wet with melted snow—or were those tears? Libertas couldn't quite tell in the dimmed light of the hallway. He hadn't budged from the wall against which he was leaning. "They came to our boathouse. How did they even find out about it?" he moaned, wiping his palms down his face in anguish.

"Have they charged her with anything?" Libertas hardly recognized her own voice.

"No," Ricci muttered into the palms still covering a face full of unspoken torment. "Just said she was under arrest and strongly advised me to mind my own affairs when I tried to protest, or I would end up in their cellar too, for obstruction of justice."

Libertas and Harro exchanged anxious glances. Was it possible that the Gestapo had been watching Gisela this entire time and had just made their move today? Did they know about Paris? Had they followed her into the Soviet Embassy? Had the Soviets tipped them off themselves, considering the contents of the papers a German provocation?

Her throat entirely dry, Libertas whispered to no one in particular, "What do we do now?"

Harro released a ragged breath and raked a hand through his hair. "Nothing rushed. The absolute worst thing we can do at this moment is panic and do something idiotic." He shifted his gaze from Libertas to Ricci. "Let's all sit down, have a drink, and talk this over."

Looking as if he'd aged ten years, Ricci dragged himself after the couple into their atelier and dropped onto the sofa, drained and without hope.

While Harro busied himself with making drinks—just to give his ice-cold, trembling hands a purpose—Libertas glued herself to the window, her eyes trained on the street below. Through the glass fogged by her breath, every shadow, every slow-moving car, took on a menacing meaning; every passer-by in a fedora was a Gestapo agent; every innocent whistle for a taxicab, a signal to go in. She felt herself jump when Harro pressed a glass with brandy on ice to her palm.

"Forgive me," she whispered, taking it from him. "It's the nerves."

He only kissed her on her temple, where his lips lingered longer than usual, as if he was reluctant to let go. It must have affected him greatly, seeing Ricci go through the anguish he would be doomed to go through as well if their worst fears turned out to be justified. But after the first jab of fear for their own lives had somewhat eased after a few deep gulps of brandy, a sucking feeling of emptiness replaced it.

Gisela. Her brave, reckless Gisela.

Discreetly, Libertas wiped the tears from her cheeks. No need for Ricci to see her cry. Bad for morale.

From the depths of the atelier, Harro's voice came, guardedly cool and reassuringly logical: "If the leather-coats knew about the documents and the Embassy, they would have arrested her much sooner. In fact, they would have intercepted her before she passed the papers to the Embassy. They simply wouldn't have risked the Soviets getting their hands on them. They didn't bring you in for questioning either, which can only mean that they don't suspect a conspiracy."

There was a pause; silence charged with tension like a taut string about to snap.

"Ricci, I need you to think hard." The sound of leather creaking as Harro shifted in his seat. "Has Gisela involved herself with anything else lately? Anything that could have provoked the arrest?"

Ricci didn't need any time to think. "No. Ever since she returned from Paris, she has been with me the entire time. I would have known if she—" Another exasperated breath. "No. There was nothing illegal. Just... that."

That. One single word, dropped almost as an accusation even if Ricci didn't mean for it to sound as such. One single word that cut against Libertas' nerves like a sharp blade, filling her with guilt and burning remorse.

"I should have gone instead," she spoke quietly against the glass. "We had no right to ask Gisela to risk her life for our affairs. My father lives in Paris with my former governess. I could have used them as an excuse." She tossed her head, annoyed with her own stupidity, her carelessness that could very well have cost Gisela her life. Or her freedom, at the very least. "I should have done it, not her—"

"Don't blame yourself, Libs." Ricci's tone had a softness to it now. "You didn't make Gisela do anything. It was her wish to go. In fact, she was most excited about it. To her, it was one big adventure." He snorted gently, barely audibly. "You know how she is. A rebel, a wild spirit who reads too many spy novels. She thought of it as a game."

Only, it wasn't a game. It was life—which now hung by a thread.

Chapter 21

On the fifth day, when Libertas couldn't bear the wait any longer, she called her uncle Wend and arranged a lunch with him. She was the first one to arrive, anxious and exhausted from sleepless nights, and checked her wristwatch every two minutes despite the fact that she was twenty minutes early and her uncle arrived punctually at five to twelve.

After kissing her ceremoniously on both cheeks, Wend held Libertas in his outstretched arms, regarding her with concern.

"Are you now well, Libby? You look awfully pale, if you forgive me for saying so. I'm only asking out of concern."

"I'm always pale, *Onkel*." She tried to smile. "Everyone in our family is, except for *Vati* with his ruddy complexion."

Wend smiled politely at her attempt at a joke and moved up a chair for her himself, ignoring the waiter. He went through the motions of perusing the list of wines and ordering their best Riesling and making small talk about weather and the insufferable issues with the road construction, but as soon as their appetizers were brought in and the waiters left them alone, Wend folded his hands atop his knee and looked at his niece pointedly.

"So, what is this all about? I don't assume you summoned me here because you missed me so."

"I did miss you." Libertas tried to smile, but her lips quivered in spite of herself.

"What is it, Libs? Is it Harro? Is he ill again?"

"No, it's not Harro." She wasn't sure how to even begin such a conversation. "It's Gisela."

"*Ach*, a very bright girl, if a bit wild." He chuckled fondly. "She lives with you, does she not?"

"She used to rent a room from us, but she moved in with her beau just before Christmas."

"That artist fellow?"

"Ricci. Yes."

"What about her then?"

Libertas searched his face for clues. *Was he pretending so well, or had he truly not heard anything about it?* The very thought of her own uncle feigning ignorance when his relative's life was in danger unnerved Libertas, and yet, it was still a possibility. Wend had proved time and again that his loyalties lay with the Party. But would he betray his own blood for money and the power it showered him with?

"She was arrested a few days ago," Libertas said in an even tone.

The genuine surprise in Wend's eyes didn't escape her. He paused mid-gulp, lowered his glass to the table, and dabbed his mouth with a napkin. "On what charges?"

"That's what I would like to know."

"You mean to tell me that they didn't charge her with anything?"

"They didn't. Ricci was present during her arrest and demanded an explanation. They simply told him to mind his own affairs and took her. Ever since, we've heard nothing."

"That's not good," Wend muttered quietly, drumming his fingers on the edge of the table. "It was the Gestapo, I assume? Not the police?"

Libertas only shook her head.

Wend nodded again, several times, to some thoughts of his own. But something shifted within Libertas at that concerned expression of his, at that mind feverishly at work. He really was blissfully ignorant then, despite his closeness with von Below and Göring.

Unless they kept him in the dark on purpose, a sudden thought occurred to Libertas. *What if in place of Röhm, a murdered SA leader, her uncle Wend had fallen out of favor for whatever reason? What if the Party leaders decided to do away with the entire family, charging them all with treason and using Gisela as an excuse?*

The glass of sparkling water nearly slipped away from her sweaty palms. Gulping it desperately, Libertas was aware of her own racing heart; racing thoughts that turned darker with every hectic breath, making her break into a cold sweat.

Through the faint ringing in her ears, Wend's voice came as though from under water. "Libs? I'm asking if you want me to ask around about her?"

With a tremendous effort, she managed to recollect herself. "Yes, please. If you can. If it's not too much trouble."

"It is unfortunate that Göring isn't in charge of the Gestapo anymore else I would have given you the news within twenty minutes. Now, it's Himmler and Heydrich's domain." Wend's expression turned visibly sour. It was obvious he didn't think much of either and chose not to deal with them if he could help it. "But don't you fret." He grinned encouragingly at his niece. "I have people who owe me a few favors. I'll tell you what's going on in a few days at the most. And now, eat. If you get any thinner, the wind will carry you away."

A sad smile crossed Libertas' face. Sometimes she wished it would. Somewhere very far away from Germany.

Wend kept his word. He came in person in the middle of the afternoon, while Harro was at work, and waved off Libertas' offer of coffee.

"No, no, don't take my coat either. My driver is waiting downstairs. It appears that our little rebel was arrested for some idiotic incident that took place years ago, back in 1934 as a matter of fact. Something about spreading anti-government propaganda, half of which she didn't even understand and, as it turned out during the interrogation, had entirely forgotten by now." Wend drew his gaze to the ceiling. "At any rate, they have sentenced her to five months of incarceration and only as a favor to me. She'll be out before you know it. Just in time for you and Harro to take her and Ricci to the marina. And now, excuse me, but I truly have to run. All that business with Austria…"

Another dramatic sigh; an obligatory peck on the forehead, and Wend was gone, leaving Libertas lightheaded and smiling faintly with exhaustion and immense relief.

Only five months. Some idiotic incident from before. They were safe. Everything should be just fine by summer.

But then March came and with it, German troops marching straight through the Austrian border and Wend's words—*all that business with Austria*—which Libertas had ignored, took on a whole new ominous meaning.

The Greater German Reich had just gobbled up another neighboring territory and no one had blinked an eye. Summer would come, but nothing would be fine. In the air, the faint acrid smell of war was spreading.

July 1938

"How do I look?" Throwing an anxious look at Harro, Libertas fixed her hair for what felt like the hundredth time.

She was soaked by the time they had reached their grim destination point—more from nerves than heat. While they'd driven, it was still tolerable with the roof down, but now, as they stood in front of their car, rivulets of sweat snaked down her back under her thin satin dress.

"So beautiful, it should be illegal," Harro replied, obviously in the hope of easing her nerves, and added with a grin, "as always."

Libertas smiled at him feebly in gratitude and took a bouquet of lilies they had bought on the Linden from his hands. *Tiger lilies. Gisela's favorite.*

At last, the gates to the Gestapo bastion groaned to life, a uniformed man stepping out to hold it open. Her heart beating in her throat, Libertas craned her neck, not realizing that she had stopped breathing altogether. But then a shadow of disappointment darkened her features as an emaciated elderly woman shuffled out of the gates, holding a canvas bag with whatever meager personal possessions she had.

Releasing a sigh and checking her wristwatch once again—the orderly they had spoken to did say four o'clock—Libertas resumed her fidgeting with the flowers.

Harro nudged her slightly in the back, his face oddly gray even under the healthy summer tan he had acquired.

Libertas regarded him quizzically—*What?*

It was then that he put his arm around her shoulders, his palm ice-cold for some unimaginable reason, and directed her, gently but firmly, in the direction of the gates that were closing once again. A wooden, unnatural smile distorted his face, looking more like a painful grimace.

"Whatever you do, Libs, just don't cry," he muttered to her through gritted teeth, his fingers digging further into her skin.

Why would I cry? Libertas almost asked him, still in denial, still too terrified to believe that this fragile shell of a woman who stood waiting for them in front of the gate was her Gisela.

Every step turned into sheer torture. Staring stubbornly at her sandaled feet (how inappropriately bright her red nail polish looked just then, she realized with mounting horror), Libertas refused to process the terrible transformation.

It had only been five months…

In what world was this possible?

"Gisela!" The artificial cheerfulness in Harro's voice startled her. "How are you, old girl? We missed you something terrible! Right, Libs?"

Another slight nudge.

Libertas willed the corners of her quivering lips to arch upward. "Terrible…" she scarcely heard herself whisper as she held the flowers before herself like a shield.

But then, ashamed of her own fear, Libertas finally lifted her head and looked into the eyes of her cousin and smiled wider, suppressing a gasp of horror, swallowing it along with a lump of tears, locking it deep inside for Gisela's sake.

It was impossible to believe that this apparition with nearly translucent skin and a net of blue veins visible under it was only twenty-seven. A woolen dress, in which she must had been arrested, hung on her skeletal frame in loose folds. Purple half-moons under her eyes had the same cadaverous tint to them as Gisela's lips that stretched into an uncertain, exhausted smile. The only bright spots in her entire appearance were her cheeks that glowed with some unnatural blush and her eyes, shining from under the heavy lids with feverish light. It was as though an invisible fire was burning inside Gisela, slowly but surely reducing her to ash.

Shuddering at the thought, Libertas grasped her cousin by her bony shoulders and kissed her on both cheeks.

At once, Gisela began to protest. It hadn't progressed to the contagious type; the prison doctors assured her of that much, but it was still best if Libertas kept her distance. Also, she wouldn't be moving back in with them. Neither with Ricci, even though he did plead with her to…

Harro was the first one to recover control of his emotions.

"Come," he said gently, taking the canvas bag from Gisela's hand, "come to the car. Let's get you seated. You must be exhausted…"

"From what?" A glimpse of the old Gisela was still discernible in this new one's smile. "I've spent the past five months on my back. Had enough rest to last me a lifetime."

"Tonight, you stay with us," Harro continued as he directed Gisela to their car, all business. Libertas knew it was easier this way for him, dealing with everything in steps. "And tomorrow, we'll start looking for a good sanatorium for you."

"The best one!" Libertas added, recovering her voice at last. "We'll find the best sanatorium possible. Mountain air is just what you need now. It'll right you in a few weeks, you'll see."

As Libertas was arranging a cover over Gisela's legs, she was looking at her cousin desperately as though craving encouragement.

Gisela took pity on her; nodded; cradled Libertas' hand in hers.

Libertas saw it in Gisela's eyes—an unannounced death sentence; sensed the putrid breath of the Grim Reaper just over her cousin's shoulder, but she didn't cry as she nestled next to her. There were three of them in the front seat, but Libertas could scarcely feel her cousin's hip against hers. Even then she didn't cry; only bit into her bottom lip, hard enough to draw blood. Harro was right about that, like he always was about everything—Gisela didn't need it.

"They don't suspect a damned thing about our Paris affair."

It took Libertas a few moments to return to the present moment; to take in the meaning of Gisela's words.

In spite of everything, one leg in her grave, Gisela was grinning triumphantly, her eyes closed against the warm summer wind. "They offered an immediate release to me, in exchange for any valuable information I could offer. Some bigwig from the Reich Main Security Office came down to see me in person, pale as death, eyes—the most disturbing I've ever seen. Entirely empty. Cold, like ice. Not a glimpse of a soul behind them."

Something rattled in her throat. An off-white handkerchief at her mouth, Gisela twisted in her seat as far from Harro and Libertas as possible until her coughing fit passed. In alarm, Libertas listened to her ragged breathing; watched beads of sweat break on Gisela's temples, round and heavy like pearls; saw her clutch her handkerchief in her fist to hide the fresh crimson spots on it.

"...Told me he'd sign my release personally if I gave him something valuable on Harro. You're on some list of theirs," Gisela said, tapping Harro's knee, concentration creasing her brow as though she struggled to delegate anything important to them as quickly as possible...

While she still had a chance, it suddenly occurred to Libertas. With a tremendous effort, she swallowed that lump as well.

"At any rate," Gisela continued, her voice hoarse and exhausted with the effort, "he wanted to know if you're up to something. I told him that you were an exemplary Reich citizen, much to my personal disappointment, and the only illegal vice of yours was your unhealthy obsession with American swing."

Harro laughed at that; through the bitter tears of gratitude, Libertas suspected.

Gisela chuckled too, choked on her laughter once again, rubbed her chest in which something kept boiling, rattling.

"Gisela, perhaps you shouldn't be talking too much," Libertas suggested softly, her hand on her cousin's back, rubbing in gentle circles, pacifying the beast raging inside.

But Gisela only waved her off. "I need to say it all while I still can. Where was I? Yes, the pale-faced bigwig. It appears he severely lacks a sense of humor as well. Not only didn't he appreciate my joke but he transferred me to the moldiest cell they had in the entire cellar, with all the tubercular cases confined to the same wing. A vindictive son of a bitch." She snorted with a mixture of sarcasm and disdain. "So, you're in the clear for now. They have nothing;

only the old *Gegner* files on you, Harro, but it's all water under the bridge. Have you heard anything from the Soviets?"

"Not yet," he responded. "But I suspect we will."

In Gisela's eyes, there was a faraway look. A faint, dreamy smile was playing on her cracked, bloodless lips. "I wish I'd live to see that day. I would know then that my life wasn't lived in vain. That I did something... remarkable."

"You already did," Libertas and Harro interjected in unison.

"Something utterly remarkable and brave," Libertas continued, clasping her cousin's narrow palm in hers. "You're a hero, Gisela. You will always be."

"Will you write about me?" Gisela asked, all playfulness gone all of a sudden. "Now that you've finally quit that idiotic job of yours and decided to become a writer."

"Oh, I'm very far from being a writer," Libertas tried to protest.

"Oh no, we're having none of that," Gisela cut her off in that no-nonsense manner of hers. "I read excerpts from your travel diaries. They gave me my freedom back, even behind the stone walls. They may have put me into that dungeon, but your words took me on such adventures, Libs! Your writing may have an impact in the most unexpected ways. Please, don't give it up. Write. You never know who needs to hear your words, whose life they will transform. Promise?"

Libertas nodded. "Solemnly swear."

"Good." Releasing a tremendous breath, Gisela finally leaned against the upholstered seat and closed her eyes, her affairs settled at last, her last will drawn, Libertas and Harro left in good hands.

Chapter 22

Zurich, Switzerland. August 1938

Seated in an outside café, Libertas was stirring a coffee that had long gone cold. All around her were women in sundresses, carefree laughter, birds singing, music filtering out of open windows, yet all the while inside of Libertas, a veritable tragedy was unraveling its dark wings. In front of her red-rimmed eyes, unseeing and glazed over, staring blankly into the void, Gisela's image swam, translucent and already dissolving into nothing.

Libertas had just visited her again, this very morning, like she had done religiously for the past few weeks since she'd followed her cousin into the best sanatorium she and Harro could find for her. She would have spent her entire days with Gisela, had doctors not explained that it would only exhaust Gisela, who needed rest most of all. Making her comfortable was of the utmost importance now, they explained in their mild, sympathetic voices, purposely avoiding Libertas' eyes.

"But there must be some treatment," Libertas kept asking, still nursing a useless hope, still refusing to surrender, "something you can do?"

Another clearing of the throat; another bland, polite smile; fittingly sorrowful eyes avoiding hers. "We'll do our utmost to make Fräulein von Pöllnitz comfortable."

Comfortable. How much she loathed that word!

With a groan, Libertas closed her eyes and rubbed them fiercely.

What could possibly be comfortable about a dying woman obsessively powdering her face that was wasting away not by days but by hours now just to "pretty herself up" before Libertas' daily visits?

What was comfortable about seeing Gisela's bloodless lips tremble as tears, huge as raindrops, rolled down her cheeks when she complained to Libertas bitterly that "that bitch of a nurse took away her mirror."

What could possibly have been comfortable about trying to come up with excuses as to why she, Libertas, couldn't give Gisela her compact powder; bursting into tears herself; running out of the room like a pathetic coward just to return thirty minutes later with a handbag full of makeup and applying it all herself to her cousin's waxy face with its purple eyelids and brightly burning cheeks.

"There. Pretty as a picture."

Libertas cringed as she recalled herself saying those words just a little over an hour ago. With a suppressed sob, she thought of how Gisela's expression had brightened when Libertas had finally handed her the mirror, how her cousin had beamed with gratitude and something that could have been relief and had asked for a cigarette. How, without hesitation, Libertas had passed her one and lit up for her. How Gisela's physician appeared in the door of her ward, alerted by the smoke no doubt; how he'd begun to say something but, seeing Libertas' expression, stopped and left, closing the door softly after himself.

Even people on the gallows were allowed their last smoke. It would have been cruel to deny Gisela that very last indulgence of hers. What bitter irony it was that as she had pulled in a long lungful of smoke, for the first time since her release from prison, for the first time since her arrival here, Gisela actually looked comfortable.

At peace.

When Libertas returned to Berlin, she found it a triumphant city decked out in bloody banners and victorious wreaths. Among celebratory crowds, cheering their Führer who had just won another war for them without a single shot fired, she alone was dressed all in black—not only for Gisela whose funeral she had arranged all by herself, but for the independent Czechoslovakia as well.

"You have heard, I assume?" Harro asked as he held her in the embrace she had missed so sorely. "The Wehrmacht has just marched into the Sudetenland. It's our German *Protectorate* now," he said, full of bitter, mocking disdain. "Herr Chamberlain has just offered it to Hitler on a silver plate to 'preserve peace' in the region."

Libertas only shrugged, too tired from the road and the events of the past two months. It had been difficult to be the only person present at Gisela's funeral besides the minister and two gravediggers, but that was Gisela's own last wish: to be buried in the peaceful Swiss ground and be remembered for how she lived instead of how she died. She hadn't wanted to be seen withered and sick; instead, she had hoped to remain forever youthful and rebellious in her lovers', friends', and relatives' minds. Libertas had understood it all too well and hadn't argued.

"To be frank, I didn't expect any heroics from the British." She sighed in response to Harro's remark. "You remember what Evan said when we asked him to deliver our reports to his government? *Not our business what Hitler does in Europe. We've had enough of the first war; we don't want the second one.*"

"Only, appeasement doesn't work with dictators. Now that they've allowed him to gobble up Sudetenland without even inviting the Czechoslovakian president to the table, Hitler will only want more. Now, he must really feel omnipotent, unstoppable. This is what happens when you don't check the power and when the man who abuses it doesn't face any repercussions. This is how dictators are born. This is how nations die."

That evening, they stayed inside and brooded in silence. The next morning, when the city still slept, its streets littered with confetti, little red flags, and wilting flowers, they rose early and began to plot.

Because someone had to stay behind to fight.

Because someone had to stop the bloodthirsty dictator before it got too late.

Because, in the face of injustice and in the name of freedom, even the smallest act of rebellion counted.

They began to plot, in Gisela's name.

Chapter 23

October 1938

The sun had sunk beyond the roofs a long time ago. The streets were mere shadows now, a labyrinth of alleyways and silver-roofed buildings, dark and slumbering. And among all this darkness, a single beacon of light, a dim ember gleaming softly in the night—the atelier on the most bohemian of all Berlin streets, the Kurfürstendamm, where conspirators had gathered, resolved to fight against the regime that had just claimed another one of their own. Before it could claim many more.

No music this time—they were still in mourning. No laughter either; the occasion was far too grave. No mutual acquaintances or lady friends or boyfriends who dropped by either; only a small, intimate circle of friends who knew they could trust each other with their lives. Who would give those lives to protect the others, just as brave Gisela had selflessly done.

"I don't think I need to explain the gravity of the situation," Harro opened the meeting after everyone had settled down on a carpet in front of the fireplace, all eyes on the map of Europe—a new one, freshly printed, with borders of the Greater German Reich spreading further and further like an oily stain in clear blue water. "No matter how many times he's promised the contrary, Hitler won't stop after slicing himself a piece of Czechoslovakia. He wants world domination; subjugation of all the nations that can present even the vaguest threat, and total annihilation of any race he considers subhuman. He needs to be stopped."

Tense silence hung over the room. One by one, Harro looked into the eyes of the friends sitting shoulder to shoulder. Walter Küchenmeister and Dr. Elfriede Paul, the inseparable couple who aided the persecuted people to immigrate; Kurt Schumacher with his frank blue eyes, wheat-blond hair, and artistic hands, and his wife Lisl, herself a *Mischling*, a half-breed, according to the Nuremberg Laws, who had helped Harro condense sheets and sheets of documents into stamp-sized miniatures which Gisela, in turn, had passed to the Soviets in one small envelope. In the eyes of all four reflected the fiery determination that burned in Harro's gaze, just as it did in Libertas'.

Three couples, firmly set on changing the course of history itself.

Or giving their lives in the process.

"Harro and I have been talking," Libertas picked up where her husband had left off. "Our biggest trouble as of now is misinformation. I worked at MGM and am somewhat familiar with how Goebbels' *Promi* works," she proceeded, calling the Propaganda Ministry by its nickname. "After it acquired full control of the media, the German people have only been getting their information from him. Now, I need hardly explain to everyone gathered that Goebbels is a propagandist, not an impartial, objective source of information by any measure. Therefore, the entire nation is only consuming the information—or should I better say, propaganda—Goebbels himself feeds them. All other sources have conveniently been silenced."

Another pause, almost a minute of silence for Martin, for Henry, for Harro himself who had scarcely escaped with his life and would always carry the scars from his encounter with the Gestapo.

"If you heard the national news, Germany is doing splendidly," Harro continued. In the frantically dancing shadows thrown off by the fire, his features were set—serious, noble. "Unemployment is remarkably low, birth rates have skyrocketed, industry is booming, and our strength is growing by the day. Now, it has been omitted, of course, that unemployment is so low because whoever hasn't been drafted into the new Wehrmacht is busy building the autobahns for the German Army and the birth rates have only skyrocketed because women have been pushed out of workplaces and confined to the kitchen and nursery once again."

"And industry is booming because we're actively rearming," Walt quipped. A journalist to the marrow of his bones, he made it a point of honor to remain informed of all current affairs, even if the new administration had banned him from practicing his profession due to his "leftist" views. "Even though it's directly against the Versailles Treaty."

"Precisely," Harro confirmed. "But ordinary people never hear about that."

"Nor do they care, for the most part," Libertas added. "As long as Hitler keeps them occupied, fed, and bursting with pride for their heritage, they don't care one way or the other who pays for it. It's easy for them to look away when their Jewish neighbors are being dragged off or their Social-Democrat colleagues are arrested for speaking their mind."

"Therefore, we need to target intellectuals first and foremost," Harro said. "People who tend to lean left as it is and who always question everything but simply don't have the means of accessing independent information sources."

"How are we going to do it?" Elfriede asked, practical as always.

"A leaflet," Libertas announced with barely contained excitement, jumping to her feet. In a few instants, she returned with a template in her hands, which she laid out atop the map.

"*Der Stoßtrupp*," Kurt read the title drawn on top of the page. "The Raiding Party?"

"You don't like it?" Harro asked.

"I do, actually." Kurt was grinning now, leaning over the leaflet with interest. "Catchy."

"Bold," Lisl agreed, smiling mischievously as well. "It gets my vote."

"…The annexation of the Sudetenland is an act of aggression in itself," Elfriede began to read under her breath. "There is no indication that the ethnic Germans living there have ever been persecuted and harassed by the local population. The entire conflict has been artificially created by the German Propaganda Ministry with Minister Goebbels as its mastermind—"

"We're naming names?" Walt's eyes were positively shining with excitement now. "I'm tickled pink! That's an actual crime against the state."

"Only if we get caught committing it," Libertas said in an even tone, shrugging slightly.

"So how do we *not* get caught producing it?" Walt asked, rubbing his hands in anticipation. It appeared he was ready to grab the template and go to a printing office himself.

"We'll need a lot of paper." Kurt, the only artist in the group, instantly livened up. "I have plenty at my studio, but I can always get more from the wholesaler I deal with without raising any suspicions."

"That's taken care of then." Harro nodded. "What about the distribution?"

"What did you have in mind?" Lisl asked.

"The names of our targets we'll get from the telephone book," Libertas explained. "All doctors, lawyers, writers, professors are listed there. We can drop the leaflet off personally, wearing gloves, of course, in order not to leave fingerprints."

"Or we can mail them," Harro proceeded. "We just aren't sure which option is riskier."

"I'd say dropping them off personally is," Walt ventured after a pause. "There are so many informants nowadays, one can never be certain who's watching. Before too long, some harmless grandmother who sees you entering the building will make a phone call and it'll be off with our heads."

"Walt's right," Elfriede said. "It'll be much more inconspicuous to mail them."

"What about stamps?" Harro asked. "How do we acquire so many without raising suspicion?"

"We each buy four or five at different U-Bahn stations," Lisl ventured. "There are always so many people underground, they'll never remember our faces if we don't buy too many."

"And I can drop them off at different mailboxes as I drive for my errands," Elfriede suggested. "I'm a physician. I visit several patients daily, in different parts of the city. I can easily mail them on my way."

"Good. That's very good." Now it was Harro's turn to rub his hands in anticipation. "We'll start small. A few dozen, to begin with. But those few dozen will spread like wildfire among like-minded friends and acquaintances of those intellectuals we're targeting. Granted, a few may be reported, but if we're careful, handle everything only in gloves, and never leave a trail, we should avoid detection just fine."

"Everyone on board?" Libertas asked.

Judging by everyone's grins, she didn't have to.

Golden October days followed. Days during which the six of them worked like a well-oiled machine; days during which The Raiding Party pamphlet descended upon the city of Berlin in a torrent of fallen leaves, revolutionary red, bleeding truth from its pages.

Drowning the need for sleep in buckets of coffee, Libertas typed the same text over and over, well into the night, so Lisl could pick them up early in the morning and deliver them to her husband Kurt for the finishing touch—the title that accused and called to action with its angry red letters he personally painted on each pamphlet. It was Elfriede who then stuffed them in her physician's leather bag and set off on her rounds, flooding the affluent areas of the city with envelopes containing the inconvenient, bitter truth—of German aggression, of the upcoming war, of all the victims of the regime who had already suffered for their beliefs, and many more who should suffer still. And each day without fail, it was Walt who supplied his physician lady friend with stamps and envelopes he and Lisl purchased in different parts of the city, mockingly thanking the regime that had prohibited them from practicing their respective professions, thus allowing them plenty of time to go about their anti-governmental affairs.

By the end of the following week, they ran out of paper. Kurt offered to purchase more, but Harro refused categorically to take the risk.

"We're just starting," he explained with a warm palm on Kurt's shoulder to soften the artist's disappointment. "It would be idiotic to attract attention to ourselves now and botch the entire business."

"Elfriede said it right," Libertas added with a smile at the physician. "Dead, we are of no use to anyone. Let's wait and see how people react."

"Yes," Elfriede nodded her agreement. "Let's see if there's even a point to this entire enterprise."

"Judging from the papers, there is," Walt announced, looking positively coy. "So far, only twelve pamphlets were reported to the police. I saw it just this morning in the *Beobachter*."

"Which means hundreds and hundreds are presently circulating all around Berlin," Harro whispered as though too afraid to believe such good fortune.

"People are keeping them, sharing them." In her excitement, Lisl found and pressed Kurt's hand. A warm, amber glow illuminated her face; danced with mirth in her liquid black eyes. "Perhaps, they're talking about them this very moment, just like us."

"We can only hope," Harro concluded. "*Damen und Herren,* since we're all still alive and very much kicking, I announce operation 'Raiding Party' a success," he jested darkly, raising his glass in a toast.

They celebrated that evening, but at night, Libertas awoke alone once again, with Harro's cold pillow by her side.

It was ridiculous to hope otherwise; naturally, the dangerous affair had taken its toll on his health. The old wounds inflicted by the Gestapo had reopened, as though to remind him of the cost of resistance, the price of one's decision to fight.

"Harro?" Barefoot and shivering against the chilly night air, Libertas tapped gently on the bathroom door. "Do you need anything? I have some morphine for the pain… Whatever Gisela did not use."

She heard him chuckle softly on the other side. "I'm not dying yet."

"I hope not. I still have plans for you."

The gentle clicking of the lock.

Libertas squinted against the bright light, but smiled all the same, at the sheer fact that he'd let her in. Ordinarily, Harro chose to suffer in silence, away from her eyes. But something had shifted in him since Gisela's passing. No longer was he embarrassed of pain or his perceived weakness. Gisela had been reduced to a former shell of herself after her incarceration and yet, neither Libertas nor Harro had ever encountered a stronger person than their brave comrade. Pain was a badge of honor now. Harro decided to wear it proudly.

"You need a vacation, my dear husband," Libertas said, lowering onto the rug next to the claw-foot bathtub.

Harro, who lay on the bare tiles, hands folded atop his scarred stomach, managed a pained grin. "I would be a complete muttonhead to argue the point, my dear wife."

"We both do."

He looked at her tenderly and reached for her hand. "Yes, we do. Forgive me, please. I never thanked you for staying with Gisela to the last."

"It was the least I could do."

"It must have been difficult. Seeing her like that."

"Very." It tore her heart to shreds.

"She deserves a statue to be erected in her honor."

"She does. Perhaps, someday. When people come to their senses."

"Do you think we'll live to see it?"

For a long time, Libertas remained silent, hesitating between ludicrous hope and grim reality.

"I don't know," she confessed at last, caressing Harro's fingers with hers. "But while you're with me, while we're fighting for it side by side, it doesn't really matter. Sometimes the journey is just as important as the destination. And I'm honored to be making this journey with you, my brave freedom fighter."

Harro lifted himself up onto one elbow, thoroughly concealing the pain it had caused, and kissed Libertas' knee.

"I want to make an actual journey with you," he said as Libertas lowered his head to her lap, tangling her fingers in his gilded hair. "I want to see as much as I can with you. While we're still alive and breathing."

A sharp pang of grief pierced Libertas' heart at those words. They both carried Gisela's memory in them much deeper than they thought. Her death had changed a great many things but, most of all, it had changed them.

"Let's go to Italy. Let's drive through the Alps," he continued, his voice gathering force and passion. "Let's hold hands as we rock on the waves in a gondola. Let's make love in an open field, under the starry skies. Let's do it all before it's too late."

Her heart throbbing with infinite love and wistful longing, Libertas lowered her lips to his and kissed him on his open mouth. Harro's hand was still on the back of her head when Libertas pulled away slightly.

"Italy it is then, husband. Before it's too late."

Venice. October 1938

In the gathering twilight, the old city was breathing dreams and magic. All around them, stained-glass windows burst into a myriad of colors in the last rays of the setting sun. Old, crumbling palazzos full of former grandiosity stirred to life, enveloped in shadows that concealed the net of cracks in their walls. From the balconies, notes of a lovelorn guitar poured down the street. In the warm, musty air hung the vague scent of excitement and something foreign and exotic.

As Libertas gazed around her, eyes full of wonder, Harro drove slowly along the narrow street, a map of the city opened on his lap.

"There's a garage two streets away," he said, eyes shifting from the map to the street signs and back. "We can leave the car there. It'll be easier to use local means of transportation, I gather," he joked, tossing his head in the direction of the canal just visible through the gap of the buildings as they approached the intersection.

Gondolas glided along it, expertly navigated by men with strong, bronzed arms and faces obscured by hats. Tucked inside, couples cradled each other in their arms. It was a land of sea-scented air and romance, lost in time and space, a piece of paradise crossed with arched bridges and guarded by stone-faced gargoyles and, suddenly, Libertas wished to blend with it and dissolve into its bliss, forever.

They lost themselves to its charm for days they didn't care to count, wandering the maze of streets hand in hand, dipping fresh-baked bread in olive oil in open cafés and drinking ruby-red wine not by the glass but by the bottle, intoxicated on Pinot Noir and each other.

On an impulse, they bought first-class tickets for a cruise across the Adriatic and ended up stranded in Dubrovnik, an ancient city even more exotic than Venice due to the Oriental influences seeping into its architecture and dialect they didn't quite understand. Through an ancient-looking Austrian émigré, they discovered the city's shopping district, where the eclectic choice of antiques mixed with handmade goods sold for dinars, the exchange rate of which they hadn't the faintest idea about.

"We only live once," Harro declared, handing the line-faced seller, who was missing quite a few front teeth, German Reichsmarks for the handmade leather belt and a vest the seller's wife had knitted herself.

"Yes, we do," Libertas agreed, shelling out more banknotes for the antique brooch that would go marvelously with the silk black dress she had purchased at the Wertheim, and gasped, only now noticing an antique familial crest hanging on the back wall. It was almost lost among taxidermized animal heads and ancient-looking clocks and African tribal face masks. But all the tribal masks in the world couldn't dim the proud glimmer of silver crossed with red and black—its bold, fearless inscription bearing its motto and her own name: *Libertas*.

"Harro!" she cried, shivering with excitement. "Look!"

The light that had ignited in her husband's eyes didn't escape her. "Oh, Libs," he muttered, his hand on the small of her back. "But we simply must get it."

"We'll hang it on the wall of our atelier."

Where the portrait of the Führer was supposed to hang.

"Yes." Harro nodded. "We most certainly will."

They dragged the crest with them onto the steamer heading to the island of Korcula, too fearful to leave it alone in their rented room in Dubrovnik. They left their clothes on it when they went swimming in the still-warm waters at night, after drinking too much of the heady Yugoslavian wine.

On this island, it was impossible to believe that it was already winter in Germany, that trees in the Tiergarten had lost the last of their leaves, that officers had donned their winter overcoats and the first flurries of snow dusted the cobbled streets, instantly crushed under the steel-lined boots of the marching soldiers. They hadn't seen a single uniform here; hadn't heard a single political speech.

Here, it was all songs and cicadas and water lapping gently at their bare feet.

Here, Germany with its bloody banners and even bloodier laws had acquired a distant, nightmarish quality, already dissolving at the first rays of the rising sun—a bad dream one would forget by breakfast of dumplings and sour cream.

"We could stay here." Libertas finally said what she knew Harro was thinking as well. "Just… not go back."

"We could." He looked like he had been considering the very same thing for quite a while now.

"The climate has already done wonders for you."

"It has. And the people are so nice. And we wouldn't be the first ones to leave, either. Thomas Mann left. Erich Maria Remarque left. Fritz Lang left. And those are just famous names. How many ordinary people have emigrated? Elfriede has lost count of all the passports she has supplied them with."

"That much is true," Libertas agreed readily.

They needed to persuade themselves in this, to pacify their own consciences. There was nothing shameful about leaving the country that had gone to the devil. They had stayed longer than others at any rate; did what they could, risking their lives and losing friends to the cause they so fiercely believed in. Not a soul would be able to reproach them for finally throwing in the towel. After all, how much could they do against the entire regime?

But then, simultaneously, their gazes turned to the crest and its bold black letters.

Libertas.

Freedom or death.

"But if we all leave, who shall be left to fight?" she whispered hoarsely and bitterly.

Harro made no reply. Only looked with infinite longing at the azure sky melting into the turquoise water gilded with the sun as though committing it all to his memory.

The following day, they gathered their meager belongings, boarded a steamer in silence, and traveled back to Venice to retrieve their car.

On November 8, they crossed from Switzerland into Germany, their mood somber and subdued. Immersed in their brooding, they failed to notice the lights dimmed along the Kurfürstendamm, closed blinds in the apartments above, the abundance of Brownshirts clustering on the corners, hawkish eyes trained on passers-by, wooden batons tapping impatiently against their thighs.

Only when the first sounds of glass bursting under the vicious blows reached their apartment on the top floor did they realize what precisely they had returned to. As the savage crowd unleashed their hatred on Berlin Jews, hurling rocks at the storefronts of their businesses and dragging the owners themselves outside to beat them senseless, Libertas and Harro looked on, seething with helpless ire but refusing to avert their eyes. For they needed to witness the atrocities committed to describe them in their testimony against the regime that craved blood and put them into powerful, wrathful words in the next pamphlet that they would distribute in thousands—and not only in Berlin this time, but all over Germany, all over Europe if possible, through the connections they'd made, through the people who refused to avert their eyes and claim that the suffering of others was not their problem.

In the darkness of their apartment, the silvery shadow loomed from the opposite wall, a war cry against the injustice, a call for resistance against the dictator.

Libertas.

Freedom or death.

Chapter 24

Berlin. October 1939

Sleep escaping her once again, Libertas sat on the wide windowsill, beneath which the central heating element was softly hissing, and smoked her third cigarette in a row. From time to time, she rolled her shoulders, gleaming faintly marble-white in the dark. They were still sore from arranging the furniture—whatever she could move herself, that is—and unpacking countless boxes with books, linen, and dishes that she and Harro had brought from the old apartment.

Their new residence on the Altenburger Allee 19 was even bigger than the old one—an airy, spacious penthouse overlooking the former Olympic stadium, equipped with all modern utilities, hot water, and central heating. With Harro's latest promotion, it was only natural to leave the bohemian Kurfürstendamm behind and settle into something befitting an officer assigned to Reichsmarschall Göring's personal headquarters at Wildpark-West, a forest near Potsdam. Libertas was aware that she ought to be grateful that Harro hadn't been sent to the front at least and could still travel back to Berlin to visit her every weekend. But she still felt his absence much too sharply and particularly at night when sleep wouldn't come and the silence pressed down on her with its intolerable weight and the other side of the bed was much too cold, the warmth of the heating element not even enough to reach it.

Over a year had passed since their return to Germany—one miserable year that felt like a lifetime. Now, alone and unsettled, Libertas spent her nights plagued with thoughts each darker than the last, wondering if they had made the right choice returning to

Berlin just before all hell broke loose and set the black-clad devils free in the aftermath of the *Kristallnacht*, even more dangerous and bloodthirsty than before.

Outside, the searchlights probed the night sky for enemy aircraft; otherwise, Berlin was shrouded in darkness. It was odd and disconcerting to imagine that somewhere in the east, the war was unraveling its dark wings, but here in the capital, only vague echoes of it reverberated along the maze of its streets. In the former Olympic stadium, football matches still took place as they were scheduled. Stores still brimmed with goods, but in place of Reichsmarks, ration cards had now been introduced and, suddenly, Libertas couldn't purchase two pairs of leather boots but only one. Helpless and missing Harro terribly, she chain-smoked and cursed the rationing and simultaneously said her blessing for the black market that was thriving once again, supplying everyone who could afford it with luxuries of the pre-war past. Writing was also out of the question now. Even paper was rationed and so, Libertas was left to fight all of her demons without the possibility of committing them to paper and therefore releasing them. Everything was bleak, muted somehow and without hope.

But while Libertas felt restless and lost, Harro appeared to thrive in the charged atmosphere of danger and death. Shoulders no longer hunched, he walked with purpose in his step now; in his sharp, intelligent face, his eyes gleamed with fierce resolve. Thanks to Libertas' charming Göring into taking Harro under his wing, he had moved swiftly through the Luftwaffe hierarchy. Playing a devoted Nazi for years had paid off as well. He was in the very lair of the wolf now, observing, listening closely, gathering information, readying himself to strike at the first convenient moment.

Begrudgingly, Libertas released Harro from her embrace when, having just arrived on his short weekend leave, he would set off for one clandestine meeting or another, looking profoundly miserable for abandoning her in such a manner but having no other choice.

Their Raiding Party operation had borne fruit and now, Harro spent his short weekends traversing from industrial Spandau to the leafy Wilmersdorf and to the formerly "red" Pankow to organize carefully made connections, to recruit more freedom fighters, to mark more Luftwaffe and Wehrmacht strategic positions on the map, extracting them from the depths of his photographic memory. Not a minute was squandered for leisure. Not a word spoken without purpose. Not a single invitation wasted on people who wouldn't prove to be useful to the cause.

Libertas never complained and was careful to conceal her disappointment when Harro would dress hastily at the first rays of the rising sun. Duty first; she was mature enough to realize. It was Harro himself who couldn't bear the pain of separation any longer and, having swung sharply round on his heel one day, looked at Libertas and asked gravely and with hope trembling softly in his voice, "Do you want to come with me?"

A smile of extraordinary happiness blossomed on Libertas' face. Without an instant's hesitation, she snatched her coat from the hanger, pulled on her tall rainproof boots, wrapped a scarf around her neck, and put her arm through the crook of her husband's—just where it had always belonged, from the very beginning.

From that day on, they only took trains together. Together, they met people under the cover of the Grunwald's alleys. Together, they screened new recruits and accepted invitations from the "undecided" ones, as Harro called them in jest—people, mostly from the upper middle class, with plenty to lose but consciences that wouldn't let them sleep; people who had come by the Raiding Party leaflets and hadn't been the same since. People who wished to know if anything could be done and how precisely they ought to go about it.

It was through her husband that Libertas had come to know Heinrich Scheel, a Social-Democrat from a progressive family, who began writing pamphlets long before Harro, during the

Röhm purges, "before it turned into a neck-risking fashion," as Heinrich loved to jest as they strolled along the banks of the Spree or navigated the pathways of the Tiergarten, all deserted, even on weekends, due to the war.

It was also through Harro that she met Heinrich's best friend Hans Coppi, still a boy really, with downy growth on his cheeks, eyes full of dreams behind comically thick lenses and lips that smiled all too readily. But in Coppi's case, his innocently youthful appearance was rather deceptive, as Libertas had come to learn. A radical communist, he had been arrested at the tender age of eighteen and had already seen the insides of Oranienburg concentration camp, bore scars from the SS guards' horsewhips, and cracks in his ribs from their wooden batons. Only, what the SS hoped to break, they had inadvertently forged into something formidable and slightly terrifying. Coppi had been to hell and came back to tell about it; he'd come face to face with the devil and laughed about the experience. There was nothing else they could possibly threaten him with. He had left all his fear behind the barbed wire and that alone made him into a force to be reckoned with.

But Harro's most important connection, in Libertas' eyes at least, was a lovely couple living in a lovely apartment near the Tiergarten with just-as-lovely a friend from the American Embassy, to whom the couple passed information in a fascinatingly shameless manner.

"I'm an American myself," Mildred Harnack had explained with a coy grin during their very first meeting one particularly dismal October evening. A bit older than Libertas, she was tall and blond, attired in a simple black dress accented by a string of pearls, elegant in an effortless way that only enhanced her natural beauty. To Libertas, Mildred reminded her painfully of Gisela with her vivacious, outspoken manner; only softer around the edges, less reckless somehow. A former literary critic, she was brilliant to the extreme but savvy enough to conceal it from outsiders. "So, it doesn't cause any suspicion, our associating with other Americans.

And besides, I'm just a silly blond girl. What harm can one expect from a silly blond girl?"

Only, that was just an excellent ruse. When the doors were tightly closed, the blackout curtains tightly drawn and the four of them gathered around the table for dinner and discussion, Mildred quickly demonstrated the true degree of her intellect. Sharp as a whip, she was not only up to date with all recent political, economic, and diplomatic developments, but could analyze any possible outcome with a strategy that would put any chess player to shame.

Arvid, her husband, took unconcealed pride in his brilliant spouse's arguments and often watched her talk with a faint, loving smile. A descendant from a family of intellectuals and an academic himself, he didn't seem to mind in the slightest whenever Mildred took the lead, only listened to her attentively with his head slightly inclined and nodded sagely to certain thoughts of hers. Compared to Mildred, he was rather plain-looking—eyes of some bland gray color; his hair, also not quite blond, not quite brown, receding prematurely; steel-rimmed glasses that thousands of Berliners wore. All in all, a man entirely undistinguishable in a crowd.

"Which is also a brilliant ruse," Harro had commented when Libertas and he were back in their apartment, changing out of their evening clothes. "Whenever he sets off to meet someone, he never attracts attention."

Libertas had to agree; she had just spent over three hours with the Harnacks and yet, Arvid's features were already blurring, dissolving in her memory. A brilliant ruse indeed, no camouflage needed.

And so, Harro and Libertas' eclectic circle of co-conspirators had taken root, begun to sprout all over Berlin—a communist branch here, an American intelligence there, even a Soviet connection Hans Coppi had mentioned—as long as it was directed against fascism and everything it stood for, Harro wasn't too selective. They had no common origin, no common class or ideology. Only their love of freedom, and that was enough.

In the fall of 1939, the seeds of the resistance had taken root. Now, they only had to wait for them to bear fruit. And so, Libertas smoked and waited, gazing out into the darkness, probing the sky for answers, just like searchlights probed it for the enemy.

Summer 1940

"*Victorious German Army is in Paris!*"

Libertas grimaced slightly as she read the block-lettered headline on the round news column near Alexanderplatz U-Bahn station. She was grateful for the sunglasses she was wearing: they concealed the sadness in her eyes from her fellow Berliners. Below the gothic script, the propaganda poster featured a photo of an officer saluting the troops from the height of his horse with the Arc de Triomphe in the background.

Victorious German Army in Paris…

Only, there was nothing victorious about Libertas' mood. *Whatever was going to happen to her father's fashion studio now? Whatever was going to happen to Valerie, the woman who had raised her and shaped Libertas into the woman she had become?*

With a rush of anguish, Libertas clutched at the cigarette pack inside her handbag. She smoked a great deal too much and she knew it, but there was nothing else around to calm her nerves.

"Libs? Is that you, old girl?"

Startled, Libertas swung round to the voice and dropped her silver lighter.

Günther Weisenborn—a former dramaturg, Harro's friend from the old *Gegner* days, the first man who had seen talent in Libertas' traveling diaries before war broke out and put an end to her literary aspirations—picked it up and offered it to her with a gallant, somewhat theatrical bow. He hadn't changed a bit, hadn't aged a day, Libertas noticed right that instant. The same debonair look about him, the same wry grin in its place, the same mischievous gleam in his eyes. No uniform either, despite the fact that most men of serviceable age had been conscripted to different army branches or departments.

"Günther!" A cigarette and the lighter now clasped in her hand, Libertas threw her arms around him, genuinely happy to see him.

"Quit it with such public displays of affection, you shameless harlot! I don't fancy being shot in my male parts by Harro." His tone was serious, but in his nearly black eyes, mirth was dancing.

Torn between laughing and crying—from the sheer joy of encountering a sliver of the past, pre-war life—Libertas moved her sunglasses to the top of her head and felt her lips quiver even more at the look of sympathy in Günther's eyes.

"Harro's not here, is he?" he asked quietly.

Libertas only shook her head.

"At the front?"

"No, thank heavens. At the Luftwaffe's general staff's headquarters in the east."

"That's not too bad."

"No, considering." She quickly swiped at the tears gathering in the corners of her eyes. "What about you? Not drafted yet?"

"Ha, they don't draft politically unreliable fellows like myself. We'll ruin the entire morale of the troops."

"They found out about your past?" Libertas asked, regarding him with concern.

But Günther didn't appear to be bothered in the slightest. "I told them myself, when I came to the drafting office, or whatever they call it." Fascinatingly unconcerned, he gestured toward Libertas' unlit cigarette. After she'd offered him her pack and they'd lit up, he proceeded, "I need hardly add, they weren't too thrilled, but given that I presently work as a journalist and write reviews for Goebbels' propaganda films, they let me be. Propaganda at the time of war is essential and so people who write it are essential as well. As long as we contribute, they don't bother with us. What about you, old girl?"

"Slowly going mad with boredom."

"What of your great German novel? I thought that would keep you occupied?"

Libertas merely gave him a certain look. "With present-day rationing, all I can write is a title for that great German novel before I run out of paper."

Günther snorted. "Not working then?"

"No."

"The German Women's League will come for you soon, with such an attitude." Back to jesting with Günther; only Libertas was far too aware that despite the playful tone, the message was serious. "A German woman's duty is to pop out blond babies for the Reich. If you're not busy doing that, you ought to contribute in other ways. Watch it or they will conscript you to field duty. They'll make you dig out potatoes somewhere near Liebenberg."

"Liebenberg is all set." Libertas sighed, still reeling from her last visit to the familial estate. "Polish and French prisoners of war are working the fields. As for me, I've already paid my fine for being a housewife this month."

Günther narrowed his eyes as he pulled on his cigarette, mulling something over. "Why don't you become a film reviewer as well?" he asked out of the blue. "The work is simple and the pay is ridiculously high. You already have experience after working for MGM. I could recommend you highly. Then, next time the *Frauenschaft* ladies come for you, you'll show them your employment papers and they'll piss right off."

Libertas nearly choked on the remnants of smoke in her throat. "Günther!" She play-swatted him on his arm, vainly trying to suppress her laughter. The street was swarming with people; plain-clothed informants could be standing next to them and there he stood, badmouthing the German Women's League.

But Günther only shrugged, unconcerned. "I'm an unreliable. What else do you expect from someone with my reputation?"

"You'll end up in one camp or another for your long tongue."

"That's a very strong possibility. Now, what of that job offer? It pays eight hundred marks."

Libertas' hand, with the cigarette in it, stopped within centimeters of her open mouth. She stared at Günther in stunned silence, wondering if it was one of his jokes or if she had misheard him altogether.

"Eight hundred?" she finally managed.

"That's what I said."

"A month?"

"A month."

"Harro makes only five hundred!"

"I did say *ridiculously* well-paid, didn't I?" Günther arched a brow, grinning wryly.

But only after Libertas picked up her copy of the *Zeitschriften-Dienst*—a special list of instructions distributed to all the writers by the Propaganda Ministry—did she understand why the job was so absurdly overpaid. She had just signed her employment contract at the prestigious *National-Zeitung*—the same paper Günther worked for—and the first thing the editor of the culture section had mentioned was that all reviews must be written according to the guidelines of the *Zeitschriften-Dienst*.

"And, Frau Schulze-Boysen?" The editor's hand lingered atop the thick leaflet. "This list must never be brought to the attention of the general public, you understand? Do not even speak of it to your closest friends. It is of paramount importance that it stays between the Propaganda Ministry and our staff."

Libertas nodded dutifully, her hands itching to open the guidelines and see what was so peculiar about them that her new boss had nearly classed them as state secret papers. And then, on the park bench across from her new office, Libertas understood it all.

The writers—liberals at heart, just like Günther, just like Martin was, just like herself—were being blatantly bribed for writing what they would never have considered writing without a gentle but firm push from Goebbels' *Promi*. From every page, from every line, Goebbels' bigotry and lies spread their poison, tainted whatever they would come in contact with.

"In essence, we are being told to write that receiving a bullet in his guts is the best fate of a German man." With great sarcasm, Libertas divulged the news to Harro when he arrived home for the weekend. "And also, that anything that goes wrong—even the latest drought—can be blamed on international Jewry. It's them who are, apparently, sabotaging their crops. It's also them who make Karl the street-sweep drink himself blind and beat on his wife. Because of them the heating pipes break in winter and good, honest German men catch syphilis in the trenches."

Harro exploded at Libertas' last remark. "What do Jews have to do with syphilis infections?"

"And that's what we, Reich journalists, are getting paid so much for—to invent a plausible reason and sell it to an ordinary, plain person in the street who doesn't know any better." Libertas snorted with disdain and went silent for a while. "I suppose, it's a bit easier for me. With my former experience, I shall only be writing film reviews. But whoever reports the news, I feel for them, poor devils. They will have to twist themselves into pretzels to present the facts to the public in such a manner that will leave Goebbels satisfied. And we both know that after they undergo the *Promi's* censoring, they won't be facts anymore. Thoroughly prepared propaganda, chewed-up and shoved right down the throats of unsuspecting people."

Reaching out, Harro squeezed her knee with affection. "At least those women from the *Frauenschaft* won't bother you anymore."

"That's what Günther has said as well."

"And, Libs?" He waited for her to look at him before proceeding. "Don't beat yourself up over it. I have to do the exact same thing daily. We have to pretend to be good, conscientious Germans in order to keep fighting them from the inside."

"I know. It still bothers me."

"And that's why I'll always love you so much. Because it bothers you when it has long stopped bothering everyone else. Because you sing French songs to the prisoners of war who work on Liebenberg's fields. Because you smuggle mail for the Polish ones. Because you refused to just up and leave, and to the devil with Germany, and instead, force yourself to face the enemy daily and fight for the ones who can't fight for themselves. Because you're so very strong, Libs…" He brought her hand to his lips and kissed it with great passion. "Because you make *me* strong. Without you, I'm nothing."

"And I'm nothing, without you," she whispered through a film of tears.

"We'll get through, love. We just need to stick it out for a little longer. It won't last forever, this war. And hopefully, we'll help end it sooner rather than later. Together."

"Yes. Together."

Chapter 25

September 1940

Feeding the birds pretzel pieces in the time of rationing earned them disapproving sideways glances, but neither Libertas nor Mildred cared much for the public's opinion. In the course of the past few months, they had become fast friends, meeting up for walks and ersatz coffee and switching roles in hosting dinners. The more she got to know the American, the more Mildred reminded Libertas of Gisela, whom she dearly missed; the same fire in her eyes and the same reckless, almost suicidal love of freedom, no matter the cost. Or perhaps it was the fact that Mildred anchored Libertas during the days when Harro was away and she felt swept away by the tide of events she had no control over. Whatever was the case, Libertas sought Mildred's company for those walks in the Tiergarten, a mere five minutes from the Harnacks' apartment, and for the healing, soothing balm of her words—*everything shall turn out just fine for us, Libby, you'll see! We're on the right side of history. Our cause is right and, therefore, we shall win, one way or the other.*

But today, Mildred lacked her usual laidback attitude. Under the seemingly cool blue of her eyes, something sharp and excited lurked. She could barely sit still for more than five minutes, her eyes shifting from one passer-by to another as though she was annoyed with their sheer presence. Finally, she lost the last of her patience, grabbed Libertas by the sleeve of her knitted cardigan, and pulled her toward one of the shadowy alleys.

It occurred to Libertas that Mildred was itching to impart some sort of important news, but the announcement that came minutes later was nothing that she had expected.

"A man came to see Arvid last night," Mildred spoke barely audibly and in English. "I opened the door. He lifted his felt hat, introduced himself. Alexander Erdberg, he said his name was. Handsome, but not exceedingly so; very well-spoken, a heavily Viennese accent. At first, I thought he was selling something. But then he asked for my husband. Naturally, I inquired what business he might have with Arvid."

Libertas listened closely, not realizing that she was holding her breath.

"Now what comes next is out of some spy thriller, I swear!" Mildred continued, lowering her voice even more. "That Erdberg fellow asks if he may come in, positively refusing to say what it is that he wants. I'm thinking that all this is rather strange, to say the least, but he is dressed with great taste and looks like an intellectual, and I'm a curious woman, you see? So, I let him in and call Arvid from his study."

Mildred went silent as a bicyclist sped by them and resumed her story only after he was out of earshot.

"As soon as they shake hands, Erdberg asks Arvid if he can speak freely in front of me. Arvid says yes. And then—don't faint when you hear this—Erdberg goes and announces that his real name is actually Alexander Korotkov and he's an envoy for the director of the field office of the NKVD."

"Soviet Intelligence?" Libertas gaped at her friend in stunned amazement.

"The very same." Mildred was becoming giddier and giddier. "But you wait, it gets more interesting here. Arvid studies him closely for some time and then asks, 'My good Herr Erdberg, just why don't you think we won't call the Gestapo on you right this instant? We are good, law-abiding Germans—' Arvid thought that Erdberg, or whatever his real name was, was a Gestapo provocateur."

"That's a safe assumption nowadays," Libertas conceded, trying to recover from the shock.

"Such a possibility occurred to me as well, believe me. But this Soviet fellow only grins very amiably and says, 'My good Herr Harnack, you won't call anyone because you were in contact with our people back in 1935, before that contact was lost.'"

"Was Arvid really?"

"Yes, he was, and only a real Soviet intelligence officer would know all the details and that Korotkov/Erdberg fellow surely did. After that, Arvid relaxed visibly and offered the man a drink. Erdberg accepted and raised a toast to Soviet-German antifascist coalition. I have to say, he was very straightforward about everything. It appears, despite the Soviet-German non-aggression pact Hitler and Stalin signed a year ago, the NKVD—Stalin's secret police—are very suspicious of Hitler and rightfully so."

"Harro says the same. Hitler has been eyeing Soviet lands for quite some time."

"See? Those NKVD comrades are not stupid. At any rate, Arvid told Erdberg openly that he also works with the American intelligence."

"What did Erdberg say?"

"That it doesn't concern him in the slightest. Explained that the Soviets are more than willing to abandon their ideological differences with the capitalist countries for the sake of achieving the common goal—eliminating fascism in Europe, that is."

"Sensible. I must admit, I never suspected them of being so flexible in their views."

"Me neither, but there you have it." Mildred was positively beaming now. "Libby, it looks like we're in business. Arvid has already agreed to pass whatever information he has to the Soviets, but he only has contacts in the Wehrmacht. Now, he didn't mention Harro, but if Harro is willing—"

"Harro is very willing," Libertas announced with firm resolve. "He's been itching to find a reliable contact for years. I told you that my cousin Gisela passed documents to their embassy, but we haven't heard anything since."

"Well, you didn't quite leave them your names or return address, I assume?" Mildred grinned. "They only met Gisela and she died soon after," she finished with audible sympathy in her voice.

It had never occurred to Libertas that this was the reason for the radio silence on the Soviet's part—Gisela's arrest and passing and their move soon after. Even if the Soviets traced Gisela's relative who visited her in Switzerland, Libertas no longer lived at the same address. And then that trip to Italy and Yugoslavia! She nearly slapped her own forehead at her stupidity.

"Moving was incredibly idiotic of us, wasn't it?" she asked Mildred quietly.

"Don't kill yourself over it." Mildred squeezed her arm reassuringly. "We have our contact now. That's all that matters."

A small smile began to break on Libertas' face. "Yes. That's all that matters," she repeated, as though to assure herself of the reality of all of this truly happening.

"So, the information chain is as follows: Harro directly to Arvid and Arvid to Erdberg, or—when Harro can't make it—Harro to you, you to me? And I pass it all to the men?"

A tingle of excitement creeping from the small of her back and slowly raising the hairs along her spine, Libertas looked at Mildred and wondered: *Will it truly be us who shall help end all this? And if so, at what price?*

But Libertas swiftly shoved that last part to the very back of her mind. As long as the dictator was dead and his empire crumbling, they didn't risk their lives in vain. In the end, it was all that mattered.

*

January 1941

Blackout drapes firmly drawn, Libertas' and Harro's apartment was immersed in shadows and tense excitement. Mildred and Arvid were already there when Harro arrived, bringing with him the icy taste of winter and the vague scent of the war emblazoned into the blue-gray leather of his Luftwaffe overcoat. Quickly kissing Libertas with his cold, chapped lips, he greeted the Harnacks and immediately pulled out copies of the maps and photos from the secret compartment of his service valise.

The three pairs of eyes followed his every movement, riveted to the aerial shots taken from a very low altitude.

"Leningrad," Harro announced, pointing at one of the aerial photos. "Island of Kotlin."

He didn't need to add anything else. It was obvious that German intelligence didn't take photos of crucial sea ports and railway junctions just for the fun of it. It was also obvious that no peace-loving country would stamp their maps with *Luftwaffe Russia Department* at the top right corner, just under the eagle holding a swastika in its claws.

"They even created a special department for it, eh?" Arvid asked in a low, pensive voice as though reading Libertas' thoughts.

"Yes," Harro replied. "Fortunately for me, I'm the contact point for all the Luftwaffe attachés. Essentially it means that not a single foreign Luftwaffe department chief can sneeze without me getting a report about it to pass to Göring's table."

"It wasn't just our paranoia or suspicion then?" Mildred asked. "We're indeed actively preparing for war with the Soviets?"

"We are. And I'll need you two to pass all of this information, along with the maps and photos, to your Soviet contact so they can do something about it before it's too late," Harro finished in a grim tone.

"Do you think Stalin will confront Hitler?" Libertas regarded the maps dubiously.

"I'm afraid I have no sight into Stalin's heart," Harro sighed. "If he has one, that is. But even if he doesn't confront Hitler, perhaps he'll fortify his borders at least."

"Stalin should never have begun those Red Army purges against his own officers." Arvid shook his head, the diplomat in him marveling at such grave strategic oversight. "They did away with the crème de la crème of their military elite. So many truly talented strategists—all gone, shot for nothing. Who shall command their armies now?"

"They have so many people, I don't think it shall be an issue." Mildred snorted softly.

"*Ach*, quantity versus quality, my love," Arvid argued in a gentle voice, smiling tenderly at his spouse. "It still takes a good strategist to command all of those people. Without a good commander, they're just a useless crowd."

"Still, it is my profound conviction that the Soviets will win." When everyone regarded him dubiously, Harro explained, "Eventually, with great losses, but they will. Napoleon Bonaparte made the very same mistake, marching into Russia with his troops. We all remember quite well how that ended up for him and his soldiers."

"Yes, but we aren't fighting with horses and muskets now," Libertas argued. "The German war machine has already shown that it can conquer entire countries in a matter of days. Look what happened to France, Belgium, Norway. Doesn't it frighten you just a little?"

"To be frank with you, no. They do move fast—true," Harro conceded. "But it takes days for the infantry to catch up with the panzer divisions. Also, to get all of those motorized divisions moving, they need fuel. European countries are much smaller in size. The Soviet Union is tremendous. Our troops shall stretch themselves too thin at one point or another. They'll get bogged down in the infamous Russian mud. They'll have to wait for the infantry to catch up with the vanguard, which will run out of fuel sooner or later and just that shall kill their Blitzkrieg."

"So, if the Soviets will win at any rate... why not just let them do it?" Mildred suggested.

Harro looked at her, sadly and gravely. "Because we don't want this war to break out in the first place, Mildred," he said in a mild voice. "I loathe our leaders, but I still love my country and my people. I don't want my fellow countrymen to die for nothing. I don't want them to set out for that march altogether."

"Perhaps it would help to sabotage the German OKW's plans from the inside?" Libertas suggested.

Harro turned to her, interested.

"I was thinking, another Raiding Party pamphlet perhaps?" Libertas probed. "But this time aimed not at the intellectuals but at the troops? Lisl, and Kurt with his art studio, can make as many photocopies as we need."

Harro's expression visibly brightened. He grasped Libertas' face in his palms and kissed her on her forehead with great enthusiasm. "You're my brilliant girl, Libs! That's a grand idea! We shall write the text for it tonight, so you can take it to Kurt right after I leave for the headquarters."

That evening, the four of them ate their dinner with great appetite, their spirits soaring high once again at the promise of glimpsing peace somewhere in between the heavy gray clouds of the gathering storm. And only two days later, Libertas, dressed in a military-style trench coat and tall boots, set off in the direction of Kurt's studio, her inner pocket burning with the fiery speech she and Harro had conceived in the middle of the night, with the single candle burning at their bedside where they had just made love and where they were plotting peace when the very air around them was scented with war.

Germany can't afford to be dragged into a war that can't possibly be won! Raid your libraries, revisit your history books, remind your political and military leaders of Napoleon's fate! He, too, was acting on the pretense of restoring France's natural borders; he, too, was blinded by his recent successes and thought his military genius was above all; he, too, considered his armies undefeatable. But when French soldiers got bogged down in Russia's marshes and mud; when they began freezing to death in subzero temperatures; when it became obvious that victory would never be possible, Napoleon's own political circles turned their backs on him.

How can anyone, in all good conscience, doom his own people to a similar fate? How can any leader place his own ego above the fate of the entire nation? How can anyone close their eyes to the unraveling tragedy that shall doom us all, as it has doomed the French armies? Enough of this compliant silence! Speak up! Demand sticking to the conditions of the non-aggression pact with the Soviets! Write, speak, scream against the war! The voice of one shall be silenced, but the voices of thousands shall echo thunderously over Germany's cities. Our strength is in numbers, so rise up, speak up, and do not surrender until victory is ours. The victory of peace—the most glorious of all.

Chapter 26

March 1941

It was nearing eleven in the morning, and the words still wouldn't come. Lost in thought, Libertas tapped her pencil absently on the desk, littered with the latest releases requiring her immediate attention, but her attention was elsewhere. That morning, Harro was meeting Alexander Erdberg/Korotkov in person for the first time. Work all but forgotten, Libertas' mind was at the Wannsee, wandering the banks of the still-frozen lake, following the imaginary conversation of the two men who could very well change the fate of millions, of entire Europe, if they played their cards right.

Just hours ago, Libertas had kissed Harro gently on his lips, fixed his scarf under his winter Luftwaffe overcoat, and begged him to be careful.

Of course, he would be; he always was, her Harro. He would shake the Soviet agent's hand in a polite manner but keep his distance all the same; he would speak openly but with a certain aloofness that Korotkov would most likely consider typically German, Libertas thought with a faint grin. As they strolled along the snow-dusted banks, Harro would keep his gloved hands folded behind his back as he explained in frightening detail what danger the Soviet Union was facing from Hitler's armies. Korotkov would believe him—or not—but in any case, he would ask for further cooperation, because it was only sensible, to have their own man who saw Göring's war maps with his own eyes daily.

According to Arvid, the NKVD agent knew of their fresh Raiding Party pamphlets already—how exactly he had discovered them was anyone's guess. But the fact remained; not only did Korotkov know of their existence, but he even brought one of the leaflets to the meeting with the Harnacks and read out passages he found particularly interesting, then grimaced slightly and explained that it was all fine and well and very noble but dangerous all the same.

Perhaps, Korotkov had asked for a personal meeting with Harro to tell him that face to face. Perhaps, he would ask Harro to cease the production of the leaflets for the time being. He was already committing treason passing top-secret information to the Soviets; why have the Gestapo breathing down his neck for some idiotic pacifist leaflets?

However, Harro would only shake his head slowly and explain to Herr Erdberg—he would address him by his German nom de guerre, he had already told that much to Libertas—that he was a German patriot first and foremost and that he would loathe to see all of his compatriots driven to their deaths by some maniac obsessed with world domination. *If Herr Erdberg could accept that fact, they could do business together*, Libertas imagined Harro saying. She had never met the Russian, but it was her profound conviction that he would grin at this, with a certain degree of admiration for his counterpart's iron principles, and offer Harro his hand, palm up, to seal the deal.

The shrill ringing of the phone made her jump in her chair, yanking her abruptly out of her reverie.

"Libertas Schulze-Boysen," she said, rubbing her chest to still her nerves.

"Hello, Frau Schulze-Boysen." A pleasant male voice. "I hope you will forgive me for introducing myself over the phone, but I fear, I had no other choice. My name is Otto Lutz and I work for Agence Havas."

He paused, letting the information sink in. Libertas only blinked, mystified. Agence Havas was the biggest French news agency; under a new German "management," granted, but an informational mammoth all the same.

"We've been reorganizing our staff for the past few months and we have an opening for a position in the cultural section here, in Paris. Several of our editors have recommended your work highly and I, myself, find your writing positively refreshing; in short, just what we've been looking for. Is that something you would be interested in discussing?"

For a few moments, Libertas lost all faculty of speech. She'd been so preoccupied with Harro's and her illegal affairs with the Harnacks and the Soviets, she scarcely paid attention to her work as a film reviewer. She wrote her articles quickly, almost always right after watching the picture in question, in one café or another, and submitted them sometimes without as much as proofreading her texts. After all, Günther Weisenborn, who had found her this job, was of the same precise opinion: *why waste our breath on sheer propaganda? It's bad enough that we accept our thirty shekels for feeding it to the public, it would be utterly without conscience to put actual effort into making it as attractive as possible.*

But, apparently, even her negligent writing was good enough for Herr—*what was his name? Otto something?*—in Paris.

"I'll be in Berlin for the Führer's birthday on April 20," he continued, without waiting for Libertas' response. "If you don't have any other plans for the day—I suppose you do have plans for the evening, it's Hitler's birthday, after all, haha—I suggest we meet at the Propaganda Ministry and talk it over."

"All right."

"You won't forget the date, will you?"

His attempt at a joke was lost on Libertas. "No."

"Splendid. It's all settled then. I shall call you a day or two in advance and we can agree on the time."

"I'll be waiting," Libertas replied mechanically.

*

Tears of melting snow rolled slowly down the window glass, collecting at the bottom and spilling onto the plasterwork, also gray and tearstained. A cigarette in her hand, Libertas gazed at the crying city and tried to remember if Harro had an umbrella with him. Had Korotkov? Would he share it with Harro? Or would they duck inside the nearest tavern and order two coffees, pretending to be friends catching up after a long separation?

Paris… She would be near her father, working at the fashion capital of the world, just as Valerie, her governess, had always dreamt she would. Valerie was safe for now, protected by Libertas' father's influential name, recognized as an essential worker. But it wouldn't hurt for Libertas to bring her own influence as well to keep Valerie from harm. Surely, the local German command would do this favor for their new cultural section chief. But, most importantly, she would be away from all these intrigues, from all the danger hanging like an ax over her and Harro's necks, from the conspiracies and clandestine meetings that had been draining her for the past few years, claiming her loved ones, making her paranoid and sick with worry, constantly looking over her shoulder, jumping at every sound, wondering if Harro would come back or if he had already been arrested by the sinister Gestapo…

Another phone call. This time Libertas scarcely heard it behind the whirlwind of her thoughts.

"Libertas Schulze-Boysen."

"Have I told you recently how much I love it when you say Schulze-Boysen, Frau Libs?"

In spite of herself, Libertas felt a warm smile blossoming on her lips. "No. You've been very preoccupied lately, Herr Harro, and have been neglecting me in a most unapologetic manner."

He laughed softly into the receiver.

"Have you been caught in the rain?" Libertas asked, squeezing the phone harder. "Do you want me to come and bring you a change of clothes?"

"I'm fine. It's been misty here all morning but no rain. We're both fine," Harro finished, meaning something completely different.

"Thank God," Libertas whispered, releasing the breath she hadn't realized she'd been holding.

"Libs? Alex wanted to know if you'd be interested in meeting up for a picnic on April 20? To celebrate the Führer's birthday." There was a barely recognizable tension in Harro's voice despite the seemingly upbeat, nonchalant tone. He needed her to be there; for whatever reason, but he did. "And can you bring Lisl with you? I would love to introduce them as well. Something tells me they shall hit it off instantly, these two." He laughed. It came out almost natural.

"Do I have to give the answer now?"

"I'm afraid so. Alex is leaving for Vienna tonight and you know how his work is. He may be away on his sales business and won't be able to contact us from abroad."

Naturally, he wouldn't, Libertas thought with an inward sigh.

In Paris, there was The Ritz and balconies with wrought-iron railings and macaroons and the Maxim, where oysters were always fresh and champagne cold.

But here, in Berlin, was Harro. Harro and death, already breathing its putrid breath just over her shoulder.

Pulling the smoke deep into her lungs with her free hand, Libertas wondered why the obvious choice was suddenly so difficult...

And so very easy, at the same time.

"Tell Alex I'll be there. With Lisl," she said and felt immense relief. It contradicted all laws of logic; it was outright life-risking and impossibly reckless, and yet, Libertas had never been more certain of her decision.

It must always feel this way, when one decides according to one's heart and not one's mind, no matter how much the mind screams in protest.

"I love you, Frau Schulze-Boysen."

"And I love you, *Herr Leutnant*. More than anything in the whole wide world."

More than life itself, she finished mentally.

Libertas didn't have to say it to him. He knew it already. Knew, and loved her back just as much.

April 20, 1941

Her insides twisting with angst, Libertas plastered a bright smile on her face and waved. Harro and his companion—around thirty, very good-looking, with chestnut hair ruffled slightly by the wind and the body of an athlete under seemingly casual clothes—waved back at the two women and rose from the bench to greet them. It had been previously decided that they would all arrive here, at Marquardt, a small fishing town near Potsdam, separately: Libertas and Lisl by train and Harro would take his bicycle. No one knew how Korotkov had gotten here, but according to the Harnacks, that was always the case with the Soviet agent—he materialized seemingly out of thin air and disappeared back into the shadows.

Korotkov greeted the women in flawless German and shook their hands with typical Viennese gallantry before escorting them to an open café on the riverbank where they could speak in private without causing any suspicion. Selecting a wrought-iron table that stood nearest to the loudspeaker, Korotkov moved a chair for Lisl, while Harro did the same for Libertas and ordered beers and a few dishes they could all share. The fact that they could only talk over the loud music by leaning close to each other didn't escape Libertas. Korotkov knew how to strategically choose the position, it seemed.

As she watched his mannerisms and listened to his jests and an occasional curse, for which he would instantly apologize, Libertas found it difficult to believe that the man was not, in fact, an Austrian native. Viennese slang rolled much too smoothly off his tongue; he held his expensive, imported cigarette much too elegantly in his manicured hands.

"I play the piano," he said, catching Libertas off guard.

It was impossible to see his eyes behind the dark shades, but for some reason, Libertas was sure that they were crinkling mischievously at the corners.

"I didn't say anything," Libertas muttered, feeling the blush creep into her cheeks. Could he read minds too? Had he figured out that she was wondering whether he was a double agent?

"You were studying my hands very intently," Korotkov explained with a friendly grin. "And not just studying, but scowling with suspicion. Not how you imagined an agent's hands would look?" He nodded in understanding before Libertas could say anything in her defense. "It's all right, you have every right to be suspicious. I'm here to put your mind at ease. And as I have already said, I play the piano. I don't dig trenches and neither do I fight other agents, no matter how much spy films that are so popular nowadays will try to persuade you otherwise. Now, let me guess what you play."

He pulled a bit closer and gently took Libertas' hand in his. For some reason, a chill ran through her, as though she was near a wild animal that had suddenly sought to be petted.

"Also piano and... accordion?" He looked up, head slightly inclined.

"You didn't just guess it." Libertas looked at him hard. "You knew it."

"I did," Korotkov conceded surprisingly easily. "I shouldn't have tried to trick you. Harro has already warned me that you aren't easily tricked."

"What else do you know?" Libertas demanded, suddenly emboldened.

"That you're missing a very important interview at the Propaganda Ministry because of yours truly. Please, allow me to say, I'm really grateful that you've chosen my company."

"How do you—" Libertas stopped abruptly. She hadn't even told Harro about Otto-from-Paris' call. Just how had Korotkov possibly unearthed that information? "Have you been listening to our phone conversations?" she asked as the realization dawned on her.

Korotkov grimaced slightly. "Guilty as charged. In my defense, I figured if the Gestapo taps into Berliners' conversations, why not us as well?"

To be sure, he meant the NKVD.

Libertas' expression must have been more than eloquent, for Korotkov lifted a conciliatory hand before she had a chance to give him a magisterial dressing-down for intruding on her privacy in such an insolent manner.

"I stopped the practice after my meeting with Harro. He knows about it, in case you were curious. I never concealed anything from your husband and have been extremely forward with him; you can ask him yourself."

Libertas shifted her gaze to her husband and saw him nod. In the Soviet agent's presence, he seemed remarkably relaxed and at ease, but then again, Harro had always been a better judge of character than Libertas. If he trusted the man, she would just have to learn to trust him too.

"And as for listening to your phone conversations, it was sheer necessity rather than the unhealthy curiosity of a bored agent, I assure you," Korotkov continued. "My superiors had to be certain that we could trust you and Harro before we could proceed with further cooperation. In our business, you never know who truly wishes to help and who is a Gestapo provocateur. You must understand, you have just suspected me of being one yourself." He gave Libertas a disarming smile.

After a moment's hesitation, she finally permitted a grin as well. "You're forgiven, Herr Erdberg."

"Call me Alex. We're all friends here, no?" Breaking into another friendly smile, he waved to the waiter, indicating that he would like another round of beers.

Astounded, Libertas noticed that the harassed-looking waiter simply smiled back at the Russian. It appeared Korotkov managed to charm just about anyone coming into contact with him. Even Libertas' icy demeanor began to thaw little by little. But perhaps that was his strategy all along? She had expected to see the stereotypical Slav that Goebbels depicted in his propaganda films, uncouth and smelling sharply of makhorka, with an atrocious accent, cagey eyes, and a constant grimace of discontent. Instead, there sat the life of the party, a Viennese bohemian dressed expensively and with great taste, with a golden wristwatch and hair that was slightly too long, which he kept raking back with his long, elegant fingers, laughing heartily at jokes and supplying his own in spades, flirting with Lisl in between plotting against Hitler's government and asking Libertas if she would become their cell's radio operator in the same cheerful tone so she almost choked on the fish she was eating.

As Harro thumped her on the back, Korotkov quickly moved a glass of water toward her. "I would never insist on it, if you feel that you're not ready," he said. "We have already discussed it with Harro, and since he's away five days a week and we may have something urgent to transmit, we need someone who's always in Berlin. It doesn't have to be you. It can be Lisl, if she is up to the challenge." He winked at Lisl, who broke into an embarrassed, beaming smile. "Or I can ask Arvid."

"But neither of us knows how to operate it," Libertas said, finally recovering her breath.

"Oh, very simple! I'll teach you in two minutes. It's easier for someone who plays a piano because you'll have to spend a long time working with your fingers. That's why I had you in mind, piano-accordion girl." Another playful grin, as though he wasn't suggesting something for which the Gestapo cut people's heads off with an ax. "I'll teach you coding and decoding, too. Our coding system is the best in the world. Nearly infallible. So, as long as you follow it to a T, no Gestapo agent will be able to decode it, even if they intercept it."

"That's a lot to ask," Libertas muttered, lowering her fork. The fresh fish had suddenly lost all of its flavor.

"I understand that. You have every right to refuse."

Libertas looked at Harro. He met her gaze but said nothing at all; didn't betray his emotions with a single twitch of a brow. It was her decision and hers alone. He refused to push her in any way, only took hold of her hand and gave it a slight pressure. *Whatever you decide, I shall support you and respect you for your decision*; his hand said what his lips didn't. And Libertas loved him all the more for not forcing her into the noose, no matter how much was at stake.

Perhaps, that's what made her decision so easy.

"Lisl and I, we'll do it," she said, looking Korotkov firmly in the eyes. "But still, teach Arvid and Mildred, too. In case…" She let out the breath, bracing herself for what she was about to say. "In case something happens to us."

"Will do," Korotkov promised simply and lifted his beer in a toast. "To victory!" he bellowed loudly, prompting cheers and toasts from the neighboring tables. "To *our* victory," he said softer as they brought their glasses together, a hawkish gleam in his eyes.

*

June 1941

Inside Libertas' and Harro's apartment, all windows stood open, curtains billowing in the breeze like the sails of a great ship. From the Olympic stadium, the wind carried loud cheers of football fans—Germany was playing against Switzerland. Summer was in the air, sultry and blossom-scented, with a painfully blue sky and birds singing loudly in the emerald domes of the trees. Only Libertas remained gravely silent as she opened a vulcanized fiber case brought by Korotkov, suntanned and dressed in short-sleeves, looking like someone without a care in the world despite the fact that Harro had just told him, on the most reliable authority, that the German forces would attack the Soviet Union on June 21, both from the air and the ground.

"It's a battery-powered transceiver that can be operated any-where," Korotkov explained, patting himself—for cigarettes, Libertas assumed. Instead, he produced a small book from the back pocket of his linen trousers. "You happen to like poetry, from what I gathered. Here's some poetry for you."

Mystified, Libertas turned a small tome of Schiller in her hands.

"This is your codebook." Korotkov smiled. "The key code is created by using a certain word order from a random book—in your case, Schiller. Only the agent on our side will know which sentence you're using to decipher the code..."

In the next hour, Libertas felt herself drowning in the informa-tion Korotkov was pouring forth, quoting numbers and technical details out of his seemingly bottomless, eidetic memory.

"Now, it is of the utmost importance that you broadcast only from 02.00 to 03.15 local time, with the wavelength set at 52.63 meters, or from 16.15 to 17.30—also local time—on the wave-length 42.50 meters. The third time slot is from 22.30 to 23.15, and the wavelength for that one is 46.10 meters. For a call signal, you must use the fourth, first, and sixth letters of the name of the day when you're transmitting. For instance, when you transmit on Monday—*Montag*—you use TMG."

"Wait, wait, Alex; can I at least write it down? Just for now?"

He laughed, regarding Libertas as though he was finding her positively amusing. "Funny joke. Appreciated. Now, let's continue."

Long shadows stretched along the sun-warmed hardwood floors by the time Korotkov checked his wristwatch and clapped Libertas on her shoulder, sending another jolt of pain into her already splitting head. In the past few hours, he had made her repeat the numbers and coding techniques until she could do so without having to think twice and could replace a battery in the receiver with her eyes closed. The dining table's cloth had disappeared entirely under cups of coffee, overflowing ashtrays, and sheets of paper on which Libertas was practicing the coding under Korotkov's guidance as Harro looked on. He had already passed his course on Luftwaffe radio communications, but after everything he'd witnessed, Harro admitted that the Soviet technique was much more sophisticated.

"Let's just hope it works," Korotkov replied, collecting the used sheets of paper and heading to the bathroom to burn them and flush the ashes.

After he returned, he offered his hand first to Harro, then to Libertas, looking each deep in the eyes and holding their palms longer than usual.

"It's been a pleasure working with you, comrades." The very first time he had used the term. In his voice, thick with emotion, it sounded almost like an endearment. "I don't know whether I'll be recalled in the case of war or... I don't know if we'll see each other again, so let me just thank you for everything and wish you luck. You'll need it. We'll all need it. And... try to stay alive, will you? Because I would really like to celebrate victory together with you, when all this is over."

When Harro closed the door after him, Libertas looked at the calendar hanging in the hallway.

It was June 18.

In three days, the war started.

Chapter 27

Schloss Liebenberg. Summer 1941

Absently, Libertas stirred her lemonade with a straw as she stared through the void somewhere above Uncle Wend's shoulder. Summer looked good on him. It bleached his hair with its silver strands to a halo of shining platinum and made his blue eyes stand out even more against his tanned skin. He was in a rare mood that afternoon, too: the German Army was ramming through the Soviet defenses with such lightning speed, he had a bet going with someone from the Reichstag that the Wehrmacht would reach Moscow by September 1.

"And then, ladies and gentlemen," he announced, roving his gaze around the summer veranda on which, besides Libertas' mother, half a dozen of his colleagues were relaxing, "we'll be rolling in Soviet black gold."

That caught Libertas' attention. She straightened scarcely visibly in her seat, forgetting all about her drink. "Black gold?"

"Oil, my precious one," Wend explained with an indulgent smile. "I'm talking about their Caucasian oil. Moscow and Leningrad, that's all fine and well, but they're far from being primary objectives. Something to stroke the Führer's ego, is all. But once we get our hands on their oil, our forces shall truly become unstoppable."

"I imagine they won't even know what hit them when we strike them in the south," one of Wend's guests chuckled wryly into his fist, his black signet ring sparkling ominously in the sun.

Libertas stifled a yawn, feigning boredom, and turned her attention back to a *Film Kurier* magazine, all the while Wend and his guests traded jests and top-secret information, never suspecting the girl in the thin sundress was committing every detail to her memory.

Misinterpreting his niece's indifference, Wend tapped her shoulder with his fingertips to call her attention. "Your good friend Minister Goebbels sends his greetings."

He's not my friend, she was just about to throw back poisonously but bit her tongue in time.

"He mentioned a few of the reviews you wrote for several recent motion pictures," Wend continued.

The prideful glance he threw at his colleagues didn't escape Libertas. It both amused and upset her that Wend still held this idealized opinion of her. She had always been his golden girl—a perfect, blue-blooded Aryan princess to parade in front of his comrades and colleagues, much as he did with his prized racehorses. When she was a child, he'd make her recite poetry for them. When she became a gangly teenager constantly switching boarding schools, he would ask her to play the accordion and sing the French songs she had learned in Paris. Later, she had become an officer's wife and now, a film critic whose articles Minister Goebbels himself enjoyed. Suppressing a grin, Libertas imagined how long Uncle Wend's face would become when he learned what his golden girl was up to and how little she had in common with the Libertas he imagined she was.

"He says you have such an eye for details," Wend continued, entirely oblivious to Libertas' thoughts, "you should try filmmaking. *Herr* Minister said you have all the prerequisites to be an even better film director than Leni Riefenstahl," he finished to a few chuckles from his uniformed audience.

Libertas beamed politely, knowing exactly why Goebbels still had it in for Leni Riefenstahl, who had not only dared to reject his advances but become a successful director without any help from his side.

"In fact, the *Promi* has just founded a new agency in charge of production of short films—ten, fifteen minutes at the most—which will run before any film presentations at theaters. When we're back in Berlin," Wend proceeded, lighting a cigar, "go to the German Documentary Film Institute office. *Deutsche Kulturfilm-Zentrale,* Jägerstraße 26, right on Gendarmenmarkt Square. Give them your name at the reception and mention Minister Goebbels. I can guarantee they shall accept you on the spot."

"I know nothing about filmmaking."

"You'll learn," Wend said, unconcerned. "Isn't that what you always wanted?"

Libertas made no reply. The truth was, she didn't know what she wanted anymore.

"A thousand greetings to all our friends." She broadcasted the encrypted message during the assigned time slot, just past twenty-two hundred hours, just as Korotkov had instructed.

All around her, Schloss Liebenberg forest rustled softly, as though stilling itself as much as possible for her clandestine work to go smoothly. In the distance, Libertas' horse snorted from time to time, tearing blades of grass out of the ground. An owl hooted sharply, invisible and amber-eyed, the guardian of the night. But Libertas paid no heed to it all. Her brows drawn sharply in concentration, she listened intently for the confirmation that wouldn't come.

In the course of the past few weeks, Libertas had tried to broadcast countless times, only to be met with an impenetrable wall of silence from the Soviet side.

"I must be doing something wrong," she had told Harro after the first few unsuccessful attempts. He had appeared doubtful but tried the radio himself and got the same result.

"It's not you," he had declared in the end. "Something is wrong at their end. Take it to Lisl, let her or Kurt try."

But, just their fortune, Kurt had been drafted to the Wehrmacht, and Lisl had soon returned the device, shaking her head in resignation.

For a couple of weeks, the transmitter had taken up residence at the Harnacks', only to be returned to its original owner with their sincerest apologies.

And now, Libertas was risking her life, dragging it to her familial estate with the rest of her luggage, but the small transmitter with its radio silence mocked her all the same.

Libertas checked her watch—thank heavens for the bright moonlight—and attempted another broadcast, just to grit her teeth in helpless ire when minutes passed without any response. She had firsthand attack plans, a wealth of information from the very top, and no one to receive it. Hissing curses under her breath, she tore the headphones off and threw them onto the dewy grass, suddenly missing Korotkov and his devil-may-care attitude and expensive Austrian cigarettes. What she wouldn't give just then for him to appear out of nowhere, put his pianist's hands on the receiver, and fix everything within minutes. Fix this entire damned war…

But no one came out of the forest. Libertas was alone.

For a few split seconds of sheer desperation, she envied Gisela and Martin because they didn't have to witness it all—the mess their beloved country had become; the mess that only very few people like Harro, like Arvid and Mildred, like her and Lisl, were desperately trying to fix, only to fail miserably.

No one was coming to save them. They had to fight for themselves.

Berlin. October 1941

The office of the German Documentary Film Institute still bore faint traces of fresh paint and floor wax. Neo-Germanic classicism was reflected in every detail, beginning with grand marble staircases, sculptures, and posters of stern-looking Teutonic knights and Aryan women adorned with nothing but flowers and Nordic pride. Along the walls of the endless corridors, crimson *Hakenkreuz* banners were stretched tightly, framed by marble columns and crowned by golden wreaths in eagles' claws. It only took Libertas one look around to realize what sort of films would be made within its walls.

"You have an excellent résumé, Frau Schulze-Boysen," the man in charge of personnel, who had introduced himself as Herr Tikalsky, declared, visibly impressed. The manner in which he balanced his glasses on the very tip of his nose, looking at Libertas over them and then lowering his eyes again to her résumé, made her wonder by what miracle they remained there in the first place. "With your experience, I can easily offer you a position of film censor. As a stepping stone, naturally," he rushed to clarify.

It occurred to Libertas that Uncle Wend hadn't lied. They indeed expected her here, whoever the recommendation came from.

"I've been told you're interested in making films yourself?" Another inquisitive glance over the thick lenses.

"Yes," Libertas replied, after clearing her throat.

It happened to her often in recent times, this odd dissociation from reality. One part of her tried to live as she should, applying for jobs, trying to build a career, going shopping and setting off for a run at the Olympic stadium in the mornings to keep herself in shape, but all those actions were blurred somehow, mechanical, as though happening to someone in a feature film she was watching. It was the other part that was always sharp and on guard, always listening, always seeking out connections, always waiting for a moment to strike, for a signal to attack—a fighter in the shadows only pretending to be the Libertas that Herr Tikalsky was presently talking to.

"I assume you have guidelines of sorts?" Libertas asked after collecting herself, all business once again.

Tikalsky brightened at once. "Art, German land, and people."
Blood and race, in other words. Familiar rot. Just as she had
assumed.

"Filmmakers will be submitting their concepts or finished
films to you directly," Tikalsky continued. "It will be up to you
to decide whether they adhere to the Party line or not. I need
hardly add that we must never release any of that pacifistic garbage
some of them insist on making. One idiot has come up with an
idea to make a film about German and French troops playing
a football match on Christmas Day, during the Great War." He
chuckled, coughed into his fist, and chuckled again, as though
embarrassed to be even relating such a ridiculous concept to his
newest employee.

"You're quite right. That's unacceptable. He should have offered
to make a documentary about German and Soviet troops playing
a conciliatory football match," Libertas said with a straight face.
"That's much more relevant."

Her deadpan manner must have been persuasive indeed as
Tikalsky paled slightly, only breaking into relieved chortles when
Libertas grinned with the corner of her mouth. *Just a joke, Herr
Tikalsky. Don't get yourself in an uproar.*

By the afternoon, she had finished signing all the necessary
papers. A secretary at the personnel office handed Libertas a key to
her new office and congratulated her on the new position. Libertas
thanked the woman politely, signed in a journal for the key and her
new ration card, and left the office just in time to catch a U-Bahn
train back home.

She heard the phone ring from the staircase. Shoving the key
into the lock, Libertas hurried inside, feeling her heart beating
wildly in her throat for a reason she couldn't quite explain. Some
recently acquired fighter's instinct reported something and, without
thinking twice, she dropped her bag on the floor and rushed across
the hallway to grasp the phone before the line went silent.

"Libertas Schulze-Boysen," she rasped into the receiver, her breath still hectic from her wild sprint.

"Yes, hello?" A male voice, unfamiliar, heavily accented. "Your friend gave me your number."

"Which friend?" Libertas asked, feverishly working things out in her mind. The accent wasn't Russian; Spanish, if anything. She didn't know any Spaniards.

"My name is Vincente Sierra. I'm here on business for my company."

"What company?"

"Simexco. Our headquarters are in Belgium. We do a lot of business with Germans. I understand that you have a relative in Paris who has a fashion studio?"

"Yes. My father." Libertas was even more at a loss.

"Splendid! Is it possible for us to meet to discuss our possible business with your family anytime this week? I'm afraid I have to leave for Brussels soon and don't have much time."

"You never said which friend gave you my number."

"*Ach*! Apologies." Libertas imagined him slapping himself on his forehead. "Alex Erdberg, my business competitor and very good friend."

Libertas' stomach did a somersault. *Korotkov had found a way to contact them after all!*

"Yes, Herr… Forgive me, please—"

"Sierra. And no need to apologize. Foreign names." He chuckled politely. "The Tiergarten Zoo? Say, Saturday at twelve? Would that work for you?"

"Yes. Yes, it would work just fine."

Lowering the phone, Libertas released a tremendous breath, feeling as though a great weight had been lifted from her shoulders.

Chapter 28

Libertas shivered in her ermine-collar coat as she waited in front of the Zoologischer Garten U-Bahn station, more from nerves than the chilly October afternoon. All around her, people hurried to and fro, collars turned up high, hats pulled down onto scowling foreheads, wet newspapers clutched firmly in gloved hands. The weather itself couldn't decide between rain and snow and drizzled something nasty for countless days in a row.

"Horrid weather for the troops," an occasional passer-by speculated with a knowing look about him to his fellow commuter. "Russia is infamous for its muddy roads. Tanks and all other machinery are getting bogged down. That's why there isn't much progress…"

A harsh gust of wind picked up the rest of his words and scattered them along with yellow leaves and old newspapers full of former glories and promises of swift victory by September 1. It suddenly occurred to Libertas that Uncle Wend had lost his bet to someone from the Reichstag. With a chilling lack of interest, she wondered if he was more upset about losing the money or the fact that he wasn't drinking champagne in the Kremlin as he predicted he would have been by now.

"Frau Schulze-Boysen?"

A startled gasp caught in Libertas' throat. Swinging round on her heel, she came face to face with a man dressed expensively, if much too warm for the weather, who was smiling apologetically at her.

"Forgive me please for startling you," he said by means of introduction and lifted his felt hat, bowing his head slightly. "It was never my intention. Vincente Sierra. It's a pleasure to make your acquaintance."

Recovering herself, Libertas shook his hand encased in a tailored leather glove, all the while studying the Soviet agent's face closely. Shorter than her in stature, with darker coloring, black liquid eyes, and a five-o'clock shadow already forming on his face despite the fact that he had clearly shaved recently, Libertas understood why the Soviets gave Herr Sierra a Uruguayan passport instead of trying to pass him off as a local as they did with his counterpart, Alex Korotkov. Sierra's German was also heavily accented, unlike Korotkov's flawless Viennese-flavored speech, but in his eyes Libertas instantly recognized the same sharp gleam, the same fiery intelligence, the same steely will.

"Shall we head out?" Sierra pulled his head into his shoulders against a particularly sharp gust of wind. "I hope you forgive me for saying so, but I can't bear your Berlin winters for the life of me."

"It's only October," Libertas remarked, confused.

"*Ach*, but that's not Uruguay for you," Sierra protested cheerfully and extracted a pipe out of his pocket. "You don't mind, do you? Keeps me warm."

Only then did the realization dawn on Libertas. To any curious eyes, he appeared perfectly harmless, a somewhat funny-looking South American businessman braving the German cold to secure a deal with the daughter of a Parisian fashion designer.

Keeping to his story, he babbled loudly about Brussels and some raincoat company that had just been re-oriented to produce waterproof clothing for the brave German troops; about someone named Bock and what excellent champagne they drank at The Ritz in Paris; about the possibility of opening a second fashion house under Libertas' father's name here, in Berlin—*the second fashion capital of the world, so many beautiful ladies, so many handsome military gentlemen who all need uniforms, and it would be his utmost pleasure—*

Sierra's tone changed abruptly as soon as they entered the Zoo and found themselves near the secluded enclosure of the bald-headed eagles. "Whatever happened to the promised transmissions?"

Caught off guard, Libertas swallowed nervously, suddenly finding herself face to face with an intelligence operative and not some harmless salesman.

"We have been trying this entire time, I swear!" Like a student accused of not completing an assignment, Libertas began enumerating the time slots and wavelengths and whatnot just to persuade the Russian that she wasn't some empty-headed amateur, that she indeed gave it all she had, that she—

Sierra waved her off generously. "Never mind then. The transmitter could have been defective. So many people trying, including your husband, couldn't have failed if it weren't. It's all right, I'll report it to the center. We'll get you a new one within days. I'll test it myself to make sure that it works."

"Thank you so much, Herr Sierra. We won't disappoint you this time, you have my word."

"No harm done, Frau Schulze-Boysen. Such things happen in our line of work."

No harm done was a doubtful statement. Libertas heard from Harro firsthand how many Soviet soldiers had been encircled and transported to countless POW camps springing up throughout occupied territories like mushrooms after the rain. How many of them had already perished from starvation, disease, and exposure to the elements. And how many of those deaths could have been prevented, had the transmitter worked as it should have.

"Is Alexander all right?" Libertas asked, not quite counting on the answer.

"Alexander is more than all right." Sierra chuckled. "He's a big shot in the Lubyanka NKVD office now. It was on his recommendation that your case has been transferred to us."

Libertas didn't ask who "us" was but assumed that Sierra must have meant the GRU—the Soviet counterpart of the German *Abwehr*, the foreign intelligence service.

"He must be terribly disappointed in us," Libertas muttered, studying the magnificent birds.

"If he was disappointed, he would have sent your file to the archives and forgotten you like a bad dream."

"Still."

From Sierra, another negligent wave of the hand. "Don't concern yourself with the past. It's the future that we must think about." He tapped the glass enclosure with his index finger. "Formidable creatures, aren't they?"

"They are," Libertas agreed, wondering where he was heading with this. "That's why so many countries have them as their symbols, I suppose."

"Do you know why former tsarist Russia had a double-headed eagle?"

"No?"

"Because unlike other countries who only look one way, we always look both ways. One head to the east, another one to the west. And if our latest intelligence doesn't lie, the eastern threat of Japan should soon disappear entirely." Sierra's mysterious grin reflected in the glass. "Hitler is counting on Japan to attack us from the east so that we would have to fight on two fronts but according to recent reports, Japan has other plans and they have nothing to do with us."

As though hypnotized, Libertas stared at his finger glued to the glass, pointing straight at the bald-headed eagle.

"Not the United States?" she whispered incredulously, searching then the agent's impenetrable face.

"You didn't hear anything from me. Technically speaking, it doesn't concern me one way or the other what happens to them. But feel free to impart the information to your friend Arvid Harnack, who has friends at the US Embassy, from what I hear. But it is essential that you don't mention my name. It's quite against my instructions."

"Why are you telling me this then?"

Sierra released a breath. "Because your friend Arvid is married to an American citizen and because both of them have been supplying us with information relevant to the Soviet Union for quite a while. I think it's only fair to return the favor."

Libertas considered something for some time. Then she turned to Sierra with an expression of determination on her face. "My husband is coming back on his weekend leave today. Would you like to stop by and meet him? He might have some fresh information for you. I also have something of interest to share with you."

Sierra arched a curious brow, to which Libertas shrugged with a grin.

"Your double-headed eagle might have missed something looking to both sides but not up and down. And it's from the south that your next threat will come."

Something shifted in Sierra's expression. He regarded Libertas with a newfound respect. "What time?"

"Come by for dinner. Six o'clock."

"It's a date, Frau Schulze-Boysen. I'll bring great Uruguayan wine."

Libertas' widening grin mirrored Sierra's. She was beginning to like the man.

Sierra arrived punctually at two minutes to six, with flowers for the mistress of the household and a case, Libertas suspected, of the promised wine.

"Did you get here all right?" she asked, accepting his leather coat that was surprisingly perfectly dry despite the wet snow falling outside.

"Oh yes," Sierra responded with great enthusiasm. "Leutnant Spannagel from the High Command of the Wehrmacht headquarters was kind enough to offer me a ride in his staff car." He hung his hat on the rack and, with wonderful nonchalance about him, opened the case to reveal a portable transmitter sitting snugly inside. "Such a fine gentleman. I recommended your husband to him highly. And your father, of course."

"You drove in the Wehrmacht officer's car with… this?!" Libertas was at a loss for words, staring wide-eyed at the radio.

Sierra only looked at her, seemingly confused. "But, naturally. Now, if he offered me a ride and I refused it—and in such weather!—that would have raised suspicions, wouldn't it? The best way to hide something, Frau Schulze-Boysen, is right under the enemy's nose. That's how we hid our beloved Alex and that's how we're presently hiding dozens of other agents all over occupied Europe. Where can I wash my hands?"

Libertas pointed silently at the bathroom door and remained standing in the same spot, staring blankly at the transmitter, when Harro's steps echoed out of his study.

"Damned phone, always rings at the worst times," he grumbled under his breath and halted as soon as he spotted the transmitter sitting comfortably on his mail table. "Is that…?"

"Yes."

"And where's…?"

"Bathroom."

They exchanged looks and suddenly broke into laughter. Libertas knew that she had set out on an adventure when she was marrying Harro, just as he was aware that life with her would be anything but dull. However, neither of them could have ever imagined, in their wildest dreams, that they would be hosting a Soviet intelligence agent for dinner and committing a treason against the state and the Führer under that state's nose. It was both exciting and frightening, but as long as they had each other, little else mattered.

"I haven't told you in a while, but I love you more than life," Harro said softly, enclosing Libertas in his embrace.

"You don't have to tell me anything. I know," she replied, bringing her lips to his.

Later, as they took their conversation out of the dining room to the living room's couch, Harro confirmed what Libertas had told Sierra.

"Army Group South has your southern city of Maykop as their next objective," Harro said, swirling the cognac in his glass. "They're already short of fuel. They have stretched themselves too thin. Machinery can't cope with supplying the vanguard with the Romanian fuel; they're getting bogged down in your infamous Russian mud as well."

Sierra lowered his head to his glass, trying to conceal a knowing grin. "They should wait until they get acquainted with our infamous Russian winter. It's already snowing in Russia something frightful, you know. And your brave little Wehrmacht boys are all still wearing summer uniforms."

He coughed into his fist to mask his gleeful chuckling, but then saw his hosts' faces and desisted.

"Forgive me, please. I shouldn't have made that joke just now. You have welcomed me so warmly, I keep forgetting you're Germans." Sierra sighed, raising his gaze to the tall ceiling as though searching for answers in it. "I know that they're only soldiers and that most of them have been conscripted against their will and that they have been drawn into this war by those leaders of yours... It just gets to me sometimes, you understand? I'm here, living the life of a wealthy businessman, and they're trampling my country's land, killing my friends—who the devil knows? My superiors don't report anything to me. My family is in Leningrad, perhaps, starving to death... And if they had the presence of the mind to run, who knows what may have happened to them? We're Jewish, you see. I ought to be a professional, but—" He stopped abruptly, looking like he'd given up more than he should have, and wiped his hands down his face, looking tired and old all of a sudden.

"You have every right to be angry at us," Libertas said softly. "I, for one, feel very guilty."

"Whatever for?" He smiled sadly. "You haven't done anything to me."

"My people did. It is my shared responsibility."

Sierra looked at her for a very long time before shifting his gaze to Harro and raising his glass. "You married a very good woman, Harro. Make sure to take good care of her."

"It's she who's been taking care of me for the most part." Harro grinned, looking over at his wife. "But you're right. I married the best woman there is. No offense if you're married too."

"I'm not. And none taken. Just… try not to get caught, you two, will you?"

Harro snorted softly. "Funny. That's precisely what Alex told us before the war started and we lost contact."

"And I can see why." Sierra slapped his knees and rose from his chair. "All right, children. The curfew time is approaching. I must take my leave."

"Be careful, Vincente," Libertas said to him as she held out his coat to him in the hallway.

"Anatoly," he whispered so softly, she scarcely heard him.

Only after he had disappeared behind the door did it dawn on her that Sierra had just told her his real name.

Chapter 29

November 1941

It was only her second week on the new job and Libertas had already overslept. Silently cursing the alarm clock she had forgotten to wind the night before, the sleet under her feet muddying her boots, BDM girls shaking their collection boxes near the U-Bahn station, the winter relief truck gathering warm clothes for the brave soldiers fighting the Bolsheviks on the Eastern front that was parked just in front of the intersection and blocking her way, Libertas ran through the gloomy November morning into the building of the German Documentary Film Institute.

Inside, it was a beehive as always: secretaries carrying stacks of binders, artists arguing over promotional poster concepts, exasperated directors following harassed-looking censors along the hallways.

"…but, Herr Böhme, with all due respect, I have already cut the offending parts as per your notes—"

"The entire documentary is going to the trash because of your cameraman! The theme of the project is *The Soviet Paradise*. It is meant to be mocking, not literal! He should have been filming the degradation, filth, and horrendous living conditions of the Soviets, not glorifying their architecture!"

"Apologies, Herr Böhme. It was filmed near Leningrad. The architecture dates back to the tsarist times. There was no filming around it. The entire town was like a picture. We do have footage of streets bombed out by the Luftwaffe, which we can pass for damage inflicted by the Bolshevists themselves, right after the Revolution, if that will do…"

Libertas didn't catch the rest of the conversation. She was already running up the grand staircase, skipping the elevator that always took too long and moved much too slow, unlike the one in Harro's Air Ministry that made one's stomach drop, according to Harro.

Helmut, her secretary, greeted her in his usual well-regulated, professional voice and passed Libertas her morning mail.

"Coffee, Frau Schulze-Boysen?"

Libertas paused on the threshold of her office. "Is there any chance you can you make a jam sandwich happen as well? I didn't have any breakfast today."

Helmut gave her a coy grin. "Will that earn me an early dismissal on Friday?"

Libertas narrowed her eyes at him. "Do you have a date then, you weasel?"

Throwing a glance at the door, Helmut pressed his finger to his lips. "Nothing of the sort, Frau Schulze-Boysen. Just meeting a friend for drinks."

A date indeed, Libertas grinned knowingly. She was secretly pleased that Helmut had entrusted her with his secret about his amorous inclinations involving a very handsome cutter from the editing department; the secret that could earn him and his lover a one-way ticket to the concentration camp under the new Reich laws against homosexuality.

"Make it two sandwiches and you can leave at four on Friday instead of six."

Displaying two rows of enviously straight, perfectly white teeth, Helmut bolted out of the door before Libertas had a chance to ask if he needed her ration book.

Her mood somewhat improved after the friendly exchange, Libertas was sorting through her mail when a particularly thick envelope attracted her attention. Expertly slicing through the paper with her letter opener fashioned after a sword, she froze in her seat and felt the blood draining from her face as the envelope's contents spilled onto her desk.

At first, Libertas' mind refused to process the images of naked men, women, the elderly and children facing the edge of a wide ravine as soldiers wearing SS uniforms aimed rifles at their backs.

Something staged, she tried to persuade herself; *something for one new project or another. Those were actors, and only that. They received their pay at the end of the day and went home…*

It was a good thing she was sitting. Her head began to swim, waves of nausea sweeping over her.

…And those bodies in the ravine, Libertas swallowed bile rising in her throat, *just mannequins. Broken, soft-limbed, frighteningly lifelike mannequins, as in her father's fashion house. Not real.*

"Not real," she whispered, as though saying it out loud would somehow make it true.

But then her trembling, white fingers pulled a letter from under the stack of atrocities and the proud words of an SS man poured out of it, boasting the numbers of those filthy Jews he'd rid his beloved Reich of, gloating over how submissively those Slavs had gone to their deaths, anticipating the next village, the next city, the next ravine with the thrill of a demented hunter—and all of a sudden, the grim, terrifying reality of it all settled over Libertas like a dark cloud.

They weren't just a nation of warmongers. They were a nation of ruthless, soulless killers.

"We're doomed," Libertas said later to Harro as he sat before the fireplace, ashen-faced and gaunt, going over the photographs countless times. "A nation that commits this sort of crime has no right for existence any longer."

Her voice was oddly calm, tinged with gloom and cigarette smoke. She'd had a few days to think it over before Harro had returned home on leave. By the time he took her in his arms, she knew precisely where she stood in all this.

"If I had any lingering doubts before—I mean, we are dealing with the Soviets, after all, and I'm quite far from being a communist or approving of their ideas in any way—these photographs removed them for good. Harro, it doesn't matter anymore if we survive. We have no moral right to try to survive when Soviet women are being shot, still clutching children to their chests. But we have a moral obligation to do everything in our power to bring down this regime. Our lives are a small price to pay."

Harro looked up at her, misty-eyed and unusually vulnerable in his Luftwaffe uniform. "Libs, I didn't know about any of this, I swear to you…"

"I know you didn't. It's the SS. *Totenkopf.* Death's Head squads. They execute civilians."

"How did those photos make it to you in the first place?"

"Helmut." Libertas smiled weakly. "That little weasel told some numbskull with an SS relative serving on the Eastern front that his boss was gathering materials for the upcoming exhibition and that they were encouraged to send whatever they wished to my office."

"Is Helmut…?"

"He's not with any organization, no. Just a good man with a conscience, who wants atrocities exposed and perpetrators called to justice."

"It's reassuring, actually."

"What?"

"The number of people we have encountered throughout the years who are willing to help one way or another. Who still resist, no matter the danger. Who refuse to succumb to this communal hatred for everything foreign and who risk their lives just to bring peace about. It began with journalists, then spread to other intellectuals, doctors like Elfriede, diplomats like Arvid, artists and bohemians like Kurt and List, communists like Hans Coppi and now, Helmut." A smile warmed Harro's pale face. "Perhaps, nothing is lost yet. As long as they live, our cause lives."

Libertas nodded thoughtfully, gazing at the fire. "I brought these photos here just to show you and then destroy them. But you know what?" Leaving her cigarette in the crystal ashtray, Libertas headed to her study and soon returned, holding a photo album in her hands. "I'll keep them. I'll keep them, I'll preserve them as evidence, and when the time comes, I'll hand them to the people who will use them to bring justice about."

Harro rose from his chair, a familiar spark igniting in his eyes. "Yes. You do that, and I'll write a new pamphlet. And this time, we'll print tens of thousands of it and spread it all over Berlin, all over the Eastern front so that the Wehrmacht soldiers know what their counterparts from the SS are doing. And then, perhaps, they shall revolt as well and refuse to fight. Or, better yet, turn their guns on their political officers and do away with them and embrace former enemies and peace will return once again to Europe."

Libertas caught his hands in hers and looked at him for a very long moment. "I should so love to live long enough to see it happen. But even if I don't, even if it only happens after we perish, it would still mean that our fight wasn't in vain."

December 1941

Dinner at the Harnacks' wasn't a joyful occasion this time. Mildred was in a particularly subdued mood, absently poking at the food she had so carefully prepared to celebrate Harro's transfer back to Berlin and making attempts at weak smiles when Arvid or her guests tried to distract her from her unhappy musings. Libertas understood her friend only too well: Mildred was an American after all, married to a German, but an American nevertheless, and now, her adopted homeland was officially at war with her real one thanks to the Japanese attack at Pearl Harbor, and the attitudes of people who used to be so friendly to her before had shifted all of a sudden. Mildred didn't quite know what to make of it all. Yesterday, a diplomat's wife; today, an enemy alien.

Discreetly, Libertas reached under the table for Mildred's hand and gave it a warm squeeze. When Mildred looked up from her plate, the mixture of tears and profound gratitude in the American's eyes nearly tore at Libertas' heart.

"What's worse, we have lost our contact with my friend from the American Embassy," Arvid was saying, also not quite himself that evening.

"There is still Herr Sierra," Harro remarked pensively, twisting a cigarette in his restless hand. "And from what Libs told me, he isn't averse to sharing information with his American counterparts."

"His superiors may even approve of it, now that they're allies," Libertas suggested, shifting her gaze from Arvid to Harro and back.

"That's a possibility," Harro agreed.

"I think I'm being watched," Mildred announced suddenly.

Arvid regarded her sympathetically. "Sweetheart, we talked about it."

"Yes, and you said I'm only imagining it. I'm not." Her tone was sharper than usual. "I know what I feel. Those beady eyes on the back of my head, no matter where I go. Women are very sensitive to these things. We have learned to be aware of our surroundings from an early age, just to avoid being caught unawares and escape unwanted male attention. I know what being followed feels like."

"You think it's the Gestapo?" Harro pulled forward, his brows drawn tightly in concentration.

"I don't know," Mildred moaned, rubbing her forehead and suddenly looking utterly exhausted. "Who else would it be though? Some secret admirer?"

No one laughed. Silence hung over the room, heavy and oppressive. Libertas could hear her own breathing.

"In that case, I don't think it would be wise to bring the transmitter here," she said at last, biting her lips as she was working things out in her mind. "Too risky to try to transmit from here if you are indeed being watched."

"I agree with Libs." Harro nodded.

"But you can't do it out of your apartment either," Arvid argued. "The Gestapo will trace you after a couple of repeat transmissions."

"What about Hans?" Libertas turned to Harro. "Hans Coppi, that young communist fellow who worked on the pamphlets with you? No one would suspect him. He's not technically associated with our circle. Could you not train him how to work the radio? Or I could go into his apartment and transmit from there myself if—"

"Absolutely out of the question," Harro replied with a categorical shake of his head. "I don't want you anywhere near him. You associating with a communist and a former concentration camp inmate—that's just the very thing we need right now."

"But you, a Luftwaffe officer, associating with him is fine and well?" Libertas arched a skeptical brow.

Harro's expression softened. "Libs, you're already doing too much," he said with a gentle smile, a meaningful look in his eyes.

They hadn't told Arvid or Mildred about the photos flooding Libertas' desk, which she kept meticulously organizing into albums, along with the names of the perpetrators, their addresses, company and detachment numbers, and superiors' titles—a prosecutor preparing the case of her lifetime. The Harnacks had enough on their plate as it was. Why burden them with this knowledge on top of everything else?

"Let someone else be a hero for a change," Harro finished, finally bringing the light to his cigarette.

Libertas grinned tiredly and raised both hands in mock surrender. "Comrade Coppi it is then."

*

A few days later, Libertas tucked the transmitter lovingly into its case, passed her gloved hand over it, and handed it to Harro.

"Tell Hans to take good care of it, please."

"He will guard it with his life," Harro said with a knowing grin, taking the suitcase into his hand, also encased in a gray leather glove. "For him, this is the ideological fight. He would rather die than disappoint his brothers-in-arms in Moscow."

With that, he put his uniform cap on and left.

Through the frost-kissed glass, her fingers holding the heavy blackout drape, Libertas watched the silhouette of her husband walk into the city of darkness and slowly dissolve into it. Imagining the falling snow covering his tracks unsettled her for some reason, as though the winter itself was wiping Harro's existence from its memory.

Mildred's paranoia, that's all there is to it, Libertas tried desperately to persuade herself as her hand rubbed her chest of its own volition. Now, she was imagining things too. No one was following them.

And even if they were, so what? Wasn't she just telling Harro how she was prepared to die for the cause? Yet this was too soon, she hadn't amassed enough evidence yet. They hadn't done enough, hadn't helped enough...

Just a few more months, that's all she was asking whatever higher powers there were. Just a few more transmissions, just a few more albums to fill, just to nudge the Allies a tad closer to victory.

Then, she would die in peace. Then, their fight wouldn't be in vain.

Chapter 30

January 1942

Suppressing a tremor of righteous anger in her hand, Libertas carefully penned a letter to yet another SS murderer. This one had outdone even his ruthless comrades, attaching photos of a Jewish family being shot by him personally—a mother shielding an infant with her naked body and her two children, a boy and a girl, who couldn't have been older than two, clutching her doll, made of rags, to her chest in the same manner her mother was doing with her youngest sibling.

> *Dear Frau Schulze-Boysen! Greetings from the almost Jew-free Eastern front!*

In the next photograph, the same SS man was baring his teeth at the camera as his comrade was playfully aiming at the dead girl's doll—the only thing left, by some miracle, on the edge of the ravine over which the entire family had toppled moments ago.

> *It is frightfully cold here, but our love for the Reich and the Führer and the idea that we're carrying out his own mission warms my heart…*

Cold, all-consuming hatred flooding over her, Libertas grit her teeth as she began writing a reply to the killer of the innocent.

> *Dear German Hero! I can't express the extent of the gratitude we all feel for your selfless sacrifice in the name of the*

Reich! Only, it pains me that I cannot name the brave man fighting for our future as the contributor to our upcoming exhibition. Is it possible for me to learn your name so I can not only attribute your wonderful deeds, but keep you in my prayers at night?

In the past few weeks, Libertas had discovered that lies could flow ever so smoothly from her fountain pen as long as she kept the final goal in her mind: to bring all of those grinning, arrogant murderers to justice. Soviet justice, German justice, Allied justice—it mattered not who would tighten a noose around their necks. All that mattered was that the noose would wait for their return home, not the fanfares celebrating their ugly feats.

Never before had the job exhausted her mentally to such an extent that she had to drag herself back home, sick to her stomach and depressed beyond any measure, like an automaton propelled forward only by sheer hope for revenge. So, when the first RAF-carried bombs from Britain dropped on Berlin, she watched their fiery flowers bloom in the distance and reveled in the acrid smoke that the wind carried from the Mitte neighborhood.

What would have appalled Libertas a few months ago—these were innocent civilians, after all—didn't stir her in the slightest during the frostbitten January of 1942.

Not after those "innocent civilians" turned the remaining Berlin Jews away from news kiosks, waving Minister Goebbels' decree in their faces, which prohibited Jews from having access to any information whatsoever. No need for them to gloat over Germany's recent defeats near Moscow, which had thrown the Wehrmacht a good two to three hundred kilometers away from the capital. No need for them to read about ghetto liquidations in the East either; else, they would go into hiding and make catching and slaughtering them all a much more difficult business for the offices concerned.

Not after a hysterical woman pleaded tearfully with a uniformed official to leave her her dog: *her husband had died on the front, they had no children. The small fluffy mutt was the only thing in the world she had left.* The official didn't care one way or the other. The new law said that the Jews couldn't own pets and so the mutt had to go.

"But what harm does a dog do to the Reich?" the woman asked, tears rolling down her gaunt face and collecting under her chin.

The official made no reply, but Libertas, who watched the scene unravel, knew it in her aching heart. Unlike people, a dog couldn't be taught to hate. A dog loved its master unconditionally and the Nazis couldn't bear the thought that someone, even if it was only an animal, showed German Jews affection when everyone else spat in their faces.

So yes, they deserved bombs raining down on them; deserved being obliterated in the most horrific of manners because they were just as complicit as their Führer, as their brothers and sons shooting children on the front, as the man who tore the last hope out of the woman's hands.

That evening, when Libertas silently placed the photograph of the girl with the doll before Harro, he stared at it for a very long time before reaching for a stack of papers with a look of deadly resolution about him.

"I know precisely what to write in our new pamphlet," he said, sharpening his pencil. "I'll write about this horror in such a way that no one shall remain untouched by it."

The last day of January had dawned bright, smelling faintly of smoke. The night before—bombardment again, this time near the Tempelhof Airport. When the call had come a few days before that, Harro and Libertas had volunteered as air wardens for their building. Though in their case it meant chasing everyone into the underground cellar and then heading into the deserted town to mail countless pamphlets and then going back up to their penthouse, making love, drinking black-market wine and, with fatalistic nonchalance, gazing into the fiery night until the British Air Force ran out of bombs and they could sleep soundly again.

On that last day of January, Berliners woke to the words some of them kept to themselves but which now stared at them out of the small rectangular papers:

> *Get louder and louder! Stop putting up with all of it! Stop letting yourselves be ordered around! Oppose this fear all around us! We will save ourselves and the country only when we find the courage to place ourselves on the frontline in the battle against Hitler.*

Still enveloped in the warmth of Harro's embrace, Libertas imagined factory workers hiding it in the pockets of their overalls, foreign correspondents choking on their coffee and picking up their phones, the officials in the Wehrmacht's local recruiting headquarters pale in amazement and—perhaps—concealing the pamphlet to discuss it later with like-minded people who didn't fancy one bit the manner in which the war was progressing.

This time, it was an all-out assault, on all fronts, east and west. This time, Libertas and Harro and everyone else in their ever-growing circle announced that there would be no armistice, only unconditional surrender.

> *Send this letter out into the world to as many as you can! Pass it on to friends and co-workers! You are not alone!*

The leaflets poured out of people's mailboxes. They littered the streets and were glued to newsstands, storefronts, U-Bahn trains, and even columns of the Reichstag.

Fight on your own at first, then as a group! Tomorrow,
Germany will be ours!

When later that day Libertas entered the German Film Institute's building, she couldn't help but grin at the groups of people suddenly huddled together and muttering excitedly over something. Perhaps, nothing was yet lost if this could nudge them in the right direction, show them that the resistance was possible, that they weren't the only ones who loathed the current administration. Perhaps, then, together they would rise up and overthrow the dictator and extend a hand of peace to their brothers in the East and West and become the Germany they would all be proud of, not just a country for the small-minded, hateful nationalists who dared to call themselves patriots when all they did was spew hatred, approve of concentration camps, and not even blink when Jewish or Slavic children were slaughtered.

Perhaps, Germany would be theirs after all.

Perhaps, they would live long enough to see it happen.

The Gestapo agents hadn't yet torn the rest of Harro's most recent pamphlets from the tiled walls of U-Bahn stations and, much to their embarrassment and helpless ire, their own headquarters. He was already working his typewriter maniacally as Libertas watched him with infinite fondness and pride from her own study across the living room. They had rearranged their furniture in this manner on purpose; weeks of service-imposed solitude had brought them even closer together and now that Harro was back in Berlin, neither Libertas nor he could bear the thought of being separate even for a few fleeting moments. And so, they worked each in their own study but invariably exchanged winks and loving glances, comforted and inspired by one another's presence.

"You writing about that Jewish girl with her doll?" Libertas called to her husband across the room.

She suspected that this was the case after Harro had asked her for the dreadful photo and positioned it in front of his typewriter. The first leaflet was only a warm-up; now, Harro was finally mentally ready to describe the Eastern front atrocities in all their grim "glory."

"Yes," he replied without lifting his head and extracted the finished text from inside the typewriter. "I decided to do it in the form of a letter of one soldier to another. Do you want to hear what I have? It's still a rough draft, but I would welcome your opinion very much."

"Of course." Libertas felt warm inside from his words. "Read it to me."

Harro cleared his throat, shifted in his seat. It was obvious he was preparing himself. Libertas understood it all too well. It was one thing to write it; reading it out loud was a different matter entirely.

"I shot a family yesterday. A mother, her infant, two older children as well. Even the little girl's doll. Why, you ask me? Orders… Ach, you're asking, why the doll? Give me a moment and I shall tell you everything. Just let me light up first. It's easier this way. Cigarettes make everything easier, and schnapps even more so. Our commanders supply us with it in spades. Where was I? That's right. The girl. I have done away with hundreds, perhaps thousands, of similar girls by now, but this one stuck with me for some reason. I keep seeing her at night, with that idiotic doll."

Harro swallowed but didn't look up. Just paused long enough to compose himself.

"It was snowing that morning. When their turn came to undress, the mother kept asking to keep the rags around her infant. Whatever for is anyone's guess; he, too, would be shot at any rate. But the detachment commander permitted it. The woman kneeled in the snow; next to her, her young son—six or seven by the look of him. Only the girl

hesitated, but the boy took her hand and pulled her next to himself and she kneeled as well, not a question asked. Obedient children, well-bred. And then—she must have thought of it as a game of sorts, I gather—the girl puts her doll next to her in the snow and looks at me as though craving approval. Sure, I tell her, the doll shall get it too…

"The doll, I shot the last. It tumbled after the girl into the ravine and lay there, next to the girl's arm, when we began filling the ditch with the frozen earth. Why I did it, I still don't know. There is no political officer to explain it to me. Only snow-covered steppes and silence, alien and hostile, and that idiotic doll I keep seeing in my dreams. Orders…"

Harro had finished over a minute ago and Libertas still didn't know what to say. For some reason, the text affected her even more profoundly than the photo itself as though Harro had gone and turned her very soul inside out and put into words everything that she was feeling.

"Harro, it was so very horrible. Not the writing, I mean, but the feeling it left me with. *Ach*, I won't be able to sleep for weeks now."

"You wouldn't be able to anyway; the RAF bombers shall see to that." Harro tried to jest, but even his own smile came out miserable and full of pain.

"Your words… they punch right in the gut."

"Good. That's precisely what they should be doing."

"But do you think SS killers will feel remorse? Anything at all?"

"SS killers aren't my targeted audience." Harro shrugged. "They're lost causes as far as I'm concerned and I'm sincerely hoping each of them shall get a bullet at the end of this all. No, we shall spread it among Berliners, among foreign correspondents and, this time, among the regular Eastern front soldiers as well. Kurt has been drafted to the Wehrmacht. It's a risky enterprise of course, but why not try to smuggle this leaflet in one of Lisl's letters to him?"

Libertas considered. "Add a call to action to the leaflet to make it really effective."

Interested, Harro tilted his head to one side.

"Seeing that we want regular soldiers to revolt against the regime, offer them a solution that doesn't put them in a position of choosing between their conscience and death. Many of the Wehrmacht soldiers are conscripted against their will; they don't approve of the war, but they aren't heroes either. They wouldn't want to die for some vague idea. And physically attacking their commanders or simply refusing to pick up arms would result precisely in that—a court martial for them. No, offer them a choice that would keep their hands clean but leave them alive and acting nobly as well. Offer them to join the partisans. Russian forests are crawling with them. It is my profound conviction that they shall take anyone who wants to fight against the Germans, even it means taking German deserters themselves."

Libertas was still speaking when Harro began to tuck a fresh sheet of strictly rationed paper into his typewriter.

"I'll rewrite the first part," Harro said, his eyes gleaming with renewed fervor. "I'll write it from the point of view of a Wehrmacht soldier witnessing the crime. As if it's him, who's describing what he saw to a comrade of his. And then, in the end, he shall ask: *But is there a choice for us all? Aren't we doomed, no matter where we turn? Aren't we placed between one death and another when the choice stands between a noble Prussian character and the beastly cause the SS rabble is fighting for and dragging us into the abyss with them? I say, yes. If I have to choose between shooting small children or be shot myself, I would go over to the partisans. Desertion? Yes. But isn't it better to desert one's army rather than one's principles and Prussian honor?*"

Libertas, who was inching closer and closer into his study on her tiptoes so as not to disturb him in his moment of inspiration, held her hands clasped in front of her chest.

"Brilliant," she whispered breathlessly. "Absolutely brilliant! Harro, write it just as you have spoken it just now. Title it an 'Open Letter to the Eastern Front.' And I'll take it to Lisl once it's ready. Wehrmacht soldiers need to read it."

*

When Lisl opened the door several weeks later—that's how long it took to produce the leaflets without raising suspicion —Libertas hardly recognized her. In place of a vivacious young woman with brilliant black eyes and lips that never ceased smiling, a deathly-pale ghost of her friend stood, dressed all in black. Instantly, Libertas' heart sank.

"Kurt?" she whispered, fearing the worst.

Lisl only shook her head and motioned for Libertas to enter.

Inside, the apartment was shrouded in permanent twilight. Warm April sun struggled to get through the thick blackout drapes. The stale smell of cigarette smoke and dust hung in the air.

"I would have offered you coffee with scones, but I'm afraid I haven't gone out in a while," Lisl said by means of greeting. It occurred to Libertas that even an attempt to smile was beyond Lisl's powers.

"Do you have any food at all?" Libertas asked, still recovering from the shock of seeing her friend in such a state. She was bone-thin, sickly, resembling Gisela on her last breath far too much for Libertas' comfort. "You do have a ration card, don't you?" She wasn't sure where the German government stood on half-Jews, with German husbands fighting on the front, on the matter of ration cards.

"Yes, yes, of course," Lisl said absently, gathering a near-empty packet of cigarettes off the dining table, also covered with a thick layer of dust. "Want one?"

It wasn't the brand she smoked, but Libertas took it out of politeness. "Anyone I know?" she probed once again after they had both lit their cigarettes.

Once again, Lisl tossed her head. Even in the shadows, Libertas could see that her dark hair was tousled and unwashed. "My cousin's parents. A distant relation, you would think, but I used to spend more time in their apartment than I did at my own when I was a young girl." A hint of a small smile appeared on Lisl's face. "The kindest people I knew. Uncle Richard was blind, but, God, could he describe things! If you spoke to him on the phone and didn't know of his handicap, you would have thought he had the sharpest eyes that noticed everything—shapes, colors, all shades of the sky at dawn…"

She released a cloud of heavy, gray smoke.

"And Aunt Alice, she was such a sweet woman. Always spoiled us—me and my cousin—something rotten. It was Uncle Richard who taught me music. He was a musicologist, but he was also a remarkable musician with the finest ear one could only wish for." Lisl's smile slowly slipped off her face, replaced by a scowl full of grief that tore at Libertas' very soul. "If he knew them personally, he would never have hurt them. No, I refuse to believe that anyone would, if only they knew them personally."

"Who, Lisl?" Libertas reached out and gently touched Lisl's hand after she appeared to be too lost in her thoughts.

As though coming from under a spell, Lisl looked up. "*Ach*, yes. An SS man. I don't remember his name. It doesn't matter at any rate. There's nothing to be done. He got what he was after. They were Jewish, you see, and the Jews can no longer own any property. They aren't even citizens, technically speaking. Enemy aliens." Lisl snorted with cold disdain.

"He wanted their apartment?"

"Yes. Who can blame him? Such a fine real estate, right across the corner from Kaiser-Wilhelm-Straße, the building bordering the park. Five rooms, high ceilings with plasterwork, gas, hot water, hardwood floors…" Lisl's gaze went dark once again. "He was gracious enough not to deport them, he said. Just told them to gather their things and get the hell out by Easter so he could move his new wife in. I would have taken them, no questions asked, but they were a different breed of people, you see. Very proud, very… set in old ways. And so, they barricaded themselves inside and opened the gas. By the time the police broke the door, they were both dead."

"Oh, Lisl, I'm so sorry…"

From Lisl, another smile, even more miserable than the first one, and a dismissive wave of the hand. It was obvious she didn't want to discuss it any longer. The wound was too fresh.

"Forgive me for burdening you with my troubles," Lisl changed the subject, confirming Libertas' guess. "You wanted something? I assume you did; else, you would simply have called."

Libertas tugged on her cigarette, her mind at war with itself. She did want something, but how could she, in all good conscience, ask Lisl for something of this sort after her friend had just lost two very dear people to her?

As though guessing her thoughts, Lisl prodded Libertas gently. "Just tell me. I'm tougher than I look. I won't break, I promise."

Silently, Libertas produced Harro's *Open Letter to the Eastern Front* from the inside pocket of her trench coat. "We were wondering if you could pass it to Kurt in your letter to him, but if it's too—"

"Let me see."

With iron resolve, Lisl snatched the pamphlet from Libertas' hands. As she read, her brows pulled tighter and tighter together; her soft mouth turned into a harsh slash. But it was her eyes that expressed her mood best of all. Never before had Libertas seen such all-consuming hatred burning in anyone's gaze.

"Have you more with you?" Lisl asked after she was done reading.

Libertas opened her handbag and pulled another stack from under its double bottom.

"Give me another ten in addition to this one. I always send him a ten-page letter; this time, I'll send him one page of my own and the rest shall be yours. Let them read about what they're truly fighting for. Perhaps, if the truth smacks them straight in their faces, they will do an about-face after all."

"I know Kurt would."

"I know, if Harro was at the front, he would too."

They shook hands, two comrades-in-arms, and then embraced tightly, for one could never be certain anymore if another day would come for them to see each other.

"Good luck, Lisl."

"You too, Libs."

They looked into each other's eyes, feeling that the time was coming when they would need it.

Chapter 31

May–June 1942

Libertas would have preferred to relax in Harro's new boat (snidely called *Dushinka*—"Sweetheart" in Russian—as a dig against the Reich Libertas greatly approved of), but duty called. And so, wearing a somber black dress and armed with a pencil and a notebook, she was getting ready to attend Goebbels' new propaganda love child "The Soviet Paradise." The exhibition had been brought to Berlin from Prague, where it debuted in March, and presently occupied a large part of Lustgarten park. According to the catalogue distributed among the Institute's staff, the aim of the exhibition was to open the eyes of ordinary Germans to the poverty, misery, depravity, and need of their ideological enemy. According to Harro and his knowing smirk, the true idea was to distract Germans from their own troubles that kept mounting, the further the war progressed.

"Goebbels' idea is as old as the world itself," he had declared as soon as he learned of the exhibit. "Show them how supposedly terrible it is on the other side so that they forget that they have to wait in endless lines for hours just to end up with minuscule rations that only keep growing smaller and smaller; that they have a permanent bench in the cellar where they sleep now instead of their beds; and that their family members are being slaughtered in the pointless war Hitler decided to wage for no other reason but for his own ego's sake."

Libertas hadn't argued then but blinked at Harro in surprise now, when he suddenly appeared in her bedroom and asked if she had a spare ticket for him, his eyes gleaming with enthusiasm. It was obvious that one idea or another had possessed him while he was reading his smuggled copy of the Soviet newspaper *Pravda—Truth*—in its original language that morning.

"Why?" She playfully narrowed her mascaraed eyes at her husband in a look that could only be interpreted as, *details, please.*

With the air of a magician performing his most successful trick, Harro spread his hands wide in front of his face and announced in a grave voice tinged with barely contained excitement: "*Now in Germany, a permanent exhibition: The Nazi Paradise: war, hunger, lies, Gestapo.*" He beamed at Libertas. "What do you think?"

"A new pamphlet?" Harro's fervor was so contagious, Libertas felt her own breath catch in her throat.

"Better. We'll print stickers that we'll be able to glue everywhere. On every goddamned wall in this city. On every newspaper kiosk. On every government building. We'll smother Berlin in them."

Libertas swallowed once, twice. The idea was excellent, daring, no doubt, but a twinge of anxiety stirred in her stomach all the same.

"Harro, you don't think we're growing a bit reckless with all this, do you?" she probed gently, twisting the end of her belt in her fingers.

"Reckless? No. I'd say, we're perfecting our craft." Smiles chased across his face. "The Gestapo aren't smarter than us. If we stick to our routine, they'll never catch us."

Libertas still wasn't persuaded. "So far we've been incredibly fortunate," she began carefully. "That last insane idea to pass leaflets to Kurt's detachment, even that we got away with—"

"We haven't been fortunate, we've been smart," Harro argued. "We always use gloves. We buy paper in small amounts and through different channels that would never attract attention. Our envelopes are all from different makers, sold in different stores all over Berlin. There's nothing to tie us to any of those illegal activities. Trust me, Libs; I constantly think of our safety and of our friends' safety. My own life matters little, but I would never jeopardize your life or the lives of our comrades. The only way the Gestapo shall catch us is if they get their hands on one of the Soviet agents and he cracks under torture. Now, we know that Korotkov is in Russia, so that end is secure."

"Sierra is still working in Belgium," Libertas said pensively.

"Yes, but…" Harro heaved a sigh. "Sierra is a professional. It is my profound conviction that he'd never talk under torture."

"Perhaps not. But what if they get their hands on his codebook? Of messages?"

"Do you remember what Korotkov did to the papers after he showed you coding? He destroyed them immediately. They're well-trained agents, Libs. They would never just leave those messages lying around for the Gestapo to find." He circled a comforting arm around her waist. "And now, let's get going. I can't wait to see what Goebbels has invented to cover up our own government's shortcomings."

It was a welcome joke. Libertas felt her shoulders relax.

"I have to give Goebbels credit, it's exceeded even my expectations," Harro muttered into Libertas' ear as they wandered through a giant tent nestling between the National Gallery and the Berlin Cathedral.

What began with pridefully displayed captured Soviet machinery deepened and darkened the further they went. Now, they probed their way among the reconstructed ruins of Minsk streets under the stern looks of Lenin and Stalin, whose likenesses were plastered onto every wall, creating a general paranoid impression of two Soviet leaders watching them closely, no matter where they turned.

"Powerful," Libertas commented. "Frightening."

"It's supposed to be," Harro said quietly. "Last year, Goebbels inspired people to give their all—including their husbands, brothers, and sons—to fight his war. This year, inspiration won't do the trick anymore. He has to terrify them into fighting for their fatherland. He has to show them, *'See? This is the Judeo-Bolshevist enemy under whose yoke you shall all live if you don't fight well enough, don't starve yourself enough, don't work yourself to death like the government asks of you. Submit to us because we are the only ones who shall protect you from this filth, this red terror, this slavery.'* And the imagery works so well, they don't realize they're already enslaved by Hitler, Goebbels, Göring—you name it," Harro finished in a whisper tinged with anger.

As they turned the corner, where the sunlight scarcely reached at all, a reconstructed part of a Soviet grocery store came into view. Libertas' gaze slid over the empty shelves, spare a few vodka bottles, and a dusty, chipped counter with a set of green scales on it, the hand of which was already set on thirty grams.

A fellow Berliner, attired in a fashionable white dress, must have noticed it too after a close inspection. "Just look at it, Norbert!" she cried, yanking at her husband's sleeve, her accusatory red nail pointing at the arrow. "Those Jews cheat their own people out of their money!"

Libertas saw the woman's husband sneer at the shelves in disgust. "Vodka and bread, thirty grams less than it should be. A paradise indeed!"

Much to Libertas' fright, Harro swung on his heel toward the couple. She didn't like the amiable smile on his face at all.

"And now it has come to us!" Harro declared cheerfully. "Just yesterday, I went down to the Officers' Club and they have the same business there. Only, instead of vodka, we have schnapps. I wonder if the Soviet sort is more drinkable." He pretended to consider the shelves with a look of mock concentration about him.

The couple chuckled politely but were already moving step by careful step away from the insane Luftwaffe officer.

"Now, why would you go and do that?" Libertas hissed at Harro as soon as they turned another corner, finding themselves one on one with the reproduction of an NKVD torture cell, a hose lying abandoned in the middle of its tiled floor smeared with blood.

Harro shrugged, not concerned in the slightest. "Someone had to tell them the truth."

"And that someone had to be you?" Libertas continued berating him, her anger growing with every passing second. "Attracting attention in such a provocative manner! Just what we need right now, when Mildred thinks she's being followed. How do you know that we aren't?"

Harro made no reply, only stood, gazing pensively at the cell.

"What do you think," he said at length, "is it truly Soviet or ours?"

Libertas released a heavy breath, suddenly feeling infinitely exhausted. "If you keep acting like that, we shall soon find out."

"Harro, promise me that you won't try anything without me," Libertas whispered against her husband's lips, reluctant as ever to let go of the lapel of his blue-gray uniform.

They stood on the platform of the Anhalter Bahnhof that crawled with more uniforms than civilians. Libertas' train, heading to Vienna, was already belching smoke, but for the life of her, she couldn't separate herself from Harro. He kept pacifying her gently and promising to stay put, but she had seen the drafts of his Nazi Paradise leaflets. Like a dog with a bone, he wouldn't just let it go, no matter how dangerous it was.

"When I come back from Vienna, all right?" she asked once again, seeking confirmation in Harro's eyes.

"All right." He kissed her on the lips and handed Libertas her valise with the documents she had prepared for the meeting with Wien-Film, an Austrian film company. "Now, go. You can't be late for your first official business trip. If everything goes smoothly, next year you'll be heading there as a director. Wouldn't that be something?"

He was trying to distract her with a subject he knew she had passion for; in fact, filmmaking and Libertas' career was all Harro was talking about lately and particularly after the exhibition. It was as though he was gently but firmly nudging her in a direction different from his; trying to set her onto a safe path; creating a future for her which was happy and prosperous—and Libertas didn't like it one bit.

She kept obsessing over it on the way to Vienna while the train crawled slowly along bombed-out parts of the railway repaired by the prisoners of war, skeletal and begrimed. It kept prickling the back of her mind throughout the four-day meeting with the heads of the film production company with incessant discussions of plans, scripts, and new guidelines on what could and could not be shown to the public according to the *Promi*. It turned into mounting suspicion when Libertas stepped off the train in Berlin just to discover a station worker scrubbing something off a tall limestone column while two plain-clothed men stood and watched.

Promptly, Libertas averted her eyes, her sweaty palm clutching her valise with force. But it was on the U-Bahn train when one of Harro's stickers stared her directly in the face from the train's door that Libertas' state of disquiet turned into sheer despair.

"Harro, you promised!" A much-too-long contained scream tore off Libertas' lips as soon as she unlocked the door to their apartment.

"Libs!" Harro's rushed steps from the study; his loving arms around her. "Forgive me, please! I couldn't possibly involve you with this. You were right; it was too soon and too dangerous and I couldn't—"

"Then why, Harro?" Her words were a mere resigned whisper.

"Because it's working, Libs!" Harro pulled away, a familiar fiery gleam in his eyes. "Hartmut, come and bring it!" he called into the depth of the apartment. In another instant, Hartmut emerged from the living room, smiling from ear to ear.

"Hartmut! What a pleasant surprise!" Mystified, Libertas welcomed Harro's younger brother into her embrace and, somewhat embarrassed, realized that he wasn't a young boy anymore but a young man. A soldier, almost.

"Hartmut has just returned from Munich, where he traveled along with his *Hitlerjugend* troop," Harro explained, smiling, and encouraged his brother slightly forward. "Hartmut, show Libs the souvenir you brought with you!"

Positively glowing, Hartmut produced a leaflet from the pocket of his uniform shorts and handed it to Libertas. In growing disbelief, she was reading the words that could very well have been Harro's.

"What is this?"

"Another resistance cell," Harro explained, barely containing himself. "They call themselves The White Rose. Our movement is growing, Libs! We aren't alone!"

And then, for a fleeting few moments, Libertas allowed herself to believe that victory was possible, that it was only a matter of time, that the people's will would eventually triumph over the dictator's grip.

"Germany will be ours," she quoted their motto and opened her arms to both brothers—in blood and in arms.

"Yes. Germany will be ours."

Chapter 32

August 1942

August came and with it, plans to bring about the German people's revolt. Emboldened by his success and drunk on the idea that his call to arms was finally catching among like-minded people, Harro was unstoppable now. Day and night people gathered in their apartment: old friends from the *Gegner* days, fellow bohemians who had grown sick and tired of Hitler's dictatorship, artists and communists, diplomats and journalists, musicians and physicians—whoever hadn't been conscripted and therefore lost to the ever-growing circle was ready for the final battle.

"A print shop?" Lisl inquired. She still wore black, but it was no longer a color of mourning. Now, it was the color of revenge.

"An *illegal* print shop." The stress Mildred placed on the word *illegal* didn't escape Libertas' attention.

"Where are you planning to obtain the printing press?" Arvid asked Harro.

"From a friend." Harro gave a nonchalant shrug. "He has a printing business, so it won't raise any suspicions. Imagine the possibilities professional printing presses shall provide us with?" The familiar light had ignited in his eyes. "We'll be able to counter any propaganda the *Promi* puts out in their sources with our own. We'll be able to reveal the true extent of our losses on the front. We'll be able to show them the photos of atrocities Libertas has been gathering this entire time. We'll be able to drown the entire Reich in truth!"

Even though Libertas heard her name, she didn't turn away from the window by which she was standing. She could swear it was the same man reading a newspaper on a park bench who was there the day before. And the day before that. And the day before. She had only noticed him last Friday, by sheer accident, when she looked out of the window, bored to tears with her work, and caught him staring straight at her. Ever since, she'd been watching him discreetly, from behind the curtain.

Watching him watching her.

Or was she growing just as paranoid as Mildred?

"Libs?"

Awoken from her unhappy reverie, Libertas turned to Harro: "Yes?"

"I was asking if you could give me your albums, so John can make photocopies of the original photos and letters those SS soldiers sent you."

"Yes, of course," she replied absently and shifted her eyes back to the street.

The man was still there, his face obscured by the paper. It was all idiotic, of course, but still…

"Mildred," she called softly to her American friend, "could you come here for a second?"

Mildred must have spent hours watching her own ghosts, as she approached the window from the side of the wall, without revealing herself. The knowing glance she gave Libertas—*just show me where to look*—nearly broke Libertas' heart.

"That man on the bench, with the newspaper," Libertas whispered to her friend so as not to alarm anyone else. "Have you seen him before?"

She stepped away and bit into her lip as though a criminal awaiting her sentence while Mildred peeked carefully from behind the curtain. It couldn't have taken her more than ten seconds, but to Libertas, those seconds stretched into painfully long hours.

"No." Mildred moved away from the window and back into the shadows with a categorical shake of the head. "Never saw him before in my life."

Libertas was just about to release the breath she was holding when Mildred noted conversationally, "Mine is short and pudgy, with a pockmarked face. You can tell straight away he's a former bull."

In ordinary circumstances, Libertas would have appreciated her friend's use of a Berlin slang term for a policeman, but now, she suddenly couldn't force a single word out of herself.

"Noticed him a couple of months ago," Mildred continued, her eyes staring with blank resignation into the space. "Others come and go, but he's always back. They must work in shifts, I gather."

"The Gestapo?" Libertas' words trembled and died on her lips.

Mildred gave a shrug and produced a cigarette case. "They're listening to our phone."

"How do you know?"

"It's clicking all the time," Mildred explained with the same fascinating calmness.

"What does Arvid say?" Libertas threw a concerned glance at the group of friends, with Harro explaining something animatedly to them. Arvid, his hands steepled, was nodding along.

"Arvid still thinks it's telephone line damage from the bombing."

From that day on, Libertas began to listen closely whenever she picked up the phone. To be sure, there was a click each time she picked up the receiver.

Harro, however, dismissed all of her concerns with a negligent wave of his hand. "Let them listen. We aren't saying anything compromising on the phone at any rate."

"That's not the goddamned point, Harro!" Months of fried nerves had taken their toll. Libertas exploded at long last. "The point is, they *listen* to us, they *watch* our apartment for heaven's sake! Does that not bother you in the slightest?!"

"Libs, love, we've been through this," Harro countered with a mild smile. "They don't have anything to tie us to the leaflets."

"What about the radio? What if they get to Hans and make him talk?"

"They already tried, back when they seized him for his communist activities in 1933. He didn't betray his comrades then, he won't do it now. Don't fret."

That weekend, driven by his desire to provide a sense of normalcy for Libertas, Harro took her sailing on their boat. It was one of the last warm days of dying August, painfully beautiful with its glorious azure sky with whipped butter clouds and golden rays caressing their exposed limbs.

Gentle waves rocked the boat, lulling Libertas to sleep. For the first time in months—or was it years now?—she finally felt her shoulders relax. Libertas thought her happiness was complete when Harro put the oars down and placed Libertas' feet on his lap, massaging them gently as the *Dushinka* drifted serenely along the calm, warm waters.

But then the pricking sensation returned, amplified and increasingly alarming.

"Harro, don't turn around, but that man on the bank is watching us through his binoculars."

Undisturbed in the slightest, Harro turned all the same and broke into chuckles. "He's watching the birds."

"Harro, I swear, he was looking right at us," Libertas insisted, but Harro only pulled her close and began kissing her with increasing passion until she eventually grew quiet and forgot all about the man on the bank.

*

September 1 was the date. It occurred to Libertas that it must have been symbolic to Harro for several reasons: his birthday the following day, the grim anniversary of the beginning of the war. It was only logical to put the new print shop into action on that day. It would bring them luck, Harro had said. It would turn this entire rotten Hitler business around.

But Libertas wasn't around to celebrate it with him. For whatever odd reason he had, Harro had convinced her to take their convertible and go to Bremen to visit her relatives.

"The change will do you some good," he had reiterated as they were saying their goodbyes in front of their car. "You'll come back refreshed and rested."

The familiar feeling that he was sending her away just as he did back in June was gnawing on Libertas' mind, but she took the small suitcase from his hand without a word of protest and arranged it in the front passenger seat. She didn't ask any promises from him this time. Already she knew he would lie and do as he pleased at any rate, so why instill guilt in him before their parting?

Above their heads, the clouds were gathering. The air smelled of rain and ozone.

"Put the top up," Harro said. "It's going to storm soon. I don't want you to be caught in it."

He was looking at her strangely, with a mixture of infinite love and the most profound sorrow. Her heart beating itself to death in her chest, Libertas threw her arms around his neck and buried her face in the folds of Harro's shirt.

She had a feeling they were parting forever.

Compared to Berlin, Bremen was an oasis of peace and serenity. Life moved unhurriedly, people smiled at each other, and the food shortages weren't as noticeable as in the capital. But to Libertas, this idyll appeared suspiciously staged, a mere act, much like those her *Kulturfilm-Zentrale* was producing. She waded through her days as though in a dream, her phone conversations with Harro the only glimpses of reality.

But then, one evening on September 5, Harro didn't call.

"Something's wrong," Libertas declared in a no-nonsense tone to her cousin and threw her suitcase back in her car.

She drove like a madwoman along the autobahn, her foot planted firmly on the gas pedal. Towns and villages and fields with foreign workers farming them flew past her window as Libertas' mind went feverishly through hundreds of scenarios, each one more terrifying than the previous.

Harro got compromised.

Harro went into hiding.

Harro had been hunted.

Harro was announced a deserter.

Harro was arrested.

Harro was tortured right that very moment.

Harro was already dead.

Grasping the wheel with force, Libertas gritted her teeth and forced her frantic mind into a semblance of control. She needed a cool head to deal with whatever fate was ready to throw her way.

When she opened the door to their apartment a few hours later, Libertas didn't know what to expect—Gestapo agents waiting for her in the living room, overturned furniture, the corpse of her husband with a bullet wound in his temple; anything, but not this overpowering normality, not a chair out of place.

Suspicious and shivering with nerves, Libertas went through one room after another, only to find them in the same state as she had left them. In Harro's study, his papers were still on the desk. In her study, her notes appeared to be perfectly undisturbed and in order. She was just about to throw herself down on the floor to fish out a hatbox from under the bed where she had kept her albums hidden, but then she remembered that Harro had given them to his friend John to copy. Except for that, there had never been anything remotely compromising in their apartment. Following Alex Korotkov and his Soviet colleague Sierra's instructions, Harro always took care to destroy all paper trails of his illegal activities the moment he was done with them.

Her disquiet still present but somewhat subdued, Libertas decided to wait.

Evening crept up and seeped through the windows, enveloping the room in darkness. No Harro, still.

The night descended upon Berlin. Somewhere in the distance, air sirens wailed and stopped shortly after. In the sky, searchlights probed the darkness for the enemy fliers. No Harro, still.

Libertas fell asleep on the living-room's sofa, still dressed, hoping that he was with a mistress somewhere. In the morning, no Harro, still.

Libertas took a cold, sobering shower, changed her clothes, gathered her papers and went to work. But at *Kulturfilm-Zentrale* it was worse still. Her colleagues greeted her with friendly smiles and commented on her gorgeous complexion; superiors sent secretaries weighed down with binders—*So good to have you back, could we possibly have this back by Friday?*—while all Libertas wanted to do was to take them by their shoulders and give them a good thorough shake. *My husband is missing; how can you act so normal?!*

But, of course, they knew nothing about that. And was he missing after all?

By lunch, Libertas' nerves gave out. It was an idiotic idea of course, but she picked up her service phone and dialed Harro's office in the Air Ministry. The phone clicked with mocking familiarity.

On the first ring, his secretary picked up. Libertas recognized her perky voice at once.

"Hello, Frau Schulze-Boysen! *Herr Leutnant* is not here, I'm afraid."

"Where is he then?"

"Traveling on official business."

"He just left without announcing where? Without telling me?" Libertas' knuckles turned white.

"I wish I could help you, Frau Schulze-Boysen, but I truly don't know." There was an odd undertone to the girl's voice.

Libertas thought of the telling click and feverishly began to think of how to extract information out of the secretary without compromising the girl's safety. But before she could come up with something, the girl herself announced in her usual perky voice, "His sword knot is still here in his wardrobe though. Would you like to come here and pick it up for him? I finish at five. I could bring it down for you. I imagine he'll be looking for it."

He wouldn't be, Libertas thought, her heart turning to stone in her chest. An officer would never leave on official business without a crucial part of his uniform missing. Her Harro was someplace where he had no need for his sword knot.

"Yes, that would be grand," Libertas forced her voice to sound as regular as possible despite tears already stinging her eyes. "I'll be there."

She left work early, without notifying anyone. After an excruciatingly long ride on the U-Bahn train, she was in front of the Air Ministry, fifteen minutes to five. The wait dragged on impossibly long. Libertas had smoked three cigarettes by the time the staff poured out of the building.

Greta, in her smart Luftwaffe Helferin uniform, waved at her amiably from the stairs. As soon as she reached the bottom, she gathered Libertas into an unexpected embrace.

"Someone called the office September 5 just before noon," she whispered urgently in Libertas' ear. "*Herr Leutnant* told me that someone was in the building's lobby waiting for him and that he would be back soon. I never saw him again; only a man from the Gestapo came this morning and told me that *Herr Leutnant* is away on official business and that I was to say it to anyone who asked. I'm so very sorry."

She was; Libertas saw it in the girl's misty eyes.

With a hand that trembled slightly, Greta handed Libertas Harro's sword knot. "Here. I hope he gets to wear it again. I will be praying for you both."

With that, the girl disappeared into the crowd, leaving Libertas alone with her grief.

Chapter 33

It rained for the third day in a row. Libertas was slowly going mad—from the suddenly silent apartment, from the cold pillow on Harro's side of the bed, from the absence of the friends she felt sharply in her gut. From the almost physical feeling of the noose tightening around her neck, one hour at a time.

At the Harnacks', no one picked up the phone. Lisl was also gone; where, it was anyone's guess. Libertas knew where Hans Coppi, their communist-friend-turned-radio-operator lived, but she was too afraid to go there. Her watchman had changed the newspaper for a black umbrella, but he was still on his post, right outside her window, watching, waiting. No; implicating Coppi was entirely out of the question.

Driven to despair, Libertas went through her old diaries and notebooks. Filled with such youthful idealistic nonsense, she thought she would howl with helpless grief. Here was one which she had bought just before coming to Berlin to work for MGM. God, how long ago it was! Almost ten years… A third of her life.

Libertas' fingers began to tremble when she turned the page and came across a short message her then-idol, director Fritz Lang had written for her:

> Live *up to your name, little Freedom Fighter. Perhaps, one day I shall make a film about your bravery.*
>
> *Good luck!*
> *Fritz Lang.*

The lines swimming in front of her eyes, Libertas slammed the notebook shut, dropped her head atop her folded arms, and broke into sobs. She was no freedom fighter. She was no brave hero at all, just a terrified young woman who had suddenly lost everything and found herself alone against the entire hostile world.

A knock on the door. Prepared for anything, Libertas wiped the tears, adjusted her clothes, and went to open it.

Just a post lady. She exhaled with immense relief and signed for the postcard.

From Mildred. From some tiny village on the coast of the Baltic Sea.

> *Dear Libertas and Harro! Warm greetings from Preil! Heading to Königsberg soon to visit the Amber Museum. Wishing you were here! In case you decide to come, we stopped at the Kubillus Hotel. Ask for us at the front desk.*

That explained the unanswered phone. Libertas turned the postcard in her hand this way and that. But the vacation? Now? And why the odd invitation? Surely, they both knew that Harro couldn't just up and leave his service.

A sudden thought struck her. *What if not an invitation, but a warning?* Veiled advice to run while they still could. Mildred couldn't bear the cold; she would never go to the Baltic Sea willingly, even in relatively warm September.

But from the Baltic Sea, it was only a short trip to the Soviets, Libertas' mind quickly supplied, *and they had friends there, NKVD and GRU. If they decided to make a run for it...* Perhaps, so could she.

Perhaps, Lang was right all along, deciding to abandon a ship that was already doomed. Perhaps, she should follow his example, while there was still a chance.

But leave Harro? In some Gestapo dungeon?

With a pained moan, Libertas wiped her hands down her face, feeling completely and utterly at a loss.

She was still sitting in the same semi-frozen state, her thoughts racing and driving her to madness, when another knock came, more urgent than the first.

Feeling infinitely tired, Libertas rose from her seat.

Let them take her. She had lost all will to fight. Without Harro, she simply ceased to exist and cared not what would happen to her any longer.

Rather to her surprise, instead of her watchman and his underlings, Uncle Wend stood in the door, his uniform sprinkled with rain.

"Gather a small bag," he said by way of greeting, pushing his way inside the apartment and locking the door after himself. "Take only money, jewelry, and your passport. Hurry up, the train is leaving in an hour."

"What train?" Libertas blinked at him uncomprehendingly. It all resembled one very long, very bad dream from which she couldn't awaken no matter how much she tried.

"The train that shall take you to Trier." Wend was already in her bedroom, going through her dresser, pulling pearl and diamond necklaces from their respective boxes. "You'll hide it all so that passport control doesn't uncover it."

"What's in Trier?"

"Officially, friends you want to visit. Unofficially, a Swiss border which you will cross, the sooner, the better. Libertas, get your passport, now! Do you think I'm joking?!"

For the first time, she saw her uncle—ever coolheaded, ever dignified—in a state. So, the matter was serious indeed.

"*Onkel*, where is Harro?" she asked, not really hoping for an answer.

"Forget about Harro," Wend threw over his shoulder. "He should never have dragged you into all that rotten business with the Soviets!"

So, they knew about the Soviets. All the blood drained from Libertas' face. Her legs were slowly turning to jelly.

"He can get the bullet for his treason, but I'll be damned if I let anything happen to my own flesh and blood," Wend kept grumbling as he tore into Libertas' desk, searching for her passport, after she made no move to do so herself. Numbly, she watched him grope about for the documents and money, grateful that he had the presence of mind to do something in that nightmare from which she couldn't wake up with the best will in the world.

Her mind falling apart like a house of cards, Libertas scarcely remembered the rest. She could barely recall the torn pieces of memories: uncle Wend's hand clasping her lifeless wrist with force, the stifling air of his car smelling faintly of imported cigars and spilled whisky, the chaos of the Anhalter Bahnhof station and a sea of uniforms, Wend saying something to her through the opened window of her private compartment. And the final feeling of abandonment when her fingers slipped from his hand and the train began picking up speed, carrying her further away—from Harro, from Berlin, from the life that would no longer be.

Familiar stations began to flash before her eyes. Along with them, snapshots of the past—one endless motion picture reel full of love and adventure and the idealism of youth. With an aching heart, with a trembling palm pressed against the cool glass of the window, Libertas was saying goodbye to Berlin. It was the route of countless refugees before her, also torn from everything and everyone they knew and loved, but the realization of it didn't make it any less painful. Uprooted, hurled into the unknown, persecuted and stripped of all human rights, they had turned into the flotsam of Europe—Jews, communists, dissident journalists, pacifists, and writers who had too much to say for the Nazis' liking. Even in her wildest dreams, it hadn't occurred to Libertas that she would ever join their ranks, but somehow, she felt proud of such an affiliation.

At last, she surrendered herself and closed her eyes, shutting the golden autumn day just outside her window from her thoughts and falling into a deep, dreamless slumber.

When a polite knock on her private compartment door tore her from its lulling embrace, Libertas sat bolt upright, unsure where she was for a few instants, rubbing the sleep from her eyes, together with the crusted salt of dried tears.

It occurred to her that it must be a car attendant with his usual offer of tea or refreshments. However, when she opened the door to tell him that she was perfectly all right and didn't wish to be disturbed till her stop near the border, two men in civilian suits greeted her with chillingly polite smiles.

"Libertas Schulze-Boysen?" the senior one inquired, momentarily revealing his identification tag with a series of numbers under the unmistakable *Geheime Staatspolizei* engraved just above.

The Gestapo. It had been idiotic to hope that they would just let her slip away in such a manner. Their asking her name was also a pure formality. They'd been following her long enough to know what she looked like, but still, Libertas nodded, following the script out of the same politeness.

"You're under arrest," the same Gestapo officer announced with studied casualness. His underling was already holding a pair of manacles in his hand.

With a mixture of resignation and relief, Libertas offered him her wrists. It was better this way. No more agony, no more looking over her shoulder. She would be with Harro once again, even if it meant that they would ascend the scaffold together.

Yes, it was better this way. It was just the ending she had imagined for her story. The ending Fritz Lang would be proud of. Who knew, maybe he would make a film about her, at which one armchair critic or another would turn their nose and announce their somber verdict, in which no one except for their porcelain figurines would be interested, that the plot was weak and that the main protagonist unlikable.

The younger Gestapo agent looked up in alarm when Libertas burst into a scornful, mirthless laughter.

Nothing, she shook her head as he was handcuffing her. *Ignore me, it's my custom to laugh at the most inappropriate situations. Cart me off to your Nazi Paradise torture cell and make an end of it. I've had enough of this circus.*

Prison at Kaiserdamm 1. September 1942

Libertas' cell was narrow and damp, with mildewed walls and a cot so painfully uncomfortable, she eventually ended up pulling the mattress down to the floor and spending the night fighting off bedbugs and an occasional curious rat. She was brave at first, feisty. Her hair was still nicely done, her clothes still elegant and bearing the scent of expensive French perfume. She wasn't planning to deny whatever charges they would bring up against her; on the contrary, Libertas wished to take the blame on her shoulders and hers alone and sign the confession right that instant. With the only condition, of course: Harro and the others would have to be released. It was she, the sly Jezebel, who had seduced her honorable husband into this conspiracy. Harro himself would never have even entertained the idea of going against his own country. She had made him, and it was her profound conviction that he already regretted it immensely. Why not send him to some penalty Luftwaffe detachment for a few months? They would all see how good an officer he was, without her rotten influence.

Yes, she decided, measuring her cell from its metal door to its single tiny barred window at the top of the wall. *This would do nicely. This was what she would tell them.*

But an entire week passed and no one had summoned her for an interrogation. Days began to drag—dreary, growing progressively colder, one longer than another. With mounting apathy, Libertas watched her nail polish chip, layers of grime accumulate on her body, her hair stick to her scalp in oily lumps. By the end of the second week, she became increasingly aware of the smell of her own body.

It was in this state, filthy and resembling only a former shadow of herself, resigned to her fate and exhausted, did they take her upstairs one morning.

The interrogator, with an astonishingly youthful face, whistled through his teeth after he read out the list of accusations against Libertas Viktoria Schulze-Boysen, née Haas-Heye. "Writing and distribution of subversive texts, criminal support of the Jews, spreading of anti-government propaganda—oral and written— recruitment of persons with the aim of forming partisan groups in Berlin, espionage—domestic and international... I must admit, Frau Schulze-Boysen, I'm impressed!"

Libertas only stared at the paper hard.

"Where's my husband?" she asked instead and didn't recognize her own voice.

"In his cell," the interrogator replied amiably. "He gave us a fright, I must tell you! Claimed that he had copies of all top-secret Luftwaffe papers stashed someplace abroad, in a secure location, and if something happened to him or you or his friends—we've arrested all of you, by the way, in case you've been wondering—the person responsible for it would release them to the international press immediately. I need hardly add, the situation was rather delicate, and we had no other choice but to promise *Herr Leutnant* that nothing would happen to you or his friends and he, himself, would only receive a prison term in exchange for his revealing the location of the papers to us."

A hopeful smile touched upon Libertas' chapped lips fleetingly. *Harro, her brilliant, brilliant Harro!*

But the interrogator dismissed it with a single sweep of his hand. "It was just a ploy; your husband admitted that much himself. A rather smart attempt on his part—something I would have tried myself, I have to give him that. But, you must understand," the amiable, predatory grin was back on that angelic, savage face, "there can't be making deals with terrorists. And that's precisely what you are—terrorists. The good news," he proceeded, folding his hands, "is that you'll all be going to the gallows together. Now, if you could just sign right here." He was already moving the official document toward her.

"I want to see my husband."

"And I wanted to celebrate this Yuletide in the Kremlin, but it doesn't look like it's happening, so..." He uncapped a fountain pen and placed it atop the paper. "Right there, on the bottom."

And then, despite her filthy state, despite the fact that she was at his complete mercy, Libertas grinned slowly and viciously at the interrogator. "Well, *mein Herr*, I regret to inform you, but my signature isn't happening either, just like your Kremlin trip. I fear, it's simply not your year," she added with a mockingly playful shrug.

His face turned to stone. He paled visibly, set his teeth. "Fine. Have it your way," he hissed, snatching the paper back. "I don't need you signing anything, you'll all hang regardless. We have your radio operator, Coppi. In exchange for his pregnant wife's life, that Bolshevist pig sold all of you out."

"Hans isn't a pig," Libertas countered calmly. "*You* are, for threatening a man with his innocent wife and unborn child's death."

For an instant, he looked like he was about to slap her. However, then he collected himself and called for the guard to bring "the terrorist bitch" back to her cell.

"And no walks until the Reich Court-Martial!"

*

A few weeks later, a Gestapo official yanked the door to her cell open.

"Libertas Schulze-Boysen," he began in a monotone voice without a single glance at the woman sitting on the filthy cot before him. "On the charges brought against you, you are to appear before the Reich Court-Martial tomorrow morning, where you shall be judged and sentenced along with your co-conspirators. The charges against you are the following: writing and distribution of subversive texts, criminal support of the Jews, spreading of anti-government propaganda—oral and written—recruitment of persons with the aim of forming partisan groups in Berlin, espionage—domestic and international," he read out, sounding dreadfully bored and tired. "You shall also be provided with a defense council appointed to you by the state."

Libertas expected him to inquire if everything was clear to her, but apparently, enemies of the state, guilty of inciting honest Germans to riots, oughtn't to count on such courtesies from their Gestapo jailers.

"Sign here," he instructed, suppressing a yawn.

Poor devil, Libertas mused to herself with great sarcasm as she slashed her signature across the page. *Must have been up all night, extracting confessions out of her fellow "terrorists" without a wink of sleep. A true Reich servant.*

"Your mother must be really proud of you," Libertas remarked with a charming smile.

The official only glared at her but made no response. Arguing with "terrorist bitches" must have been beneath his noble Aryan self.

When the echo of his steps grew silent in the dimly lit corridor behind her cell door, Libertas only smiled in relief. The Court Martial and the charges didn't concern her much. She would see Harro again and all of her friends, and that's all that mattered.

Chapter 34

December 1942

When the doors to the grand courtroom of the Reich Court-Martial opened, the empty seats of the panel of judges weren't the first thing that Libertas' gaze fastened upon. Neither was it the oversized bust of Hitler that all but dwarfed a small blindfolded statute of Justice. No, it was Harro whom she'd sought out from the uniformed crowd. Her Harro, pale and gaunt but exuding calm confidence—confidence in their cause, in the example they had set for future generations, for the message they had plastered all over the capital and which was already sending waves all over the country.

He met her gaze, nodded at her with a smile she loved to no end, and suddenly, Libertas felt calm and at peace, a smile of her own slowly blossoming on her bloodless lips.

"As an accused, you have no right to make a Hitler salute when the judges enter," a courtroom official informed Libertas with an air of superiority about him.

"I wasn't going to," she retorted with a defiant smile that turned his arrogant expression sour.

The judges entered, ridiculous in their wigs and flowing robes; Libertas gazed at Harro.

Her interrogator—it turned out his name was Roeder—went into a lengthy accusatory speech depicting Libertas' and Harro's lifestyle as something amoral and Bolshevist at the same time. Libertas gazed at Harro.

Libertas' court-appointed lawyer, whom she had seen for the first time that morning, struggled with his monocle that kept falling out of his eye, which must have been widening time and again as he listened to the accusations made against her. Libertas gazed at Harro.

"Make no mistake," Roeder's voice screeched like a rusty nail across the iron board, "Libertas Schulze-Boysen is not an innocent party in all this. She was her husband's most zealous co-conspirator, who, along with him, carried out criminal deeds and recruited more people into their terrorist cell…"

Over the heads of all those useless, frightened men, Libertas gazed at Harro, and Harro gazed at her—her most zealous co-conspirator, her comrade-in-arms, her fellow martyr.

"It was with her help that Schulze-Boysen was able to send top-secret military secrets to Arvid Harnack intended for the enemy, both American and Soviet," Roeder continued.

"I love you," Libertas mouthed to Harro, scarcely hearing a thing. In her mind, they were alone, aboard Ricci's boat where they had first met, where they had fallen in love, where they had forever ceased to be alone and become a part of something grander, something no mortal could tear apart.

"She also provided technical help for Schulze-Boysen's illegal, seditious pamphlets…" Roeder continued wrathfully.

"I love you more," Harro mouthed back to her. "Forever and ever…"

"…Until death do us part," Libertas finished in unison with him and broke into the happiest of smiles. It had suddenly occurred to her, on that defendants' bench, that she was the luckiest woman alive.

The feeling only grew and intensified when Roeder called on the defendants and, one by one, they began admitting their own guilt and doing their utmost to protect the others.

"Yes, it was me, I was the radio operator and it was also me who encrypted the messages and transmitted them to the Soviet agents,"

Hans Coppi declared, noble and unafraid. "I have been convicted for my political views, served a term in the concentration camp, and it was only natural that I would return to my communist business as soon as the opportunity presented itself. I acted alone; the Schulze-Boysen couple are not communists, neither do they sympathize with the regime."

"I took advantage of my husband's good nature and delivered sensitive diplomatic information to my friends from the American Embassy when it was still functioning," Mildred declared, her American accent sharper than usual, her shoulders squared proudly. "My husband is a good German and an innocent party in all this."

"I have voluntarily printed leaflets that have been left by unknown persons at my husband's studio and distributed them among the population," Lisl Schumacher announced, fascinatingly calm in contrast to her lawyer, who was sweating profusely. "My husband fought bravely on the front and had not the faintest idea of all this when these people," she nearly spat out her words in disgust as she pointed an accusatory finger at Roeder and his underlings, "tore off his insignia in front of his comrades, dragged him here like some criminal, and tortured him severely—"

The frantic banging of the gavel and shouts to order drowned out the rest of her words.

When Libertas' turn came to speak in her defense, she only burst out laughing instead, finding Roeder and his reddening face positively amusing just then.

"You dare to laugh at the People's Court?!" he shrieked, his voice turning hysterical.

"Herr Roeder, this circus we're having here is the furthest thing from the People's Court. So, yes, I'm laughing at it because you're all ridiculous, trying to pass something resembling justice when the outcome is already signed by your beloved Führer."

"Very soon you won't have much to laugh about!" Roeder exploded, his eyes rolling wildly at such impudence.

"I will, as long as I have your self-important mug to stare at!"

Much to Roeder's horror, not only the rest of the defendants, but even a few of the carefully selected independent observers and bailiffs began to cough and snigger into their fists, their faces turning crimson from their efforts to contain themselves.

Libertas couldn't believe her good fortune when all of the defendants were escorted to the same waiting room during the recess. Her astonishment only grew when one of the guards, after throwing a discreet glance at the door, approached them one by one and removed their manacles. He hadn't said a single word; his gesture said thousands.

"Are we allowed contact?" Harro probed carefully.

It occurred to Libertas he didn't wish to cause any trouble for the sympathetic guards.

"Officially or no?"

Moments later after he said that, the second guard broke into a conspiratorial grin and purposely turned his back on the group. *As long as we don't see it*, his back seemed to say.

Infinitely grateful for a glimpse of humanity where they expected none, spouses threw themselves into each other's arms, friends embraced tightly after a long separation, comrades-in-arms shook hands at last and thanked one another for the honor of fighting together against the same enemy.

And amid all this, Libertas and Harro stood, arms around each other, eyes closed, reunited against all odds and blissfully happy, despite the Grim Reaper already breathing its putrid breath down their necks.

"I missed you something dreadful," Libertas confessed somewhere into the folds of Harro's jacket.

"I missed you more," he whispered into her hair, kissing it, caressing it lovingly, inhaling the familiar scent.

"Did they hurt you?" Libertas asked.

Harro shook his head. She saw in his eyes that he was lying but didn't pry any further. It didn't matter any longer.

Seated at the bare wooden table, Hans Coppi was sobbing, face hidden in his hands, begging forgiveness, which he felt he didn't deserve. He had held out under torture; they had tried to break him and failed, he swore to it. But when they'd brought his wife into his cell, his pregnant wife who didn't know a thing about the entire rotten business—

"Hans, shut your mug, will you?" Still hugging Libertas with one arm, Harro clapped Coppi on his back with such emotion—*Quit it, it's forgiven*—Hans broke into tears once again, grateful tears this time. For being understood. For being forgiven. "There are no traitors among us, only heroes. And you're one of the bravest ones."

In a surge of emotion, Coppi grasped Harro's hand and kissed it before wringing it in both of his. "I shall never forget your kindness as long as I live."

"The entire twenty-four hours?" Libertas asked with a deadpan look.

Coppi froze for an instant but then, when the joke had caught up with him, he broke into laughter along with the others.

"Libs, that's just wicked," Mildred commented, wiping her own tears—of joy, of life cut much too short, of chances taken, of going to the gallows without regrets.

"Do you think they'll hang us or shoot us?" Kurt Schumacher asked, his uniform gone, one arm planted firmly around Lisl's shoulders.

"I would think you and Harro would get a firing squad?" Libertas looked up at Harro.

Harro grimaced as he considered the question. "My money is on the noose. Hitler won't grant us the honor of being shot as military men. He and Goebbels would want to present us to the public as mere criminals. And criminals get the noose."

"To be completely frank with you, I'd much prefer a noose to an ax." Mildred shivered theatrically. "They say you still comprehend what's happening to you after an executioner cuts off your head. I don't want my last memories to be of a wicker basket!"

"You just had to go and say it!" Libertas stared at the American with mock accusation.

"What? It's true."

"You could have kept it to yourself!"

"No, it was too good not to share with you." Mildred blew Libertas a kiss.

Lisl, her pale face shining with some inner light, broke into chuckles as well. "I can't believe us. We have laughed our way through this entire resistance enterprise and we're still laughing."

Libertas grew serious. "Because laughing, and particularly in our situation, is resistance as well. They want to see us plead and cry but we'll laugh in their faces instead. We'll laugh until our last moment. We'll go out just the way we lived—proudly and with our heads held high."

Harro kissed her on her temple, pride shining in his eyes.

A guard clearing his throat interrupted the moment. Libertas had all but forgotten about their existence, but now, with puzzlement and growing wonder, she watched the courtroom staff carry in trays with food that looked like it came from a restaurant and not from the prison canteen.

"Is that... beer?" Hans Coppi blinked at the jug in the middle of the unexpected feast.

The guards only exchanged wry glances. "Officially, it's water. Unofficially..." He didn't finish, only motioned for the defendants to get at it before the Gestapo called them back into the courtroom and denied them this last pleasure.

They ate amid cordial chatter, as though they were back at Harro's and Libertas' atelier and not in the Reich Court-Martial break room. Never before had food tasted so delicious, spiced with humanity and kindness they hadn't thought to expect and instilling hope in their hearts that perhaps their example wouldn't be forgotten but, instead, would propel German people into action and do away with the dictatorship that had no right to exist.

Chapter 35

December 1942

The sun had set the courtroom aglow. After little deliberation among the judges, the verdict was pronounced.

"For the crimes, jointly committed, of conspiring to commit high treason, subverting the Wehrmacht and aiding the enemy, according to the legal provisions outlined in Section 83 Paragraph 1.3 of the Reich Penal Code; Section 57 of the Military Penal Code; and Section 5 Paragraph 1 of the Wartime Special Penal Code, no form of punishment other than execution can be considered."

Harro turned to look at Libertas and, much to Roeder's astonishment, gave his wife a playful wink. *Told you so*, his nonchalant look seemed to say. At their posts, the courtroom guards regarded the fearless man almost with admiration.

Next, Hitler's own verdict was read out, just telegraphed from his headquarters in the East, where he was apparently following the Court Martial closely: "I uphold the verdict of the Reich Court-Martial and decline to issue a pardon. Signed, Adolf Hitler."

This time it was Libertas who broke into scornful laughter. "You could have at least made an attempt to pretend that this was an independent court," she addressed the judges directly, not impressed in the slightest with their calls for order. "You're telling me to respect the court? This is not a court, this is a circus. *Der Führer's* personal show, scripted and staged. Don't point your gavel at me! What are you going to do if I don't obey? Behead me twice?"

She laughed harder. Laughed, with scorching disdain, in the red faces of the pitiful slaves of the regime. She was dying a free woman, with her conscience clean. They would have to live with themselves and their shame forever, and as far as Libertas was concerned, that was a far worse punishment than any death sentence.

Kaiserdamm 1 prison. December 1942

It was odd to be happy alone in her cell, with only hours to live, but that night, Libertas didn't have a choice. With a rush of inexplicable exhilaration, she was writing to her parents about the life she had lived without regrets and of the honorable death she would die.

> *Don't mourn me, please. I die for my people, together with Harro, and frankly, I couldn't imagine a better way to leave this life. I have fulfilled my every wish. I have done all I could, and it is my profound hope that our actions shall inspire others—to live freely and to die without fear...*

There were no tears that night, only a fire coursing through her veins and her heart drumming the music of a farewell parade. There were no sorrows either, only infinite love pouring from under her pen and spilling onto the paper almost in verses—*To Harro, my last words.*

> *I've always loved you more than life*
> *And now I can finally prove it.*
> *I've always stood by your side,*
> *And so I'll stand by you in death.*
> *It is my fate, I choose it.*
> *We shall no longer be apart;*
> *It is my biggest joy*

At dawn, to freedom we depart
Our memory shall live
That nothing will destroy.

Tenderly, Libertas pressed her lips to the paper—her farewell kiss to her beloved.

"Will you make sure that he gets it?" she asked the guard at her door.

He was a different fellow from the courtroom ones, but the sympathy in his eyes was the same.

"I shall personally see to it," he promised gravely, hiding the paper in the inner pocket of his uniform.

Almost with shame, he read out the high order for all prisoners sentenced to death to remove all their clothes and leave them on the stool beside the cell door. Looking away as respectfully as possible, he manacled Libertas' wrists and apologized once again. *Bastardly orders; he was well aware, but the Führer didn't want to risk them hanging themselves, surely, Frau Schulze-Boysen understood…*

The tinge of disgust in the guard's voice when he pronounced the title—Führer—didn't escape Libertas. With a faint smile, she padded, barefoot, to her cot. They were getting fed up with him as well. She would go to the gallows with hope in her heart.

In the morning, with the first pink rays of the rising sun, Libertas got dressed ceremoniously, grateful for the guard allowing her to take her time. She refused the chaplain's services—she had nothing to confess and no sins to be forgiven for. She pinched her cheeks and bit into her lips to bring out the color—prettying herself up for Harro.

"How do I look?" she asked the guard.

"Very beautiful." The man was of her father's age and looked as though he was about to cry.

While he was placing handcuffs on her wrists, Libertas caught his fingers for a fleeting instant. "Thank you for your kindness."

He only shook his head. *It was nothing. He wished he would have done more.*

Outside, in the frost-covered courtyard, the police van was already waiting, belching exhaust fumes into the crisp, fresh air.

Pausing momentarily, Libertas looked at the pale blue expanse above her head and inhaled a full chest.

"What a beautiful morning to die," she said with a dreamy smile and, throwing the last wave goodbye at the misty-eyed guard, stepped inside the van.

Seated opposite Kurt, Hans, and Arvid, Harro was already waiting for her, handcuffed and gazing at her with all the adoration in the world.

"Here." He patted the bench next to him. "I saved you a spot."

"How did you know I was going to come?" Libertas asked playfully before nestling next to him and losing herself to his lips once again.

"I got your note last night."

"You did?"

"I wrote you one too, but then I decided that I would rather say it all to you myself, while I'm holding your hands and looking into your beautiful eyes. My Libertas."

Through the small barred window on the back of the van, familiar sights sailed by. It occurred to Libertas that the driver, whoever he was, was purposely taking his time, as though allowing the condemned men and women to enjoy their last tour of Berlin. Their victory tour, as it soon turned out.

From the guards, Libertas was aware that Hitler and Goebbels had gone to great lengths in order to conceal the case from the memory of the people, to erase the martyrs' very names from everyone's mind. And yet, just past the Brandenburg Gate, two uniformed Wehrmacht officers stopped in their tracks and saluted to the van sharply. The bellboy at the Hotel Adlon's entrance raised his fist in the air in a grim salute. A postwoman rode her bicycle behind the van for some time, her gaze trained at the small window, one hand pressed to her heart as though to the solemn sound of an inaudible national anthem—not the Reich one, but the old Germany, back when they were all free.

"Whoever told them about our route?" Arvid voiced the question playing on everyone's mind.

"Word gets around," Harro replied with a dreamy smile, gazing contentedly at the city he was leaving in good hands. "The guards could have told their friends and they, in turn, told theirs. Or the Wehrmacht officers from the Court-Martial discussed it at the Officers' Club."

"What else do you think they discuss?" Libertas turned to him.

"Hopefully, something even bolder than we ever attempted." Harro's eyes ignited. "Hopefully, they shall have better luck than us."

Near the boarded Soviet Embassy, Lisl climbed in and fell into Kurt's embrace, much as Libertas had fallen into Harro's.

"Aren't police vans supposed to have no windows?" Lisl inquired after settling down. "Aren't they worried people shall see us and we them?"

"Officially, it should be entirely concealed." It occurred to Libertas that Harro was quoting one guard or another. "Unofficially, though... It is my profound conviction we have more people on our side than we could ever have dreamt of."

He looped his handcuffed arms and Libertas, grinning, wormed her way into his embrace.

"Remember, when we married, you promised me the world," she said, pressing her cheek against his.

"Mhm."

"You gave me something better, Harro." Libertas' gaze was fixed on a Luftwaffe officer standing beside the news column with his service dagger taken out and lifted in a silent salute. "You gave me future. Germany shall be ours."

He kissed the top of her head and, with tears of hope in his eyes, whispered, "It already is."

A Letter from Ellie

Dear Reader,

I want to say a huge thank you for choosing to read *The Girl on the Platform*. If you did enjoy it, and want to keep up to date with all my latest releases, just sign up at the following link. Your email address will never be shared and you can unsubscribe at any time.

www.bookouture.com/ellie-midwood

Thank you for reading the story of this truly remarkable woman. I hope you loved *The Girl on the Platform* and, if you did, I would be very grateful if you could write a review. I'd love to hear what you think, and it makes such a difference helping new readers to discover one of my books for the first time.

I love hearing from my readers—you can get in touch on my Facebook page, through Goodreads or my website.

Thanks,
Ellie

EllieMidwood
elliemidwood.com

Acknowledgments

First and foremost, I want to thank the wonderful Bookouture family for helping me bring Libertas' and Harro's story to light. It wouldn't be possible without the invaluable help and guidance of my incredible editor Christina Demosthenous, whose insights truly bring my characters to life and whose support and encouragement make me strive to work even harder on my novels and become a better writer. Thank you, Kim Nash and Noelle Holten, for your enthusiasm and for cheering my work all over social media. A special thanks goes to the incredible Eileen Carey, who created the cover that left me in complete and utter awe! It's been a true pleasure working with all of you and I already can't wait to create more projects under your guidance.

Mom, Granny—thank you for always asking how my novel is doing and for cheering me up at every step. Your support and faith in me make this writing journey so much easier, knowing that you always have my back and will always be my biggest fans. Thank you for all your love. Love you both to death.

Ronnie, my love—all of this wouldn't be possible without you. Every time you meet a new person, the first thing you say about me is "my fiancée is a great novelist, you simply must check out her books!" I always grumble that you're embarrassing me with all that attention, but inwardly I'm so very grateful for you being so very proud of me. Thank you for all your support and for putting up with my deadlines and all that research information I keep dumping on you. You are my rock star.

A special thanks to my two besties, Vladlena and Anastasia, for your love and support; to all of my fellow authors whom I got to know through Facebook and who became my very close friends—you all are such an inspiration! I consider you all a family.

And, of course, huge thanks to my readers for patiently waiting for new releases, for celebrating cover reveals together with me, for reading ARCs and sending me those absolutely amazing I-stayed-up-till-3am-last-night-because-I-just-had-to-finish-your-wonderful-book messages, for your reviews that always make my day, and for falling in love with my characters just as much as I do. You are the reason why I write. Thank you so much for reading my stories.

And, finally, I owe my biggest thanks to all the brave people who continue to inspire my novels. Most of them perished at the hands of the ruthless Gestapo, but it's their incredible courage, resilience, and self-sacrifice that will live on in our hearts. Their example will always inspire us to be better people, to stand up for what is right, to give a voice to the ones who have been silenced, to protect the ones who cannot protect themselves. They all are true heroes.

Note on History

Thank you so much for reading *The Girl on the Platform*! Even though it's a work of fiction, it's almost entirely based on a true story. While writing it, I relied mostly on an incredibly well-researched biography of Libertas and Harro written by Norman Ohler, *The Bohemians*, and several other sources that helped me construct a fictional narration of this incredibly inspiring true story.

Libertas' family history, her upbringing, descriptions of her familial estate, and her relationship with her relatives are all based on fact, including her warm relationship with her former governess Valerie, which must have influenced—at least in part—her attitude toward the persecution of the Jews in Germany. Libertas indeed began her career at MGM but, disillusioned with the absence of any prospects, eventually left the Berlin office of the American film studio to become a freelance writer. As described in the book, she was later employed first as a film critic and later as a film censor at the prestigious Kulturfilm-Zentrale, where she indeed began corresponding with SS men stationed in the East with the purpose of collecting evidence of the crimes against humanity committed in several photo albums, basically tricking the unsuspecting SS men into sending her photos of their gruesome deeds.

Libertas' and Harro's first meeting on the river is also based on Libertas' own memories of the event written in her diary. Harro's arrest, torture, and eventual release by the SS in early 1933 are also based on true fact, just like the murder of Harro's friend Henry Erlanger at the hands of the same SS men. Both were accused of being "radical communists" due to their liberal views expressed in their newspaper, *Gegner*. Traumatized by his arrest and torture (he indeed bore scars left from the SS bullwhip and swastikas his captors carved into his thighs), Harro fled to the Baltic coast and joined what would later be known as the Luftwaffe—armed air forces—hoping to "blend in" with the dominant militaristic sentiments of new Nazi Germany and thus spare himself and everyone around him any further trouble with the SS and Gestapo.

In my descriptions of the development and general dynamics of Libertas' and Harro's relationship, I also stuck to the historical sources, only taking creative license to fill in the gaps where historical narrative was missing. The descriptions of their common friend Ricci and his fondness for the American Harley-Davidson and rebellious leather outfits are also based on fact, just like the description of Libertas' cousin Gisela and her story of early involvement with different resistance cells, arrests, her incredibly brave deed of passing secret documentation to the Soviet Embassy in Paris, and consequent arrest and tragic, untimely death.

All the secondary characters and their involvement with Harro's resistance cell are also based on real people and their courageous actions, most of which resulted in their imprisonment and execution, as described in the novel.

Libertas and Harro indeed worked together with two Soviet agents who had contacted them via Arvid and Mildred Harnack and later became accused of being members of an espionage ring with ties to the Soviet Union dubbed by the German military intelligence, *Red Orchestra*. Their meetings with the Soviet agents and the transmission of the messages to the Soviet Union with the help of Hans Coppi are all based on historical fact, just like the contents of the illegal pamphlets Harro was writing, printing, and distributing with the help of his friends, contrary to the Soviet agents' wishes.

Libertas' and Harro's arrest, trial, and execution are also based on true facts, including the very inspiring moment with the guards removing their handcuffs and serving them beer and excellent food during the court recess, which was certainly contrary to protocol and could endanger the guards themselves if they were found out.

Neither Libertas, nor Harro were associated with certain political cells, be it the communist movement (Hans Coppi was a member), or social democratic movement. They were German patriots who believed in the freedom of speech, freedom to love whoever they wanted without fear of persecution, freedom of criticizing the government that was leading the entire nation to the abyss, and freedom to choose whether to conform or resist; to live, survive, somehow voluntarily closing their eyes to the crimes against humanity perpetrated by their fellow countrymen, or to die martyrs and inspire others to resist and follow their cause, which they, to some extent, did.

In July 1944, less than two years after their execution, the biggest assassination attempt on Hitler's life was undertaken by the German military leadership with Claus von Stauffenberg personally planting the bomb under the table in Hitler's Wolf's Lair. Countless books and movies were made based on Operation Valkyrie; hopefully, now, people will get to know the lesser-known heroes that gave their lives in the name of freedom and inspired others to follow their heroic steps—Libertas and Harro Schulze-Boysen.

Thank you for reading their incredible true story!

Made in the USA
Columbia, SC
24 May 2023

17236139R00190